Escape into Light

Also by Elizabeth Webster:

The Flight of the Swan
Johnnie Alone
To Fly a Kite
Bracken

Escape into Light

Elizabeth Webster

Fic
Webster

St. Martin's Press
New York

Library of Congress Cataloging-in-Publication Data

Webster, Elizabeth.
    Escape into light / Elizabeth Webster.
        p.   cm.
    ISBN 0-312-06964-2
    I. Title.
    PR6073.E2312E83   1992
    823'.914—dc20   91-33032
                                                                              CIP

First published in Great Britain by Souvenir Press Limited.

First U.S. Edition: January 1992
10   9   8   7   6   5   4   3   2   1

CONTENTS

PART I
HOLES IN THE GROUND

Poor Caroline got out of bed and screamed. Not aloud, of course. That would have upset her mother. But inside, deep inside, right in the heart's core, she screamed and screamed. The scream felt like a wave. It began in her toes and went up through her knees and her thighs, growing in power, tingling into her spine and all the way up to her head where it fizzed and boiled with the anguish of trying to get out. 'Let me out!' the scream said. 'Let me out! Get me away from this—somehow—anyhow . . . Just get me away!'

But there was no way out for the scream—no way out for poor Caroline—and her mother was already thumping on the floor with her stick.

Caroline wrapped herself in her tired dressing-gown and fumbled wearily for her slippers. 'Yes, mother,' she called. 'I'm coming . . .'

Her mother was sitting up in bed, two angry spots of colour in her cheeks, and a glint of more than malice in her sharp blue eyes.

'You're late,' she snapped. 'I want my breakfast. And my feet are cold.'

Caroline sighed and looked at the clock on the bedside table. 'It's only half-past seven.'

'What's that got to do with anything?' Her mother's voice was rasping and cold. It put Caroline's teeth on edge. 'If I want my breakfast early, it's because I *need* it . . . I feel faint without food.' She lay back on her pillows, looking as faint as possible. 'The doctor said I needed building up,' she added in a weak and fading tone.

'Yes, mother,' agreed Caroline, and went downstairs to the kitchen.

If only I wasn't so tired, she thought, nearly knocking the

teapot over in her exhaustion . . . Never an unbroken night—that stick rapping on the floor every half hour—a drink of water—my pillows plumped up—my hot-water-bottle filled—my sheets changed—a bedpan—another hot drink—a sleeping pill . . . *Sleeping*?

Caroline shuddered. She refilled the hot-water-bottle, poured boiling water into the teapot, rescued the toast from the toaster before it burnt, scooped a boiled egg out of the saucepan into a silver egg-cup, arranged the rest of the breakfast tray and carried it upstairs.

'Where's the sea-salt?' demanded her mother at once. 'You know I can't eat ordinary salt. And you haven't polished the silver. This egg-cup's filthy.'

Caroline went downstairs for the sea-salt and a silver cloth. 'I'll give it a rub now if you like,' she said mildly. 'But I did polish it yesterday.'

'*Yesterday*!' snorted her mother. 'You're getting slack, my girl. I expect the house is a disgrace—thank God I can't see it . . . And look at you! Not even dressed yet. Tatty old dressing-gown and down-at-heel slippers. Hair a mess. You look a sight!'

Caroline turned away from her mother's bed and caught a glimpse of herself in the mirror. Yes, she thought, she's right. I do look a sight.

What she saw was a pale, tired face with anxious eyes, a mouth that was clamped straight in case it trembled, and a cloud of wispy hair that might have been auburn if it hadn't been so lank and lustreless. She never had time to wash her own hair, somehow. She was always washing sheets, or her mother's solid, none-too-fragile body, or the ridiculous frothy nighties and bedjackets (a new one every day) that her mother insisted on wearing . . . Got to look my best, haven't I? The doctor might come . . .

'This egg's undercooked,' stated her mother.

'Shall I do you another?'

'No,' her mother snarled, pushing it away pettishly. 'What's the use? You never get anything right. I could just lie here and starve for all you care.'

'I'll do another in any case,' said Caroline, ignoring the last remark, and went downstairs again.

When she came back, the first egg—undercooked or not—had been demolished, and her mother said she didn't want another. But when Caroline turned to go back downstairs yet again, her mother changed her mind.

'I might as well eat it. Too much gets wasted in this house.'

Considering it was her mother who usually threw tantrums about her food and refused to eat it, or demanded something else, this was outrageous of her. But Caroline did not protest. Silently, she put down the second egg (in an even more highly polished silver egg-cup) on her mother's tray, and went away.

The carping voice followed her, but she didn't listen . . . She was past listening to anything any more. She got dressed in a mood of grim despair, and on an impulse which she couldn't explain put on the only bright-coloured outfit she possessed, a cherry-red wool suit which she had bought years ago. It still fitted her, though, and she felt a little less dowdy and bedraggled when she looked in the mirror again.

'What are you wearing that for?' asked her mother. 'You're not trying to go anywhere, are you?'

'No, mother. Only shopping.'

'You know I can't be left—'

'Yes, mother, I know.'

'If you go out, something will happen to me—I know it will.'

Caroline looked at her mother, suppressing another sigh. There was real panic in those malicious blue eyes, and she could not ignore it.

'It's all right,' she soothed, trying to keep exasperation out of her voice.

'It's not all right—' Her mother was working herself up again, and something inside Caroline seemed to clench itself into a knot of dread.

'It's all wrong—leaving me here alone . . . *Anything* could happen.'

'Mother,' protested Caroline, '*please*! Nothing's going to happen—and I'm not going anywhere, except to the corner shop.'

The sharp eyes were full of suspicion. 'Then why have you put on your red suit?'

'Because,' explained Caroline, with a sudden wild flick of hysterical laughter, 'I thought it might cheer me up.'

'Cheer you up?' The querulous voice was shrill with outrage. 'What've *you* got to be depressed about?' She glared at her daughter. 'You should try being me for a change—cooped up here in bed day after day . . .'

It would be a change, thought Caroline, with the same mad flick of humour, to lie in bed all day and be waited on hand and foot . . . But aloud she only said, quite kindly: 'Yes, I know it's hard for you.'

'Hard?' squeaked her mother. 'It's a nightmare!'

You're right about that at least, thought Caroline, and looked away from her mother in case her face betrayed her . . . A nightmare it surely is.

' . . . And now you're threatening to leave me—'

'Mother, I'm *not*. I'd never leave you. Surely you know that?'

Her mother began to sob. 'Abandoned,' she cried. 'Just a useless old woman . . . Nobody wants me . . . And now you—you—'

'Hush,' said Caroline, and folded her arms round her weeping mother and rocked her to and fro like a child. 'You'll make yourself ill again. No one's going to leave you. There's no need to get upset.'

'There is, there is!' wailed her mother, stiff with resistance in her arms. 'You're tired of me—your own mother . . . You don't love me any more.'

'I do,' crooned Caroline, looking over the top of her mother's head at the square of window. 'Of course I do . . .'

'You're all I've got—' The sobs were subsiding, but the voice was full of pathos. Caroline knew that heart-tugging voice . . . It was the one she dreaded most of all.

'Yes, I know.' She patted her mother briskly. 'And you're all I've got, too. So I'm not likely to desert you, am I? Now I'm going to make you another cup of tea. And while you're drinking it, I'll just slip down to the shop. You want something nice for lunch, don't you?'

Her mother sniffed and searched for a tissue. Caroline handed her one—a pink one scented with lavender, which her mother preferred.

'Can't you phone?'

'You know I can't. They don't deliver any more. No one delivers nowadays. I've got to go. But I promise not to be long . . .'

She escaped from the room with its fetid sick-room smell and its overcharged emotions, and went down to put the kettle on again. Really, she thought—all this fuss about my red suit. I wish I'd never got the darned thing out.

She carried the tea upstairs, expecting another outburst. But her mother was strangely silent, and the blue eyes were moist and mutely accusing as they watched her from the bed.

'There,' she said, falling into the old pattern of comfort and reassurance, 'drink that up and you'll soon feel better. Nothing like a good cup of tea . . . I won't be long.'

She almost ran down the stairs in case her mother called her back, but there was no following voice or rapping stick . . . Maybe, thought Caroline hopefully, she really was enjoying her cup of tea. So long as the silence held till she got out of the house.

With a sense of enormous relief, she seized her handbag and let herself out of the front door.

It was a crisp day—she had almost forgotten how bright and crisp an autumn day could be. The chestnut trees flared gold in the morning sun, and a thin rime of frost sparked on the fallen leaves.

Caroline felt like skipping. But instead she walked with brisk strides along the pavement, and lifted her face to the sun.

It didn't take long to collect the household's small supplies. She usually bought a week's food, to save just such another scene as this morning's. Her mother did so hate to be left . . .

At the last moment, she paused by the fruit counter and bought some grapes as an extra treat, and her glance fell on a small basket full of anemones which was standing beside the potato sacks. Those colours! she thought, arrested. So deep and pure, like stained-glass windows . . . vibrant and strong and filled with light. Singing colours . . . I'd like to buy the lot!

'How much?' she asked, picking out one small bunch of glowing violet and garnet red.

'Sixty pence,' said Ranjit Singh, the shopkeeper, and then—seeing the longing in Caroline's face—he found himself adding unexpectedly: 'You can have two for a pound.' He looked at her, smiling. 'Lovely colours, I am thinking.'

'Yes!' agreed Caroline. 'I am thinking so, too!' And she stooped to pick out another bunch with even brighter crimson and purple petals. 'I'll take the two, then.'

The flowers seemed almost to burn in her hand, and she carried them home like a banner.

So alive! she thought. Those marvellous colours! And the sun on the turning leaves, and the clear morning skies . . . So alive! I'd forgotten how it feels to be alive . . .

She reached the door of her mother's house, and stood for one more moment looking back at the bright day. Then she put her key in the lock and went inside.

It was very quiet indoors. The heavy furniture seemed to lie in wait, brooding and dark. The shadows on the stairs pressed round her as she stood.

'Mother?' she called. 'I'm back.'

There was no answering voice, and no imperious rapping on the floor.

She climbed the stairs with the flowers in her hand, and went to her mother's door and stood looking in. The figure on the bed looked smaller somehow, and frailer . . . And very still.

Caroline drew a sharp breath and went closer. The silver-blonde dyed hair lay spread on the pillow, framing the pale, petulant face. There were no spots of colour in the faded cheeks now . . . The absurd frilly nightdress fell away from one loosely dangling arm, and the blue eyes stared straight at Caroline and saw nothing. They seemed to reflect reproach and a faint surprise—and that was all.

Even without moving another step, Caroline knew she was dead.

She said something would happen to her if I went out, thought Caroline bleakly. And I didn't believe her . . . And now it has. And I can't even shed a tear.

All at once she became aware of the bright flowers in her hand, and something about their flaring beauty made her wince inside. So *alive*, I called them, she said to herself. And I put on my red suit today, and told myself I'd forgotten how it feels to be alive. And all the time—

Carefully, she laid the blazing anemones down on her mother's body and folded the two limp hands across them.

Then she turned and went downstairs to ring the doctor.

*   *   *

'It was my fault,' said Caroline, standing dry-eyed and stiff before her old friend Dr Ellis.

'It was nothing of the kind,' he snapped. 'She died of a heart attack—brought on, I suspect, by working herself up about nothing, as usual.'

'But I went out. She said something would happen to her if I went out.'

Dr Ellis sighed. 'Caroline—she's been saying that for years, and you know it. She used to say it to your father, long before you came home to take over . . . In fact, it was poor Jim who was driven into an early grave, not your mother. And the fact that she survived for another fifteen years is entirely due to you.'

Caroline almost wrung her hands in piteous, inarticulate self-reproach. 'All the same, I shouldn't have left her—'

William Ellis had known Caroline for years—all her life, in fact—and he had been visiting her mother all through her long, self-imposed illness. He had often told her to get up and live a normal life—people with heart trouble didn't stay in bed all day nowadays. But she took no notice. She would lie there, looking fragile and reproachful, while her young daughter ran around her in circles, getting older and more tired day by day.

'My dear girl,' he said gently, 'you have looked after your mother for most of your adult life—with the utmost devotion. I know. I've seen you. And you have absolutely nothing to reproach yourself with—*nothing*.' He looked at her with his compassionate doctor's gaze, assessing much as he went along. 'How old are you now, Caroline?'

She hesitated, almost as if the question confused her with its irrelevance. 'I'm—thirty-five.'

'Exactly. Thirty-five. You're still a young woman, you know.' He smiled at her, watching the distress and puzzlement cloud those expressive blue eyes. 'I can remember when you first came home from college, after your father's death—' He paused, picturing her in his mind. So young and ardent and pretty . . . and she'd be pretty now if she wasn't so tired . . . Young and pretty and somehow hopeful. He spoke the last word aloud.

'*Hopeful*?' She sounded totally uncomprehending.

'Yes.' William Ellis sighed again, trying to find a way to get through to her. 'How many times have you been away on holiday since then?'

She looked shocked. 'On holiday? Never.'

'For a night or two, even?'

'No, of course not. She didn't like to be left.'

'And how often during the week did you go out— dancing, perhaps? Or to a concert? . . . Or for a walk with your boyfriend?'

Caroline's mouth had almost fallen open in amazement. Now it clamped tight shut. 'You must be joking.'

'No, I'm not. I know exactly what your life has been like. I'm just pointing out that you gave up your entire existence to your mother—all your waking hours, and half the night as well, by the look of you.'

She stared at him. 'It was my choice.'

'Your choice—? To give up your degree for a dull local job in your uncle's office, and when she found that took you away from her, to give that up as well? And with it, your freedom, your independence—and your boyfriend.'

Caroline blinked. Her face, which was already pale, went even paler. 'Gerald? Actually, he gave me up.'

Ellis snorted. 'I know. The prospect of being permanently responsible for a chronic invalid daunted him. But it didn't daunt you, did it?'

'I—had no option.'

16

'Oh yes you did, my dear girl. You could have said no to all her ceaseless demands and gone back to college. You could have insisted on keeping your job—and on going out when you liked—but you didn't. You stayed in and looked after her—and she used you unmercifully.'

Caroline, knowing quite well where the doctor's abrasive kindness was leading, suddenly agreed with him, sighing. 'Yes. I know . . . But she was my mother, and I loved her—'

'Of course you did.'

'And she was frightened,' said Caroline, staring at William Ellis with those honest, far-seeing eyes. 'She was afraid of death—and I let her die alone.'

The doctor shook his head decisively. 'I doubt if she had time to be frightened. It was quite sudden. Probably almost instantaneous.'

'I should've been there.'

'It could have happened any time—while you were downstairs making tea, or anything.' He paused, and then added deliberately: 'She didn't look frightened, did she?'

Caroline's direct gaze flickered as she thought about it. 'No,' she said at last. 'Surprised.'

William Ellis laid a firm hand on her arm. 'Exactly. It just took her by surprise. No time for alarm. Much the best way . . . So you have no cause to blame yourself. And you simply mustn't let such thoughts haunt you any longer. You gave her fifteen years of happiness—much more than she had any right to expect.'

'Happiness?' said Caroline, as if it was a word in a foreign language.

The doctor's hand tightened on her arm. 'Yes. Happiness. And now it's your turn. You have a life of your own to lead now. It's high time you began to consider yourself.'

'Happiness?' repeated Caroline, in a voice between nightmare and dream . . . That heavy sick-room smell—the querulous, anxious voice, the restless limbs—that blue, accusing gaze . . .

'Are you sleeping?' Ellis broke into her thoughts.

'Sleeping?' she laughed. 'It's absurd, isn't it? I used to long for a good night's sleep—no interruptions—no demands. And now, I like awake, waiting for her voice to call

17

out . . . and her stick banging on the floor.'

'We can remedy that,' the doctor assured her, well aware that there were deeper-rooted ills that he could not remedy—yet.

'Can you?' She sounded suddenly so lost and tired that he was almost shocked. She had always been strong and enduring, young Caroline . . . And this was what fifteen years of drudgery for a possessive, ungrateful woman had done for her. He only hoped she had the stamina to pull out of it now, and start living again, poor girl.

'Of course.' He patted her kindly. 'We'll make you sleep.'

'There's the funeral to get through.'

He nodded. 'Are there relations who will help?'

She laughed again. 'Oh yes, there are relations. But whether they will help—'

She remembered the time when her father died. Aunts and uncles, black armbands and discreet sniffing into handkerchiefs. But none of them—not one of them—had offered to help the young Caroline, twenty years old, halfway through college, bewildered and scared . . . Her mother had collapsed at once and gone to bed never, as it transpired, to get up again . . . It had all been left to her— the arrangements, the house to run, the bills to pay, the stairs to climb—the endless stairs to climb . . .

'Anyway, I'll be there,' said William Ellis, seeming to understand her thoughts without being told. 'You can rely on me.'

Caroline's rare, exceedingly sweet smile flashed out. 'Haven't I always?' she said.

*　　*　　*

A lot of people came to the funeral, whom she scarcely knew. They crowded into the hall and the over-stuffed front room, making the house seem smaller and stuffier than ever. Their voices yapped and bayed in a crescendo of family gossip, with occasional lapses into the kind of hushed sepulchral tones that belonged to funerals.

Caroline, rushing in and out of the kitchen with more glasses of sherry, cups of tea and plates of sandwiches, found to her surprise that she hated them all—all of them, with their false bonhomie and their equally insincere condolences, and their beady eyes summing her up as they watched her over their teacups.

I hate them all, she said. And I wish they'd all go home and leave me in peace.

She banged down another empty tray on the kitchen table and went over to the stove to refill the teapot. But as she reached for the kettle, a snatch of clear conversation came to her from the open door into the sitting-room, and she froze, her fingers still clutching the wooden handle of the kettle.

'What are we going to do about poor Caroline?' said a voice—female and sharpish, probably Auntie Flo's.

'Oh yes, poor Caroline. It is a problem, isn't it?' Another voice, also female, slightly more non-committal.

'What are we *supposed* to do about her?' Yet another woman's voice. (What were all the men talking about, anyway?) This time it was cold and slightly defensive.

'Well—' the first voice again, a little apologetic. 'She is totally alone now, poor thing—and she's not getting any younger.'

'And I don't suppose May left her anything—except this poky little house.'

'She won't be able to stay here, will she? On her own?'

'Well, I certainly can't have her.' That was the cold voice—colder and even more defensive.

'Nor can I. Our place is *much* too small . . .'

'But what will she have to live on?' Auntie Flo again, a bit anxious this time.

'She'll have to get a job. Didn't she have one before?'

'Yes, but—it's been a long time . . . She's probably rusty—'

'And dreadfully out of touch, poor girl . . .'

'It's a shame—wasting all those years on that . . .'

'Now, Jessica,' cut in a man's voice at last, slightly warmer and full of joky reproof, 'we mustn't speak ill of the dead . . .'

'We weren't,' reported Jessica crisply. 'We were just wondering about poor Caroline—'

19

'What about her?'

'Well—how will she manage?'

'If I know anything about that girl,' said Uncle Bob, dismissing it jovially, 'she'll manage very well.'

Outside in the kitchen, Caroline seized the tin tray off the kitchen table and hurled it on the floor with a resounding crash.

That should stop them, she thought.

There was a moment's silence outside, and then the hubbub of voices began again, but a little subdued this time, and as if they had moved farther off.

Caroline found that she was trembling with anger. How dare they! she said. Poor Caroline, indeed! I'll give them poor Caroline!

She turned blindly, longing to escape from those relentlessly wagging tongues and cold, inquisitive eyes—but a quiet voice behind her said: 'Hold on. They'll be gone soon . . .' and Dr Ellis came into the kitchen, carrying a trayful of glasses.

Caroline took a deep breath. 'I'm sorry. It's just that— they were talking about me.'

'I know. I heard them.' He put down the tray with a decisive thud that made all the glasses jingle. 'Tiresome old busybodies!'

Caroline laughed.

'That's better.' The doctor grinned at her and held out a full glass of sherry. 'Can you drink this stuff? Have a swig, it'll do you good.'

Caroline took it from him, and noticed with shame that her hand still shook.

'Ah!' said another voice from the doorway. 'I'm glad *someone's* got the sense to give the girl a drink!' and Caroline's Uncle Hal came through the door.

She liked Uncle Hal. He was her father's brother—a successful solicitor, with a manner that was both dry and practical but not without humanity. It was in his dusty office that she had pursued her dull clerk's job until her mother objected to her absence.

William Ellis quite liked Hal, too—though he wasn't a patch on his brother, James, who had been William's friend and had died much too soon . . .

'Hal,' he said, 'I think she's had about enough of those old biddies out there. Can't you shift 'em?'

Hal rubbed a hand round his elegant silver tonsure and gave a rueful grin. 'I will do my best,' he said sedately. 'But first, I want a word with Caroline.'

The doctor smiled and made a move to go. But Hal lifted a peremptory hand. 'Don't go, William. You've looked after this family for more years than I care to remember—and you were very good to my brother, James . . .'

'Didn't have much chance,' growled William Ellis, who found that he still minded somehow about James's death.

'Well, anyway, you've been more help to Caroline than the lot of us put together,' said Hal, sounding for once quite straightforward and not a bit pedantic. 'So you might as well stay.' He turned to Caroline, and laid a thin, dry hand on her arm. 'I only want to say this now, my dear girl. You needn't worry about the future—not yet at any rate. There's a bit of money to come—and there's the house. No need to take any decisions at the moment—and no need to take any notice of *them*, either!' He jerked his narrow head in the direction of the chattering voices beyond. 'Come and see me in my office—tomorrow, if you can. We'll sort everything out then. All right?'

'Yes, Uncle Hal . . . Thanks.' But she found his sudden kindness perilous, and taking up yet another tray and wielding it as a kind of barrier, she hurried out of the room.

Hal looked after her shrewdly. 'Not sleeping much?'

'Not a lot, I'm afraid.'

'Surely, William, you could—?'.

'I have,' snapped William, pretending to be affronted. 'What d'you take me for? But it takes time to unwind. Give her a chance.'

'Yes,' agreed Hal soberly. 'That's exactly what I do want to give her.'

'Don't we all?' sighed William Ellis.

*　　*　　*

21

Caroline meant to go and see Uncle Hal in his office that morning, but somehow it didn't work out quite like that.

To begin with, she decided to walk through the park, and to call in at the corner shop on the way. Ranjit Singh had sent flowers to her mother's funeral. He was the only one who had in that quiet keep-yourself-to-yourself neighbourhood, and he had even put in some brilliant anemones among the stiff chrysanthemums, perhaps remembering how Caroline's eyes had seemed to rejoice at their bright colours in his crowded shop. Caroline had noticed them at the funeral, but she hadn't had time to look at them properly, and anyway, she had told herself sternly, it was no time for rejoicing about colours or anything else . . . But now, she could at least tell him she was pleased.

There was something odd about the world this morning, though, and she found it quite difficult to walk calmly along the pavement towards Mr Singh's shop. The paving stones seemed to grow wider as she walked, and to stretch into endless, frightening distance, and the tall terraced houses seemed to tower and lean over her, as if they would like to crush her into the ground. The traffic, too, seemed bent on her destruction. It roared and screeched in her ears, and great juggernauts hurtled past all the crossroads in an unending, menacing stream . . . Everything seemed too big and too loud, and she found herself cringing whenever a bus or a lorry swept by, and even when she encountered anyone on the pavement . . . She was trembling and sweating when she reached the shop on the corner. What on earth was the matter with her?

'Good morning, Miss Gilmour. It is a beautiful day,' said Ranjit Singh, looking at Caroline with dark, observant eyes. He rather admired her. He knew what she had endured over the years with that difficult customer, Mrs May Gilmour. But she had always been pleasant and polite to him, never one to complain. He would have liked to say something to her—something encouraging and kind—but he couldn't quite think how to say it without sounding presumptuous. So he contented himself with that gentle platitude about the weather.

'Yes,' agreed Caroline, surprised to find herself panting a

little with fright about nothing. 'L-lovely sunshine . . .' She
drew in a shaky breath, and added: 'It was so kind of you to
send the flowers . . .'

Ranjit Singh was looking at her anxiously. 'Would you be
sitting down?' he asked, producing a chair from behind the
counter. 'I am thinking you have been hurrying too much.'
He watched her debating in her mind whether she ought to
give in to weakness, and whether it was proper to sit down
in his shop.

'Thank you,' she sighed, for in truth she was feeling
rather peculiar—her heart seemed to be thumping so
wildly and loudly. Maybe Mr Singh could hear it, too, and
that was why he was being so solicitous?

'I am making a cup of tea,' he announced, and bustled off
into the tiny kitchen at the back of the shop.

Caroline looked at the shelves of goods around her—but
they seemed to be growing taller too, and to be leaning
towards her, leering. She closed her eyes.

I ought not to be doing this, she thought—sitting here,
idling . . . There's so much to do. All mother's things to
sort . . . And what about Uncle Hal? . . . But somehow she
couldn't get up just yet. Her legs were shaking too much,
and the noisy thumping of her heart confused her.

'It is the best Darjeeling,' said Ranjit Singh, holding out
the cup of tea with hopeful deference. 'I hope you will be
liking it?'

Caroline smiled with pale determination and took it from
him. But her hand shook so much that she nearly dropped
it. 'Thank you,' she said again, and tried to sip it calmly.

'Would you be taking sugar?' asked Ranjit, wanting to
ask something much more urgent.

'No—I—I don't think so . . .' She sounded a little
uncertain.

'It is being very good for shock,' said Ranjit, greatly
daring. He held out the bowl of sugar, and then, seeing her
trembling hands, carefully spooned some sugar into her
cup and stirred it for her.

'I'm sorry . . .' she began, apologising for her extraordinary collapse, 'it's all so big, you see . . .'

Ranjit Singh stared at her. 'Big?' But he did not sound

surprised. Not many things surprised Ranjit Singh any more. It was almost as if he understood her.

'Too big . . .' sighed Caroline. 'All that—out there—' She waved a still-shaky hand towards the open door of the shop. All those buildings . . . and the traffic . . . And those pavements, miles and miles of them . . . too big and too loud . . . And I'm getting smaller and smaller, like Alice . . . Smaller and smaller . . . I might even slip down a crack . . .

She looked up into Ranjit Singh's concerned brown face. 'The cracks are getting wider, you see,' she said.

Ranjit Singh nodded. 'It is being a very frightening world we live in, Miss Gilmour—these days.' He paused, wondering if a little soothing conversation would give the tea time to work. 'Before I am coming to England,' he said in his gentle, lilting voice, 'I was being part of a big family in a small village . . . We all knew each other. If some sadness happened to one of us, we could all help . . . If there was a happiness, we all rejoiced mightily and there would be a party . . .' He smiled, remembering with affection and not a little sadness those far-off days. And if there was a sick old woman to look after, we all looked after her, he reflected. We didn't all go away and leave it to one daughter . . . But of course he could not say this to Miss Gilmour.

'No pavements?' said Caroline.

'No. Only baked earth. And dust.' His smile grew wider. 'Plenty of dust.'

'I don't mind dust,' murmured Caroline. And then, more insistently: 'No cracks?'

'Oh yes.' He nodded his dark head. 'In the summer, when it was hot, there were many cracks . . .' His glance slid sideways to her face, and he added with swift reassurance: 'But they were only little ones.'

Caroline leant back in her chair, seeming comforted. She drank the rest of her tea in silence, and then carefully set the cup down on the counter before getting up.

Ranjit Singh watched her covertly and saw that she was still not very steady on her feet.

'I must be going now,' she said, with an attempt at

24

brightness. 'Thank you for the tea, Mr Singh. You've been most kind.'

He smiled at her without speaking. But he was worried. Did she know where she was going? She didn't seem herself at all . . . And the strange, frightened glitter was still in her eyes when she looked out of the door at the busy street beyond.

'Where would you be going now, Miss Gilmour?' he asked, trying to sound as ordinary as possible. 'Is there anything I can be doing for you?'

She shook her head. 'No thank you, Mr Singh. I'm only going to my uncle's office.' She drew an uneven breath of resolve. 'I thought I'd go through the park . . . ' Her voice wavered a little, and then she added—still with the same studied brightness: 'No pavements there, you know . . . and not much room for cracks.' She smiled at him again with sudden dazzling brilliance. 'I shall be quite all right if I'm careful.'

She went out of the shop, erect and purposeful, and started to walk very carefully between the cracks of the pavements towards the park.

Behind her, Ranjit Singh stood and watched her go, and then even more purposefully went to the back of his shop to the telephone.

'Dr Ellis?' he said. 'This is Ranjit Singh at the corner shop.'

'Oh yes, Ranjit. What can I do for you?'

'It is not me, Dr Ellis, it is being Miss Gilmour.'

'Miss Gilmour? Caroline?'

'Yes. Miss Caroline. She was in my shop, and I am thinking she is not very well . . . ' He hesitated, not knowing how to explain it.

'What do you mean?'

'She was being frightened.'

'Frightened? What about?'

'I do not quite know, Dr Ellis. But I am thinking it was the world. She said it was too big.'

There was a pause at the other end. William Ellis was no fool. He heard the anxiety in Ranjit Singh's voice. And he understood, in a flash of professional insight, exactly what

25

was happening to poor Caroline. In fact he had been expecting something of the sort . . . 'Where is she now?' he asked, rapidly running his eye down his appointment pad on his desk.

'She said she was going to her uncle's office—through the park.'

'Through the park?' He sounded startled. 'That's a long way round.'

'It was—because of the pavements,' explained Ranjit, hoping it didn't sound too unlikely.

'The pavements?'

'The cracks in them,' he added painstakingly. 'They frightened her.'

'I see,' said William Ellis gravely.

'I did try to keep her here,' Ranjit sounded quite upset by now. 'I was giving her a cup of tea . . . but she would not stay.'

'That's all right, Ranjit. You did your best, I'm sure. I'll get over there right away and see if I can find her . . . She's had a lot of worry lately.'

'I know.' The lilting voice was still full of distress. 'I would go myself, but I cannot leave the shop . . .'

'Don't distress yourself, Ranjit. You stay there where I can reach you. In case I need your help.'

'I will do that, Dr Ellis,' assented Ranjit thankfully. 'I will be here—if there is being anything I can do . . .'

William Ellis rang off, seized his raincoat and his doctor's case, left a stream of instructions with his receptionist for his other partners, and went striding away down the road towards the park. No use taking the car if that was the way she had gone . . . He wondered what had triggered this off, and how bad it really was. He knew she was living somewhat on a knife-edge of control, and that she might well slip over it. But he hadn't thought it was this near. He only hoped she was not in real trouble—and that he would be in time.

*　　*　　*

In spite of walking very carefully, Caroline was almost panic-stricken by the time she got to the park. The cracks had grown bigger, she was sure, and the pavements stretched farther and farther, like a giant chessboard with holes where the joins were . . . She had to cross the road to get to the park, and after waiting in vain for the stream of lorries to stop, she ran desperately through the traffic, dodging buses and taxis and careless private cars, in a frantic dash for the quiet grass and tree-lined walks behind the iron gates of Coronation Park.

It was better inside. She was still panting and frightened, but the gravel paths were smooth with no cracks in them, and the shadows under the trees were cool and silent. A litter of red leaves lay scattered on the grass, and at first they delighted her with their glowing colours and she enjoyed the crunchy feel of them under her feet. But then she suddenly thought that they might be hiding the cracks under the grass, and she ran away from them rather swiftly, back to the swept paths, and found her way to a bench in the sun.

Gratefully, she sank down and tried to still her shaking limbs. It's all right here, she told herself. Nothing is threatening me. The sun is shining, warm on my face, and the trees are kind . . .

But then she noticed that even the trees were leaning towards her—particularly that great cedar by the edge of the grass—and they seemed to be growing taller and wider and more menacing even as she watched. So she looked away hastily, and it was then that she saw the crack. It was a trench, actually, that the gardener had dug ready for some autumn planting. But it was brown and dark and it gaped wide open, just at her feet, like a grave widening ready for her to fall in.

Leaping up on to the faded green slats of the bench, Caroline screamed. Up till now, the screams inside her head had stayed in, unuttered—just fizzing and boiling with the unresolved struggle to get out. But this one escaped, and came out loud and clear. She stood there, frozen into upright terror, a rigid, petrified figure on top of the bench, while the scream rang around her.

Almost at once, things began to happen. One of the gardeners and a park-keeper came running, thoughts of muggings and sex attacks uppermost in their minds. And several ordinary strollers stopped in their tracks and turned back to see what was happening. Before long a small crowd was gathered round the bench, while the park-keeper tried in vain to understand what had frightened the hysterical lady standing rigid on top of it.

Could she have been attacked? Was it a flasher in the bushes? Or one of the old meths drinkers who liked to sleep on park benches? Or a practical joker, or some kids with firecrackers? . . . Or could she just have seen a mouse?

While they were debating this, and asking ineffectual questions, and scratching their heads and looking at one another in dismay, and Caroline went on screaming, a calm, rather sunburnt man with a camera came along the path, pushed through the little crowd of helpless onlookers, and got up on the bench beside Caroline. Then he did two things. First, he smacked her face very smartly, and then he put his arms round her and hugged her.

Caroline gasped, choked, and stopped screaming.

'It's all right,' he said. 'I've got you. Nothing can touch you now.'

Caroline's laboured breathing came out in great gasps that were almost sobs—but not quite. She hadn't cried since her mother's death—not for years and years, in fact—but now it was not far off, and the man holding her so steadily in his arms seemed to know this.

He looked over her head at the anxious little crowd, and spoke directly to the park-keeper. 'Is the cafeteria open? Do you think someone could bring her a cup of tea? She'll be all right in a minute.'

But he could feel Caroline still shaking in his arms, and he tightened his grip on her and added gently: 'Hold on. I'm here.'

The park-keeper took his cue and dispersed the small crowd with soothing words, despatching his gardener to fetch a cup of tea.

'Something frightened the lady. She's all right now. No

28

harm done. Nothing to worry about . . . Her friend will look after her.'

Still making soothing noises, he shepherded the curious strollers and would-be helpers away.

But he's not my friend, thought Caroline, sudden clarity coming to her bruised mind for a moment. I don't even know him . . . Yet somehow she felt that she did, and his arms—still round her—felt familiar and safe.

'Now,' he said, 'let's sit down . . . You're not afraid of the bench, are you?'

'No,' whispered Caroline. 'It's—the crack.'

The brown man turned to look down at the trench and then lifted his head and smiled directly into Caroline's dilated eyes. 'Oh, *that*,' he said. 'That's not a crack.'

'Isn't it?'

'No. That's a trench.'

'A trench? . . . Are you sure?'

'Of course I'm sure. I should know a trench when I see one.' For a moment there was a certain grimness in his voice and a hard gleam in his eye.

Caroline looked from him to the trench and back again. 'But not for war?' she murmured.

'Certainly not. For geraniums and things. It'll be filled up soon.' He kept one arm round her, still holding her firmly, and unslung his camera with the other. 'Tell you what—I'll photograph it. Then you can tear it up.'

'What?'

'Tear it up.' His smile was clear and reassuring. 'This is one of those instant things . . . See?'

He focused his camera, stooping to see the offending trench through his sights, and clicked the switch. There was the usual buzzing sound, and Caroline watched fascinated while the picture developed under her eyes and came out of the slot.

'There you are,' he said, handing it to her. 'One hole. Now, tear it up.'

Caroline looked at him, bewildered. 'T-tear it up?'

'Yes. Then it will be gone.'

She looked down at the real trench uncertainly. 'But it's still there.'

'No,' said the man decisively. 'Not as far as you're concerned. Once you've torn it up, it can't get at you. Try.'

Obediently, Caroline tore it up. Her fingers were still stiff with fright, but she managed it somehow.

'Now,' said the stranger, still brisk and cheerful, 'give the bits to me. I'll drop them in the litter bin and they'll be gone. Can't have that park-keeper after us, can we?'

By this time, somehow, Caroline was sitting down beside him on the bench, his arm was still round her, and yes, he was right, the trench was no longer trying to swallow her.

'Tell me,' he said chattily, 'how long have they been getting at you?'

'Only—only today.' Caroline's voice was still shaken and ashamed. 'I think . . .'

He nodded. 'That's not too bad, is it? We'll master 'em. They can't have got a real hold in one day.'

'C-can't they?'

'No.' He was quite definite. 'They need more time than that.' He gave her shoulders a reassuring hug. 'They creep up on you,' he said, 'if you give 'em half a chance. But we won't let 'em.'

Caroline closed her eyes against the sudden tears that rose up, threatening to swamp her. It was so good, so extraordinarily good, to be on the receiving end of this unknown stranger's kindness—even if only for a minute. She couldn't remember ever feeling so cherished and protected before.

'Bear up,' he said, seeing the sheen of tears on her lashes. 'Here comes your tea.'

The gardener came hurrying, with tea in a plastic beaker, relieved to find Caroline sitting down and behaving normally. It took all sorts, he reflected, handing over the tea, and maybe the poor lady had troubles he didn't know about.

'No,' he protested, as the sunburnt man felt in his pocket for change. 'Mr Simms says compliments of the Parks Department, and he hopes the lady's feeling better.'

'Oh, she is,' smiled the man. 'Much better, thanks.'

Gravely, he took the plastic beaker and folded Caroline's cold fingers round it. He watched the rigid paleness recede from her face, and a faint colour rise in her cheeks as she struggled for composure. The tears still clung to her lashes, but she did not let them fall. She did not know it, but she looked suddenly very young and vulnerable, sitting there in the golden autumn sunshine—like a small girl after a tantrum, trying to be good.

'Drink up,' he said. 'All over now.'

But it wasn't, and Caroline knew it. The world still lay in wait for her out there. But here, in this quiet oasis of warmth and light, she was protected by a stranger with strong arms and a brown-velvet voice that sang with certainty and kindness. She wanted to stay here for ever . . .

Carefully, she began to drink her tea, and her companion sat on beside her in peaceful silence, with his arm still comfortably round her shoulders.

It was to this curiously touching scene that William Ellis came hurrying through the park, foreboding and self-reproach in his conscientious doctor's heart. He stopped when he saw them, and approached more cautiously. Who was the man she was with? Certainly not the ex-boyfriend who had fled from trouble. This was an older man, and he didn't seem to be afraid of responsibility . . . and she seemed to know him well.

'Caroline?' he said. And waited for her to look at him, or for the man beside her to give some sign. He wasn't quite sure what to expect.

'Oh, Dr Ellis . . .' Caroline's hand holding the beaker suddenly shook. 'I've been . . . so stupid . . .'

'No,' said the man beside her, with intent. 'Not stupid. Frightened.' He gave her another small hug of reassurance. 'But you're not frightened now, are you?'

'N-no,' admitted Caroline, and tried to smile. It was a dim, tired smile, but it still held a curious radiance, and both her companion and Dr Ellis seemed to wince a little as they saw it.

'Maybe I should take you home?' suggested the doctor, seeing that the stranger had managed to calm her down. But this was stupid of William—only he couldn't have known, of course, how it would take Caroline.

She suddenly began to shake again, and clutched the tea

so hard that the plastic cup bent and the hot liquid spilled out onto her hand. 'No!' she whispered. 'No! I can't go home . . . Not to that house . . . Not ever again . . . It's waiting for me . . . I *can't*.'

'Hush!' said her companion, and looked over her head at Dr Ellis. 'No one's going to make you go home . . . It's all right.'

'It'll get me.'

'No, it won't. I told you. I'm here. We won't let it.'

Caroline shuddered in his arms, and tried to steady her breathing. 'I'm sorry . . .' she gasped, 'so sorry . . . to be such a nuisance . . .' For a moment, the real Caroline looked out of her eyes at her old friend Dr Ellis, but then that brilliant clarity receded, and she saw him as an enemy who wanted her to go home to that heavy, brooding house and its menacing shadows.

'No!' she whispered again, and tried to retreat still farther, shrinking away along the bench. 'I can't go back—I *can't*.'

The two men looked at one another, and something seemed to pass between them.

'I know where we'll go,' said the man, holding Caroline's shaking body still beneath his sheltering arm. 'There's a place I know . . . It's not far from here.'

Caroline drew a quivering breath. 'Safe?'

'Very safe.'

'No—no cracks?'

'No cracks. All smooth grass outside. And smooth floors inside. Not a single join. You'll see.' He turned to Dr Ellis with easy deference. 'You'd better come and inspect it. Then she'll know it's safe.'

Caroline felt, obscurely, that she had been unfair to Dr Ellis. He was her ally—he had never been her enemy. What was she thinking of? 'Yes,' she said. 'Please come too . . .' And once again, tremulously, she tried to smile.

Together, the two men helped her to her feet. She was trembling again now, and her legs would scarcely support her. But she struggled to hold on to the tilting land-scape, and let them lead her gently between them. The brown man kept a firm arm round her, and she could feel

32

the warmth and reassurance of his presence even as she stumbled on—and dear old Dr Ellis had hold of her, too, and she knew dimly that his touch was also safe and kind. Yes, she was well protected . . . But the world still waited there, outside her charmed circle, ready to pounce . . .

They got her to the garden door before she collapsed completely. But she was far out by now, and scarcely heard what they said to her, or to one another. The whirling shadows and crouching beasts came closer and closer until they fell on her, and she was swallowed up in blackness . . . Poor Caroline was gone.

PART II
NO HOLES IN LIGHT

She woke to light. Light and space, and immense quiet. The room was awash with light—the walls, the ceiling, the furniture, all a pale rosy-white, repeated in the filmy curtains blowing round the open window. Outside the window was sunlight on golden trees and a glimpse of pale blue sky with white clouds moving across it. But even they seemed to reflect the same pale rose-gold light, and an echo of it danced on one wall in a shimmer of moving tree-patterns.

'Light . . .' she murmured, her voice slow and dream-laden.

'Yes, Miss Gilmour . . . Daylight. And a lovely day at that.'

'Which day?' she asked, drowsily unconcerned.

'Friday . . . You've slept a long time.' The voice was kind and calm, and blessedly neutral. It required no answer, no response.

'Friday?' It meant nothing to her . . . Sighing, she sank, fathoms deep, drowned in rose-gold light.

*　　*　　*

'Jon Armorel,' said the brown man, holding out his hand to Dr Ellis. 'Photographer. Late of Trans-global, Middle East. Sorry I took over.'

'Sorry?' William Ellis grasped the firm hand in his. 'I should think you were a godsend.' He looked at the younger man keenly, liking what he saw. The sunburnt face was explained by that brief, laconic description. Middle East . . . but *late* of' . . . ? There was a certain look of pain about that straight and disciplined mouth—Dr Ellis knew pain when he saw it—and the dark blue eyes were

37

curiously bleak. 'What I don't understand,' he said carefully, 'is how you knew so exactly how to handle it.'

The bleak eyes lit briefly in a gleam of humour. 'Been in the same boat myself. Didn't you realise?' He glanced round the long, graceful room with its wide French windows opening onto green lawns. (He had been right about the grass being smooth, thought the doctor, half-smiling). There were a few other people in the room, sitting together in small groups, or reading quietly alone. It was peaceful and silent, and the muted greens of the furnishings against the white walls were restful to the eye.

'You were a patient here yourself?'

'I still am.' He got up to help himself to some tea from the trolley close beside him, and brought over a cup to the doctor. 'Can you drink this stuff? It's all they allow here.'

Dr Ellis smiled. 'I know.'

The other man laughed a little. 'I thought you must. If you've got a practice in this town, you must know Ferguson.'

'Oh yes, indeed. I've even sent him patients of my own from time to time.' He hesitated and looked at Jon Armorel with enquiry. 'He does excellent work.'

'Sure.' Jon sipped at his tea, and made a wry face over it. 'And I know he has to cope with all sorts—junkies and alcoholics as well as simple nervous wrecks like me—!' His voice was malicious. 'But I must confess I do long for a real drink now and then . . . It's an occupational hazard.'

William Ellis was watching that grin, and decided to be inquisitive. 'You said *late* of'—?'

A shadow seemed to cross Jon's face, and the eyes grew bleaker. 'Ah well, you know how it is. You outrun your usefulness—or you stop producing the goods they want.'

Ellis thought this wasn't the whole of the story. 'There's usually a reason.'

Jon glanced at him shrewdly. 'Yes, well . . . When you go out on a blazingly unlikely story from a notoriously shaky contact, and get your partner killed in the process—' He took a rather desperate gulp at his tea, 'and get yourself shot up as well, and then find the whole thing was a plant—'

The doctor's face was grim with sympathy. 'Nasty.'

Jon put his cup down with a decisive click. 'It was. Very. and when I got home with bits of shrapnel in my lungs, the office decided I'd shot my bolt, as it were . . . School sports days and peace marches from now on . . .'

Ellis laughed. 'They can be quite bloody, too.'

Jon nodded morosely. But he did not laugh.

'So what happened?'

'Happened?' He looked at the doctor with flat calm. 'I had the father and mother of a breakdown . . . It was Richard's death, of course, mostly . . . I blamed myself for it—still do, as a matter of fact. They said it was a kind of "shell-shock",—we'd been working under fire in the Israeli-Lebanon war for months . . . But I think it was just guilt.' He sighed, and stared out of the window, away from William Ellis's too-penetrating gaze.

'It usually is,' said William, and repressed a sigh of his own. He was thinking of his patient, Caroline, and her taut, self-accusing voice saying: 'She was frightened—and I let her die alone . . .'

'What about your patient—Caroline, was it?' asked Jon, more or less reading his mind. 'Can you tell me about her?'

William Ellis hesitated for a moment. But then he decided that he could trust this man, and he would probably be here for a while yet and could maybe continue to be of some help to Caroline. He had been very useful so far, and he seemed to know very well how to get through to her.

'Why not?' he said slowly. 'She is suffering from a sense of guilt, too—and just as undeserved.' And he told Jon Armorel the whole story. He described the young Caroline when she first came home from university—brave and ardent and pretty, with that glowing auburn hair and those clear, fearless blue eyes . . .

'What was she reading?' interrupted Jon, already protesting inside at the waste of a keen young mind—let alone all that childish beauty and eagerness for life that the doctor described.

'Reading? Oh, modern languages, I think—and history of art. She was always quite keen on painting—and she meant to travel and get jobs in foreign art galleries and museums.' He looked at Jon sadly. 'She never did, of course.'

'She will have time now,' said Jon. He leant forward suddenly and laid a brown hand on William's arm. 'They'll get her well, you know . . . They nearly always do, here.'

'Yes,' agreed William. 'I'm sure they will.'

'I suppose you've seen Ferguson?'

'Yes. As soon as we brought her in. He was very hopeful.' He glanced a little warily at Jon. 'He said . . . they mostly make them sleep for a week first.'

Jon grinned. 'That's what they did to me.'

'But you're all right now.' It was a question really, and a lot lay behind it that William did not like to say.

'More or less,' assented Jon. 'Though my lungs aren't in the clear yet, and I still get nightmares. That's why they're keeping me a bit longer. I can go and come as I like now, of course. But they like to see me tucked up in bed at night.' His voice was sardonic. 'And I'm not too safe with cameras.'

The doctor looked startled. 'With cameras?'

'Yes. Some hang-up from the job and Richard's death . . .' He seemed unwilling to go on, but William wanted to know more.

'So?'

Jon gave a non-committal shrug. 'They brought me some of my old equipment.'

'Who did?'

'My erstwhile colleagues. Thought it would cheer me up to get back behind the lenses.'

'And?'

'I got up in the night and smashed the lot.'

Dr Ellis whistled. 'Expensive.'

'I'll say . . . That's why I was playing about with this silly thing.' He held up the small instant camera.

'Served its purpose, though,' smiled William.

'Yes.' Jon paused, and then added seriously: 'And I know what you're driving at.'

'You do?'

'I'll be here a while longer—and, yes, I will keep an eye on her, if you like.'

'I would be grateful,' said William. 'Especially as you seem to talk the same language.'

'As to that—' Jon answered carelessly, 'it takes an *aficionado* to recognise the language of despair.'

William nodded. He did not miss the anguish behind that flippant tone, but he was much too wise to say so. Anyway, he rather felt that mutual despairs had a way of cancelling each other out—given time . . . He sincerely hoped so.

With this faint hope in mind, he got to his feet and said goodbye to Jon, and went back to have a quick look at Caroline—still fathom's deep in drugged sleep—before he went home to his evening surgery.

Behind him, Jon lit a cigarette in spite of his damaged lungs, and thought of the panic in that girl's eyes . . . He was glad he'd been able to quench it a little. My God, he said to himself, sardonically, I'm actually thinking of someone else for a change . . .

Sighing, he got up from his chair and went over to play chess with the lonely colonel in the corner.

*   *   *

The next time she woke, the same iridescent light bathed the room, and she seemed to float in it . . . She felt like the leaf-shadows on the wall, vague and unfocused, drifting on rose-gold sunlight and blue air . . . Nothing troubled her . . . nothing ached . . . no weariness assailed her. She lay in a trance of well-being, tranquil and at peace . . .

'Peace . . .' she said aloud, watching the shimmering reflections on the wall.

No one answered her. No sound reached her—except, far out in the gold trees of the garden, some drowsy woodbird called . . .

Smiling, she sank back into dream . . . Light filled her tired mind . . . her tired soul . . . There was no pressing need, no obligation, no duty unfulfilled, no weight of long responsibility, no crisis, no danger . . . only light . . .

But presently she swam up into golden day again, and knew that someone was beside her.

41

She lay for a while watching the moving patterns on the wall, and then realised that she was looking at the profile of a man. It was a quiet face, brooding and still—the forehead high, with dark hair springing away, the nose straight, and the chin firm beneath a mouth that was sad. She could not see the eyes, for they were fixed on the distant trees of the garden beyond the window, but the whole cast of face and line of head seemed remote and sorrowful.

'Sorrowful . . .' she whispered.

The man turned his head and she saw his eyes—and then she remembered him. She remembered the trees of the park in the autumn sun, and some unexplained moment of terror—and his arms round her, warm and comforting . . . Or had she dreamed it . . . ?

'It was you . . .' she said.

He smiled, but did not get up from his chair by the window. 'You don't have to remember,' he said gently, and the dark blue eyes seemed to wait for any sign of panic to return. But there was none, and at length he spoke again, in the same quiet voice: 'They thought you might like a friendly face when you woke up . . .'

'They . . . ?'

But he did not answer that. Instead, he pointed with a brown hand to the trees outside the window, and murmured peacefully: 'Golden October . . . Soon you'll be well enough to sit out on the terrace.'

'Have I been ill?' She sounded puzzled, but not alarmed.

'Somewhat. Overtired, I should say . . . But you're better now.'

She lay looking at him, accepting the reassurance in his eyes, unsurprised by the sense of warmth it gave her. 'I don't know who you are.' She was smiling a little.

His answering smile was friendly, but still laced with sadness. 'Me? I'm Jon. Jon Armorel. I live here at the moment because I've been ill, too.' He thought that might reassure her still more. But her next words startled him.

'I don't know who I am, either.'

His eyes seemed to grow darker with concern. 'Don't you remember?'

She turned her head in a vaguely dismissive movement

and said quite calmly: 'Oh yes, I remember. But I'm not her any more.'

He waited, and when she didn't go on, prompted her gently: 'Not her?'

'Not poor Caroline. Not ever poor Caroline again.'

He nodded. 'So . . . who do you want to be?'

She looked thoughtful. 'I don't know.'

'Who were you before?'

She began to smile again. 'At school . . . I was called Turps.'

For a moment he was nonplussed. Then he laughed. 'I know. "Queen, queen Caroline, Washed her hair in turpentine . . ."'

'"Turpentine, To make it shine, Poor Queen Caroline."' She was laughing a little too, now, but she went on: 'You see? It was *poor* Caroline even then.'

'At least you were a queen,' he said, smiling. And then, pursuing it: 'What about—at university?'

Her eyes widened. How did he know so much about her? But somehow, she was comforted by this rather than surprised.

'I was Charley there . . .'

He grinned. 'Yes. You look like a Charley.'

'A proper Charley?'

'I didn't say so!'

She lay back against the pillows, still smiling. 'I am, though . . .'

'It's quite a good idea,' he said slowly, 'to admit your limitations . . . Personally, I rather like Charley.'

She looked at him with sudden, vivid sadness. 'My father liked it, too.'

At that revealing look, his expression changed. 'Then that settles it.' He spoke with decision. He got up and came over to the bed and took her hand in his. 'Welcome to the world, Charley—your brave new world.'

'New?' she said, feeling extraordinarily calm and secure under his touch.

'New,' he repeated. 'As from today, Charley—entirely new.'

*　　*　　*

43

But of course, she couldn't leave the old world out altogether. It was bound to encroach. Dr Ellis, calling conscientiously to see how his patient was progressing, carefully said nothing about her past life, or her future plans, but contented himself with a couple of shrewd summing-up glances, a kindly pat and the encouraging words: 'You'll do!' . . . But there was Uncle Hal waiting for instructions. She knew she ought to see him. She knew there were things to discuss and papers to sign. But the thought unnerved her. It made her tremble and sweat just to contemplate it . . . She simply wasn't ready for decisions yet . . . It was as much as she could do to get out of bed and sit by the window. Even that small effort made her knees shake and her head swim—and when the friendly young nurse brought her a menu and asked her what she would like for lunch, it threw her into a panic and she couldn't make any choice.

She was looking out at the long shadows of trees on the grass in the garden below her, when someone else came in to see her.

'You won't know me yet,' he said, smiling, 'but I've looked in on you quite a few times while you were asleep.'

'Have you?' She stared at him attentively.

He was tall, she noticed, and a little stooping, with a long, easy body and a clever-shaped head surmounted by a shock of dark hair with white streaks at either side. His face seemed as relaxed and mobile as his body, and there was a definite quirk of humour lurking at the edge of his mouth. His eyes, regarding her with lively intelligence, also reflected sparks of humour, and though they were clearly engaged in summing her up, they did not seem in any way formidable.

He held out his hand. 'I'm Dr Ferguson. And you are Charley, Jon tells me.'

She smiled, accepting, and put her hand trustfully in his. The fingers felt cool and firm as they grasped hers—and somehow full of quiet strength. 'And Jon tells me you are called the Guvnor.'

He laughed. 'True. Though I don't do much governing.'

'Not?' She tilted her head to one side, watching the

sunlight pick out the two white streaks in his hair. Her eyes kept settling on trivial details, she reflected, while a thousand unanswered questions burned in her mind.

'No. Only—suggesting.' His smile was real, she thought, and not a bit bland. 'D'you mind if I sit down? I've been walking round all day.' He came and sat beside her on the window-seat.

She realised suddenly, still without any sense of surprise or embarrassment, that she was wearing a neat, unfamiliar robe over a borrowed nightie, and she had no idea how she had acquired either.

'I know there must be a lot of questions in your mind,' he said, interpreting her bewildered glance correctly. 'But maybe I can resolve some of them.'

She looked at him then and said flatly: 'What's been wrong with me?'

He answered without evasion. 'We call it nervous exhaustion.'

'A breakdown?'

He frowned. 'No. Nothing so serious . . . At least—yes, I suppose you could say it was a breakdown of will.'

'Will?'

'Mind over matter.' He grinned. 'You were just very tired—frightfully tired and over-driven. So you seized up, just like a car.'

She laughed. Then grew grave. 'What happens now?'

'You rest.'

'How long for?'

'Until mind and matter recover.' His smile was somehow infectious. 'Or—if we're talking of cars—until the battery is recharged.'

'Am I on charge?'

'What do you think?' He waved a hand at the sun-gilded garden. 'It's all waiting for you out there. Sunshine, fresh air, plenty of good food which you haven't had to cook— and positively no worries.'

She sighed. 'It sounds wonderful.'

'But—?'

She hesitated. 'I don't know . . . I suppose I'm not used to being self-indulgent . . . or idle.' Her smile was shy and a little perilous this time. 'I keep thinking I ought to—to—'

'Pull yourself together?' The dazzling quirk of humour had somehow got entangled in his eyebrows.

'Yes . . . and—and do something positive.'

'Such as?'

'Oh, I don't know . . . Make plans . . . rearrange my life . . . organise my future . . .' She shuddered.

'But you don't want to?'

'N-not yet.'

He nodded. 'Good girl. At least you're honest about it.' He turned to face her seriously. 'You really must give yourself a chance, you know . . . You've been quite ill. Just take your time, and don't do anything until you feel ready. There's no hurry.'

She twisted her hands together and said painfully: 'There's one thing I want to know—'

'Yes?'

'Who's paying for all this?'

Dr Ferguson's calm gaze did not change. 'Oh, so that's what's worrying you. Your uncle—Henry Gilmour.'

'*Uncle Hal?*'

He grinned. 'Why not? Is it so unlikely?'

'He's never paid for anything for me before.'

For a moment Ferguson looked quite stern. He did not say: Then it's high time he did—but she could see the thought quite clearly in his eyes. Instead, he said neutrally: 'Well, he seems very concerned about you now.'

'Does he?'

'Certainly. He has rung up several times to inquire after you. And he asked me to tell you not to worry about anything—it's all being taken care of,' his smile regained its former strength, 'including all your expenses.'

She looked astonished.

He leant forward and patted her shoulder, almost affectionately. 'My dear Charley, I don't know why you should assume no one cares what happens to you. Your uncle wants to come and see you—but I told him to wait until you were a bit stronger.'

'That was . . . very considerate of you.' She found that his sudden kindness had made her close to tears.

He saw this, and got up quietly and stood looking down at her. 'You're tired now. I'll come in and see you again soon . . .'

She nodded, feeling the room swim round her—the moving sun-patterns on the walls laced now with the extra shimmer of tears. She closed her eyes against them, suddenly riven by the great wash of light . . .

When she opened her eyes again, she was alone.

*   *   *

It was not long after the Guvnor's visit that Evie, the young nurse, put her head round the door and said cheerfully: 'Miss Gilmour—the hairdresser's coming this morning. Would you like to have your hair done?'

Charley was startled—and instantly thrown into another panic. 'Yes, I—I think I would. But—' She went across, somewhat shakily, to peer at herself in the mirror. 'How do I want to look?' she murmured, and then, more desperately: 'I don't know what I want to look like.'

She gazed at the strange, pale face in the mirror. It didn't look much like her . . . Light from the window fell on it, burnishing the planes and contours into unfamiliar shapes. It looked younger and softer than she remembered—that would be the long days and nights of sleep, she supposed. The eyes weren't exactly frightened any more, but still a bit bewildered and thrown by decisions. They looked larger, somehow, and bluer in this light—less faded . . . And her mouth—well, it had stopped looking clamped into tight lines of control. It looked . . . gentler, somehow, and more vulnerable—dreadfully vulnerable. It was nearly trembling now . . . And her hair—that was certainly a disaster. It was really quite a good colour—a sort of tawny auburn at its best—but now it looked heavy and dull and lay flat on her head in untidy, lightless wisps. It was too long, too . . . But how should she deal with it? What ought she to do with it? Really, it was absurd to get into such a state over a mere head of hair . . .

Vaguely, she pushed it up on top of her head, and then

47

let it fall again with shaking fingers. 'I don't know what to do with it . . .'

Evie was a kind girl, and used to the fears and indecisions of her patients. She came and stood beside Charley, and smiled encouragingly. 'It's pretty hair, you know. Why don't you let her decide for you? She's the expert.'

'Yes,' sighed Charley. 'Maybe she'll know . . .' But a thought occurred to her, and she turned away from the mirror and looked up at Evie shyly. 'Is Jon—is Mr Armorel still here?' She didn't know if she ought to ask about him. But he hadn't been to see her again since that first day, and she found herself wondering why, and even wishing that he would come . . .

Evie seemed to hesitate a little. 'Yes, he is here. But he hasn't been very well for a day or two.'

Concern swept into Charley's face. 'Oh dear. I'm so sorry. Is he better now?'

'Oh yes.' The young nurse was cheerful again. 'He's downstairs today. Would you like me to—?'

'No,' said Charley, for once sounding almost decisive. 'I'll . . . Have I any clothes here?'

Evie went over to the white wall cupboard and opened it. 'The things you came in are all here.' She picked up a small pile of neatly folded clothes from the shelf and waved a brisk hand at the dark grey suit hanging on the rail. 'There's a laundry service here—we had your smalls washed for you.'

Charley got up unsteadily. 'Can I get dressed?'

'Yes, of course. Do you want a hand?'

'I—I don't know,' she confessed. 'Am I allowed downstairs?'

Evie's smile somehow conveyed approval and encouragement. Her patient had taken the next step on her own. 'You can go wherever you like—but your legs may feel a bit woolly on the stairs.'

'I think I can manage,' said Charley, and—painfully and slowly—began to get dressed.

But Evie was right, she did need help—and she was trembling with absurd exhaustion by the time she was ready to go downstairs. She didn't much like this dark charcoal-grey suit and the plain white blouse . . . It had been in respect for her mother, she remembered, with a faint flicker of distress deep down in her mind, and she had been going to see Uncle Hal in his office, so it was neat and formal . . . But now—somehow in this place of light and space and wonderful undemanding peace she longed for colour . . .

'Your uncle offered to bring in some of your other things,' said Evie, helping her into the jacket with kind and competent hands. 'But Dr Ferguson said we'd better wait until you asked for them . . .' She didn't go on, but Charley understood her.

I don't want them, she thought. I don't want to see any of them ever again . . . Or that house . . . or that awful furniture . . . Not any of it . . . But aloud she only said: 'This will do for now.'

She managed the corridor quite well, but she was glad of Evie's steadying hand on the stairs. They were wide and airy, with a beautiful curving balustrade, and tall windows looking out at green lawns and the same golden trees she could see from her own room. Downstairs, there was a big, open hall with glowing rugs on the floor, and several doorways opening out of it—all of them seeming to throw pools of light from beyond back into the central space where she stood.

'This way,' said Evie, and led her into one of the big sunny rooms.

Charley got an impression of green—soft, quiet green in the carpet on the floor, the covers of the chairs and sofas, and the curtains that framed the long French windows— and another wide view of green grass beyond.

It was a peaceful room—as filled with light and space as the rest of this gracious house—and even though there were several people in it, there was no sense of crowding or intrusive communal activity. Everyone seemed relaxed and quietly absorbed in their own pursuits. They did not stare curiously at Charley. One or two looked up and smiled— the rest went on with what they were doing and left her alone.

Jon Armorel was sitting alone by the window, gazing out

49

at the garden. But he looked up when she approached, and warmth came into his eyes as he saw her.

'Charley! You made it downstairs—congratulations!'

Evie steered her into a chair beside Jon and said, smiling: 'You'll be all right now. I'll come and fetch you when she's ready,' and went off to deal with other matters.

'When who's ready?' asked Jon.

'The hairdresser.' She looked at him anxiously. 'Jon—they said you'd been ill again. Are you all right?'

He grinned. 'I'm not complaining—except that I can't go out.'

'Why not?'

'Too damp and cold for these plaguey lungs, they say. Though it looks good enough out there to me.'

It did to Charley, too. But she said, with some asperity: 'What happened to your plaguey lungs anyway? You don't say a thing about yourself.'

His grin faded a little. 'Caution, Charley, pure caution. People here are apt to go on about their ailments . . . and I don't much like self-pity.'

She blinked a little. Was it a rebuff? Did he really hate being questioned?

But he turned his head and smiled again, aware that he had sounded unreasonably abrupt. 'It's all right, Charley—I'm prickly this morning.' He drew a rather painful breath and coughed a little. 'If you really want to know, they shot a few holes in them out in Lebanon. But they're healing up nicely, thank you—only now and again I get flare-ups. That's all.'

She gazed at him, seeming paler and more distressed than ever . . . And I make all this fuss about nothing, she thought. How can I bother him now about anything so trivial?

But Jon was regarding her with something very like affectionate amusement, and she began to smile, too.

'Well, then,' he said, 'what's on your mind, Charley? Tell Uncle Jon.'

'It seems so silly,' she began, and then plunged on in a breathless, shamed little voice: 'but I don't know what I want to look like . . .' She lifted a shaky hand and pushed it

50

crossly through her hair. 'All this fine talk about a brave new world,' she went on, with a gleam of humour, 'and I haven't the foggiest idea how to live in it! I can't even make up my mind about my own new image—let alone anything else!'

Jon laughed. 'Why ask me?'

'Because you're a photographer. You look at things like an artist. You can *see*.'

'The bones beneath the skin?' He screwed up his eyes and looked at her consideringly. 'Feathers,' he said. 'Tawny-owl style. Or it might be a young kestrel—with a chestnut mantle . . .' His voice was flecked with laughter, and sparks of the same lively humour glinted in his narrowed gaze. But even so, his appraisal was dazzlingly kind and seemed to have something in it of admiration, too, which rather puzzled Charley.

'Feathers?' She sounded doubtful.

'Yes. Tell her to cut it in feathers—short all over, but featherd round your face. And layered—so that it stands out in tongues . . .' He put out his hand and took hold of a strand of her hair and tugged it gently. 'I should think it would curl naturally, given half a chance . . .' He brushed his hand lightly over her head and added, still smiling at her confusion: 'And a few highlights—or a red rinse or something. Be dashing.'

'Shall I?'

'Why not?' His eyes were bright with challenge. 'You've got nothing to lose.'

'Nor I have,' she agreed, half-laughing, too. 'Then feathers it is.'

* * *

When Jon thought about it, he knew exactly what Charley ought to wear to celebrate her new hairstyle. She ought to wear green—vivid emerald green, the colour of spring, the colour of life and youth . . . And he knew, without being told, exactly what the clothes would be like that she had left behind in that house which made her shudder even to think of returning to. They would be dull and plain, well

51

brushed and cared for, neat and colourless and out of date, and she would hate them . . . He also knew that she was not ready yet to go out shopping in the crowded town stores . . . He was a born organiser, Jon. He was used to setting up a scene, telling people how to look and what to wear, stage-managing a dramatic incident . . . That is, he had been until he went out to the Middle East war and saw real-life dramas that needed no stage-management. Human suffering on a scale he'd never imagined. Things that his camera recorded which required no setting up by him . . . Until, of course, he was set up himself—set up with Richard the innocent victim . . .

Here, as always, his thoughts ground to a halt. It was no good. No good remembering. No good blaming himself any longer. It wouldn't bring Richard back . . . But all the same, something inside him grieved continuously for a tall, rangy man with a honeyed reporter's tongue and a handsome, mobile face that looked into the camera with a seraphic but wholly deceptive smile; a drinking companion of the utmost reliability, hard as nails and brave as a lion—a bit flamboyant, perhaps, and inclined to take unnecessary risks . . . until one day he took a risk not of his own choosing—the ultimate risk—and lost.

No, said Jon, getting to his feet. I must not remember. Not yet. Ferguson is right. I must go out and do something positive.

So he went out into the town, regardless of the chill in the autumn wind, and bought an emerald green dress for Charley.

When he got back, he sent it up in its carrier bag via young Evie, with a note inside which read: 'Dear Charley, Green for new life. I think it should go with your hair. Try it and see, Jon.'

He wondered if she would be offended and refuse to accept it, but somehow he thought not. Beneath the rigid respectability of the existence she had endured for so long, Charley was anything but conventional, and in this brand new life of hers she was like a child on the threshold of adventure, eager but scared.

So he was not really surprised when she came down the

stairs towards him, glowing in emerald green. But he was surprised at the transformation. Even he had not expected such a change.

The hairdresser had been clever. The short, faintly curling mass was just disciplined enough to show off the delicate shape of her head, and the feathery ends clung round her face, framing it in tawny red-gold tongues. The colour was good, too—a rich and vibrant auburn, just as he'd imagined. It made her look younger and more vulnerable—but also vividly alive.

Yes! he said to himself, I was right. And then to her shy and apprehensive gaze, he called up the stairs: 'Charley— you look simply wonderful!'

She paused for a moment, as if not quite sure of herself, and then came on down to him with her hands outstretched. 'Oh Jon, thank you. How did you know I was starved for colour? It's beautiful—but I must pay you back, of course.'

'Of course,' agreed Jon, smiling. 'But now come and let me show you off. Have you seen yourself in a mirror?'

'Yes.' She was smiling too, now.

'Well? What did you think?'

'I could hardly believe it was me.'

He took her over to the big gilt mirror in the hall and solemnly placed her in front of it.

'It's you all right,' he said. 'Allow me to introduce you. Charley—this is Charley. Brand new and good enough to eat . . . You'll know her next time you see her, won't you?'

She looked at herself in wonder, and then began to laugh. 'Yes,' she said. 'Yes, Jon. I believe I will.'

*   *   *

After this, she thought she could face Uncle Hal. It was time she put her life in order. But even so, once she had sent for him, she was a bit apprehensive.

He came on a windy morning, while she was watching the leaves whirl off the trees in the garden.

She had decided not to go downstairs to meet him. There were things to discuss which had to be said in private—

53

better to stay up here in her room, at least for the first part of the interview. Maybe she could introduce him to Jon later on . . . Besides, she must deal with this on her own, not in a place where Jon was within call. She relied on him too much already.

When Henry Gilmour saw her sitting on the window-seat, he couldn't believe his eyes. He had left behind in that funereal house a tired, pale woman in dowdy black, with faded hair and shadowed eyes that were dull with fatigue and pain . . . But here was a young, slender creature in vivid green, with a small, graceful head glowing with vibrant colour, and eyes that were a clear, far-seeing blue— serenely regarding him out of a delicate, heart-shaped face he scarcely recognised.

'My dear Caroline,' he said, holding out his hands to her, 'you look a different girl.'

'I am a different girl,' said Charley. Then she smiled and waved him to a chair. 'Do sit down, Uncle Hal. I know we have a lot to discuss.'

He was looking at her in astonishment—and some relief. This quietly confident girl was very different from what he had been expecting. The interview might well be easier than he had anticipated. He set his briefcase down on the floor beside him and leant back in his chair.

'I need hardly ask if you are better—you look wonderful. But I did take the precaution of consulting Dr Ferguson before I came.'

Charley smiled. 'What did the Guvnor say?'

Uncle Hal also permitted himself a small smile. 'He said you were responding very well to a regime of rest and no worries, and he was pleased with you—but you need time.'

Charley nodded. Time, she thought. Time to breathe . . . to let the slow days go by in this lovely house . . . time to explore the long shadows of the garden and the flaring autumn trees . . . time to walk on the green lawns and talk to Jon . . .

'As to that—' she began, and hesitated. 'It must be costing you an awful lot. I will try to—'

'No,' said Hal firmly. He shook his narrow silver head at

54

her (like her father's, but thinner and sharper). 'You must stay as long as you need to, my dear girl . . . It is clearly doing you a great deal of good. I don't want you to leave a day sooner than necessary—and certainly not before Ferguson says you are ready.'

'But—' She was still a little anxious.

Uncle Hal leant forward suddenly and laid a thin, narrow hand on her arm. 'Caroline—look at it this way. I could have helped with your mother all these years. After all, she was my brother's widow. But I left it all to you. For fifteen years, you took full responsibility . . . with dire consequences for yourself. Now, maybe, I can make some small recompense.' His eyes seemed to sharpen for a moment against some inner flick of self-reproach. 'It's about time.'

'You shouldn't feel like that.'

'But I do. I feel I owe it to you—on behalf of the whole family.'

Charley looked at him with sudden compassion. Her Uncle Hal really minded about this—he was quite upset.

'If you put it like that—'

'Of course I do.' He was brisk again. 'We'll say no more about it. Now, to business—' He got out some papers from his briefcase and laid them on his knee. 'The house and its contents are yours, of course . . . and there's the life insurance.'

She stared. 'What life insurance?'

'Your mother's.'

'I didn't know she had any.'

'No.' The same small smile hovered at the edge of her uncle's mouth. 'She made very sure of that.'

'What do you mean?'

He shook his head at her in smiling reproof. 'You always did make excuses for her. Caroline, your father knew he was a sick man—a good while before he died. And he knew what May was like, and what your life would be like when he wasn't there to take care of her.'

'So?'

'So he took out two life insurances—one for himself and one for May. He tied up quite a lot of his money in this way—so that when finally you were on your own, there

55

would be something left for you.'

Charley was puzzled. 'I suppose . . . my mother knew?'

'Oh yes. She was very annoyed at the time. She wanted the money to use as and when she chose, but she couldn't touch it—except possibly borrow against it. But I wouldn't let her do that. It was, in effect, your inheritance.'

She was silent for a moment. Then she said slowly: 'I wish I'd known . . . I could have—'

Her uncle cut in smoothly. 'Yes. I'm sure. You could have made things a little easier for her then, Caroline. But it was Jim's wish that it should come to you intact, and I had to respect that.'

'Why did you say "she made very sure" I didn't know about it?'

Uncle Hal gave a short, mirthless little bark of laughter. 'Can't you guess? Because she thought you might try to bump her off a little early if you knew.'

Charley stared at him in disbelief. 'You can't be serious.'

'Oh yes, I am. She told me so. That was the reason she gave for my strict instructions not to tell you.'

She sat gazing—shocked into renewed silence.

'Caroline,' he said, quite gently now, 'it is time you saw things clearly. Ferguson tells me you are still suffering from a sense of misplaced guilt about your mother. But you don't have to. I know you were fond of her, and did what you had to do most devotedly. But she used you, Caroline— unmercifully. And even with all your care for her, she didn't trust you. She expected you to be as grasping and self-centred as she was.'

Charley blinked. 'She was ill and old. People who are ill have sick fancies . . .' I should know, she thought. I've been ill. I've had sick fancies myself. Oh, poor mother!

Uncle Hal was looking at her curiously. 'I know I've spoken bluntly . . . I was very fond of your father, you know . . . But you still don't blame her, do you?'

Charley sighed. 'How can I? She couldn't help being what she was.'

As to that, Hal Gilmour had his own private doubts. But he said only: 'I hoped to release you from—any sense of obligation.'

56

After a pause, while she considered this, Charley smiled at him and said quietly: 'Yes, Uncle Hal. I think you have.'

He looked relieved. 'Well, then—you will have a lump sum—'

'How much?'

'Twenty thousand pounds.'

She looked startled. 'So much?'

'It won't go all that far these days.' His voice was dry. 'But it will give you time.' He glanced at her. 'As to the future—I don't know what plans you may have . . . But if you want to return to work in my office, there will always be a place for you.'

Charley swallowed a rising lump of panic. 'Thank you, Uncle Hal . . . That's kind of you . . . But I—I haven't made any plans yet . . .'

'Quite so.' He paused, and then added in a different, warmer voice: 'You might want to do something quite different.'

She smiled. 'I might.'

'Well—' Once again he paused for a moment. 'In the meantime, since your mother's estate will be frozen until probate is granted, I'm depositing an interim payment in your account to be going on with. I'm sure you'll want some new clothes and things—especially now you're looking so glamorous.'

She looked at him in surprise. There was actually approval in her uncle's voice—and in his appraising glance.

'I—it was actually Jon—Jon Armorel who gave me the courage,' she explained.

'Ah yes. Mr Armorel. William Ellis told me about him. He has been very helpful, I believe.' But the dryness was back in his voice now, and the gleam of approval was gone. 'Caroline,' he said, and hesitated and cleared his throat, obviously embarrassed.

'Yes?' She could not for the moment understand his discomfiture.

'Since neither your father nor your mother is alive—and you've lived such a—such an isolated kind of existence . . .' He floundered again, not knowing how to put it. 'I am your only close relative—' he added helplessly.

'Yes, Uncle Hal? What is it?'

'It's just—I'm sure this Jon Armorel is a good enough fellow—been ill himself, I'm told. I'm sure he has no—er—ulterior motive . . . But—but do be careful, my dear girl . . . The world is full of the most unscrupulous people, you know, and I—I wouldn't like you to get hurt.'

She was staring at him in astonishment now. But she understood him, and even forgave him his kindly old-fashioned doubts. How could he know about Jon? . . . A man deeper in despair than ever she had been, who knew how to meet catastrophe with common sense and whose very coolness and detachment was a comfort and relief . . .

'It's all right, Uncle Hal,' she said carefully. 'I have no intention of getting involved with anyone at present.' (Or ever, she told herself, fiercely. Not ever. From now on, I'm staying free. No ties. No responsibilities. No tugging of heartstrings. Just me, Charley—and the whole wide world to play in . . . But even to her, it sounded defiant and childish. And somehow the thought did not please her. In fact, it rather frightened her.)

'I'm afraid I've tired you,' said her uncle's voice. 'We'll leave all the details till later. But I should advise you not to say too much about your financial affairs—to anyone.' And when she made no response, he went on briskly: 'In the meantime, you'd better just sign these . . .'

Dutifully, she signed. But the same sense of unreality was growing—and with it the old, mounting terror. She didn't know what she was afraid of . . . but she was afraid.

She scarcely noticed when her uncle, feeling a little anxious now, said goodbye and almost tiptoed out of the room . . . But the room wasn't empty . . . It was full of shadows waiting to pounce . . . and the beautiful open spaces and shifting patterns of light in the place that she loved were suddenly full of menace . . . It wasn't safe any more . . . They were coming for her—even here . . . Trembling, she climbed under the window-seat where perhaps they would not find her, and crouched there, hidden, too terrified to move.

It was little nurse Evie who found her. She came into the room and saw the crouching figure under the window-seat,

58

and being a sensible girl who was used to assessing the most practical course of action in an emergency, she went running for Jon Armorel who seemed to be the one person who knew how to talk to Charley.

Jon was tired that day, and had been half-dozing over a book in a corner of the big drawing-room. But he came running, too.

He took one look at Charley's desolate figure, and simply came forward and folded her in his arms.

'It's all right, Charley. It's all right. It's me—Jon.' He glanced over her head through the wide windows at the rainswept garden and saw the cloud-shadows chasing across the grass followed by brilliant fingers of sunshine. 'Look,' he said, drawing Charley up beside him, 'the shadows are all going . . . the light's coming back.'

The young nurse, Evie, stood looking at Charley's ashen face for a moment. But when she saw returning warmth creep into it, she turned on her heel and went away. Jon Armorel knew what he was doing. Better leave him to it. Besides, she ought to report to the Guvnor about this latest setback.

By the time she returned with Dr Ferguson at her side, the room was empty, and Charley and Jon were walking side by side across the sun-dappled lawns of the garden. Ferguson stood for a moment watching them, and then turned to Evie cheerfully. 'Well, Jon Armorel seems to have the magic touch.'

'I hope I did right?'

'Certainly. It's better this way.' He smiled at her reassuringly. 'Not so alarming for Charley. Besides, it's good for Jon to feel useful.'

Nurse Evie was no fool. And she liked Jon Armorel. Most of the staff did, come to that. He was no trouble—except when he had nightmares; and though he was a bit moody at times, he was always ready to help in a crisis. She also liked Charley and was sorry that this setback should have occurred after she had begun to look so well and attractive . . .

'I'm sorry it happened. I should have gone in as soon as her uncle left.'

He smiled and shook his head. 'I doubt if you'd have prevented it. The past still has power to hurt, that's all. She'll grow stronger.'

Evie nodded. 'Shall I—? Do you want to see her later?'

'Not today. Let Jon be the doctor today . . . I'll see her tomorrow. It won't seem so frightening then.' He turned to his young nurse kindly, knowing that she was the kind that cared about her patient's progress—and God knew they were rare enough. 'Don't worry, Evie. She's doing very well. There are bound to be small setbacks at first.'

Together they turned away from the window and went back to work—the Guvnor to see another patient, Evie to push the tea trolley into the green drawing-room. They both heaved an inner sigh of relief that another small crisis had been overcome.

*   *   *

Outside in the damp and gleaming garden, Charley seemed almost dazzled by the colours. Every fallen leaf was polished with rain, glowing in crimson and fiery orange pools under the naked trees. Even the bark of the wind-shaken branches seemed rich with golden light—their sober brown transformed. Late chrysanthemums and dahlias almost shouted their brilliance at her from the borders by the high brick wall. The sun laid bright hands on every twig and blade of grass.

'I'd forgotten . . .' she murmured.

'How clear the colours are after rain? So had I.'

'But you're a *photographer*,' she protested. 'You can't have.'

'I haven't exactly been looking at the glorious English countryside just lately,' he said drily. Mostly dust and bombed buildings . . . bodies and rubble . . . Bodies like Richard's, lying spread out and helpless in yet more dust . . .

At his bleak look, Charley was sorry. Clumsily, she tried to distract him. 'But now—there's this!' She waved a hand at the jewelled garden. 'Tell me about this place, Jon. I seem to have been too vague to ask.'

60

He laughed. 'The Rehab House, the Guvnor calls it. He says it isn't a nursing home and it isn't a clinic. It's just a place where people start again.'

Charley nodded. 'That makes sense.'

'It does, doesn't it? Ferguson is very keen on light and space—airy rooms and this wide-open garden to walk in. He believes that lots of rest and taking off the pressure is what people need most . . . And once they learn to relax and enjoy these tranquil surroundings, the rest will follow.'

'Does it?'

He glanced at her, half-smiling. 'Usually.'

'What about you?'

The smile faded a little. 'Me? I'm fairly tranquil—at least by day.'

'But at night?'

He stopped and looked up at the windows of the house, now ablaze with crimson from the setting sun. 'I shout,' he said. 'So they tell me . . .' Then he turned his head and smiled at her again. 'But it's getting better.'

Charley drew a slow, steadying breath. 'I suppose . . . I could say that, too?'

'Of course.' He tucked her arm through his and gave it a small, encouraging squeeze. 'Almost completely better, I'd say . . . This was only what they call a "temporary set-back".' He was almost laughing, and she found herself smiling in response.

'All the same, I ought to—'

He stopped again, and looked at her seriously. 'Charley—we all have our moments of panic. But they're soon over, and they get *less*, I promise you.' His gaze was steady and full of quiet assurance. 'You're doing fine.'

'Am I?' There was still uncertainty in her voice, and a faint bewilderment at her own absurd weakness.

'Yes,' he said firmly. 'Yes, young Charley! Come on, I want to show you the herb border. It's made like an Elizabethan knot-garden . . .'

They walked on, arm-in-arm through the gleaming rain-wet leaves, their faces lifted to the saffron sky and the fast-sinking rose-red disc of the sun.

* * *

61

In the end it was an outsider who made up her mind for her and gave her the courage she needed. Gerald Farmer came to see her. She didn't know how he found out where she was, or why he was allowed in—but there he was, large as life, with his yellow hair and his ingratiating smile, and his podgy damp hands clutching a bunch of chrysanthemums. She suddenly found that she was angry, enormously angry, and all her uncertainty and doubt about the future seemed to dissolve so that she knew exactly what she wanted to do.

He came towards her, treading cautiously across the green carpet of the quiet drawing-room, and she saw with some satisfaction how his eyes widened in surprise as he recognised her.

She was drinking a cup of tea at the time, and she had a sudden urgent desire to throw it in his face. But no, that would be extravagant—even a little hysterical. And anyway, it was not what the new, brave Charley would do.

Even so, she drew a sharp breath of resolution—like someone going into battle—and Jon, playing chess farther down the room, looked up in swift concern. He did not move, but he watched her quietly from then on—and Charley knew it.

'Caroline? How well you are looking. Are you surprised to see me?'

She looked at him coolly. 'Yes, Gerald. I am.'

He stood over her awkwardly, not sure whether to sit down or not. Finally, he thrust the flowers at her and said in a jocular tone: 'Had to come and see how you were getting on, didn't I?'

'Did you, Gerald? Why?"

He was stumped by this and began to bluster. 'Oh well, you know—worried and all that . . . Wanted to know—'

'Wanted to know what?' Her voice was still calm and flat.

He looked at her now more warily. What was she playing at? This visit, which he had thought would be easy—full of magnanimous condescension on his part and abject gratitude on hers—was not going according to plan.

'Why—er—how you were.'

'I am very well, thank you, Gerald.'

He seemed confused by her straight, unyielding stare, and turned round to look for a chair. There was one not far away, and he drew it nearer and sat down. She made no attempt to put him at his ease, but sat there calmly looking at him over the rim of her teacup.

'I thought—' he began, and actually cleared his throat in a manner that was clearly nervous.

'Yes?'

'Maybe you could do with some help.'

'About what?'

'Well,—you'll be coming home soon, won't you? It's a big house to manage on your own. Probably you'll want to make a few changes . . . I could help shift the furniture around—or do some redecorating. I'm a dab hand with a paintbrush.'

Charley gazed at him in disbelief. The ten years of loneliness and rejection she had lived through since he had walked out on her might never have existed . . . Did he really think he could stroll back into her life as if nothing had happened? And carry on towards the same cozy future he had talked of before? She had a sudden recollection of her Uncle Hal saying: 'The world is full of unscrupulous people . . . I wouldn't want you to be hurt,' and warning her not to discuss her financial affairs . . . How had Gerald found out? Or was he merely guessing—assuming she would be well off enough to be worth pursuing after all? There was the house . . . and furniture . . . and some undisclosed legacy? It all added up, she supposed, to a solid enough expectation, with a docile and ever-grateful dull little wife thrown in . . .

When she thought about it, she began to find it funny, especially as Uncle Hal had meant Jon—kind, undemanding Jon—in his careful warning, not Gerald Farmer at all.

'Actually,' she said, and could hardly control the desire to laugh, 'I shan't be coming home.'

'Not coming home?' He was astounded.

'No. I'm not keeping the house. It's going to be sold. And all the furniture. Lock, stock and barrel.'

'Sold?' His voice was almost a squeak. 'Are you sure you know what you're doing?'

'Quite sure, Gerald, thank you.'

'But—' he was nearly too shocked to speak, 'where will you live?'

She smiled at him with sudden, dazzling sweetness. 'I'm not sure yet. Somewhere far away from this place. I have no intention of staying here—or of ever returning.'

His jaw had dropped a little. He really looked extremely foolish, she thought, and could not suppress a small snort of amusement.

'I see,' he said. And then his eyes narrowed a little as he saw her laughing, and he leant forward in apparent concern. 'Of course, you *have* been quite ill.' There was deliberate malice in the significant tone now. 'Does your uncle know about this?'

Charley clenched her hand suddenly, longing to hit him, and the cup broke between her fingers.

Jon, who had been observing the rising tension for some time, got to his feet and came over unhurriedly. He took the shattered cup out of her hand and said in a mild tone: 'Good thing it's not the Guvnor's best Crown Derby! Shall I get you some more?'

She looked up at him in relief. 'No thanks, Jon.' Her voice was still cool and calm, but there was a faint tremor in it, and Jon was not sure if it was laughter or something else. 'Mr Farmer is just going.' She stared at Gerald—and Jon seemed to be staring at him too in a kind of waiting silence.

Discomfited, Gerald got to his feet. Charley got up too, and stood politely beside Jon.

'Well—' he held out his hand uncertainly. Charley ignored it.

'Goodbye, Gerald,' she said. 'I am sure you can find your own way out.'

He hesitated—and then could not resist one parting shot. 'I'm glad you are so much better—though convalescence can be very deceptive, I'm told.'

She looked at him gravely. 'Deceptive? In what way?'

'Euphoric,' he pronounced. 'Not the best time for long-term decisions.' His voice seemed smooth again—but

64

venomous. 'I do hope you won't regret it.'

Charley smiled. 'Oh no,' she said. 'Never. It's the best decision I ever made.'

He went away then. There was nothing else he could do. And Jon and Charley stood looking after him in silence. But presently Jon felt her begin to shake beside him, and looked at her in swift alarm.

'Are you all right?'

But she wasn't upset. She was laughing—and suddenly the laughter spilled out of her, startling the other residents in the long, cool room.

'Oh!' she spluttered. 'Oh, Jon—you should've seen his face!'

'I did.' He was laughing too, with some relief.

'It's exactly what Uncle Hal said . . .' She began to laugh again, the tears rising in her eyes, 'only he meant *you*.'

'Me?' Jon was mystified.

'Unscrupulous . . .' she gasped, 'ulterior motives . . . Oh!' and she doubled up with renewed laughter at Jon's bewildered expression.

'Oh, I see,' he said at last. 'After the loot, am I?' His grin was entirely without reproof. 'Well, he's quite right.'

'He is?' She was still giggling helplessly.

'About being careful—yes.' He looked at her half-seriously. 'Have you got any?'

'What—loot?'

'Yes.'

'Not a lot.'

'That's what I thought.' He grinned again, and put a steadying hand on her arm. He knew how perilous her laughter was. 'Well—keep it in the bank.'

'I intend to.'

He said soberly: 'Charley—do I understand you've arrived at a decision?'

'I have.' She was still smiling. 'Though I haven't made up my mind what to do about it yet.'

'Give yourself a chance!' His calming hand was still on her arm, and he could feel the tension retreating. 'One decision is quite enough for today.'

'And I haven't fallen to pieces. I *must* be better.'

His grin returned. 'Well, thank God for that!' he said.

*   *   *

It was old Dr Ellis who sparked off her next decision. He brought her a present. He came stumping across the green drawing-room and stood beside her chair, holding out various packages and looking both gruff and shy at once.

'I brought you these,' he said.

Charley opened them and found a big sketch pad, a selection of drawing pencils and rubbers, a box of good water-colours and some brushes.

'I didn't bring oils,' he explained doubtfully, 'because—'

'You were quite right.' Charley was looking at him with the glowing delight of a child. 'They need a lot of space—and they'd be too messy for a place like this. But these are perfect.'

He was clearly pleased.

'What made you think of it?'

'I remembered,' he said slowly. 'I remembered you loved it before . . . and how you used to look at colours.' His eyes rested on her, still rather shyly. 'And you always meant to go and look at galleries . . .'

She smiled. 'So I did. That was a long time ago.'

'It's not too late,' he said.

Charley's clear gaze softened. Her old friend the doctor seemed to understand a lot more about her than she had realised.

'When do you think I'll be ready to leave here?'

He looked at her consideringly. 'Do you want to leave here?'

Charley hesitated. 'In some ways . . . though I love it here, it's so peaceful.' She paused, thinking it out honestly. 'And the thought of going out still rather scares me.'

'Then you are not quite ready yet,' he said, and smiled at her. 'Though by the look of you, it won't be long.'

She laughed. 'You approve of the new me?'

'My dear girl—you look about twenty again! And so elegant! I would scarcely have known you.' He grinned and

66

then said deliberately: 'No wonder Gerald Farmer came running.'

Her eyes went wide. 'You heard about that?'

'I did.' His jaw tightened. 'And that you sent him packing.' He permitted himself another small grin.

'How—?'

'He came to see me.' A faint, contemptuous crispness crept into his voice. 'He seemed to think I would have some influence with you over your decision, or that I would persuade your uncle to intervene.'

'He *what*?' She was outraged. 'And what did you tell him?'

'That I wouldn't dream of discussing my patient's affairs with him or anyone else. That it was none of his business— and anyway, you seemed to have made an entirely sane and rational decision of which I heartily approved.'

Charley laughed. 'Good for you!' She was somehow enormously comforted by his approval. 'What did Gerald say?'

'Nothing. He went straight round to complain to your Uncle Hal.'

She looked at him in amazement. Was there no end to Gerald Farmer's presumption? 'And—?'

The doctor's grin was entirely malicious. 'I believe he threw him out.'

Charley began to laugh. 'Poor Gerald. He didn't have much luck, did he?'

'I'm glad to say—no.'

They grinned at one another.

'It isn't exactly as if I was a great heiress!' murmured Charley, still smiling to herself. 'How did he know I was here, anyway? I didn't tell anyone.'

The doctor's smile faded a little. 'I'm afraid that may have been my fault—inadvertently. That nice Indian shop-keeper, Ranjit Singh, kept asking after you. He was the one who alerted me that day, you know, and helped me to find you.'

'I didn't know that.'

'No. He was very concerned. Kept wanting to send you flowers, and fruit and anything that might please you . . . I

67

told him to wait till you were better.' He was serious for a moment. 'I wasn't sure you would want to be reminded of—the old days.'

She smiled. 'It doesn't bother me now.'

He nodded approval. 'Anyway, I assume Gerald Farmer must have found your house shut up and gone down to the shop to enquire. Poor Ranjit wouldn't have realised, and I'm afraid it never occurred to me that anyone else would bother you—least of all our friend Mr Farmer.'

'He's no friend of mine.'

'I'm glad to hear it.' He reached down into his black doctor's bag beside him, and—surprisingly—produced a large bunch of anemones and a neat, cellophane-wrapped bowl of fruit. 'So—today I told Ranjit you were better, and this is the result.' He laid the fruit on the small table beside her, and put the flowers into her hands. 'He said you liked the colours.'

Charley gazed from the brilliant anemones to the equally vibrant colours in the basket of fruit—orange, yellow and glowing red, the creamy blush of peaches and the cool green and purple bloom of grapes. There was even a rosy mango among them . . . Yes, singing colours, shouting colours, vivid with life, seeming almost to pulsate with light as a gleam of sunshine from the wide windows fell on them . . .

'I could paint them,' she murmured.

Dr Ellis smiled at her rapt expression. 'You look just like the girl I used to know, young Charley.'

'Do I?' She was still thinking about colours, and her gaze left the crimson and violet petals of the anemones almost with reluctance. 'In what way?'

'The way you were admiring the colours. You used to look out at the world with such delight. And now—'

The blue, far-seeing eyes looked into his and then beyond him at the garden outside the windows and the long shadows of the trees on the grass.

'And now I am beginning to see it like that again,' she said softly. 'Yes. It was so clever of you to bring the paints just at this moment.'

William Ellis began to look gruff and shy again, and

seemed about to get up and leave, but Charley stopped him.

'Dr Ellis—can I ask you something . . . personal?'

'Why not?' His expression changed and became instantly the kind and compassionate doctor's.

'It's about Jon—Jon Armorel.'

'Yes?'

'He said you and he had talked a bit . . . after I—after you brought me in?'

'We did.'

'Enough to—form an impression?'

He smiled. 'What are you trying to say?'

She shook her head ruefully. 'I don't know how to put it. You see, he's been wonderfully kind to me . . . I don't know how I'd have managed here without him . . . He even seems to know how to cope with me at my worst . . .' Her smile was still rueful. 'But Uncle Hal said . . . to be careful . . . And then there was Gerald being so—so blatantly grasping . . .' She broke off, floundering and distressed. 'But I—with Jon it seems so absurd. He's so steady and calm, and somehow un—unconcerned with outside opinion . . . What do you think?'

William Ellis looked at her straight. 'I think you can trust him. I also think he is a man who has been through such a lot that our everyday worries seem rather trivial.'

'Yes,' she agreed.

'And probably, being some help to a fellow human being in trouble has made him feel a bit less isolated.'

She looked surprised at that. 'Do you think so?'

He nodded. 'The only warning I might give is that you yourself are in a somewhat vulnerable state at present—and it is a fairly novel experience for you to have someone being kind to you for a change.'

She began to protest. 'That isn't true—'

'Oh yes, it is.' He got up and patted her arm. 'But I daresay you'll get used to it in time.'

He stood there smiling down at her, and Charley was suddenly overwhelmed with affection for this wise and kindly man who had guided her through so many family crises and traumatic events. She got swiftly to her feet and without pausing for thought, flung her arms round his neck.

'Thank you for everything—especially the paints!'

William Ellis was touched to the depths of his craggy old heart. But he wasn't going to say so. 'I shall expect a masterpiece, mind,' he said, laughing, and stumped off without looking back.

*　　*　　*

She was painting in the garden when Jon found her. It was a mild and sparkling morning, with dew on the grass, sunlight gilding every leaf and twig, and clear, washed skies above. Charley was trying to set down the special glow of an autumn day and finding it hard.

Jon stopped to look over her shoulder and exclaimed: 'Charley—that's beautiful.'

She shook her head ruefully. 'Not beautiful enough.' Her hand stroked in a wash of fiery colour where the cherry tree was burning away in crimson and gold. 'I'm trying to paint light . . .' she murmured. 'And it's impossible . . .'

'Light?' He looked from the painting to the sunlit garden and back to Charley's absorbed and equally sunlit face. 'Wouldn't oils be better?'

'Yes,' she sighed. 'But impossible here. You need so much more space for all that clutter—canvases and easels and . . .' she began to laugh, 'and turps.'

He grinned. 'Was that why? Were you always painting?'

She looked vaguely apologetic. 'I suppose I was rather obsessed . . .' The concentration was creeping back into her voice and her hand as she spoke. 'Turner could do it . . .' she muttered, sketching in a sheaf of cloud above the flaring trees. 'And Rembrandt . . .'

'And Monet,' added Jon, smiling. 'Light on the Seine . . . and on the waterlilies.'

'Not on them—*in* them,' she murmured, struggling to do just that with a leaf silhouetted in a shaft of sunlight. She laid down her brush and considered her painting sadly. 'How did they do it?'

'They probably spent years and years finding out,' said

Jon. She nodded. 'I ought to go and look at them all.'

'*All?*'

'Well—some of them . . .' She was gazing out across the garden, scarcely aware of Jon, repeating the names of her gods in a voice of dream. 'Rembrandt in Amsterdam—and the Hermitage . . . The Impressionists in Paris . . . El Greco at the Prado . . .'

'And Turner at the Tate,' added Jon, with intent.

She turned to him, startled. 'What?'

Jon sat down on the garden bench beside her. 'Charley, you've got to start somewhere small first. Not that London's all that small!' His smile was infectious.

'What are you suggesting?' She couldn't help echoing his smile.

'I'm suggesting that you are going to find all that travelling a bit exhausting—and a bit nerve-racking at first.' He looked at her, waiting for her faint nod of agreement.

'So?'

'So I suggest we go to the Tate and the National Gallery first.'

Her eyes went wide. 'We?'

'Of course. We.' There was mischief in his glance. 'The blind leading the blind.'

Charley picked up her brush and clutched it in taut fingers as she looked at him. 'Jon—I can't go on using you like this.'

'Why not?'

'Because I—I've got to learn to stand on my own feet.'

His smile was full of approval. It made Charley feel warm inside just to look at it, though she knew she ought not to succumb to its charm. 'You are learning, Charley,' he said gently. 'You're learning fast. But a little support won't do you any harm.'

'Won't it?'

'No.' He was still smiling, but now there was sudden appeal in his glance. 'Besides—' He sounded almost shy for him. 'I need company at present.'

Charley's expression changed. 'Well—if you put it like that . . .'

71

He looked at her straight. 'It is like that,' he said simply. So they went to London together.

* * *

They looked at light. Light on water, on Turner's fiery sunset Thames, on 'rain, steam and train', and light coming from behind the clouds in great washed skies . . . They looked at light on people's faces and people's hands—shining out of the darkness of Rembrandt's mysterious backgrounds; and they looked at the interior light behind the leaves and floating translucent chalices of Monet's waterlilies.

And here—in front of the green-gold sweep of Monet's lily pool on the curved wall in the National Gallery, Jon stood beside Charley looking down at it from the rail of the little balcony and said: 'Will you be all right for a while if I leave you here?'

For a moment, panic swept over Charley. She had found it much more difficult and confusing than she had expected to cope with the crowds and the noisy Underground, and all the seething traffic round Trafalgar Square. The Tate Gallery had been a bit better—less full of pushing people—and the Embankment traffic had been less thick and less violent, somehow . . . And there was the Thames to look at, the quiet grey Thames with its glinting eddies and majestic slow-moving tide . . . They had leant over the Embankment wall and watched the water surging up river towards the next bridge. And Jon had said: 'Lots of light—even in the muddy old Thames. Turner saw it,' and had led her without haste into the long cool galleries where the Turners burned and pulsed with their strange visionary light.

But here, it was harder. At least it had been till they reached the Rembrandts, and then it was quiet, and the light in his pictures seemed to burn deep and rich like the glow of a candle flame . . . After that, there was more noise and jostling crowds of students, and chattering people pushing in every direction, until they stood before the Monet waterlilies; and then it was quiet again, and all her

72

day seemed to flower in that cool green shade, among those marvellous shimmers of water . . .

She would be all right here. Of course she would. She could stay and gaze at those pale, ghostly lilies, and absorb the width and calm of that huge canvas, and not go anywhere at all till Jon came back . . . She would be all right. Before that encompassing green and golden world, she could not fail to be . . .

'Yes,' she said, and smiled at him. 'I'll stay here. I think I'm in love, anyway,' and her eyes returned to the Monet in fascination.

Jon nodded once, gave her arm a brief, encouraging squeeze, and left her alone.

*   *   *

She had been leaning there against the railing for some time, gazing dreamily at the painting, when the man next to her spoke.

'Lovely, isn't it?'

'Yes,' she sighed, not looking at him. 'Lovely.'

He seemed to come a bit nearer, and Charley instinctively moved along a little.

'Makes you feel good, doesn't it?' The voice was soft, insistent.

'Mm.' She was trying to sound as non-committal and distant as possible.

'Relaxing, you might say,' went on the voice, and the man's arm casually brushed against hers.

She could feel his eyes upon her, sizing her up, not looking at the Monet at all, and she felt a small stir of panic beginning again inside her. He seemed to like what he saw, for he drew nearer. But that didn't comfort her one bit.

'On your own?' he asked, casually laying his hand beside hers on the rail.

Charley turned and looked at him. She saw a smallish, weedy-looking man in a grubby raincoat, with wisps of sandy hair sticking out above his collar. His face was London-pale, and there was something oddly wrong about the eyes—they were a flat, glassy blue, curiously opaque,

73

and though they were sparkless, they were hot.

Charley shut down the rising panic and spoke crisply: 'No. I'm waiting for someone. He'll be here directly.' She turned away, hoping the man would not persist and those hot, predatory eyes would look somewhere else.

But he moved nearer, and one arm came round her shoulders. 'A long time coming, isn't he? Sure he hasn't forgotten?'

Charley stiffened. Suppose Jon *had* forgotten? Suppose he had never meant to return? . . . Suppose he thought it would be good for her to find her own way home? . . . Could she do it? Did she even remember which bus to catch? Which Underground? Which train? . . . The panic began to rise.

On the other side of her, a woman suddenly spoke. 'Bothering you, is he, dear? Shall I fetch one of the attendants?' Her voice was sharp and carrying, full of bright Cockney determination. 'There's one just there by the door,' it added, loud and clear.

The man dropped his arm from Charley's stiff shoulders, and fled.

Charley turned her head and smiled at her rescuer. She saw a little birdlike woman with a sharp, pointed nose and faded blonde hair that was a bit thin and frizzy. But the eyes—unlike those others that had frightened Charley— were warm and sparky and full of tired understanding.

'A menace, aren't they?' she said, and laughed.

Charley agreed.

The woman waved a hand at the Monet lilies drowsing in the heat, and said unexpectedly: 'You could be safe in there.'

Charley looked at her in surprise. 'Yes . . . you could.'

'A frog—' the sharp Cockney voice was suddenly soft and dreaming, 'on one of them lily pads . . . Or maybe a dragonfly or somethink . . . Just living there, in all that green . . .' She sighed. 'Peaceful, it'd be . . . No 'oles.'

Charley jumped. 'What?'

'No 'oles . . . All smooth water—and lily pads . . .' The sharp, thin face was looking at her now, and the weary eyes seemed to be offering some kind of recognition.

74

'Safe . . .' the dreaming voice continued.

Charley let out a long, quivering breath of retreating panic. Could this really be someone who understood her— who knew about the dangerous cracks in this brittle world?

'Holes?' she murmured, aloud. 'I thought they were cracks.'

'Same thing.' The woman smiled at her, and the voice regained some of its cheerful brightness. 'Papered over mostly, of course. But they're there all right.' Once more she waved a gnarled and workworn hand at the painting on the wall. ''E knew, didn't 'e?'

'Do you think so?'

'Course. So 'e paints everythink smooth, see? Well, not smooth exackly, but all wide and un—un—?'

'Unbroken.'

'That's it. Unflippin'-broken.'

Charley smiled. 'It's the light I came for . . .' She spoke softly, half to herself.

'Ah, light,' said the woman, nodding sagely. 'No 'oles in light.'

Charley was struck dumb. It was the perfect answer. *No holes in light* . . . She was amazed to have her thoughts so perfectly expressed, to be so perfectly understood.

She stood there for a while thinking about light, and when she turned to explain her thoughts to the woman, she found herself alone.

For a moment she felt a piercing sense of loss. It had been the most fleeting of conversations, but to find someone who knew without being told how perilous the world felt to Charley—how fragile each day and each moment of happiness, how dangerous each new step across unknown paths . . . Someone who seemed to know how the light-filled mirages of Turner and Monet spoke of different worlds— unsullied and unbroken—their shimmering radiance a shield against darkness . . . *No holes in light*.

She sighed, aware with a sense of shame that she had at last broken out of her self-absorption just enough to recognise a fellow human being. She had been too cut off—too shut up in her own terrors—to realise that there were other people out there, people with fears and terrors like her own, who needed comfort just as much as she did . . . And who came alone, small and wispy and tired, to look at Monet for reassurance . . .

She was ashamed. And she thought of Jon—kind, unselfish Jon—who never spoke of his own despair and had clearly been much more ill than she was, and who never failed to respond when she turned to him for help. Until now she had seen no one but Jon in her darkened world, and it was time she came out of the shadows and stopped being frightened. Time she stopped relying on Jon, whom she had used unmercifully, without thought for his own needs . . .

Jon. He hadn't come back. And she badly needed to find the cloakroom. She would have to risk it—go down the stairs through the crowds, find her way, and fight her way back here afterwards. He had said he'd come back here, so he would, she felt sure. Jon would not desert her. She must just stop panicking and find her way about, and return here to wait for him. Simple. Nothing to worry about.

She turned rather blindly away from the quiet green oasis, and struggled down the stairs to the crowded foyer. There, she asked her way, and fought on down the stairs on shaking legs . . . The corridors down below seemed endless, cavernous and echoing—but there were no cracks that she could see, no holes . . . *No holes in light*, she told herself. Remember that . . . She walked on, her footsteps sounding loud beside her, and at last found the door and the clean, tiled floor within . . . *Tiled?* . . . There were cracks between tiles . . . Nonsense, she said, they are perfectly smooth, not a single crack anywhere, and anyway *I will not look!* . . . Resolutely, she kept her eyes on the brightly-lit walls and would not look at the floor.

When she came out, she got lost. The corridors seemed longer than ever, and people seemed to be hurrying down them in all directions. Beginning to panic a little, she started to run. There must be a way out of this place somewhere, and she had got to find it. She ran breathlessly up some stairs and cannoned sharply into someone who put out his arms to save her.

76

'*Charley,*' he said, and held her close. 'Where've you been?'

'I—g-got lost,' she said, and for a moment allowed herself to rest thankfully within the circle of Jon's arms.

'I'm sorry I was so long,' he said. 'Come on. Let's go and get some coffee.'

* * *

Over coffee in the cafeteria, Charley's limbs stopped trembling, and she began to look at Jon more attentively. She thought he seemed tired and a little abstracted, and the dark shadow of sorrow was back in his eyes again.

He caught her anxious gaze and smiled at once. 'It's all right, Charley. I've been back to my office. It always unsettles me.'

'Weren't they pleased to see you?'

'Oh yes. Very.' But he fell silent again, and did not seem inclined to continue. At last he seemed to withdraw from distant thought and return to her. 'How did you get on without me?'

I panicked, she thought, ashamed. I was hopelessly lost and frightened. If Jon hadn't found me then . . . But aloud she only said: 'I managed . . .' and then she added in a different tone: 'Jon, I had a most extraordinary conversation.'

'Did you? Who with?'

'A woman. A little dried-up Cockney woman. She was looking at the Monet beside me.'

'And?'

'She seemed to think like me . . .' She hesitated, suddenly shy.

'Tell me about it.' Jon was looking at her now.

So she told him, and afterwards Jon sighed and smiled at her again and said: 'Oh, Charley—why should you think you are the only one to be afraid?'

Her eyes widened as she stared at him. Jon? Wise, steady Jon—afraid? 'You?' she said.

'Of course, me.'

She shook her head. 'But you're so calm.'

77

'Am I? Outwardly, perhaps . . . That's only experience, Charley.' His eyes were crinkling at the edges now with the old glint of humour. But she still thought he looked tired. 'I think you'll find most people are—underneath. They cover it up in different wild and desperate ways, Charley, but they all know—we all know—how thin the crust is.'

She shivered. 'You make it sound—incurable.'

'Awareness of the abyss? It is, Charley. Incurable.' His smile seemed to cancel out his own sadness. 'But there are compensations.'

'Such as?'

'Such as Monet's waterlilies . . .' He laughed a little. 'And the poor old fragile world itself . . . Everything looks more beautiful when it is threatened—including you.'

'Me?' She was astonished.

'Yes, you.' His smile was openly loving now, still laced with humour. 'I've watched you blossoming, Charley, like a late flower after frost. You know roses, how the petals look when they flower in winter? Kind of transparent? And desperately brave and fragile—like an army with banners . . .'

She stared at him. 'Jon, you're a poet.'

He shook his head and sighed. 'No. Richard was the poet. I was just his eye.'

It was the first time he had spoken openly of his old friend and colleague, Richard—and she didn't know how to answer him. But he seemed to know her uncertainty, and reached out and patted her hand. 'Don't fret, Charley. You're one of the compensations—didn't you know?'

She shook her head wordlessly, confused by his sudden, devastating kindness.

'What would you like to do now?' he asked, smiling at her confusion.

She looked doubtful. 'I—meant to do some shopping, but—'

'The crowds appalled you?'

'Yes.'

He considered. 'I think we should go and look at the ducks in the park. And then we should have a quiet, elegant dinner and go to hear Sibelius at the Festival Hall.'

'Sibelius?'

'Light, Charley. Shimmers and scurries. He understood light—just as much as Turner or Monet . . . All those wide silver lakes and the reflections of dark forest trees in the water, and that cold, clear northern light . . .'

'You sound as if you knew that country.'

'Oh yes,' he smiled. 'I've been to Finland. But you don't need to go to see it. Sibelius does it for you.' He looked at her enquiringly. 'Would you like that?'

'It sounds wonderful,' she sighed—and wondered if she was being selfish. Jon looked so tired.

'It's a rest, Charley,' he murmured softly. 'Believe me— music is a rest.'

'I believe you,' she said.

*   *   *

The lake in St James's Park was silver-grey, and a blue London dusk was coming down between the trees, but overhead the sky was still lit with the afterglow of sunset. They stood on the bridge side by side and looked down at the ducks swimming hopefully about below them, waiting for someone's sandwiches. Charley felt calmed by the silken expanse of water, and the ever-changing patterns of light and shadow on its smooth surface—and she found herself smiling at the antics of the ducks.

'What's that one?' Jon pointed suddenly. 'That one with the brilliant colours?'

'That's a mandarin,' she answered without hesitation.

'And that one?'

'A pintail, I think.'

'And what about the one with the long neck?'

'Idiot,' Charley laughed. 'That's not a duck at all. It's a goose . . . a greylag, is it?'

'They come in for the winter,' murmured Jon, looking up at the sky as if he might see the next flight coming any minute. 'I always wonder how they know exactly when to come—and where to land.'

Charley looked up, too, into the fading apricot glow in the west. 'They don't mostly stop here, though, do they?'

'Oh no. Most of them go over to Slimbridge in the west country . . . But you can hear them honking sometimes as they pass . . .' He glanced at Charley with an oddly intent stare. 'How come you know about ducks?'

'I used to paint them. Long ago. I got interested in their markings. Some of their colours are marvellous. I mean, look at the sheen on that drake's head.'

Jon looked. But he also noticed that Charley was shivering slightly. She was only wearing her thin suit jacket over the emerald green dress, and the evening was growing chilly.

'You know,' he said, 'in spite of what you thought about shopping, I think we'd better go and buy you a coat.'

'What, now?'

'Yes, now. I know somewhere that's open late. Come on, we'll take a taxi.'

He took her to a small boutique in a back street off Regent Street, and when she asked him about colours, he was as definite as she had been about the ducks.

'Oh, white, I think. With that dress—and that hair. Yes. White wool.'

Charley found what he asked for, and when she inspected herself in the mirror she agreed with him.

'Smashing,' he said. 'Put the collar up—it'll frame your face, and make you feel all warm and protected.'

Charley obeyed, smiling. But she reflected that it was Jon, not the coat, that made her feel all warm and protected—though of course she could not tell him so.

They had the promised elegant dinner rather early, and then it was the mighty voice of Sibelius that took over. She wasn't warm and protected any more, but swept by hurricanes and engulfed in tidal waves, and frozen on icy peaks, and lifted on eagle's wings, and drenched and drowned in light . . .

'You said music was a rest!' she gasped when they came out.

Jon laughed and steered her towards the river walk so that they could watch the lights on the Thames and wait for the Sibelius shimmers to subside.

Charley was silent for a long time, and then she turned to

80

Jon and murmured: 'She was right, you know. There are no holes in light.'

Jon nodded. 'Just keep believing that, Charley—and you'll do fine!'

'I'm doing fine already,' she answered, laughing, 'thanks to you.'

'So you are,' agreed Jon, and his grin was wide.

'But you'd better be careful,' she told him, 'if you fill me up with light like this any more, I'll probably explode.'

'I shouldn't do that,' replied Jon gravely. 'Fireworks are very pretty, but they don't last.'

They turned and walked along the Embankment, and went at last to catch their train, and it seemed to Charley that some of the light had spilled out and got into Jon's face as well as her own. But that, she knew, couldn't last either.

*   *   *

For a day or two, Charley went back to painting light—or trying to. She began on a dreamy study of the glinting Thames with all its reflections of the lights across the river, as she had seen it from the South Bank late that night with Jon . . . And she tried to capture the shot-silk lake in St James's Park and the brilliant trim of the mandarin ducks, spending a lot of time on the apricot afterglow of the evening sky, and the iridescent sheen on a mallard's head . . . She wasn't satisfied with either attempt, but they had at least taught her how difficult it was to put light on to paper or canvas—and what marvellous painters Monet and Turner were . . .

It was clear to her now that she was almost ready to leave the safety and peace of the Guvnor's Rehab House—but she was still no nearer to a decision on where she wanted to go or what she wanted to do. And she was a bit shaken by the discovery on her trip to London that she was still scared of the noisy crowds and still so easily driven to panic. How would she cope out there on her own, with no Jon to run to? For it was also clear to her that she was beginning to rely on Jon far too much, and to find his support much too comforting for safety.

81

Safety? What exactly did she mean by that? Was she afraid of getting too fond of Jon? Or simply ashamed of exploiting his kindness? Or both . . . ?

Still pondering these problems in her mind beneath the surface of her concentration, she finished off one more green and golden mallard's head and went to show the result to Jon. At least she could consult him about the impersonal question of light on a feathered head, even if she had to solve the rest of her problems herself.

Jon was not in the cool green drawing-room, and not in the garden. Come to think of it, she hadn't seen him at all this morning. The colonel with whom he often played chess was sitting alone in his corner, looking disconsolate.

Charley was at last beginning to see her fellow sufferers more clearly, and to view them with sympathy. She was no longer so caught up in her own struggle against irrational terrors. So she noticed the crumpled, grey-brown face of the colonel, and the lost look in his eyes.

'Hello, Colonel,' she said. 'Not playing chess today?'

'No one to play with,' he grunted, and shot her a brief, hopeful glance. 'You play?'

'I'm afraid not.' She smiled at him apologetically.

'My wife used to play,' he said, gazing away from her out of the window. 'Even when she was very ill, she still liked a game . . .'

Charley was silent. She thought she saw the glitter of tears in the fierce old eyes. At last she said gently: 'I expect Jon will come soon.'

He shook his head. 'Jon's gone.'

Charley felt herself go cold. The shock of his words was like a physical blow. 'Gone?'

The pale, rheumy eyes came back from their distance and fixed themselves on her face. 'Discharged himself. Said he was better. Don't think the Guvnor approved.'

Charley stared at him, appalled. Jon gone? Without a word? Without saying goodbye? It was so unlike him . . . Or was it? He had always been very silent about his own affairs—full of generous concern about her, but curiously reticent about himself. Maybe he wanted to slip away without fuss. Maybe he realised how much Charley was coming to rely on him, and thought he'd better get out while the going was good. Maybe, after their day in London, he had seen the red light and run screaming.

Cold with shame at these thoughts, she turned away from the colonel's penetrating gaze and began to walk out of the room. But then she remembered the lost look in his eyes and turned back. The colonel missed Jon too—and he was lonely.

'I'm sorry your partner's gone,' she said and managed to produce a pale and riven smile.

I'm sorry your partner's gone . . . I'm sorry my partner's gone . . . Oh, Jon—did I drive you away? He said the Guvnor didn't approve . . . Did you go out too soon? Are you well enough to cope?

Still shocked by the dreadful sense of loss that the colonel's news had brought, she went out into the garden and walked up and down, distracted by doubts, until she had made up her mind what to do next. At last she went in search of little nurse Evie and demanded to see the Guvnor forthwith.

'Now?' asked Evie, surprised.

'Please.' Charley's voice was calm and definite. But there was a hard core of grief inside her that she could not dispel.

It was a rule in the Rehab House that if any patient asked to see Dr Ferguson, he or she must be allowed to do so as soon as possible. Evie saw the shock in Charley's face and hurried off to find the Guvnor.

She came back almost at once and said: 'He's in his office. Shall I show you the way?'

'Please,' said Charley again, and sternly quelled the awful desire to weep that was growing inside her.

Jon gone? How could she manage without Jon? He was the only one who understood her fears and reasonless terrors. He was the only one who had ever been simply kind to her—kind and undemanding. He was the only one she had dared to get fond of, knowing her growing affection would not be exploited . . . Yes, fond of—yes, growing affection . . . Why not face it? Dear, kind, undemanding Jon, whom she trusted above all others and

was beginning to care about much more than she knew . . .
And Jon was gone.

'Hallo, Charley,' said Dr Ferguson, noting with a professional eye her paleness and her new, hard-held resolve. 'Sit down. What can I do for you today?'

Charley sat down and clasped her hands together. 'Dr Ferguson—do you think I am ready to leave here?'

'Do you want to go?'

She hesitated. 'Not altogether. But I think I must.'

'Why?'

'Because I—I've been a coward long enough. It's time I got on with my life and stopped moaning.'

He smiled. 'I haven't noticed you moaning.'

Charley pushed the hair out of her eyes and sighed. 'I do inside, she thought. I'm moaning now. Jon's gone, and I'm behaving like a lovesick cow bellowing in an empty field. Aloud she said, trying to keep the self-contempt out of her voice: 'Well, anyway, I've got to start doing something practical.'

The Guvnor was looking at her attentively. He did not miss the signs of stress, or the flick of anger directed against herself. 'Such as?' he inquired.

'Oh—well, first of all I've got to sort things out at my mother's house. I've been dreading it, but I must do it. And then I—I think I'll get a ticket to Paris—or Amsterdam.' Monets or Rembrandts? she thought, with a wild moment of laughter—which shall it be?

'It will be something of an ordeal for you.' The Guvnor spoke gravely.

'What?'

'Sorting out the house.'

'Oh. Oh yes.'

'May I make a suggestion?'

'Please.'

'Come back here to sleep—for the first few days. You'll find it hard enough coping with all that, without having to find a room in a hotel or something as well. And I don't think you should attempt to sleep in that house again—not yet.' He saw her hesitate, and went on quietly: 'In any case, your fees are already paid here up to the end of the

84

month—you might as well make use of them.'

'Are they?' She was surprised. Uncle Hal had been extraordinarily generous. Or was he paying the fees out of her mother's estate? . . . That dreadful business of the life insurance?

'That would mean you could fix up your tickets at your local travel agent and book yourself somewhere to stay before you left here.' He smiled at her encouragingly. 'You can't just plunge out into the world with nowhere to go.'

Can't I? she thought. That's what I am doing, really. What does it matter where I go? . . . I shall pursue light. It's the only purpose I've got.

Dr Ferguson was still watching the thoughts chase themselves across her expressive face. He did not miss much. 'How did you get on in London? He asked suddenly.

Charley felt herself go even paler. In London? With Jon? That wonderful day of sunlight and shadow, of Turners and Rembrandts and Monets, Sibelius and light on the Thames, light on the lake, light on a drake's head, light on Jon's face . . .

'It was all right,' she said. 'Jon was a great help. But I admit I got a bit panicky on my own.'

He nodded, hearing the note of pain in her voice, and drawing his own conclusions. But he seemed to be smiling to himself about something.

'Yes,' he said at last. 'That's why I suggest you take the next step by stages. It won't be easy.'

No. It won't be easy, she thought bleakly. But I must do it. On my own. I have been protected and spoiled and cosseted long enough.

Dr Ferguson thought it was a short enough time to compensate for fifteen years of virtual slavery. But he did not say so.

'Will you do that?' he insisted.

Charley looked into his face directly for the first time, and saw the compassion there, and a curious, waiting expectancy. He really seemed concerned about her decision.

'Very well,' she said.

There seemed some relief in his steady gaze as he smiled at her. 'Take one thing at a time,' he murmured. 'Don't

85

finalise your plans too soon . . . They usually resolve themselves—one way or another.'

Charley assented, thought she couldn't really make out what he was talking about. Resolve themselves? She was the one who needed resolve. And courage. She supposed she would find some somewhere.

'Be patient,' said the Guvnor, leaning across to pat her arm gently. 'It will come.'

Charley did not dare to answer. His intuition was uncanny.

*　　*　　*

She was painfully sorting her mother's clothes and her own into tidy piles for Oxfam, when the doorbell rang.

Charley straightened her back, pushed the hair out of her eyes, and stood still. Who could it be? Not Gerald Farmer again, surely. No one knew she was here. And she didn't want anyone to know. For a moment she was inclined to stay where she was and not answer the door at all. But then the bell rang again, shrilling insistently through the house, and she knew she would have to go down.

She descended the stairs reluctantly—how she hated those stairs—and crossed the dark little hall to the front door. Slowly she lifted her hand to pull back the latch, opened the door and peered out.

On the step stood Jon.

Charley let her hand fall and seemed almost about to fall herself, she looked so pale and shaken. 'Jon?' she whispered. 'I thought—'

He took a step forward and steadied her with one hand on her arm. 'You thought I would walk out on you without a word?' His smile was reproachful. 'Oh, Charley!'

She was so confused that she could hardly speak, but a deep well of gladness seemed to be growing within her.

'Can I come in?' he asked, and then—seeing her ashen face—he changed his mind. 'Or have you had enough of this place? Shall we go out to lunch?'

'Yes, please.' Charley's voice was small, like a chastened child's, but she was beginning to smile a little.

'Come on, then.' He waited for her to pick up her handbag from the hall table, and then led her away down the steps. 'I've got lots to tell you,' he said, and laughed at her bewildered expression.

Charley laughed too, but she didn't quite know why.

* * *

Over lunch in the nearby hotel, Jon didn't say much. He contented himself with watching the colour come back into Charley's face and the dazed look of shock retreat from her eyes.

But afterwards he ordered coffee in the quietest corner of the lounge, and settled her beside the blazing log fire and prepared to talk. He also ordered her a brandy, for she still seemed curiously shaken.

'Charley,' he began, 'I want to ask you a question.'

'Yes?' She caught the serious note in his voice, and sat up attentively.

'After our day out in London, did you feel confident that you were ready to go off on your own all over Europe?'

She stared at him, looking pale and resolute. 'That's not a fair question.'

'Yes, it is,' he insisted. 'I want to know.'

She hesitated, and then said in a strange, abrupt tone: 'No. Of course not. But I've got to try.'

Jon nodded, as if her words confirmed something in his mind. Then he said deliberately: 'You don't have to, Charley. Not yet.'

She glanced at him, almost with contempt. 'If you're suggesting I should stay on at the Rehab House—'

'I'm not suggesting any such thing.'

She looked bewildered. 'Then—what?'

Jon lit a cigarette (against his doctor's orders) and leant back in his chair. 'Charley—bear with me while I explain.' He looked at her, half-smiling, and waited for her quick nod of consent. 'When I went back to the office the other day, they offered me a job—or rather, a free-lance assignment.'

'What kind of assignment?' She was looking at him now,

87

almost with alarm. 'You said they wouldn't let you go back to the Middle East.'

'Not to the war zones—no. I'm not fit enough. But this is in Tunisia—doing a special wildlife study on some threatened lake.'

'Wildlife? Is that your sort of thing?'

'It was once. Before I got involved in human carnage.' His voice was dry. 'In fact, I was rather good at it,' he added to her doubtful face.

'Will you like that?'

'Oh yes. I get quite involved once I start. It's a lot less demoralising than photographing rubble and bodies.' He paused, considering how to put it. 'And it's a fascinating story, Charley. There's this lake, you see—inland but near the sea—miles of clear, unpolluted fresh water in winter when it rains and the rivers fill up. All kinds of wildfowl come to winter there—it's on the migration route. But in summer, the streams dry up, the fresh water flows out to the sea, the level drops and the sea flows back into the lake, making it salt.'

Charley was listening intently now, fascinated. 'What happens to the birds?'

'A totally different lot come in then—on to the salt marshes . . . and there's even a different kind of plant that tolerates salt water for them to feed on . . .'

'Extraordinary.'

'Yes. But the whole cycle is under threat.'

'Why?'

'Shortage of water. They are damming a couple of the rivers. So the lake will lose much of its new supply of fresh water . . . so they've decided to dam the outflow of the lake so that the fresh water can't flow out to the sea and get lost.'

'But that means the salt water can't flow in.'

'Exactly. The whole cycle will be lost.'

'Can't they be stopped?'

He sighed. 'Maybe. Conservationists are trying. But in the meantime I have to try and record what is there now. Before it's too late.'

Charley's voice was warm with approval. 'Sounds a wonderful job.'

'Yes.' He glanced at her sideways, and then said coolly: 'But I turned it down.'

'You *what*?'

'Turned it down.'

'Why?'

'I said I couldn't do it alone.'

Charley was silent for a moment, remembering Jon's old friend, Richard, and how they had always gone on assignments together. She knew he missed him badly—he had told her so in an unguarded moment—but surely he knew he had got to get back to work sometime, alone or not.

'Jon, you can't—'

'Wait, Charley,' he interrupted swiftly. 'Let me finish.'

She waited, confused by his abrupt change of mood.

'I told them, Charley, that I wanted to take an assistant with me. Someone to keep notes and a record of the birds, and help catalogue things ready for the narration. Someone to carry bits and pieces of equipment for me and keep them in order . . . And someone to talk to, Charley. It's not all that good for me to be alone at present. I get too broody.' His smile was fleeting. 'But also someone who understands stillness and knows when to keep quiet.'

Charley grinned. 'Sounds a tall order.'

'No it isn't, Charley. I know just the person.' He was looking at her directly now, but his smile was still tentative. 'Will you come?'

She stared. 'Me?'

'Yes, you.' He saw the disbelief in her eyes and went on quickly. 'Please, Charley. I can't think of anyone else I'd rather have with me at present. I couldn't work with another colleague after Richard—not yet, anyway. And on this sort of assignment it doesn't need a full-time journalist as well as a cameraman . . . And three or four months in the sun would do us both good. Think, Charley, think of the light on all that water . . . You could paint it—and you could paint the birds as well.'

'Jon,' she interrupted, clasping her hands in distress. 'Jon, please stop!'

He paused, uncertain of her reaction. 'What?'

'I can't, Jon . . . I simply can't.'

'Why not?'

'Because—because I'd be *using* you . . . again. Don't you see? I'd be no good to you as an assistant. I'm not trained in that sort of thing.' She pushed the hair out of her eyes and looked at him with her honest, troubled gaze. 'I'm not trained in anything, come to that,' she added, with some bitterness.

'You're a damn good painter—don't you know that?'

'Am I?'

'You could keep a sort of illustrated record . . . Between us, we might even make a book—who knows?'

She shook her head. 'That's just a fairy tale.'

Jon grinned. 'Don't you believe in fairy tales?'

She smiled back, but beneath the glimmer there was still gravity. 'I rather think I do, Jon. Fairy godfathers, at least. But it won't work.'

'Why won't it work?'

'Because it would be so unequal. I'd be mostly a liability, anyway—and you've got enough to contend with, what with your health and the job itself. You don't want to saddle yourself with another lame duck.'

Jon began to laugh. 'They're all ducks out there, Charley. What's one among so many?'

'Jon, be serious.'

He looked at her straight. 'I am serious. Perfectly serious. I want you to come.'

She sighed. 'How am I ever going to learn to cope on my own if you keep on sheltering me? I've got to—to—'

'Stand on your own lame webbed feet?' The laughter was back. 'Oh, Charley—give yourself a chance. A few months' respite will do you no harm. Time to recover your poise. You'll be ready then to go off on your own wherever the fancy takes you. But now, let's face it, you're not.'

'That doesn't make it right to burden you.'

He ran a hand through his hair in exasperation. 'Charley, you're *not* a burden. It's about time you stopped under-valuing yourself. You'd be a *help*—not a hindrance.'

She still looked doubtful.

'Or—' he hesitated fractionally, 'there'd be no strings, Charley. Is that what's bothering you?'

90

'No.' She sounded quite definite about that. But she went on slowly: 'But have you thought, Jon, that you might be taking on more than you bargained for? . . . I mean, old Dr Ellis said I was in a—a very vulnerable state, and I wasn't used to people being kind to me . . .'

Jon's eyes were suddenly piercing and bleak. 'I'm not being kind, Charley. I'm lonely.'

At this, her whole expression changed. All at once, the idea that she might actually be some comfort to Jon seemed a possibility. She stared at him, trying to see through to the heart of the matter, but Jon was staring back with truth in his eyes.

'Well, if you put it like that—' she said, and her voice was soft.

*   *   *

There followed the usual flurry of departure. She went to see the bank manager and arranged about some money, though Jon had explained that their travelling and day-to-day expenses would be paid for by his office. 'And when the film's finished there'll be a lump sum for us to divide between us.'

Charley had her own ideas about the fairness of this, but she held her peace for the time being.

Next, she went to announce her plans to her Uncle Hal, who pretended to be horrified at the whole idea and gave her another stern lecture about predatory males and vulnerable young women. But when he heard she was actually going to earn some money and have her expenses paid— and leave most of her own money safely in the bank—he relented a little and gave her a cautious smile and the unexpected advice: 'Enjoy yourself. But keep your head.'

She also said goodbye to her old friend Dr Ellis, who was clearly delighted with the whole project and said simply: 'Be happy, my dear girl. It's about time.'

But the warmth of this response was almost destroyed when she ran into Gerald Farmer in the street outside the doctor's surgery.

'*Tunisia?*' he said when she told him. He sounded

incredulous, and faintly contemptuous at the same time. 'Aren't you being a little ambitious?'

Charley shrugged. 'Possibly.'

'It's hardly the sort of place to go to on your own.'

'I shan't be on my own,' said Charley, looking him straight in the eye. 'I'm going with Jon Armorel.'

He looked astounded. 'Who?'

'Oh, never mind.' She shook her head at him impatiently. 'Just someone I know who's offered me a job.'

'But who is he? Do you know anything about him? Where did you meet him?' His voice was sharp with suspicion.

Charley sighed. 'It's none of your business, Gerald—but yes, I do know something about him. I haven't time now to tell you about it, but I'm sure Uncle Hal will oblige if you ask him.'

She saw that Gerald actually blushed at this oblique reference to his attempt at interference in her plans.

'I'm only anxious about your welfare,' he muttered, sounding absurdly pompous.

Charley laughed, and held out her hand in frank and friendly forgiveness. 'Wish me luck, Gerald. I can assure you, my welfare will be in good hands.'

He blinked a little at her smiling confidence, and gave her outstretched hand an awkward shake. 'Well, of course,' he said lamely. 'Good luck. And do be careful.'

'Oh, I will,' she assured him blithely, 'I will.' But she was still laughing as she turned away and left him staring after her.

Do I know anything about Jon? she thought. Yes, I do. He is calm and kind, and unsurprised by human frailty. He doesn't judge, and he doesn't expect too much. And he is quite absurdly generous, though he pretends he isn't. And I feel safe with him, no matter how threatening life can be— entirely safe . . . Of course my welfare will be in good hands—of course! . . . But what about his?

Even this sobering thought couldn't make her anxious today. She was somehow filled with happiness—filled with hope. She would be some use to Jon. She would learn how to be a good assistant. She would try to fill his days

92

with cheerful companionship, and exorcise the nightmares that still plagued him. Somehow she would find a way to dispel his enormous sadness, and take the bleakness from his eyes . . .

Smiling a little still, she hurried on down the street. Her last call was to see Ranjit Singh at the corner shop, to thank him for his concern and the unexpected gift of fruit and flowers.

'You were so kind to me when I was ill,' she said. The dark, serious face broke into a smile. 'I was being worried,' he admitted. 'But now I am glad you are better. And you are going away?'

'A long way away, Mr Singh. Not as far as India, of course. But to Tunisia. I'll send you a postcard.'

Her smile matched his, but it was more incandescent. Rangit Singh found himself reflecting that Miss Gilmour looked at least ten years younger, and really very pretty indeed.

'I would be liking that,' he said gravely. 'And I am hoping that life will be good.'

'I am hoping so too!' agreed Charley, and almost danced out of the shop.

It was her last day at Dr Ferguson's, and she had only a few things to collect. Jon had instructed her to buy only essential clothes—mostly light summer cotton skirts and a couple of pairs of working jeans, not forgetting a pullover or two for the cooler evenings. 'And a bikini,' he added, grinning. 'We'll probably spend a lot of time in the water— one way or another.'

She had resolutely refused his help over all this and braved the shops on her own, with only a few brief moments of panic when they became too crowded or noisy. She had also offered to travel to Gatwick on her own, but this Jon would not consider at all. In any case, he said, he had things to collect from the Rehab House, and some last-minute instructions to receive from Dr Ferguson himself, so he would collect Charley as well, and they would travel on together. She was secretly relieved about this—the idea of facing so much on her own was still frightening—but she did not tell him so.

In the drawing-room she looked for the old colonel, but he was not there. The only other occupant was Louise, a tired girl with long blonde hair and wary, shadowed eyes, who sat alone in a corner resolutely trying to do some tapestry.

'I came to say goodbye,' murmured Charley.

The girl looked up and there was a darkness in her eyes that somehow made Charley ache inside. 'Well, good for you!' she said, smiling.

'Will you be going soon, too?'

She seemed to hesitate. 'Probably. Depends on the Guvnor.'

Charley smiled back. 'We all depend on the Guvnor.'

Louise bent her head over the piece of canvas and carefully inserted the needle. 'I can face most things now. Can you?'

'Most things,' agreed Charley cheerfully.

'Except a whisky bottle,' added Louise, in a bright conversational tone.

'Was that it?' Charley was suddenly almost ashamed of her own freedom, her own bubbling happiness.

The girl looked up, half-smiling. 'Classic case. Husband unfaithful. Blot it out. Husband more unfaithful. Blot it out more. Husband totally faithless. Blot it out completely.'

Charley nodded. 'What will you do? Go back?'

'No,' said Louise, stabbing viciously at the canvas with her needle. 'Go on.'

'I'm glad.' Charley held out her hand impulsively. 'Good luck.'

Louise took Charley's hand in a surprisingly firm and friendly grip. 'Thanks,' she said, 'I'll need it. And good luck to you, too.' Her smile was brief and sudden, but it made her look much younger and less worn. 'If you're looking for the Colonel,' she added, 'he went out into the garden.'

Charley smiled at her and wandered outside to look for him. She went across the lawn and down the path by the long herbaceous border where the late chrysanthemums still lifted bronze heads to the autumn sky. Beyond the border was the herb garden and the walled enclosure given over to vegetables, and then the path curved back towards

94

the house and came to the lily pond.

And here Charley stopped and drew a sharp breath of alarm. For the colonel lay face down in the lily pond, his limbs spread out and his face under water.

Without hesitation, Charley rushed forward and seized him by the shoulders, turning him over so that his mouth and nose were clear of the water. His eyes were closed and he seemed unconscious—she was not sure if he was still breathing.

For a moment the old, frightening feeling of panic came over her, and she did not know what to do. But, looking down at him, she realised at once that she needed help, so she left him lying there and ran across the grass, shouting.

People came running then. Little Nurse Evie arrived, and after her Dr Ferguson, whose competent, strong hands soon began to force air through those sodden lungs.

In a little while the colonel's limp body arched itself into a spasm, and he began to cough and retch. At last he turned his head on one side and seemed to sigh, and the blue, faded eyes opened and looked straight into Charley's, filled with reproach. 'Why?' he whispered. '*Why?*'

They took him away then, very kindly and quietly, and put him to bed with all due care and attention. And Charley was left alone in the garden, shaken to the core by that helpless, accusing stare.

Jon found her there, and came swiftly across the grass to put a comforting arm round her shoulders. 'What happened?'

She told him briefly, and added in a choked voice: 'Jon— he said "*Why?*" . . . He didn't want to come back. He hated me for interfering. What have I done?'

Jon sighed and held her close. 'Life is precious, Charley. He'll thank you in the end.'

But she refused to be comforted. 'Will he? What has life got to offer—beyond a game of chess?' She turned to him impulsively. 'You know him better than I do. What went wrong?'

Jon's gaze was compassionate. 'His life was a bit like yours, Charley—except that he was older.' He paused, looking at her thoughtfully, and then went on: 'His wife

95

was an invalid. He nursed her devotedly for twenty years. He kept it up right to the end, and then he collapsed. Now he has no one to look after, no purpose in living. It's as simple as that.'

Charley's face was as sad as Jon's. 'He's got to find something to do!'

Jon nodded. 'Yes. And he will. He's a born fighter, really.'

Charley wasn't satisfied. 'Hasn't he any family?'

'One son, I believe.'

'Who pays to keep him here, I suppose.'

'Exactly.'

'Doesn't he ever visit him?'

'Not that I know of.'

'But he must!' cried Charley, outraged. 'After this—he must accept responsibility.' Her mouth set in an absolute line. 'Jon, I want to see the Guvnor.'

Jon protested gently. 'Not our business, Charley.'

'Yes, it is.' She was adamant. 'We've got to do something *now*—before we go.' She could not explain to Jon that she was somehow ashamed of her own new-found happiness, and could not go away and leave someone else in such depths of despair.

But Jon seemed to know her thoughts without being told. Smiling a little at her insistence, he went with her to see the Guvnor. This new fighting Charley, with flaring hair and eyes like an avenging angel's was someone to be reckoned with.

The Guvnor thought so too, and smiled inwardly at the transformation from the nervous wreck he had first seen to this vividly alive, passionate girl.

'You must remember,' he said gently, 'despair is what we deal in here. It is the root of all our troubles—as you well know.'

'Yes.' She shook her hair out of her eyes impatiently. 'Only, it's different for me. I've been lucky.' She glanced at Jon with a fleeting smile. 'But what does the colonel have to look forward to?'

Dr Ferguson considered this gravely. 'Not a lot, I admit. But he will find something.'

'How?' Charley sounded downright belligerent. Then a note of pleading crept into her voice. 'People can't live without hope, Guvnor—can they?'

The Guvnor's smile was as gentle as his voice. 'We all have to find our own springs of hope, Charley—in the end.'

She gazed at him, the words of protest dying before they were uttered. He was right, of course—as usual. But that didn't help the colonel now.

There was silence for a moment while all three of them considered the colonel's future.

'Was it deliberate, do you think?' asked Charley suddenly.

Ferguson hesitated. 'No. I think not. It's not that easy to drown yourself in a foot of water. My guess is, he fell in and knocked himself out.'

'But he said *Why*?'

'Yes. Well, maybe—if he came round at all—he didn't make much effort to move. I don't think it was any more deliberate than that.'

Charley still looked sceptical.

'When are you and Jon leaving?' the Guvnor demanded abruptly.

Charley looked at Jon, and he answered for her. 'After lunch.'

Ferguson nodded. 'I'll tell you what I'll do,' he said, looking at Charley's flushed and unconvinced face with sympathy. 'The colonel's son is arriving at twelve. No doubt he will want to thank you, Charley.'

'*What for*?' muttered Charley, still sounding mutinous.

'You can ask him that, can't you?' The Guvnor's voice was smooth. And Charley, glancing up in surprise, caught a decided gleam of mischief in his eye. 'After all, you have been through the same kind of marathon as the colonel. You can speak with authority.' The smile had got into his voice now, too. 'And once you get going, Charley, nothing's going to stop you, is it?'

'No,' said Charley, mouth one straight line of determination. 'It isn't.'

The Guvnor laughed. 'And I'm not responsible for the

opinions of my patients, am I?'

'No,' agreed Charley, meeting the gleam in his eye with a spark of her own. 'So what have we got to lose?'

Their accord was complete.

Jon thought it was pretty irregular. But the Guvnor was like that. He used unconventional means to help his patients—and maybe this was a subtle way of boosting Charley's own crusading spirit as well . . . In any case, it was clear to Jon—as it undoubtedly was to Ferguson—that Charley, with her new ardent beauty and passionate concern, was a potent and powerful advocate.

The colonel's son proved to be a bit of an anti-climax, really. Charley felt tall and brave and strong, like Joan of Arc, tingling with righteous anger. But she was confronted by a mild-mannered man in a city suit, whose pale blue eyes (like the colonel's but less faded) and long, greyish face looked neither bland nor aggressive—merely neutral. Nevertheless, Charley knew she must get through to him somehow, for the colonel's sake—and it was now or never.

'He didn't want to come back,' she said baldly, looking at him with fierce insistence. 'He said "*Why*?" when he came round. And he looked sort of—heart-broken . . . as if he couldn't bear the thought of having to go on alone.' She drew a swift breath, and pushed the hair out of her eyes in the familiar gesture of stress. 'It was a terrible look, Mr Morris. Accusing, somehow. I felt more like a murderer than a rescuer.'

The pale blue eyes opposite her seemed to cloud and grow strangely opaque. 'I didn't know,' he murmured, shaken. 'How dreadful—I didn't realise.'

'Despair is dreadful, Mr Morris. Believe me—I should know.' She spoke with quiet passion, determined to get past that grey indifference. 'You have to have some reason for existing: something to look forward to—someone who needs you. Otherwise, what's the point?' She shut her eyes suddenly, remembering how it had been with her before Jon came along with his healing kindness. 'No one can live without hope,' she murmured. 'It simply isn't possible.'

There was silence in the small private room where they were sitting. Charley could hear the gentle ticking of the grandfather clock in the hall. And somewhere, Jon was waiting for her. A sudden, enormous wave of gratitude swept over her as she thought of Jon. Without him, she might have been like the colonel—purposeless and despairing. But Jon had changed all that—Jon, with his crooked smile and his bleak, honest eyes, and his final plea: '*I'm lonely* . . .' That clever, seemingly casual demand that gave her back her pride—and her sense of purpose.

'I've been lucky,' she said to the bewildered man beside her. 'Someone has offered me a whole new future—at least for the next six months. You can't imagine what that means to me. But your father—' She broke off, and made a curious, uneven gesture with her hand. 'I wish I could wave a wand for him, like Jon Armorel has done for me.' She looked at the grey man beside her with tears in her eyes, willing him to understand. 'He's lonely, you see,' she said, as if spelling it out to a child. 'Only—he hasn't got a Jon Armorel to turn to. I wish he had.'

The silence this time was more profound than ever. Charley wondered if she had said too much. Probably she had. But she didn't regret one word of it—not one word. For something within her still grieved for the colonel, still shrank from that dark, accusing gaze, still longed to put some spark of hope back into that weary, defeated face.

'I don't know this Jon Armorel,' said the colonel's son slowly. 'And I daresay I'll make a poor substitute. But at least I can try.'

He got up then, and held out his hand, almost shyly. 'Miss Gilmour. Thank you. I owe you more than I can say.'

Charley's smile was radiant, remembering suddenly that in a few moments she and Jon would be on their way to a new adventure. 'Will you give him my love—when he is better?'

'Of course I will.'

'He may come to forgive me in time,' she murmured.

The colonel's son looked at her with the same straight gaze as his father's. 'I will make sure,' he said firmly, 'that he has every reason to.' And then he actually smiled, though Charley could see that he was still shy. 'Shall we wish each other a hopeful future?'

'Why not?' Charley clasped his hand. 'What more could we ask?'

'What more, indeed?' said Jon's voice from the doorway, and he held out his hand to Charley and led her outside to where the taxi was waiting.

Their luggage was piled in. A flutter of hands waved goodbye, and the Guvnor unexpectedly came forward and hugged Charley, murmuring into her ear: 'Well done, young Charley!' Then the doors were slammed and they were away. The square bulk of the Rehab House dwindled and grew small. The long garden faded into a green and gold distant blur. Presently, it was gone altogether. Nothing remained of the old life. Ahead was something entirely new.

PART III
REFLECTIONS AND REFRACTIONS

The villa was white and cool, with blue shutters and a blue door. It presented an almost blank wall to the street, except for the blue door and the archway leading to it. But beyond, there was a courtyard surrounded by more gleaming white arches and a fountain in the middle, flanked by tubs of brilliant flowers.

Charley stood there, amazed by the light and the sense of space, and then saw, through one shadowed archway, a glimpse of the sea—quite close beyond the white walls.

'Wait there a minute,' instructed Jon, and waved a hand towards the group of white chairs set near the fountain. 'I'll go and find Ankaret.'

Gratefully, Charley sank into a chair and watched the sparkle of the fountain as it rose and fell in the sunlight.

She was tired, but the journey had not been difficult— thanks to Jon who was such an experienced traveller. The English airport had been a bit crowded and terrifying, but flying itself had been an unexpected delight. She had found herself looking down on to a dazzling ceiling of white cloud, light-filled and vast, spreading in limitless horizons as far as the eye could see, its moving shapes and towers changing and reforming in the shimmering incandescence of the pure unbroken sunlight that poured down upon it out of deep space. She watched in fascinated wonder as this whole new cloudspace unfolded before her; and then—all at once it seemed—the clouds dissolved into scattered wisps and veils of silken light and were gone, and she was looking down at blue sea and islands, coastlines and mountains and valleys, and finally the small white sugar-cubes of houses, the blue domes and minarets of Tunis as they came in to land.

Jon had organised everything very smoothly, as usual.

There was a small green jeep waiting for them to pile all their gear into, and the customs men seemed to know him well and to examine his cameras and equipment with only moderate suspicion. They did not linger, but drove out along the coast road towards Bizerta.

'We'll come back to see Tunis and Carthage when you're not tired,' he said, smiling.

She was almost too dazzled to smile back. Everything seemed so drenched in golden sunlight. She got glimpses of squat white buildings, blue-painted arches and domes, great splashes of bougainvillea spilling down walls, minarets and towers, wide streets and palm trees, narrow streets and dark alleyways, small squares and springing fountains, and in between, more glimpses of sea and shores girdled with white sand.

They went into Sidi Bou Said because Jon said Charley ought to see it on the way, and here they parked the jeep and walked up the steep cobbled main street to the Café des Nattes for her first mint tea. They sat looking down at the narrow crowded street, and listened to the call to prayer from the minaret high above the jumble of rooftops, curving domes and shadowy arches that seemed to jostle for space around them. All the houses appeared to be of the same dazzling whiteness, spiced with the same vivid blue paint—even on the intricately carved lintels and studded doorways—and more bougainvillea frothed over walls and mingled with the cascades of brilliant flowers tumbling from balconies and half-hidden courtyards.

They wandered among the small shops and friendly street traders offering their bright-coloured carpets and blankets and hand-thrown pots—but it was the ancient traditional craft of the birdcage maker that fascinated Charley most. She had never imagined so many shapes and sizes of cage, or such intricate wire-work and delicacy of design, and she found herself talking to the shopkeeper in excited and admiring French. He was charmed, and promptly invited them to take coffee with him in his dark little room behind the shop. They left eventually with much hand-shaking and smiling all round, and Charley carrying the smallest and most delicate little birdcage she could find.

'You could keep a *grillon* in it to sing to you, if you do not like to cage a bird,' said the shopkeeper, smiling.

But Charley said no, she would not even cage a cricket. She would put a flowering plant in it instead.

Jon said nothing, but watched her with smiling indulgence. She was like a child at a party.

But even in this almost too perfect village there were sudden glimpses of the other side of the coin. The smiling appearance of sun-gilded walls and cheerful tourists, the tea-drinkers and prosperous traders, was one thing. But there were dark alleys beyond the bright street displays, and small boys begging at street corners, a sudden glimpse of an old, worn face peering out from a darkened doorway, and veiled women hurrying away under hidden arches . . . Yes, there were shadows too, behind the sunlight.

However, Jon wouldn't let her explore too much that first day. Time enough, he told her, when they were less travel-weary—and seeing the question in her eyes, he added soberly: 'Yes, there are both sides, of course . . . Many sides to this complex country . . .' He gestured towards the blue minarets and the tall white tower of the lighthouse, 'both high and low . . .' he murmured, half-smiling, and led her back up the narrow streets to their jeep. 'You will have to take it slowly, Charley—though I'm afraid much of it will shock you.'

They drove on through Utica, promising to come back and look at the ruins another day. 'Though I'm not a tourist,' protested Charley, eyeing Jon with doubtful honesty. 'I'm here to work.'

'We have to play sometimes,' countered Jon, and turned off the main highway towards Raf Raf and Ghar el Melh where the sea and its white-and-gold shoreline came close, almost irresistibly inviting. And here, before the road swung away again, they came to a small row of white villas at the end of a street that dwindled into a meandering track facing the sea.

'Here we are,' said Jon.

* * *

So she sat on a white chair in the sun and dreamed. Here we are. Here I am. In all this marvellous light and warmth—and the blue sea waiting for me . . . Why do I feel as if—as if it's all a mirage that will dissolve like mist . . . and almost scared of so much richness?

Behind her she heard the soft slap of sandals against cool marble, and opened her eyes to find herself looking into the smiling face of a large, friendly woman in a large and flowing kaftan.

Ankaret Lejeune was at that time about fifty years old—a handsome, calm-eyed woman, built on a generous scale in every sense. She was tall—nearly five-foot-ten—and wide with it, though her bulk was firm amd muscular rather than merely fat, and she moved with surprising lightness of foot. Her hair was fairish, bleached by the sun and massed into an untidy coil, her skin was tanned a smooth golden brown, and her eyes were a strange mixture of amber and green. But her smile was as wide and expansive as the rest of her, and seemed to embrace the world with as much generosity as her own outstretched arms embraced a stranger at her gates, and her voice was warm and rich with reassurance.

'Welcome,' she said, folding Charley in a large embrace. 'Welcome to Tunisia, Charley . . . You must be tired. Jon's bringing out the drinks.'

Charley had somehow expected Ankaret to speak in Arabic or maybe French, and to look a good deal darker and more foreign. But this woman spoke in an easy English voice, faintly spiced with some hidden rhythm or other, and her solid bulk seemed also essentially English in spite of the tent-like blue kaftan with its golden tassels.

At this point in her thoughts, while she had still not made any reply except a murmured 'Thank you', Jon reappeared carrying a tray of drinks, followed by a small wide-eyed Arab boy of extraordinary waif-like charm.

'This is Zizi,' said Ankaret, giving the boy's dark curly head an affectionate tweak as he came up to her. 'He is very good at carrying things and running messages.'

The small boy beamed and placed a bowl of ice on the marble table, and then handed Ankaret an enormous tapestry handbag. 'You lose . . . I find,' he announced proudly, and his grin grew even wider. Then he approached Charley shyly and offered her an orange held out on a slim brown hand. *'Bienvenu,'* he said.

Charley was enchanted. She took the orange, and gravely shook the small brown hand. *'Enchantée,'* she replied.

Ankaret and Jon looked at one another and smiled. It was clear that they were old friends and that they were saying to each other: 'She'll do.'

They sat sipping long lemon drinks in the cool courtyard, with young Zizi sitting crosslegged on the floor beside them, and then Ankaret said suddenly to Charley: 'I expect you'd like to swim.'

'I'd love to.' Charley's eyes had kept straying through the shadowed archway to that glimpse of startlingly blue water beyond.

'The water's still quite warm at this time of year,' Ankaret glanced at Jon enquiringly, 'but maybe you—?'

'Just a little splash,' said Jon ruefully. 'No serious swimming allowed just yet. I can watch Charley.'

Charley pushed the hair out of her eyes. 'I'm not very good . . .'

Ankaret laughed. 'You don't have to be, here.' She looked at Charley with massive calm. 'That's the joy of this place. You don't have to *be* anything. Just *be*.'

Charley nodded, aware that Ankaret was as perceptive as she was kind.

'I'll show you your rooms,' said Ankaret, rising to her feet and proceeding before them like a ship in full sail.

They went through another archway which revealed a row of small blue-painted doors, all leading into the main part of the house.

'All the rooms come out into the courtyard,' Ankaret explained, 'and most of the windows look the other way, out to sea. You can swim from the house. It's easier than undressing on the beach—the local Muslims don't much like it.'

Jon grinned. 'You mean they threw their hands up in horror, and have a good look.'

Ankaret's laughter was like the rest of her—mountainous and full of warmth. 'Exactly . . . This is yours, Charley. Zizi's already put your case there, I see . . . And Jon's is two doors along.' She turned to Jon seriously. 'I've done what you asked about a projection room. That end one there is always empty anyway, and it has heavy shutters so it will make quite a decent dark room . . . And I thought Charley could use it as a studio when you're not editing film.'

Charley was amazed. 'Me? A studio? You're joking.'

'No, I'm not. Jon was most insistent. Space for canvases and an easel, he said.'

'I'm—overwhelmed.' She turned to Jon. 'I never expected—'

'Go and get changed,' growled Jon. 'I'll overwhelm you in the sea.'

* * *

They played and splashed like children in the warm shallows, but then Jon seemed to tire suddenly and went to lie on the sand, while Charley floated on her back in the water and gazed at the sky. All around her was blue and gold water and blue and gold air. The light poured down upon her out of a flawless sky. She felt relaxed and weightless, floating in a timeless world of sun and shadow, and a silence only enhanced by the soft whisper of the shore-line waves . . . I am a mote, she dreamed, a drop in the ocean, a fleck of foam . . . and she felt the gentle lift and fall of the sea take her into its wide, encompassing embrace. Father Poseidon, hold me, she thought. No, that's ancient Greece . . . Who was the sea-god to the Phoenicians? . . . Or the Carthaginians? . . . Or the Romans? . . . Neptune? . . . The same, she thought, turning lazily in a quiet, iridescent swirl, the name doesn't matter. They still exist, the ancient gods. 'You don't have to *be* anything—just *be* . . .' Smiling, she turned again and began a slow, unhurried crawl back to the long white beach and its absurd picture postcard palm trees, where Jon lay waiting for her.

'Tell me about Ankaret,' she said, as they lay side by side

on the warm sand in the evening sun.

Jon rolled over lazily and propped himself up on one arm so that he could look at her. 'Ankaret? What do you want to know?'

'Well, first of all—I was expecting someone who spoke Arabic, or at best French, whereas—'

'Whereas she's as English as you are—or Welsh, rather.'

'*Welsh*?'

'Couldn't you hear the lilt?' He smiled at her.

'I could, as a matter of fact. But with that name—'

'Ankaret *is* Welsh. It means "beloved", I believe—and she is, really, by most people.'

'I can believe that.'

His smile grew warmer. 'She came out to Tunisia about fifteen years ago, and met Jacques Lejeune in the course of her job. They were married within six months, I believe . . . He was a successful lawyer—and they were very happy.' He paused for a moment, and then added in a dry voice: 'Unfortunately, he died in a car accident last year.'

'Oh!' Charley's face was full of distress. 'I'm so sorry.'

'Yes. It was a bad time for her. She decided in the end to keep the villa here and stay on. She's not short of money, though she does let out rooms to selected friends now and then . . . But she's not here all the time, anyway.'

'Why not?'

'She goes off on relief work from time to time.'

'Relief work?'

'Yes. When the rains fail and the famines come . . . She's been in Chad recently, with a French team of doctors and nurses. And before that, Ethiopia . . .' He sighed. 'Young Zizi is the product of one of her trips.'

Charley was not surprised when she thought about it. 'No wonder he's so devoted . . .'

'Yes. No parents left, no history—just a number in a refugee camp.'

'Has she adopted him?'

'Not yet . . . the procedures are very complicated. But she's made herself responsible for his welfare.'

'What will happen to him?'

'Oh, she's teaching him French and a bit of English . . .

109

He'll go to school a bit, and work a bit, I suppose. And later on, she'll find him a trade or a job . . . He won't starve, and he'll grow up independent.'

'Wonderful,' breathed Charley.

'She's always doing it. The house is apt to be full of Ankaret's rescued strays.'

Like me? thought Charley, but she kept her eyes shut against the sun and did not say it.

'Don't be prickly, Charley,' said Jon's voice softly beside her.

Her eyes flew open. 'I didn't mean—'

He smiled, and reached out on long finger to brush some sand off her cheek. 'Won't you be happy here?'

'You know I will. It's . . . out of this world.'

Jon's laughter startled a dozing seabird on the shore. 'It is rather, isn't it?'

'I can't tell you—' Charley waved a hand round at the long, sparkling vista of sea and sand and palm trees, 'the space and airiness of everything, and this marvellous light . . . And Ankaret's villa, so cool and beautiful, all those graceful rooms . . . and *no stairs*.' She began to laugh a little, too. 'I used to promise myself that I'd never live in a house with stairs again!'

Jon nodded, but he didn't interrupt Charley's rhapsody.

'I don't suppose you realised—oh yes, maybe you did, you're so clever.'

'I am? Why?'

'Well, I mean, there couldn't be a greater contrast to the dark little world I was living in, could there? I don't have to *pursue* light here. It's all round me.'

'No holes?'

She looked at him soberly. 'None.' By this time she too was leaning up on an elbow, looking away from Jon towards the sea.

'But—?' Jon's voice was gentle.

She turned her head. 'I didn't say "but".'

'Your face did.'

She was silent, and then slowly shook her head. 'It's only that—it's almost too good to be true.'

'And you're not used to lotus-eating.'

'No.' Her voice was wondering rather than sad.

Jon laid a hand on her arm. 'Listen, Charley. I'll explain our work schedule, and then you won't feel so bad. Tonight we'll dine with Ankaret. She likes entertaining, and it will make her happy. OK?'

Charley smiled. 'Of course.'

'And then an early night, I think, because it's been a long trip. And tomorrow you're going to get up before dawn.'

'Am I?'

'Yes. We have to be at Lake Ichkeul before first light . . . The thing is, Charley, we're at the end of the summer—as far as the lake is concerned. It's at its lowest and driest, the sea end is at its saltiest, and so the sea-birds are there. But not for long. Understand?'

'Yes.'

'It's on the migration path, too. All sorts of long-distance travellers will stop off there for a rest on their way south. And soon the rains will come. The rivers will fill up, the lake will change back to its fresh-water habitat, and the wintering birds will come . . . I have to capture the first stage before it changes—and record the passing visitors, too— otherwise I'll have to wait till next August or so to get the salt marshes again and complete the cycle.'

'Yes, I see. Do they overlap?'

'The birds? Yes, sometimes. It depends on the rains. We may get a patch when almost *everything* is there.'

'What do we do then?'

'Record like mad. That's where you come in. I want you to take endless notes of what we see, identify the birds and make quick sketches if you can, so that you can work from them in the studio when we're not filming. Then we can compare your lists with my film and see what we've missed. Between us, we should pick up most of them.'

'What happens when the rains come?'

'It's not usually prolonged up here in the north—or so torrential that you can't work in between. But there will be studio days, which are necessary anyway. And I have to take the cans of film into Tunis to be processed before we can run them through.' He grinned at her absorbed expression. 'We could fit in a spot of sightseeing there.'

Charley protested again, rising to the bait. 'Jon, I came to work!'

'And work you will. But there'll be time for a little fun, too. In this country time seems to stretch anyway.' He hesitated a moment, and then he turned back to her seriously. 'Charley, you must make allowance for a little self-indulgence . . . on my behalf, at least.'

'*Your* behalf?'

He looked at her, half-smiling. He wanted to say: I don't suppose you've any idea what a joy you are to take to new places. Sometimes you look like young Zizi—all eyes and wonder. It makes me feel like God . . .

But aloud, he said obscurely: 'You're not the only one searching for light, young Charley!' And, to her mystified expression, he added: 'So don't allow your puritan conscience to have too much voice!'

She gazed at him, still puzzled by his words. 'Puritan?'

He laughed, and rubbed a sandy hand through his hair. 'I'm sorry, Charley. I only meant, be happy while you've got the chance. It may never come again—this halcyon time.'

This halcyon time, thought Charley helplessly. So beautiful and so fragile. And he cannot know how much it means to me.

'You make me want to walk on eggshells,' she murmured.

'Come on.' He pulled her to her feet. 'You'll get cold sitting here being lectured. The temperature drops very fast when the sun goes down.' He held her still for a moment, looking into her face with sudden intensity.

Then Charley stood on tiptoe like a child and put her arms round his neck and kissed him. 'Thank you for making all this possible,' she said, and turned and ran across the empty sands to the villa garden and its cool white arches beyond.

*　　*　　*

The lake was still when they got there—calm and quiet under a dark sky already flushed with dawn.

112

They had parked the jeep a little way off, hoping the noise of its engine would not disturb the birds too much, and had unloaded Jon's equipment quietly. But even so, a great rush of wings went up, high voices called in the air, and the sky seemed to grow alive with wheeling birds. As the first rays of the sun crept over the horizon, Charley saw what she thought was a pink cloud coming towards her, circling the lake. But it wasn't a cloud—it was flamingoes, thousands of them, pink and white and black, turning in the sun and settling again to wade in the salty shallows, fishing for shrimps at the far seaward end of the lake.

'OH!' breathed Charley. 'Aren't they beautiful!'

Jon had already seized his camera and was busy filming. He was looking along the shore-line, focusing on the circling flamingoes in the distance, and then on the more clear-cut birds nearby as they came down into the water.

Charley had been doing her homework, and she recognised a whole lot of different waders strolling about on their spindly legs in the mudflats at the edge of the lake—little stints and sandpipers, black-winged stilts on long red legs, dotterels, redsnanks and greenshanks, and darting avocets with their long, curved bills; delicate little egrets with their fluffy crests and wing plumes and long black legs on thin yellow feet, and the less pure white cattle egret with its golden-buff plumes on its crown, and the curiously untidy-looking squacco heron . . . So many, so sprightly and delicate, wading through the shallow water, darting and diving for food, strutting and preening, calling to each other across the quiet lake, their slender shapes reflected in the pale silver-grey surface beneath them.

She was already frantically making notes, and scribbling lightning sketches beside her excited lists of discoveries.

So far, she had been looking at the waders in the salt-marsh shallows, but now she looked round at the main expanse of water—and here there seemed to be a whole different population of birds swimming and diving, flying in curving sweeps and flashes of wing, alighting in long swirls and cascades of water. First of all there were the greylag geese—thousands of them—and the noise of their voices and the beat of their wings as they flew up and settled again was almost deafening. Then there were the fussy little coots and purple gallinules, pintails and shovelers with their beautiful, vivid markings, and red-crested pochards, mallards and redbreasted mergansers. And when she looked up at the myriad wings in the sky, she thought she caught a glimpse of the more sinister shadow of a marsh harrier hovering over the trees at the edge of the far shore-line.

After the first desperate attempt to note down every bird she saw, Charley drew breath and began to look around her in more detail. The lake was big and wide, with many reedy islets floating on its surface, and the seaward side was flat and marshy. But across the water on the other shore, a tall mountain—Jebel Ichkeul—rose in lofty wooded splendour. Jon had already told her how Jebel Ichkeul had been a royal hunting reserve for many centuries, and that there were still descendants of the original pair of imported buffalo roaming the high rocky slopes. They didn't seem to be visible today, but the mountain looked dark and mysterious across the shining expanse of water, and Charley found herself longing to go over and explore it. They said there were wild boar there, and an occasional jackal, and you could sometimes see an otter swimming across the more distant reaches of the lake—but today nothing stirred except the endless flights of birds.

She realised almost at once that Jon was unstoppable when he was working. He went on and on, hardly pausing for breath or anything else, his camera whirring and his photographer's eye perpetually on the watch for the best and most dramatic shots. His camera was heavy, and Charley felt sure the weight of it must make his arms ache; she wondered what prolonged crouching and wading through mudflats and shallow water might do to his damaged lungs. But he seemed tireless and oblivious of discomfort.

She had tried to familiarise herself with all his equipment so that she could bring anything to him that he wanted—lenses and filters, light meters and tripods, and the smaller video camera which was much lighter to carry but Jon said did not give him the best results.

She had also remembered that they would be out all day and would need something to eat and drink. She had consulted Ankaret about this, and had come armed with a basket of cheese and fruit, a couple of fresh *casse-croûtes* and Tunisian *briks* filled with tuna fish and meat, and a long loaf of new bread. She had slipped out and bought these from the village bakehouse which seemed to be open and filled with baking bread from about four in the morning. The smiling baker paused in his endless task of sliding trays of long loaves in and out of the big black ovens, and told Charley that his *briks* and *casse-croûtes* were fresh and hot and the best that could be bought, and he would have some for her every day if she came at this hour. Besides these local offerings, there was a flask of coffee, and a bottle of wine which she had laid in the shallows to cool. She hoped all this would satisfy Jon when he paused long enough to remember that he was tired and hungry.

In the meantime she was so enchanted with the place itself and all its countless birds that she had no idea how fast the morning had gone until she looked up and realised that the noonday sun was high overhead and blazing down in splinters of light on the shimmering water.

She glanced down the lake and saw Jon far out, wading towards a small reedy islet where there was actually a tree growing out of the water, with an old heron's nest at its top. She waited patiently while he filmed the tall, sentinel heron standing stock still in the water below, and then went towards him as he splashed away from the reedbeds back to the shore.

'Can you stop for a while?' she called. 'Food's ready.'

'Food?' he said, and rubbed a muddy hand over his face. 'Sounds good.'

'And coffee.'

'Wonderful.' He lowered his camera carefully on to dry ground and collapsed in a heap beside it. 'Gosh, my arms ache,' he said in surprise.

Charley made no comment, but handed him a hunk of cheese, a wedge of bread, two clementines, a *casse-croûte* filled with tuna and olives, a couple of *briks* that had been so tightly wrapped in their cloth that they were still vaguely

115

warm, and a large plum tomato. 'Will this do?'

He grinned and took a bite at his cheese. 'I'm not complaining.'

Companionably, they sat side by side in the tufty reeds and grasses, and watched the birds intent on their own perpetual foraging. As they sat there, one or two bright green lizards slid away in the grasses, and a larger gecko sat and sunned itself on a stone, regarding them with a black, beady eye.

'Look!' said Charley, pointing. 'Isn't that a bee-eater? I didn't have that on my list . . . Do they really come this far?'

'In summer—they breed here, I think. Over there in those sandy cliffs below the mountain. This must be a late one that hasn't gone yet . . . ' He smiled at her eager face. 'I told you we might get both migrations meeting if we were lucky—there are even some storks left on that farmhouse roof over there . . . '

'The colours!' murmured Charley, still watching the bee-eater as it hovered in the sun. 'Like a harlequin.' And she sat spellbound as the iridescent blue-green breast flashed in the light, and the brilliant reds and yellows and vibrant chestnut of its head and mantle glowed as it perched and swung and hovered in darting flight across the shore-line into the trees.

'There's a mallard here that seems almost tame,' she said, throwing a crumb into the water. 'He keeps swimming close to have a look at us. See him? I've christened him James.'

'Why?'

'St James's Park,' she reminded him, smiling.

Jon laughed. 'Maybe he took a fancy to you and followed you out here.' He too tossed a small crumb into the water. James, the green-headed mallard drake, dived for it and came up wagging his perky tail.

'What's that funny little thing?' he asked, pointing suddenly at a small brown cream-throated bird that was running along the water margins of the lake in swift, darting movements.

Charley consulted her notes. 'That's a pratincole,' she announced, 'but I can't tell you which kind till it flies.' As

116

she spoke, the bird took off into the air with a flash of chestnut underwing, and joined a whole sweeping flock of its fellows, looking like darting swallows with their forked tails and scything wings spiralling upwards into the blue air.

'Like swallows,' murmured Jon, tilting his head to watch them.

'Collared pratincoles,' said Charley precisely. 'The black-winged ones don't have any red on them . . .' She paused, and then added, making another quick note on her pad: 'And that's a cream-coloured courser—I think. It's supposed to run and crouch . . . Yes, look, there it goes . . .'

Jon was smiling at her intent face. 'You're a marvel, Charley. You seem to know them all.'

'Not *all*!' She looked up in startled protest. 'There are supposed to be over four hundred species here at one time or another.'

'Are there?' He laid a hand on his camera, as if he meant to get up and start again at once. 'I can see I'm going to be busy.'

'Oh, not yet, Jon.' Charley held out another *casse-croûte* filled with green and red peppers topped with egg and cheese. 'You'll wear yourself out before you've begun.'

He turned lazily and took the proffered roll, and he did not refuse the glass of wine she held out to him.

She watched him for a moment in silence and then said: 'Can I make a suggestion?'

'Why not?' He spoke with his mouth full, and crinkled his eyes at her against the sun.

'That camera of yours is pretty heavy, and crouching about in wet marshes is fairly exhausting. I think you should take a good long siesta—even though it isn't high summer—and compare notes with me before you go on to the next bit . . .' She looked at him earnestly. 'I mean—I'm sure you're a better cameraman when you're not tired.'

He was silent for a moment, and then he grinned at her anxious face. 'Don't look so terrified. What you say makes good sense.'

She sighed with relief. 'More wine?'

'I shall go to sleep.'

117

'Good idea.'

He laughed. 'I'll waste time on one condition.'

'What's that?'

'You do the same.'

'As to that,' said Charley primly, 'I want to settle down to some real sketching. These lightning scribbles are no good at all!'

So she sat in the filtered sunlight under some tall reeds at the edge of the water, sketching the bright red head of a pochard, while Jon lay back in the tufts of summer-dried grasses and dozed gently among the darting lizards and vivid scarab beetles scurrying about beside him.

It was very peaceful, very quiet—only the endless voices of the birds calling to one another across the shining water broke the drowsing noonday silence.

Charley began to look at the light on the lake with rapt attention. It seemed to pour down out of that flawless sky and spread and shimmer all round her . . . She knew what kind of a painting she would like to make of it, though probably she would never be able to capture that elusive radiance. But she would have to try . . . So she took her water-colours and a new page of her sketch pad and began to make a preliminary impression of the whole wide expanse before her, setting down what she could of the pale, far shore, the reedy islets, the reflections and tall leaning reeds at the water margins, the drifting, endlessly moving population of flying and floating birds, and the smooth, translucent surface of the water like shot-silk in the sun . . .

She was too deeply absorbed to notice the passing of time, but when she glanced up at Jon she saw that he was deeply asleep.

She did not wake him.

But presently a particularly noisy and quarrelsome pair of geese came swimming close to the water's edge and shouted in his ear. Jon stirred, stretched and sat up, smiling at the talkative birds.

'What's all that about?'

'They're having an argument,' said Charley, laying a gentle wash of silvery blue on her lake reflections, and leaving the tall dark shape of Jebel Ichkeul upside

118

down in the water at the farthest edge.

Jon got up and stood looking over her shoulder for a moment, saying nothing. Then he spoke softly, almost to himself. 'The spirit of place . . . I hope I can catch it on film, too . . .'

Charley smiled at him, and watched him pick up his camera and wander off to another part of the lake.

*   *   *

That evening when they got back to the villa, Ankaret had a meal waiting for them in the long, arched living-room that opened on to the little courtyard. Young Zizi helped to serve it, gravely carrying bread in a long basket and setting it down on the table, and going back for a dish of aubergines and peppers which he placed in front of Ankaret beside the main dish of grilled red mullet.

'I didn't make *couscous* for you,' Ankaret apologised, smiling, 'though I am quite good at it. But I thought you might like to sample it in one of the local restaurants.'

'This looks lovely.' Charley sniffed appreciatively at the mixture of herbs and spiced sauce. 'Is the fish local, too?'

'Oh yes. Caught today. All our fish is fresh-caught. The little fishing fleet goes out every night.' She turned to Jon. 'And you may hear some repercussions about that from Lake Ichkeul.'

'How do you mean?'

'The fishing in the lake is very good, and there has always been a small fleet of fishing boats working there. Now they say their livelihood will be threatened by this new scheme to dam the lake. None of the sea fish will be able to come in to breed, and the small fry won't be able to swim out to sea . . .'

Jon sighed. 'Yes. The whole life-cycle of all sorts of creatures will be threatened.' He looked away through the long window facing out to sea. 'These hydro-electric boffins,' he murmured, 'they don't think of the conse-quences to the environment—only of their immediate needs *now!*'

Ankaret nodded. 'We're trying to enlighten them.'

'We?' He turned back to her enquiringly.

'The conservationists. I'm only one of them, but there are some pretty powerful ones making their voices heard. We are hoping they will be listened to.'

'Good for you.' He grinned at Ankaret in the manner of an old comrade-at-arms. 'You can be pretty formidable yourself when you try!'

Ankaret laughed, and appealed to Charley. 'Do I look formidable?'

Charley put her head on one side and considered Ankaret gravely. 'Not now. But I daresay you could be. Let's ask Zizi.' She turned, smiling, to the small boy who was standing beside her.

'*Formidable!*' said Zizi, pronouncing it French fashion—and by the gleam in his eye, he was well aware of its different meaning.

They all laughed at this, and Zizi, who had been waiting patiently to offer Charley a wedge of lemon for her fish, held out the dish to her with a shy, hopeful smile and asked: 'You like?'

'I like,' agreed Charley, and took a large mouthful of fish and nodded her head in smiling confirmation.

Jon was curiously silent during the rest of the meal, and Charley supposed he was tired. But when Ankaret asked how the day had been, he smiled at Charley and said: 'Fantastic. I've never seen so many different birds . . . All of them incredibly photogenic.' He reached out and helped himself to more fish. 'I nearly went mad trying to get them on film . . .' Once again he glanced at Charley and laughed. 'But Charley kept me in my place.'

Charley looked reproachful. 'I only said—'

'I know. And you kept beautiful orderly records and thumbnail sketches while I fell asleep!'

The laughter was general again, and Zizi asked in a small, wistful voice:

'Many birds? All different?'

'Not *all*,' explained Charley. 'There were great flocks of flamingoes, and lots and lots of geese. But quite a lot of rare birds—in pairs mostly.'

The boy's dark eyes were fixed on her face, as if he was

120

trying to see what Charley had seen. It was clear that he was longing to come with them but was much too shy to say so.

Presently, Jon drifted off to his room to fix some equipment, and Charley stayed to help Ankaret clear the table.

'Is he all right?' asked Ankaret, turning her massive frame to look after him.

Charley hesitated. 'I think he still gets very tired.'

Ankaret nodded. 'And he's always been a bit obsessive about work. I'm glad you stopped him.'

'It wasn't easy.' Charley was smiling. 'I thought he was going to get angry. But those *casse-croûtes* were irresistible!'

Ankaret laughed. 'You can usually tame 'em with food—can't you, Zizi?' She laid a casual hand on Zizi's curly head and gave it a playful push.

Zizi answered gravely, out of a refugee's wisdom: 'Food is good.'

The two women looked at one another and sighed.

'How long have you known Jon?' asked Charley, heaping plates on to a tray.

Ankaret paused for thought. 'About . . . ten years. I met Richard first—and then he brought Jon along on his next assignment . . . They were in Ethiopia then, covering the famine.'

'And . . . you were there doing relief work?'

The big woman turned away with an armful of crockery and led the way to the kitchen, talking as she went. 'Yes. For a time. A friend of mine—a French doctor called Jean-Paul Lafitte—was running a clinic out there. I . . . just went along to help for a while.'

She stood at the sink, looking out of the window at a silvery moonlit arch and a glimpse of dark, moonwashed sea beyond. 'It's awful, you know, Charley—there's so much to do out there, and so few people to do it . . . The problems are enormous . . . I always feel so—inadequate somehow.'

'But you do go—' Charley blurted out. 'You do *something*.'

Ankaret turned and looked at her. 'Are you tired of the easy life already?'

121

Charley looked shocked. 'No, of course not. It's absolutely wonderful—-the job, this place, and your lovely villa. But—she paused helplessly.

'I think you are like me, Charley. You need to feel useful.' Her voice was only faintly saddened by memory. 'It was different when Jacques was alive. We were useful to each other, and that was enough . . . But now—'

Charley glanced down at Zizi, who was patiently drying glasses on a spotless white tea-cloth at the sink. 'There is Zizi . . .' she murmured softly, and watched the smile return to Ankaret's strange, hazel eyes.

'Yes, so there is . . . And there is Jon, who badly needs company just now. So we have both got plenty to do!'

Charley's grin was a shade rueful. 'I expect I'm a poor substitute for Richard. What was he like?'

Ankaret considered. 'Very charming—a typical television journalist with a gift of the gab . . . No, not typical. He was better than most. Rather a burning brand, you know, a crusader—looking into Jon's camera and willing the public to care.'

Charley nodded. 'Yes. Jon once said: "Richard was the poet. I was just his eye."'

Ankaret looked thoughtful. 'Mm . . . though Jon's camera work can be sheer poetry, too—believe me.'

'I do believe you,' agreed Charley soberly.

There was silence for a moment, and then Ankaret said suddenly: 'It wasn't Jon's fault, you know. It's utter nonsense. Richard's girlfriend, Selina, told me.'

'Told you what?'

'That last story they went out on—it was Richard's idea. He got the tip-off and insisted on going. Jon tried to stop him. But he would go. And when they realised it was a setup, Jon tried to drag him away and got shot up in the process . . . Richard was always reckless.'

Charley was silent, understanding a lot more about Jon and his hidden, interior grief. The mention of Selina had set her thinking, too—rather with relief. For she had wondered about Jon and Richard—and whether there was more to Jon's excessive grief than met the eye . . . But if there was a girlfriend—probably not. It was just the normal camaraderie of two colleagues of long-standing, and the natural rage of a man against the waste of a young and useful life.

Presently she said: 'The girl—Selina—how did she know?'

Ankaret shrugged her wide shoulders. 'One of the other journalists was in the street at the time—he saw it all.' She looked at Charley with a shrewd and penetrating glance. 'Selina is the kind of girl who gets information out of people when she wants it—particularly men.'

Charley returned her look with a searching one of her own. 'You're not very enthusiastic about her?'

'No. A little worried.'

'Why?'

Ankaret sighed gustily. 'She wants to come out here to see Jon.'

Charley was startled. 'Here? How does she know where he is?'

'She works in his London office.'

'Oh, I see . . .' Charley paused for thought. 'And—you don't think it's a good idea?'

'I think it might unsettle him, bring back all that tiresome business with Richard . . . just when he's beginning to get over it and starting to work again . . .' She smiled at Charley. 'And looking much more cheerful.'

'Is he?'

'Oh yes. You're very good for him.'

It was Charley's turn to sigh. 'I hope you're right.' She too looked out of the window at the bright moonlight on the sea. 'What does she want exactly?'

'I rather think—Jon.'

Charley's eyes opened wide. 'Was it like that—before?'

Ankaret's mouth had a slightly contemptuous curl. 'She did her best to play off one against the other, but Jon wasn't having any. He was always absurdly loyal.'

Charley grunted. 'Sounds a bit of a trouble-maker.'

'You could say so.'

'Can't you put her off?'

'I can try. But I have a suspicion she'll come out anyway.'

'Oh dear.' Charley drew a determined breath. 'Well,

123

we'll just have to fend her off, and keep Jon happy. Maybe I could dunk her in the lake.'

Ankaret laughed. 'Charley—you're my kind of girl!'

Beside her, Zizi, who was leaning against her ample form half-asleep, looked up and asked: 'What is "my-kind-of-girl"?'

'Special,' said Ankaret. 'Like my kind of boy,' and she took his small brown hand in hers. Zizi gave her a seraphic smile and reached for Charley's hand, too.

* * *

Late in the night, Charley woke with a start, hearing a voice shouting something in the echoing silence.

She lay listening for a moment to the sounds of the night—a barking dog, a persistent Scops owl in a nearby tree—and then the shouting came again. 'No!' it said. 'No! Get down! Get down!' and it was Jon's voice calling.

Charley leapt out of bed, flung on her towelling beach robe, and went running down the corridor to Jon's door. Here she hesitated briefly, then took a swift breath of resolve, turned the handle and went into his room. Moonlight flooded through the window and lay in bars of light across the bed. Jon lay there, threshing and muttering but still clearly asleep, and even as Charley approached the bed, he began to shout again: 'No! Richard, for God's sake get down!' and he flung his arms out as if to ward off a blow or shield someone from attack.

Charley reached the bed and took hold of Jon's shoulders and shook him. 'Wake up, Jon! . . . It's all right . . . *Wake up!*'

For a moment he went on tossing and muttering, stiff and unyielding under her hands, but she shook him again, harder this time, and then folded her arms right round him and rocked him to and fro, repeating: 'It's all right . . . *It's all right!*' over and over again until her voice got through to him.

At last the fight seemed to go out of him and he went limp in her arms and opened his eyes. At first they didn't seem to focus, but then they fastened on Charley's face in a gaze of piercing awareness. Charley was caught in the same sudden intensity, and found herself gazing back, unable to look away, shaken to the heart's core by the look of startled recognition in his eyes.

But then Jon's glance seemed to cloud and soften in the moonlight and he murmured in a bewildered voice: 'Charley? . . . What's the matter?'

'You were dreaming,' she said, feeling his body shaken with deep tremors within her embrace. 'A nightmare or something . . . But it's all right now.'

'Was I shouting?'

'A bit . . .' She released him gently and laid him back against the pillows. He still seemed confused and terribly shaken.

He sighed, and rubbed a hand over his hair. 'I'm sorry, Charley. Did I frighten you?'

'No.' She sat down on the bed in the moonlight. 'But I thought you needed waking.' She waited to hear his breathing steady a little and then asked gently: 'Are you back with us?'

'More or less . . .' He was clearly struggling for composure. 'It's being back behind a camera, I expect . . . I was a bit afraid something like this might happen . . .' His voice was breathless and shamed.

Charley couldn't bear it. 'Don't *apologise*. Anyone can have bad dreams.' She paused and then said in a carefully brisk and cheerful tone: 'Shall I make some tea or something?'

He took a long, quivering breath. 'That would be nice . . .'

She got up and stood looking down at him in the white light of the moon. Even now she was not sure he had really extricated himself from his own dark dream.

'I'll . . . join you . . .' he said. 'Do me good to get up . . .' and he swung his legs over the bed and sat there, still only half-awake, staring up at Charley. He looked, she thought, like a tousled small boy caught out in some misdemeanour he could not hide.

She leant down and patted his arm with sudden undisguised affection: 'Nothing to worry about . . .' she

125

murmured. 'Just take it easy . . . I'll put the kettle on . . .' and went quickly out of the room.

In a few moments a bleary-eyed Jon, also wrapped in a towelling robe, joined her in the kitchen.

They sat for a while in companionable silence, drinking tea, while Charley wondered what she could say to him of reassurance or comfort, and came to the conclusion that she could say nothing that would not sound trite or clumsy. She had a sudden recollection of walking with Jon in the neat gardens of the Rehab House in the pale English sunshine, while Jon cheerfully reduced the shadows to normal size. Out here there were shadows too, but bright moonlight was pouring down on to the sea, turning the world to silver . . . and it wasn't a bit like an English garden . . .

'I know what I'd like—' she said suddenly.

Jon looked up from his tea enquiringly.

'I'd like to swim.'

'Now?'

'By moonlight. Would it be cold?'

'Not in the water—it might be, coming out.'

'Then we won't linger.' She grinned at him like a conspiratorial child. 'Come on—I'm going to get into my bikini.'

Jon looked at her, also grinning. 'You'll scarcely need it. No one will be looking.'

Charley's expression assumed a mock severity. 'Mr Armorel,' she said, 'I was not suggesting that kind of moonlit frolic.'

Jon observed the spark in her eye and began to laugh. 'All right. Have it your own way,' he said.

*   *   *

They swam side by side along the path of the moon. It was like swimming in liquid silver. Gleaming eddies swirled round their arms, shimmering droplets clung to their skin, the swelling curve of an oncoming wave bloomed into silver as it rose up past them—even the small white plumes of spray turned to silver as they tossed themselves softly into the shining air. The sea was full of iridescent phosphorescence, and even the few small fish that swam below the surface or leapt out of the water from time to time seemed to have a ring of white fire round them . . .

The water was warm, like silk, and the moonlight beat down on Charley's eyes in dazzling purity.

'Beautiful . . .' she murmured to herself, 'so beautiful . . .' and felt as if she was drowning in light.

But Jon was not supposed to swim for too long with those damaged lungs of his, and she knew that her own private rhapsodies were not necessarily his. Gently, she laid a wet hand on his arm and turned him round towards the shore, smiling at his unguarded half-dreaming face.

This was how Jon should look, she thought—younger and calm, untouched by dark memory, filled with untroubled peace . . . She wished, sighing a little inside, that it could always be so.

They wandered back to the villa through moonlight and shadow, not talking much, still somewhat held in thrall by the magical night, and then, as they reached the darkened archways of the villa terrace, Jon stopped and laid a hand on Charley's damp hair.

'Charley—'

'Mm?'

'Thank you.'

'For what?'

'For not lecturing me—'

'I seem to remember,' she said, smiling at him in the moonlight, 'that you never lectured me—even at my worst!'

He laughed. 'I didn't dare.'

'Well, I didn't dare, either.' She was laughing, too. There were things she wanted to say to Jon about all this—but now was not the time, she thought. 'It's too late to go back to bed now,' she said. 'I shall cook us a large English breakfast, and then we can get off to the lake early.'

'Go to work on an egg?'

'Why not?'

He grinned and rumpled her hair with a careless hand. 'Dear Charley—you are a blessing, do you know that?'

But before she could reply, he had turned away and gone in through the blue and white arches to his room.

So she cooked him an enormous breakfast, reflecting ruefully on Ankaret's earlier dictum: 'You can usually tame 'em with food.'

*   *   *

Their days fell into a regular pattern from then on. They got up early while it was still dark, ate Charley's carefully ample English breakfast, collected their equipment and some picnic food for the day, and were out at the lakeside by first light. Sometimes they came home early, but mostly they stayed until sunset when many of the birds came back to the lake to roost or to sleep on the quiet water.

Jon was tireless. He watched and waited for the best shots, waded and crept through bushes and tufts of reeds, patiently built himself small hides and look-outs, and once even climbed a tree with the smaller video camera strapped to his chest.

Charley took endless notes, drew quantities of lightning sketches, and longed for a wet day to give her time to consolidate some of her work into more detailed form— and time for her light-painting which she was aching to begin. But the weather stayed warm and settled, with cloudless skies and long hours of ceaseless sunshine.

They grew brown and healthy under this regime, and much of the inner tension seemed to be draining out of Jon as he watched and recorded the endlessly fascinating conflicts and triumphs of the birds.

Sometimes they were alone all day, but once or twice Ankaret drove out with Zizi to join them, often bringing some fresh-cooked *briks* with her from one of the stalls in the town. And once or twice Zizi came with them in the early morning when Ankaret was going to be away all day. He was never any trouble—silent and helpful, moving about quietly on his bare brown feet, carrying bits of equipment and not dropping them in the water, getting out the food when Charley told him, and going off to fetch Jon

128

from some distant patch of reed to have a well-earned break.

The small boy's face was intent and rapt as he watched the antics of the birds, and sometimes he would point to one particularly spectacular creature displaying its glorious colours, or some special little commotion and flurry of spray on the water, and ask in a small, hushed voice: 'Charlee—what is that?'

Charley did her best to know all the answers, but often she was unsure and had to consult her manuals and lists. Zizi would watch her intently, and follow her eyes down the page and then point with a triumphant finger: '*Voilà, Charlee, c'est ça!*' and they would laugh together and Charley would write in her notebook: 'Grey crane: red crown—*Grus grus*?' and then add as a reminder: 'Coming in to lake in V formation—must be migrating?' Or 'Moussier's Redstart—black and white, reddish tail . . .' And young Zizi would dance about with excitement and treat it as a personal triumph that they had identified yet another new bird.

There were other things to look at, too, and Jon faithfully tried to record on film every side of the teeming life of Lake Ichkeul. Once they saw a mongoose run through the tufty grass and pounce on a small, thin water snake in the shallows—or it might have been an eel, Charley thought. And even in early November there were flowers which seemed to have sprung up after the first rain—yellow broom flowering on the slopes of Jebel Ichkeul, tall verbenas and wild gladioli, blue-eyed chicory in the dry stony patches, and oleander and wild geraniums still cascading down over walls and banks . . .

'Charlee,' said Zizi, coming up to her with something held carefully in his cupped hands, 'for you—' and he opened his fingers to show her a big brown cricket sitting on his palm. Another time it was a butterfly with wings as blue as the sky . . . And one very still day, they caught a glimpse of the buffalo herd on Jebel Ichkeul, silhouetted against the sky as they moved in a brown, stocky mass down towards the water's edge to drink.

One day Jon decreed that they should pack up early and

drive into Bizerta where he had to make certain arrangements about processing his film, or—he told them—he might have to go down to Tunis if Bizerta seemed unsatisfactory.

They stopped in the beautiful *vieux port* and sat at a café table in the sun, drinking the inevitable mint tea and watching the fishing boats come in to unload their catches of squid and tunny, red mullet and octopus. They went through the entrance of the *kasbah*, between its tall blank walls, and wandered into the *medina* with its maze of narrow streets and *souks* filled with carpets, copper, kaftans, scented heaps of spices and herbs, and embossed leather bags . . . Charley was fascinated by all of it, and by the smiling stallholders in their *jellabas* and red *chechia* skull-caps, the veiled women in *sifsaris* slipping quietly away from prying tourist eyes, the sudden snatches of thin music from open doorways, and the black-clothed old men sitting at café tables watching the world go by . . .

But once again she was made aware of the dark side of a Tunisian town. She almost fell over a bundle of filthy rags in the street and was shocked to find herself looking down at the paper-thin face of an ancient beggar, asleep (or dying?) in the dust. She raised horrified eyes to Jon, but he only said grimly: 'Yes. Poverty is everywhere.'

There were other beggars, almost at every corner—wizened old men and whip-thin young boys, patiently holding out clawlike hands for alms, and looking at the passers-by with eyes devoid of hope . . .

And then there were the animals—the cringing dogs and cats and browbeaten donkeys of the *souks*, unfed and unloved, as thin as the child beggars, their ribs sticking out from taut and scabby skin, the donkeys struggling without protest under impossible loads, the dogs and cats endlessly scrounging under the market stalls for scraps and trying to dodge the well-aimed kicks of the stallholders.

Charley shivered. 'Don't they care?' she whispered to Jon.

'Not a lot,' he said, his mouth still very straight. 'Life is cheap out here. The only animal they look after is their camel—but that's because it's vital to them in the desert.'

130

'And—and the children?'

'I told you—life is cheap. Some get rich with the tourists. Others starve. There is a huge contrast . . .' He sighed. 'The good ones care for their children, of course. They're very family-minded and affectionate. The bad ones throw them out.'

'On—on to the streets?'

He nodded, and waved a brief flick of hand at Zizi who was dancing ahead in and out of the market stalls. 'He was one of them.'

Charley was appalled. 'Like—like these?'

Jon nodded. 'Ankaret found him starving in some gutter, curled up like a dog in the rain . . .' He glanced at Charley, still rather grimly. 'He'd been beaten so badly he couldn't stand.'

Charley's face stiffened with anger. 'Who by?'

He shrugged. 'His "master"', he said. Some of them run child-beggar rackets in the streets . . . and some—' he hesitated and then went on in a cold voice: 'Some use them as child prostitutes.'

Charley was almost too outraged to speak. 'What did Ankaret do?'

'She bought him.'

'What?'

'She found out who the "master" was, and bought him.' His dark glance rested on Charley's face. 'That was so that the man could have no further claim on him. Otherwise, he might've tried to grab him back—or finish him off with another worse beating.'

Charley shivered. 'But—he wasn't his father, was he?'

'Oh no . . . though it has been known to happen . . .' He kicked moodily at a coke tin in the street. 'No. Zizi was an orphan—parents unknown . . . no history. In a way, that made it easier . . . But when it comes to adoption, it is harder. No papers, no records—a non-existent, stateless small boy.'

She saw Zizi stop by a stall selling copper pots, and turn to wait for them. 'Will it be all right?'

Jon smiled at her, and Charley felt her own heart lighten

131

with relief. 'Oh yes. Ankaret is very persistent. Zizi will be hers—eventually.'

'The Mosque is here,' said Zizi's small clear voice. 'Can we go in?'

So they went into the Grand Mosque, leaving their shoes outside like the faithful, in a neat row among the bright-coloured prayer mats spread on the floor. Charley wondered if she would be allowed in, but Jon said cheerfully: 'You look like a boy anyway, with those jeans and that haircut. They won't question you.' Indeed, she did look like a slim, brown boy with her new tan and her short, feathery curls—a boy who walked with a spring in his step and a glow of eager delight in all he saw round him . . . Charley had not looked in a mirror lately, but the change in her was startling. She saw the change in Jon, too. He was at last beginning to look relaxed and less tired, and his usual leanness and brownness now seemed to spark with suppleness and energy rather than hard-held control.

Zizi went into the Mosque with Charley's hand held firmly in his, seeming a little awestruck. He looked round at the wide spaces and echoing arches and up to the high domed roof, and listened to the voice of the *Muezzin* in the octagonal minaret far above them, calling the faithful to prayer.

'High-place for priest?' asked Zizi, pointing to the dais above the flight of steps in the holiest corner.

Jon nodded.

'High-place for God?' pursued Zizi, his voice now hushed, as he pointed upwards into the farthest spaces of the dome.

'Yes,' agreed Jon, smiling a little at the small, awestruck face beside him. 'But the sky above Lake Ichkeul is higher.'

The three of them looked at each other with perfect understanding.

* * *

There were days when the rain fell and work at the lake became impossible, and on one of these no-go days Jon left

Charley painting at the villa while he went off to get his film processed.

Charley finished off several neat bird studies and then settled to her longed-for painting of light on Lake Ichkeul. She got so absorbed that she forgot the time, and only surfaced when the light in the studio began to fade. She rubbed a weary hand over her eyes and put down her brushes, and went across to the kitchen to make herself some tea.

As she came into the room, she saw Ankaret leaning against a table, with one hand pressed hard against her side. She seemed so taut and rigid with pain that Charley was frightened. She went across to her at once and put an arm round her shoulders. 'Ankaret? Are you all right?'

The big woman pulled herself upright, turned her head and smiled. 'Of course. Just a stitch . . . It's nothing.'

But it wasn't nothing, and Charley knew it. 'Sit down a minute—I'll make you some tea . . . Or would you like coffee?'

'Tea would be nice,' murmured Ankaret, in a voice that was a shade too breathless. She sank down into the nearest chair and sat looking down at her hands clasped before her on the table.

'Here.' Charley placed the tea in front of her. 'You've been doing too much . . . Can we take Zizi off your hands a bit more often?'

Ankaret nodded. 'Yes . . . as a matter of fact, I was going to ask you. Jean-Paul is coming through soon on his way back to France. He'll probably stop over for Christmas, and I think I may go with him to Paris for a few days.'

'Sounds like a good idea. You need a break.'

'We're going to collect funds for his next relief trip. He has a team of workers in Paris, raising money . . . And he has to report back to his hospital anyway.'

'Is he employed by them out in Africa?'

'Yes. Studying tropical diseases . . . and the effects of malnutrition. That's why they encourage him to run his clinics out in the wilds.'

'I see. When will he go back?'

'I'm not sure. In a couple of months, perhaps. When he's filed his report.'

'Will you go with him?'

Ankaret seemed to hesitate. 'I—might. It depends.'

Charley didn't like to ask what her plans depended on. She hoped it was not Jon and her. 'We're not cramping your style, are we?' she asked at last.

'No, of course not. I love having you here—and it's company for Zizi. He's taken quite a fancy to you.'

'He's a lovely little boy,' said Charley, her voice warm with approval.

'I know.' Ankaret's voice was warm, too.

Charley was looking at her critically now, assessing her pallor beneath the Tunisian tan, and taking note of the curiously tense set of her mouth.

'Is your friend Jean-Paul an ordinary doctor, too?' she asked suddenly.

'Yes, of course. He deals with almost anything at his clinics in the back of beyond. Why?'

'I just wondered . . . if he could take a look at you.'

Ankaret's strange hazel eyes came to rest on Charley's face. 'You don't miss much, do you?'

'You forget,' replied Charley primly, 'I've nursed an invalid for fifteen years. You get to recognise the genuine and the spurious.'

'I suppose you do . . . ' murmured Ankaret, sounding a little confused. Then she drew a resolute breath and said briskly: 'Anyway, it's nothing to worry about. And I shall consult Jean-Paul if it seems necessary.'

'Mind you do,' said Charley severely. But somehow she knew Ankaret would not bother.

Zizi came in then, carrying a small basket of nectarines and clementines, some of them still with their leaves on. He handed the basket to Ankaret and carefully counted out some change into the palm of her hand.

'OK?' he asked, with his wide, shy grin.

Ankaret gravely received the coins and then handed him back a few millimes. 'Put them in your money-box,' she instructed.

Zizi grinned. 'Mia-Ankar, I will be rich,' he chanted, and

scampered off with the coins clutched tight in his hand.

Ankaret sighed a little at some interior thought and looked after him affectionately.

'What did he call you?' asked Charley.

'Mia-Ankar. It's his own invention . . . A mixture of mother-mine and my name, I suppose . . .' She smiled at Charley. 'It seems to satisfy him.' For a moment she looked a little anxious, but then her natural optimism seemed to take over and she shrugged her broad shoulders. 'His adoption papers are being processed, but these things take time. Sooner or later, his future will be a bit more secure.'

'I think he's very lucky already.'

Ankaret nodded comfortably. 'So am I.'

* * *

Charley hadn't thought about Christmas till Ankaret mentioned it in connection with Jean-Paul's coming. It didn't seem to go with the blue Tunisian skies and the hot mid-day sun. But she thought she'd better ask Jon what people out here did about it.

'Not much,' Jon told her. 'It's not a Muslim festival. New Year is much more important. But the English people celebrate it, of course, and there are a lot of Catholics here.'

'What will Ankaret do?'

'Oh, she's a traditionalist. And besides, she'll want to make it a fun-day for Zizi.'

'Then we'd better spend the next wet day buying a few presents.'

Jon made a face at her. He hated wasting time, and when the rains came he could stay in and edit his film. But he saw the logic of it. They owed Ankaret a lot, after all. Besides, Charley needed a fun-day herself now and then.

So the day before Christmas Eve—when it conveniently rained at lunchtime—they packed up Jon's cameras and their uneaten picnic and drove into Bizerta. They ate in a waterside café, rather late, and waited for the mid-day siesta to be over and the shops to re-open. Then they wandered happily through the *souks* and the tourist shops and came back laughing and penniless with an armload of

135

presents. Charley was always glad when she managed to make Jon laugh. He was still much too sad. Maybe she could make the shadows retreat still farther on Christmas Day.

On Christmas Eve, Jean-Paul Lafitte arrived. He was brown and wiry, with dark hair falling in a boyish sweep over his forehead, eloquent, extremely persuasive dark eyes, a patrician nose and a straight mouth that could curve into an impish grin, and plenty of gallic charm.

It was clear that he and Ankaret were old friends and working companions—but it was also clear from the start that he was enchanted by Charley.

'I should like to show you my *clinique*,' he said, leaning forward earnestly across the dinner table. 'You are so *sympathique*.'

Jon laughed. 'Oh, she's *sympathique* all right,' he said. 'It's been her downfall.'

Charley looked at him, startled by the sudden note of bitterness in his voice. 'Jon?'

'Don't mind me,' he said, and took a gulp of wine from his glass. 'But watch out for Jean-Paul. He could persuade a Tunisian stork to fly backwards if it suited him!'

Everyone laughed, and Charley saw with relief that Jon and the French doctor really got on very well—but she was still a little puzzled by that faint edge to Jon's voice.

After dinner, Ankaret brought out a small, white-painted branch set in an earthenware pot, and Charley helped her to decorate it with a few shiny baubles and some brightly-wrapped little presents for Zizi. Ankaret explained that trees were precious in Tunisia—there was even a special tree-planting day in the calendar—so the Christmas tree trade had never really taken off. People would have been shocked at the idea of mounds of throw-away trees in the *souks*, and anyway, conifers would not really grow in this climate, even if they had roots to begin with. But, of course, something had to be done for Zizi. He loved ceremonies; and so, Ankaret confessed, did she.

In spite of her enthusiasm, though, Charley thought she seemed curiously tired by her efforts; and when Charley

136

offered to cook the Christmas dinner next day, Ankaret thankfully agreed.

They had a cheerful, carefree day—though it seemed strange to be swimming in a lukewarm sea on Christmas Day.

Zizi received his presents with a mixture of incredulity and prancing joy. Jean-Paul produced a carved wooden rhino for Zizi, and a string of tourmaline beads for Ankaret—both of them local products from the wild country round his latest *clinique*. Charley had bought Zizi a small box of paints and a sketching block because he was always trying to do things 'like her', and on the same theme, she had got one of her bird studies framed for Ankaret. For Jon she had finished the first of her 'light' pictures—which she gave to him rather shyly, not sure that he would like it.

He stood looking at it in silence for some time, and then said softly: 'No holes there . . . Oh, Charley, how strong you've grown.'

Jean-Paul heard this remark, and looked from one to the other of them with bright, observant eyes, but he said nothing except: 'What a marvellous study in tranquillity. *Merveilleux*.'

Jon, meanwhile, had given Zizi his present—a useful-looking penknife with a shiny mother-of-pearl handle—and begged him earnestly not to cut himself. For Ankaret, he had found one of the beautiful silk scarves that she loved; now he gave Charley her small parcel and stood rather anxiously beside her while she opened it. When she took off the last layer of tissue-paper, she found herself holding a perfect crystal globe brimming with light, smooth and flawless and seemingly without any seam or join.

'You see?' said Jon, smiling. 'No holes in that, either. But you scarcely need it now!'

For answer, Charley put her arms round him and kissed him, saying: 'Oh yes, I do. It will be my talisman—always!'

And then it was time for the meal, and Charley brought it in amid enthusiastic cheers. It was a joint of lamb—not traditional turkey—but Charley had found rosemary to flavour it, and aubergines to go with it, and there were courgettes and tomatoes as well. Everyone seemed very happy with it, and Zizi's eyes sparkled when she brought in her alternative to Christmas Pudding—a colourful iced bombe filled with strawberries from the Sahara oases.

Presently, during the course of conversation, someone mentioned the ruins of Carthage, and Jean-Paul, seeing Charley's uncomprehending look, turned to her in astonishment. 'You are in Tunisia for a visit, and you haven't seen Carthage? Or Utica? Or the Bardo?' His brown eyes flashed theatrical reproach at Jon. 'Jon, *mon ami*, what have you been doing?'

'Working,' growled Jon.

'Then you must take a day off while I am here—tomorrow! Ankaret, you must come too, you are the expert on antiquities.' He turned back, smiling, to a bewildered Charley. 'I shall enjoy showing Charley the sights.'

'I'll bet you will,' muttered Jon ungraciously.

'Oh come, *mon vieux*. Life is for enjoying, *non*? One cannot work all the time.'

'True,' agreed Jon, who knew very well that Dr Lafitte worked tirelessly and ceaselessly at his African *clinique* and his researches into tropical diseases. If he was intent on a small period of respite now, who could blame him?

'We will start early,' said Jean-Paul firmly. 'That will give us a whole day for Carthage and the Bardo.'

'Will it be open tomorrow?' asked Charley.

Jean-Paul laughed. 'Why not? It is not a public holiday out here.'

'We should see Utica at sunset,' said Ankaret suddenly, a strange, wistful note creeping into her voice. 'On the way back . . . It is very beautiful then.'

Jon pushed his chair back and spoke sharply. 'By all means take Charley. She deserves a break. But I've got work to do.'

'Won't it keep?'

He hesitated. 'Not really. We're on the migration path, you see. The birds keep changing. Each day they're different . . . Some are flying on across the Sahara. Some are coming down from Europe. Some are coming up from the south for the winter feeding grounds . . . It's like Piccadilly Circus out there—and I might miss something.'

Jean-Paul eyed him shrewdly. 'Would it matter?'

Jon rubbed a hand crossly over his hair. 'Yes!' he said, and then feeling that he was being boorish and unfriendly, he gave a brief, creaky smile and added: 'But I'll let Charley off.'

Charley, with a stern set to her mouth and a glint in her eye, got sharply to her feet. 'Stop talking about me as if I was a parcel. Don't I have any say in the matter?' She turned to Jean-Paul, looking down at his charming rueful smile without regret. 'It's very kind of you to suggest it, Jean-Paul, but I am here to work too, you know. And if Jon wants to work, we work.' She paused fractionally, not even looking at Jon's astonished face. 'And if he suggests a day off—he takes one too.'

There was a startled silence. Then Ankaret laughed softly. 'Good for you, Charley. That's the way to treat a workaholic.' She turned comfortably and looked up at Jon, folding her arms into a solid, challenging knot. 'Well?'

Jon stood there, curiously angry and at bay for a moment. But then his anger seemed to dissolve and he looked at Charley and grinned a little sheepishly. 'OK, Charley. You win.'

Jean-Paul reached for the wine bottle and poured some into Jon's empty glass. 'That's better. Now we will have a day of *culture superbe*.'

In the laughter, Zizi's small voice piped up. '*Moi aussi*?'

*　　*　　*

To Charley, the site of ancient Carthage seemed huge and bewildering. Long flat stretches of paved 'streets', a broken pillar or two, low walls rebuilt with bits of stelae and shards of pottery embedded in them . . . Here a bit of faded mosaic, there a brighter, more vivid one with a wooden covering to protect it from the sun . . . A heap of fallen stone, a broken capital with the acanthus leaves still crisp in their carved marble symmetry; a headless statue, half-hidden in an unexpected little grove of oleander and bougainvillea; bright lizards sunning themselves on the walls and darting away from your feet. And beyond it

139

all, cool white villas shaded by eucalyptus and acacia trees, fringed by palm trees and the vivid blue of the sea.

Young Zizi was standing with his arms round a small fragment of marble pillar, running his brown fingers down its fluted sides. *'Tu es très vieux, non?'* he crooned to it. *'Très vieux?'*

He looked up at Charley for confirmation. She smiled and nodded. 'Very, very old,' she agreed. 'But still beautiful.'

All the same, the wide sunbaked spaces of ruined Carthage were not altogether a delight to Charley. She felt strangely oppressed by them, as if all the centuries of blood sacrifices and fierce, annihilating wars had left their pitiless imprint on the very stones she walked on . . . She shivered a little in the warm sun and began to walk rather blindly away from the *tophet* of Tanit and Baal, almost hearing the cries of the sacrificial victims as they lay on the blood-soaked altars . . . And as she walked, for a moment the old frightening sense of disorientation and terror returned to her—and the cracks between the paved walkways on the baked earth seemed to gape at her in their old, snarling gaps of black menace . . .

She took a deep, calming breath and said to herself determinedly: It's only an illusion. Here I am on a perfectly harmless stretch of unbroken ground, with my friends round me, on an ordinary, sunlit twentieth century day . . . The horrors of the past are long since gone. They can't touch me now . . .

But even so, she could feel the dark pulse of ancient terror beating up at her through the tortured ground—and now there were tears on her face as she tried to escape from the earth's age-old anger.

'Charley . . .' murmured Jon's voice close beside her, 'stop letting history haunt you.' A firm brown hand grasped her arm and swung her round to face him. 'There's nothing here but sunshine and lizards,' he said softly, and leant forward to brush the tears from her face with a gentle hand.

'Come,' said Jean-Paul, also at her elbow, 'you will be

140

exhausted. We will all go and have a drink at the Hotel Reine Didon.'

Thankfully, they all followed Jean-Paul and soon found themselves sipping long cool *oranges-pressés*, and admiring the ancient hill of Bosra just beyond.

'If we climb up there,' said Jean-Paul with indefatigable zeal, 'and go to the top of the spiral staircase in the Cathedrale de St Louis, we can see the whole site . . .'

Ankaret groaned. 'I shall sit here and wait for you.'

'So shall I,' stated Jon firmly.

Jean-Paul looked hopefully at Charley. 'Are you as lazy as these people?'

She hesitated and looked at Jon, but he merely picked up his drink and waved a vague hand in the direction of the honey-coloured stone of the cathedral.

'Oh, all right, I'll come,' said Charley, easing her tired feet back into their leather-thonged sandals.

'*Moi aussi?*' begged Zizi, all huge eyes and excitement.

'*Naturellement,*' agreed Charley, laughing, and held out her hand to him.

She fancied that Jean-Paul was a little put out at this, and it only made her smile wider.

At the top of the spiral staircase, they paused to look round them at the sun-drenched landscape and the sea stretching back all the way to Tunis. Zizi was fascinated by the museum interior which seemed to blaze with colour—gold fleurs-de-lys and golden Ionic capitols, bright blue vaulting, brilliant coats of arms, many-coloured marbles and carved alabaster. It was too ornate for Charley with its flamboyant mixture of east and west, but Zizi loved it. He put his fingers in the fretwork of some delicate alabaster carving and said: '*Comme dentelle . . .*'

Outside, they wandered into yet more gardens, with cyprus trees for shade and flowerbeds bursting with yet more colour, and birds flying in and out of the sweet-scented undergrowth. One glowing, pinkish bird in particular caught Charley's attention with its tall, black-tipped crest and long curved back and strange black-and-white barred wings . . .

141

'Jon . . .' she said, returning breathless to their table on the hotel terrace, 'I saw a hoopoe.'

He looked up and smiled, thinking to himself that Charley didn't look much older than Zizi today, with her flushed, eager face and sun-dazzled eyes . . .

Ankaret got to her feet and said sedately: 'We will go and look at mosaics in the Bardo. It will be cool in there.'

In fact, it was not particularly hot outside—about 70°F, like a comfortable English summer day—but the sky was cloudless and the sun beat down upon the dust and broken shards so that the whole site seemed to shimmer with heat, and the small marble lion at the foot of the steps almost seemed to breathe . . .

'Ah!' roared Zizi into the little lion's face. 'Ah! *Tu es feroce, n'est pas?*' But the little lion only looked at him out of its stony eyes and smiled.

In the Bardo Museum, Charley was dazzled with yet more magnificence—painted ceilings, tiled walls and mosaics, carved wooden vaulting, urns and sarcophagi, bronze statues, stained glass, mother of pearl and ivory . . . Zizi stayed to stare, but Ankaret walked unerringly to the mosaic 'The Triumph of Neptune', brought up from Sousse and relaid. Charley was captivated—the chariot pulled by sea-horses, the phosphorescent sea-grottoes, Amphitrite in her golden necklace, with her shimmering red-gold hair, the leaping sea tiger and the floating sirens and centaurs . . . It was the colours that fascinated her, for the craft of mosaic-laying had reached a peak of excellence just then, and every conceivable colour and shade seemed to be reproduced in the tiny fragments of marble. Blues and greens, reds and golds and yellows, pale creams and pinks and sunset-flames, and even browns and blacks . . . They were all there, the scenes 'painted' in exquisite, delicate gradations of shade from a shimmer of white foam round a goddess's feet to the deepest night sky with stars.

They also found Odysseus lashed to the mast of his ship, with his sailors round him, while the sirens tried to lure him to his death. 'Oh,' whispered Zizi, enchanted. '*Le bateau!* . . . *Le joli bateau!*' and reached out a hand to trace the shape of the high prow and the bellying sail.

When they were tired of too many beautiful things—including some spectacular Berber jewellery which Ankaret pointed out to Charley in one special case—they retired to yet another café table for more drinks.

Jon was strangely silent during most of the day, though Jean-Paul chattered on with undiminished ebullience and answered all Zizi's questions with a flood of cheerful information. Charley had still felt a little over-awed by the Carthage site, though for Jean-Paul's sake she had done her best to be enthusiastic. But in the end she was glad to return to the flowers and trees and flamboyant birds of the little parks. They, she felt, were less frightening in their tumbling, extravagant beauty.

Jon had watched her reaction, understanding it well, but he had said nothing further. He let Jean-Paul lead her on into yet more revelations and discoveries, and hoped she would not be too disturbed by them. She was, he reflected, far too sensitive to atmosphere for comfort.

Now the long day was nearly over, and they were approaching Utica at sunset, as Ankaret had requested.

It was quite different from Carthage—much smaller, and somehow much more beautiful, and filled with the ancient sadness of shattered glories. Among the fallen pillars and scattered stones and broken capitals, geraniums bloomed. Small mosaics lay exposed to the fading sun—and one or two were carefully uncovered by the slow-moving old custodian who smiled at Charley and showed her how a wetted finger brought up the brilliant colours of a swimming fish. Most of the smaller mosaics seemed to belong at the bottom of ancient pools and waterfalls—long since dried up and forgotten. There was even a palace called 'the House of the Waterfall'. And everywhere there were wild flowers, bright-eyed lizards, and even a praying mantis motionless on an oleander leaf.

Charley walked off away from the others and stood looking out at the sunset sky and the curling silhouette of an acanthus-crowned column standing black against the brilliant flamingo-tinted west . . . But in a little while she became aware that she was not looking at the shape of a marble pillar, but at the clear-cut image of a man standing

143

alone in the oncoming darkness . . . the profile of a man she knew . . .

'Jon?' she said, going towards him quietly in the dusk. 'What is it? You've been sad all day.'

He stirred and sighed. 'Have I, Charley? I didn't mean to cast a shadow over the proceedings.'

'You didn't.' Her voice was still quiet. 'It's been a wonderful day. But I should like to think you'd enjoyed it too.'

'I have, Charley . . .' He turned his head towards her and seemed to be smiling a little. 'It's just that I take my pleasures sadly . . . Not like our exuberant friend Jean-Paul.'

Charley laughed. 'He does rather go on . . .' Then she fell silent again, gazing out at the lengthening shadows and the fading, fiery sky. 'This place is sad, though,' she murmured.

'I suppose all fading magnificence is sad,' answered Jon, his eyes also watching the dying glow in the west.

'D'you remember Ozymandias?' said Charley suddenly. 'I remember when I first read it—when I was quite a little girl—it made me cry . . . All that splendour and grandeur . . . and nothing left but two lumps of stone in the sand . . .'

'"My name is Ozymandias, king of kings,"' declaimed Jon in a voice that was unexpectedly deep and powerful, '"Look on my works, ye mighty, and despair!"'

Charley smiled and looked round at the fallen pillars and shattered pediments, the crumbling remains of a once-beautiful and powerful city . . .

'Even the sea has left it,' murmured Jon. 'It was a wonderful harbour once. Can't you just see it?—the quinqueremes, the galleys, the traders . . . and then the Corsairs roaring in . . .' He stood looking out across the flat, silted-up stretch of land below the little plateau, out towards the far-distant line of the darkening sea.

'But the birds still keep coming,' said Charley softly.

'What?'

'The flamingoes still fishing in the lake . . . The storks still flying across the Sahara, and the swallows . . . And the greylags flying in from Europe for the winter . . . After two

144

thousand years, they are still coming . . .' Her face was turned towards Jon's in the dusk. 'I think they're braver than people.'

'More enduring, certainly.'

Far above them in the evening sky, they saw a thin arrow of birds pass across the glowing west towards Lake Ichkeul, their high, faint voices calling to one another as they flew.

'There they go . . .' murmured Jon. 'Safe home for the night.'

Charley put her arm through his and drew him away. 'That goes for us, too,' she said, and led him back to the others who were busy planning a splendid meal in Ghar-el-Melh to round off the day.

* * *

'You must have *couscous*,' said Jean-Paul, looking at Charley with smiling determination. 'And before that, *méchouia*—mustn't she, Ankaret?'

Ankaret laughed with her usual comfortable tolerance. 'I promise you won't be poisoned, Charley—only rather full.'

Charley grinned and pushed the hair out of her eyes. 'I'll try anything once.'

'Famous last words,' growled Jon. But he was smiling, too.

'What will Zizi have?' asked Jean-Paul.

Charley looked at Ankaret enquiringly.

'A plate.'

'*Un plat*?' Jean-Paul looked doubtful. '*Un plat du jour*?'

'No. A plate.' Ankaret was laughing, but quite definite.

Mystified, Jean-Paul asked for a plate.

Then Ankaret spooned some of her food on to it, and passed the plate round to everyone else. That way, Zizi got to taste everything they had. The smiling waiter seemed to approve of this, and even went off and fetched Zizi a few more exotic delicacies to try, including an oyster and a sheep's eye—but this he refused to touch.

They got home late and tired to the cool arches of the

145

villa, and all sat round drinking tea while Zizi stumbled off to bed.

Charley rather wanted to talk to Jean-Paul, if she could persuade him to be serious for a moment, but she didn't quite know how to arrange it. Before, Zizi had been with them, which made it impossible, and now both Ankaret and Jon seemed disposed to linger over their tea and talk nostalgically of earlier times when they had all been together in Ethiopia.

So she was almost relieved when Jean-Paul got to his feet and said: 'I'm going to stroll down to the sea before I fall asleep . . . Charley, will you crown my day by coming moon-gazing?'

'Why not?' she agreed, laughing at his extravagance. 'It's too beautiful to ignore.'

'So are you,' said Jean-Paul, taking her hand with mock gallantry.

They went out together, still laughing, and left Jon and Ankaret looking after them. But once outside, as they reached the silvered night-time shore, Charley dropped her cheerful manner and turned to Jean-Paul seriously in the moonlight.

'Jean-Paul, can I ask you something?'

He began to say 'anything', with his hand on his heart in another absurd gesture, but something in her manner brought him up short. 'Yes, of course.'

'How well do you know Ankaret?'

He hesitated, and then said neutrally: 'Well enough.'

'Well enough to ask her about her health?'

He glanced at her sharply. 'What is wrong with her health?'

'That's what I want you to find out.' Her voice was firm.

Jean-Paul was looking at her intently. 'Tell me what you mean.'

Charley sighed. 'I can only tell you what I saw. She was holding on to her side as if she was in considerable pain. When I asked what was wrong, she said it was only a stitch. But it wasn't, Jean-Paul. She was very pale and very exhausted . . . And today, it was the same thing. She made excuses about the heat, but it wasn't very hot. And it

146

seemed to me that she got much too tired. Didn't you notice?'

Jean-Paul nodded slowly. 'Now that you come to mention it—yes.'

'If she is going to Paris with you, might she also be persuaded to go to your hospital for a check-up?' She looked at him urgently. 'I just feel . . . there are some things that ought not to be allowed to drift.'

He nodded. 'Did you ask if she'd seen a doctor?'

Charley's face seemed a bit stern in the bright moonlight. 'I asked if she would consult you . . . and she said she would if it were necessary. But I feel sure she won't bother.'

'Well, we shall see about that,' said Jean-Paul, looking for once as stern as Charley. He grasped her arm briefly in sudden totally unflirtatious warmth. 'Thank you for telling me.'

Charley turned to go in, and said over her shoulder: 'It's only that . . . she's so special . . . and I've got so fond of her . . . and then there's Zizi . . .'

'Yes,' he agreed. 'I know.' He was silent for a moment and then he said softly as they came back to the villa terrace: 'Leave it to me.'

Thankfully, Charley relinquished responsibility and went inside. Ankaret was still sitting at the table dreaming, with a cup of tea still in her hands. There was no sign of Jon.

She looked up when Charley came in and said: 'Jon's gone off. He says don't get up early tomorrow—you'll be tired.'

Charley had her own ideas about that, and was about to protest when Ankaret added in a serenely unworried voice: 'I'll be going with Jean-Paul tomorrow. You'll keep an eye on Zizi, won't you?'

'Of course.'

'I'll only be a few days . . . He'll be all right with you.'

'Will he mind?'

'I shouldn't think so. I've left him before. He's very adaptable, really—so long as he knows I won't be away long.' She smiled at Charley. 'Anyway, he likes you. It won't be any hardship—for him.'

'Nor for me,' responded Charley, smiling back. 'But he'd

better get up early, because I know Jon would rather catch the dawn flights—and I'm going to tell him so.'

She marched off down the corridor and rapped smartly on Jon's door, half expecting to hear a sleepy voice from the bed. But Jon came to the door fully dressed and looking anything but sleepy—and anything but pleased.

'Yes?'

'I just came to say, I don't need cosseting. I'll be ready at the usual time.'

He stared at her. 'But—'

'Jon. We took a day off. And it was lovely. But tomorrow we work. OK?'

He laughed suddenly. 'Oh, Charley! You've got on your avenging angel face. Yes, of course it's OK. I only meant—'

'I know what you meant. I could play about with Jean-Paul in the moonlight to my heart's content and sleep it off in the morning.' She grinned at his outraged face. 'Well, thanks—but I prefer our shining morning lake to breakfast in bed.'

'You do?'

'Of course I do.' She reached up suddenly and kissed him, seeing something in his face that needed consolation. 'Goodnight, dear Jon,' she murmured, and went away before he could say a word.

*   *   *

When they stopped for lunch the next day, Zizi ran off to talk to some fishermen who had tied up a string of small boats at the end of the lake, and Jon suddenly launched an unexpected attack.

'You were a bit fierce about Jean-Paul's moonlight dalliance last night. Didn't you enjoy his attentions?'

Charley laughed. 'Of course. Very good for my ego. But you couldn't take him seriously.'

'Oh, I don't know. Jean-Paul can be perfectly serious when he wants to.'

'I'm sure. About his work. But not about women.' She was still laughing. 'I think it's all a wonderfully accomplished game to him.'

'Don't you like games?'

Charley was watching a pair of shovelers bobbing about near the water's edge, the drake's bright plumage gleaming in the sun. 'I think the birds play their mating games with more elegance . . . and only in the spring, and only with one partner.'

Jon glanced at her sharply. There was an edge of asperity in her voice that he did not expect.

'What is it, Charley?' he asked in a mild tone. 'You haven't let that awful oaf, Gerald, put you off men for life, have you?'

She seemed curiously tense as she answered. 'No, of course not. But—but I don't think I'm any good at light-hearted adventures.' She was not looking at Jon, but kept her eyes fixed on the multitudinous birds and their busy comings and goings on the lake. 'I don't like promiscuity,' she said, sounding somehow distressed at her own short-comings, '—even without the risk of AIDS these days . . .'

Jon looked shocked. 'Jean-Paul is busy fighting AIDS, you know. It is rife in Africa. I don't think you need have any fears on that score from him!'

Charley shook her head. 'Oh, I know . . . I just meant, the kind of games that trivialise love leave me cold—and I'm a coward about serious relationships, anyway.' She seemed downright furious with herself by now.

Jon laid a hand on her shoulder and turned her to face him. 'What's the matter, Charley?'

'The matter?' she said, drawing a sharp breath. 'I'm a selfish, ungrateful, cold-hearted bitch—that's what.'

Jon almost laughed, but he saw that she was really upset, so instead he tried with great patience to get her to explain. 'Charley—don't sound so angry. You don't owe Jean-Paul anything.'

'Jean-Paul?' said Charley blankly—and then suddenly began to laugh. She could not tell him that she saw, behind the beautiful smiling face of the quiet lake, Jon's own riven face waking out of nightmare, and her arms holding him, her traitorous body aching to bring him the comfort he needed, her stricken heart shaking with futile longing, her halting tongue unable to murmur the words of love and

149

reassurance she longed to be able to say . . .

She could only sit there, under the light pressure of his hands on her shoulders, afraid to meet the searching darkness of his eyes.

'Charley?' he persisted, his voice suddenly gentle.

'I'm no use,' she whispered, a weight of tears making her throat ache as she spoke. 'No use at all . . .'

Jon smiled and reached out a hand to smooth down the springing tongues of hair on her tense, sun-burnished head. 'But you are, Charley—you don't know how much.'

She was silent under his touch, and then spoke suddenly out of her own painful thoughts. 'All I could offer you was tea . . .'

He looked at her and laughed a little. 'The universal saviour—but that was exactly what I needed.'

'Was it?'

'You see,' he said, still speaking gently and quietly, 'I think I am like you, Charley. Casual adventures aren't my style either. I'm no Jean-Paul.' He watched to see her begin to smile. 'And as for serious relationships—I'm as much a coward as you are.'

Her eyes widened. She had never thought of Jon as a coward—about anything.

'So—' he went on, giving one rebellious tongue of hair a small affectionate tug, 'leave well alone, young Charley . . . and stop having a conscience about nothing. I am very happy as I am—aren't you?'

She nodded, afraid to speak in case he could hear the tears behind her voice. But they had brimmed into her eyes anyway, and one telltale one fell out.

Jon laid a brown finger on her cheek and brushed the tear away.

'All the same,' she said, turning quickly away to find the wine bottle and pour him another glassful with trembling fingers, 'I'll bet the tiresome Selina would be more of a comfort than I am!'

He looked thunderstruck. '*Selina*? What the hell are you talking about?'

Charley held out the glass to him, almost like a challenge. 'She's coming out to see you—Ankaret says.'

'Good God, that's all I need!' muttered Jon, and took a large gulp of wine.

'Is it like that? Ankaret said she was rather—persistent.'

'It is like that,' agreed Jon darkly. 'And if she does come, don't ever leave us alone, d'you hear?'

Charley laughed. 'Is that an order?'

He grinned. 'A frantic appeal.'

'OK.' She sounded tranquil now, and turned again to sort out the food basket and hand him another *casse-croûte*. 'Was she always like that about you? I thought she was Richard's girlfriend.'

His face was as dark as his voice. 'She was. But that didn't prevent her from playing the field . . . Selina is a first-class predator. She can cause a lot of trouble, one way and another. So just keep her out of my hair, that's all!'

Charley's grin was entirely mischievous. 'I told Ankaret I could always dunk her in the lake.'

'You do that,' agreed Jon dourly. 'Cool her ardour. That I would like to see.' And then he began to laugh.

So, thankfully, they steered themselves out of deep water into the safe shallows of laughter. And into this cheerful moment of luke-warm wine and tuna sandwiches came Zizi, swinging three gleaming fish on a stick.

'For supper,' he announced, laying them at Charley's feet. 'The fish-men gave. OK?'

'OK indeed,' agreed Jon. 'What are they, I wonder? They look like sea-trout.'

Charley got up and found some thick fronds of fern to wrap them in, and finally laid the bundle in an oozy patch of water to keep cool. Beyond her, the friendly mallard kept swimming about near the edge, bobbing from time to time below the surface in search of food, but clearly also waiting for crumbs.

'Look, Zizi,' she said, 'give him a bit of bread. He's awfully tame.'

Zizi obliged, and the bright-headed bird swam close and gulped and dived and wagged his tail with delight.

'*Il est content maintenant?*' murmured Zizi, automatically slipping a hand into Charley's as he stood beside her.

151

'Moi aussi,' countered Jon, echoing Zizi's usual cry with intent. He took the other small hand in his, but his smile was for Charley.

PART IV
SHADOWS IN THE SUN

When they got back to the villa that evening, there was a strange man sitting on the terrace overlooking the beach. He was smallish and dark, more Turkish than Arabic, and his smile was ingratiating and a shade too wide. He looked at Charley and Jon out of sharply observant eyes that seemed to flicker like a darting lizard's, though he did not move his head or make any attempt to get out of his chair.

Charley found herself actually stiffening with anger—or was it alarm?—and Zizi seemed to feel the same, for he shrank behind her and hid in the shadows.

'Yes?' queried Jon's voice, crisp and unwelcoming beside her. 'Can I help you?'

The stranger got up then and held out his hand. 'Selim Aziz. I am a former colleague of Jacques Lejeune. Is Madame Lejeune at home?'

'She is not.' Jon still sounded clipped and uncompromising. 'She is away at present.'

'A pity.' The smile flashed out and then seemed to grow thinner at Jon's unmoving stare. 'I shall have to call again when she returns.'

'Yes,' agreed Jon coolly. 'You do that.'

'Will she be away long?'

'I can't say.' Jon's clear gaze met the dark, clever eyes of Selim Aziz with calm challenge.

'I see . . .' The smile returned, bright and unabashed. 'I will come back to inquire . . . from time to time.' He strolled unhurriedly towards the archway leading to the path down to the beach. 'Perhaps you would tell Madame Lejeune that I called?'

'Perhaps,' said Jon, and waited politely for him to go.

'Phew!' breathed Charley, looking after the retreating figure with relief. 'You certainly froze him out.'

'Didn't you want me to?'

'Yes,' she said fervently. 'I was just admiring your technique!'

Jon grinned. 'Occupational hazard—persistent creeps who wants interviews. And the ones *you* want, *don't*!'

Charley laughed—and then looked round rather anxiously at the open verandah. 'All the same—can anyone just walk in off the beach and sit here?'

'In theory, yes. But mostly they don't.' He also looked thoughtfully at the terraced slope down to the beach. 'There is a sort of garden gate,' he observed. 'Look . . . But no one ever seems to lock it . . .'

Charley saw that there was a small wrought-iron gate at the end of the whitewashed boundary wall of the villa garden, but it was standing open, rusty and lopsided, looking as if it hadn't been shut for years.

'Myrrha has key,' said Zizi's voice suddenly from behind Charley. He was still standing in the shadows, looking scared.

Charley turned and put out an arm to draw him close beside her. 'Who's Myrrha?'

'She's the girl who comes in to do the cleaning,' said Jon, watching the anxiety fade from Zizi's wary brown eyes.

'Why haven't I met her?'

'Because,' his mischievous grin had returned, 'we get up too early.'

'Oh, I see.' Charley was also smiling. 'Hadn't we better tell her about this man, Aziz?'

Jon sighed. 'I suppose we'd better. We'll go in late tomorrow.'

Charley heard the reluctance in his voice and was a little puzzled by it. She laid an impulsive hand on his arm and said gently: 'Surely—the lake will still be there?'

He rubbed a weary hand through his hair and sighed again at his own impatience. 'Yes, of course. It's only that— I get haunted by the things I miss . . . It's as I said to Jean-Paul—some of the birds are only passing through, going on to winter farther south, like the swifts . . .'

'You can't hope to get them *all* on film . . .'

His mouth set in an obstinate line. 'I can have a damn good try.'

'Aren't you being too conscientious?'

'Yes,' agreed Jon bleakly. 'Besetting sin.'

Charley smiled at him. 'Come on. You're tired. I'll get some supper. I'm sure Zizi's hungry.'

'So am I,' Jon admitted, sounding so surprised at himself that Charley began to laugh again.

Even Zizi laughed, though he wasn't sure exactly what the joke was. But he followed his favourite people into the cool villa kitchen and settled happily at the table.

Over supper, Charley looked round the room and said in a reflective tone: 'I don't suppose Ankaret keeps anything really valuable here?'

Jon's eyes followed hers round the simply-furnished spaces of the kitchen. 'I shouldn't think so . . . She doesn't believe much in cluttering herself up with possessions.'

'That's what I thought.'

He was considering the matter. 'A few bits of furniture are good—French colonial stuff, mostly—and that chest in the living-room is old, Moroccan, I think . . .'

'But nothing worth stealing?'

He shrugged. 'Anything is worth stealing, if you can sell it.'

She nodded.

Zizi said suddenly: 'There is the necklace.'

'What necklace?' Jon's voice was sharp, and its crispness seemed to alarm Zizi, who shrank against the table.

Charley leant over and laid her hand over his small brown one. 'It's all right, Zizi. Jon only wants to protect Ankaret's belongings. What necklace are you talking about?'

'She showed me . . .' explained Zizi, his face puckered with the effort of marshalling his thoughts into English. '*Son mari* . . . Her man gave it to her . . . a long time ago.'

'Jacques gave it to her?' Jon's voice was gentler this time.

Zizi nodded. '*Oui*. It is old. Very old . . .' He hesitated and then turned to Charley earnestly. '*Comme les autres*— like the ones in the big glass box in the place of things . . .'

157

'The Bardo?' Charley was looking at him attentively. 'But that was *Berber* jewellery.'

Zizi nodded again, even more vigorously. '*Oui*. Berber. Very old.'

Charley and Jon looked at each other.

'An antique Berber necklace?' murmured Jon. 'It would be the sort of thing Jacques would buy . . .'

'Would it be worth a lot?'

'Depends on the age—and the workmanship . . . Some of them are priceless.'

Charley whistled. 'Could that be it?'

Jon shook his head doubtfully. 'I don't know . . . I suppose he could know about it—especially if he knew Jacques before. Might even have helped him locate it in the first place . . .' He looked puzzled for a moment, and murmured: 'They don't usually part with them . . . They're handed down as heirlooms.'

There was silence while they considered the implications.

'Where did she keep it, Zizi? Locked up, I hope?'

The small boy seemed to grow pale under his golden skin. 'I must not tell,' he said, and his mouth shut tight with resolve.

'But it is locked up safe?' persisted Charley.

He shot her a wary glance. 'Safe,' he agreed shortly, and would say no more.

'Well—' Charley spoke after some thought, 'we'd better talk to Myrrha tomorrow about locking all the doors. That's all we can do for the moment.'

'Ankaret never locked anything,' said Jon, still sounding a little puzzled.

'That's what I mean!' agreed Charley, smiling.

Zizi moved along the table and leant confidingly against Charley's consoling arm. 'Safe?' he asked, a question deep in his dark eyes.

Charley looked down at him and nodded. 'Safe,' she repeated, and waited to see him smile.

*   *   *

That night something woke Charley, and she got up and went to her door, thinking it might be Jon having another of his nightmares. But when she opened her door, she nearly stumbled over Zizi, lying stretched out like a little dog across the threshold.

He woke when she stooped over him, and smiled up at her sleepily.

'Zizi? What are you doing here?'

The smiled clouded a little. 'You do not like?' It seemed perfectly natural to him to sleep on the ground, wherever he chose. He always had, as far back as he could remember.

'Where do you usually sleep?'

The smile was quite gone now, and he looked both anxious and frightened. 'In Mia-Ankar's room . . . but she is not there.'

'And you were lonely?'

'*Oui. Tout seul.*'

Charley leant down and scooped the small boy up into her arms. 'Come on, then. You can sleep in my room tonight.' She carried him over to her bed and laid him down on it. He seemed surprised by this and stretched himself out on it rather cautiously. 'Don't you have a bed of your own?'

He shook his head, and then added by way of explanation: 'A sleeping mat is easier. You can take it where you like.'

Charley saw the logic of this. But he hadn't brought it to sleep on outside her door. Why not? Was he afraid it would look too pushing? Or maybe he wanted to keep his link with Ankaret secure.

'We'll fetch it tomorrow,' she said, pulling the covers over him gently. 'Now you must sleep. It's late.'

He closed his eyes obediently. But all at once they flew open again and he said in a pleading whisper: 'Charlee?'

'Yes?'

'Mia-Ankar is coming back?'

Charley leant forward and hugged him close. 'Of course, Zizi. Of *course* she is.'

'Sure?'

She realised then, hearing the fear and longing in that

young voice, how much Zizi had endured, how much he had already suffered of separation and loss, and how uncertain he still was that anything good would last, or that life could ever be settled and secure.

'Sure,' she agreed firmly. 'Ankaret loves you. She has only gone to Paris to get some money to help Jean-Paul's sick children. She'll be back soon.'

'Soon?'

'*Very* soon.'

Zizi sighed, and settled himself more comfortably against Charley's arm. The dark lashes fanned out across the shadowy line of his cheekbones, and the small anxious frown smoothed itself out into sleep.

But Charley lay awake for a long time, with the sleeping child in her arms.

* * *

The next morning they stayed at home to wait for Myrrha, and since it was by way of being a holiday, they all had an early swim and then sat late over a long and leisurely breakfast. Zizi dodged in and out of the water, frolicking in the sea like a cheerful puppy, scattering sand and spray in all directions. The dark anxieties of the night seemed to have left him completely on this bright morning. But Charley was still a little bemused by her own dark thoughts.

Jon glanced at her once or twice in a puzzled way, but he forbore to say anything. It was clear to him that Charley had her own private problems to solve.

Myrrha, when she came, was a slim, dark Arab girl, dressed from head to toe in a white *sifsari*. But when she got inside the kitchen, she laid aside her veiled robe and appeared in a perfectly ordinary western-style cotton dress, a very English-housewife print apron, and bright red platform sandals. She spoke beautiful French, and about as much English as Zizi.

Yes, she agreed, she had the key to the little gate. But it was very rusty. It had not been used for years. Perhaps if *Monsieur Jean* would oil it for her, they might persuade it to

160

lock? Also, she said reproachfully, she always locked every other door when she left, and as *Monsieur Jean* had a key to the villa front door, near where he parked his jeep, that should mean everything was secure when they were out.

But when Charley asked in her own fluent French whether Myrrha had ever seen the man, Aziz, hanging about outside the villa before, she nodded vigorously.

'*Oui. Quelque fois.*'

'Inside the garden? *Dans le jardin?*'

'*Sur la terrasse—oui.*' Her smooth, oval face was indignant. 'I told him—get lost!'

Charley laughed, and Myrrha's expressive face relaxed and she laughed, too. 'I was right—no?'

'You were right,' growled Jon.

Zizi said in the clear, hard voice of experience. 'He is bad, that one. I do not like.'

Charley put an arm round him and agreed. 'None of us do, Zizi . . . It's all right. Everyone will be on their guard now.'

Zizi's small, tense body seemed to give a little with relief. 'I am glad,' he said.

*   *   *

That afternoon, the lake was as tranquil as ever, and Jon seemed totally absorbed in capturing on film the antics of a pair of little egrets at the water's edge. But presently he waded ashore, carrying his camera on his shoulder, and came to flop down beside Charley where she was busily sketching on the sedgy grass.

'Charley,' he said, 'what about your painting?'

She looked up, surprised. 'What about it?'

'You haven't been doing much.'

'I haven't had much chance!' Her retort was playful, but even so, Jon looked guilty.

'I know I'm a slave-driver.'

'You drive yourself harder.'

'Maybe—but that's my own choice.'

Charley looked at him tranquilly. 'So is this.'

161

He was doubtful. 'Really?'

Charley sighed. 'Jon. How many times must I tell you? I love every aspect of this work . . . even my wet feet.'

He laughed, and Charley handed him a mug of coffee from the thermos. 'You know what? You're tired. You always have doubts when you're tired.'

'Do I?' He sipped his coffee gratefully. 'I suppose so . . .' Then he grew determined again. 'But I mean it about your painting. It's too important to neglect.'

'Is it?' She paused and then said seriously: 'Well, I'm working on two more pictures of the lake. One is for Ankaret, and the other is for you . . . And they're both a mess.'

He laughed. 'How d'you mean—a mess?'

'Well, for a start, they're so full of light there's nothing else there at all!'

His laughter became somehow flecked with sadness, and he looked at Charley lovingly.

'But that's just it, Charley, isn't it? Nothing else but the sun pouring down on this flawless water. Shimmers and reflections—and a sort of timeless stillness . . .'

Charley gazed at him in astonishment. 'I thought you said you weren't a poet.'

He sighed. 'I'm not, Charley . . . And I'm finding it just as hard as you to capture all this on a piece of unfeeling film.'

She smiled. 'Ankaret said your films were filled with poetic images.'

It was his turn to look astonished. 'Did she?' He shook his head. 'My God, I hope she's right.'

In front of them on the silver water, the little mallard christened James by Charley stood on his head and wagged his tail at them. Jon laughed, and watched Zizi go forward to throw the perky bird some crumbs.

'They make our preoccupations look foolish, don't they?' he said, still laughing.

Charley, watching the play of reflection and sunlight on his face, thought: At last the shadows are going . . . He looks absurdly young when he is carefree.

'Tomorrow,' announced Jon, 'I am going to fetch another

162

batch of film, and you can paint all day . . . and I shall probably be editing all night!'

Charley looked at him severely. 'In that case,' she said in a prim voice, 'you'd better get some sleep tonight.'

He glared at her mutinously, but he did not make any protest. Instead, he patted her arm and said obscurely: 'The light gets in everywhere, doesn't it?'

*　　*　　*

Charley worked all day, alone in the studio, trying to set down light and space on to unyielding canvas. She tried transparent washes which left the whiteness of the canvas showing through. She tried to flake white on blue, and blue on flake white, and gold shafts of sunlight on still, translucent water, and the greenness of trees shimmering in their own reflections, and a pale dream-cloud of pink flamingoes flying in from a pure, far sky . . . But nothing satisfied her, and she worked on and on, experimenting and struggling, while—almost without her volition—the painting grew in power under her searching brush-strokes.

She was so absorbed that she didn't hear anyone approaching until a voice called something from outside on the terrace. Zizi, she knew, had gone shopping with Myrrha and was spending the rest of the day at her house, playing with her young brothers and sisters. He liked Myrrha, and often spent time with her and her family when Ankaret was busy. And this time, Charley felt sure, Jon had firmly arranged it so that she could paint in uninterrupted solitude . . . So it couldn't be Zizi. Or Myrrha. But it wasn't a man's voice. So it couldn't be the tiresome Aziz . . . All the same, she'd better have a look.

Sighing, she laid down her brushes, wiped her hands on her paint-stained jeans, and emerged blinking into the corridor. She went into the kitchen and stood looking out through the window to the verandah and the clear blue sea beyond. They hadn't locked the garden gate, since Charley was at home all day, but since she knew she would be too absorbed to notice much, she had taken the precaution of turning the key in the kitchen door.

163

Now she saw someone standing outside it, looking slightly puzzled to find the door locked.

'Anyone home?' the stranger called again—and Charley suddenly knew who it was. A tall, cool girl in immaculate white jeans, a model of casual elegance from the crown of her swinging blonde hair to the delicate coral tips of her painted toenails.

Selina. Of course. It had to be.

For a moment, Charley stood still, unwilling to accept this invasion of their privacy. She was taken by surprise at her own sudden lurch of dismay at seeing the girl standing there. How would Jon react? Would she upset him? Or remind him of a tragedy he was just beginning to forget? Or would he be glad to see her, and throw off his obsession with work, and go off with this golden girl and enjoy himself? Leaving that tiresome hanger-on, Charley, behind.

My God, she said to herself in horror, I'm jealous! And she hasn't even set foot in the house yet. Guiltily, she crossed the room and unlocked the door.

'You must be Selina,' she said. 'Sorry to keep you waiting.'

The girl surveyed the paint-stained jeans, smudged fingers and tousled hair. Then she smiled a cool but surprisingly friendly smile. 'And you must be Charley.' Her eyes went beyond Charley's head to the kitchen. 'Is Jon around?'

'I'm afraid not. He's in Tunis.' Charley led her through the arched doorway. Then, seeing the girl's expression, she added kindly: 'He'll be back later on.'

'And Ankaret?'

'She's in Paris.'

There was a moment's nonplussed silence. Then Charley pushed the hair out of her eyes in her familiar gesture of faint distress and added: 'But she told me you might be coming . . . I'm sorry it's not much of a welcome. Would you like some tea?'

Selina dropped her tote bag on to the floor and sank gracefully into a chair. 'Tea would be lovely.' She was looking at Charley even more attentively now, taking in

164

the glinting tongues of bright, sunbleached auburn hair, the lightly tanned face with its dusting of freckles, the startlingly deep blue eyes, and the slim, boyish figure within the careless working clothes.

'You're not a bit like I expected,' she said, with sudden frankness.

Charley turned with the teapot in her hand, and answered smilingly: 'But you are.'

'Am I?' Selina leant back in her chair. 'How?'

'Tall, blonde and glamorous,' said Charley, laughing a little. 'All the things I'm not.' She set the teapot down on the table and poured Selina a cup. 'But I hadn't reckoned on those Zizi-style brown eyes,' she murmured, half to herself.

'Why not?' Selina was always interested in discussions about her appearance.

'Brown eyes—with that very blonde hair?'

Selina grinned. 'Mouse, originally. Not such an unusual combination. Who's Zizi?'

It was Charley's turn to grin. 'A small, extremely appealing Arab boy, whom Ankaret has more or less adopted.'

'Another of her lame ducks?' Selina's tone was still cool and careless.

'Yes,' agreed Charley, somewhat tartly. 'Like Jon and me.'

Selina looked at her and laughed. 'You don't look like a lame duck to me.' Then she paused, and added—still carelessly: 'How is Jon, anyway?'

Charley hesitated. Was it now her chance to warn this heedless, stunningly beautiful creature? Could she say anything to a total stranger about Jon's long fight to recover health and equilibrium? Could she mention those dark, shouting nightmares—or the way he suddenly flagged, pale with exhaustion, when he had been filming for too long? Could she say: Don't disturb him. Don't stir up past griefs and losses. He's happy here—more or less—and calm. He loves his work and the long peaceful hours on our tranquil lake . . . Leave him in peace. *Please* leave him in peace.

But she could not say it. Not without betraying Jon himself. He was engaged in his own private inner struggle towards acceptance and renewal. She hadn't the right to speak of it to anyone.

So she looked at Selina, almost pleadingly, and only said: 'He's a lot better. But he still gets very tired suddenly if he does too much.'

'And of course he does.'

'Of course.'

Selina nodded, and the bright cap of hair swung in the sunlight. 'He always did.' She stretched out a hand and reached for the teapot to pour herself another cup of tea and added, smiling: 'I'll have to see if I can distract him, won't I?'

Charley's heart sank. She knew how Jon felt about his work, and how interruptions annoyed him.

'You're looking disapproving,' said Selina, still smiling at Charley's clouded face. 'But a little relaxation won't do him any harm. All work and no play, you know—it's a bad scenario.'

Charley was about to agree, albeit reluctantly, when she heard Jon come through the front door. 'There he is now,' she said, rising to get another cup from the dresser. 'You can tell him your plans yourself!'

Selina's brown eyes, shrewd and watchful, were assessing Charley thoughtfully. They seemed to be wondering whether she was an enemy or an ally.

But then Jon strode into the kitchen, carrying several shiny cans of film, and she got swiftly to her feet and enfolded him in an enthusiastic embrace.

'Jon, darling. How are you? Lovely to see you.'

He almost dropped the film, but managed to extricate himself and put the slippery cans down on the table.

'Selina. What brings you here?'

'You, Jon dear, of course.'

Jon groaned. 'I was afraid of that.'

'Aren't you pleased to see me?'

'Not very.' He laid a hand on the cans of film. 'As you can see, I'm rather busy.'

'I can see you're rather bad-tempered,' said Selina

166

sweetly, 'but that's nothing new.'

Charley had watched this exchange with some amazement, and it occurred to her that perhaps there was something between these two after all if they got so belligerent.

She hastily put a cup of tea in front of Jon and pushed him down into the nearest chair. Her hands lingered for a moment on his shoulders, trying to ease the tension in his angry body.

'Have some tea,' she said mildly. 'You must be tired.'

'Tunis was hot,' he admitted, and had the grace to smile apologetically at Selina. 'Sorry. I know I'm prickly.'

'You can say that again,' agreed Selina, and laughed. She didn't seem to bear any malice, and Charley was somehow oddly reassured by the lack of spite in those large brown eyes.

Brown eyes . . . 'Zizi's late,' she said suddenly. 'I wonder where he's got to.'

'Wasn't he with Myrrha?'

'Yes. But she usually sends him home by now.'

'He'll turn up at supper-time,' said Jon, smiling, and got to his feet. He reached for the cans of film. 'I must get on.'

'Oh Jon, not now!' protested Selina. 'I've only just arrived.'

Jon's mouth set obstinately. 'I've got a lot of editing to do.'

'Won't it keep?'

'No.'

Selina sighed. 'I'll have to tell the office you're overworking.'

'You do that,' snapped Jon, 'and see if they care.' He went into the studio where Charley's painting still stood on its easel, and slammed the door.

The two women looked at one another, and Selina raised delicate eyebrows. 'Is he always like this?'

'No,' said Charley truthfully. 'He's usually very easy. He must be feeling the heat or something.' She also got up and stood looking out of the kitchen door towards the evening sky. As usual, there was a golden sunset, but behind the fiery glow there was a dark mass of cloud building in the west.

167

'There's a storm coming,' she murmured, feeling the heaviness of the air press on her. 'Maybe that's the trouble.'

She turned back to Selina kindly. 'We'd better get a meal together. Maybe that'll pacify him!' She remembered Ankaret's warm, comfortable voice saying to her: '*You can usually tame 'em with food*' and she suddenly longed for Ankaret's calm, uncensorious presence in this stormy situation.

It was at this point that the telephone rang. Charley went across to the small table where it stood, in the archway between the kitchen and living-room.

'Hello?'

'Charley?' said the disembodied voice, with its unmistakably charming French accent.

'Jean-Paul? Where are you?'

'I'm ringing from Paris. I'm afraid I have news that is not good.'

'About Ankaret?'

'*Oui*. You were right to insist, Charley. She agreed to an examination—and the result is too serious to ignore.'

Charley sighed. 'What do you propose to do?'

'We have kept her in hospital. We shall be operating tomorrow.'

'So soon?'

'It is urgent, Charley. We cannot wait.'

Charley heard the anxiety behind the calm voice. Jean-Paul was fond of Ankaret—just as she was. 'How—how serious is it?'

'Very. But she has a good chance. She will need treatment afterwards, of course. And after that—a good deal of care at home.' He seemed to pause before continuing. 'The question is, Charley, can you and Jon keep an eye on Zizi? . . . And can you be there when she comes home?'

'Of course,' said Charley at once. 'Of course I can. I'm not sure about Jon—he may have to take the film back to London—but I can be here.'

She heard Jean-Paul sigh a little. 'Oh, Charley—I know you have just escaped from all that, but she has no one else now that Jacques has gone.'

'It's all right.' She spoke with curious gentleness. 'I

168

would want to help anyway. I'm fond of her too, you know.'

There was relief in his voice. 'I knew you'd feel like that, really.'

'You must tell her not to worry about a thing. We'll see to it all down here. Is there an address we can write to, Jean-Paul? Maybe we could send her some flowers?'

'Yes. Hôpital Marie-Thérèse, 8ème, ward 5 . . . Charley, there is the question of money. Is Jon there?'

'We've got enough money, Jean-Paul. You don't have to worry about that.'

'There are wages for Myrrha—and there is food for Zizi . . . And one or two other payments she was worrying about. Maybe I'd better talk to Jon.'

Charley realised that this was to reassure Ankaret, and agreed at once. 'I'll fetch him, Jean-Paul. But in the meantime, give her my love and tell her I'll be here when she comes home.'

'I'll do that, *chérie*.' His voice was warm with approval. 'Bless you, *ma petite*.'

She laid the receiver down and turned to look at Selina, who could not have failed to hear most of the conversation.

'Trouble?' asked Selina.

'I'm afraid so. Ankaret is ill. I must fetch Jon.'

'Rather you than me,' said Selina.

But Charley had no time for tantrums now. She walked into the studio and found Jon not working at his film but standing in front of her painting. He had not even closed the shutters.

'The light—' he murmured, as she came up to him. 'It's there, Charley.'

'Almost.' There was doubt in her voice. 'Jon, I'm sorry to interrupt. Jean-Paul is on the line. Ankaret's ill, and he wants to talk to you.'

Jon seemed to come out of a dream. 'Ankaret? Ill? . . . So you were right?'

'I'm afraid so—yes.'

They were walking back to the kitchen now, and Jon went swiftly across to the phone.

Charley and Selina got busy with the rest of the meal, but

169

Jon's side of the conversation still came through to them.

'In the safe? . . . No, Jean-Paul, that's not necessary . . . All right, if you say so. Yes, we'll see to it . . . Tell her not to worry . . . Charley has? Of course, she would.' He seemed to be smiling a little then. 'Will you let us know how it goes? . . . Yes, we'll be here. In the evening, yes. Give her our love—and wish her luck . . . Take care of her, Jean-Paul.'

He rang off, looking disturbed and anxious. For a moment he did not return to the kitchen, but stood there, irresolute, rubbing a weary hand through his hair.

Charley went across to him. 'May I make a suggestion?'

He looked at her, and something like relief and recognition seemed to come into his face. 'Mm?'

'Come and eat. Leave work for the moment. There's going to be a storm anyway. Probably it will rain tomorrow and you can work at home all day.'

He nodded. Then a thought seemed to strike him. He gave her arm a small, protesting shake. 'Oh, Charley—another invalid to look after. I'm so sorry.'

'Don't be.' She smiled at him. 'It's the only thing I'm really good at, you know—nursing. Besides, Ankaret has been very good to me.'

'She's been very good to us all,' said Jon sadly. 'I only hope it's going to be all right.' He sighed. 'What do we say to Zizi?'

'I'll tell him,' volunteered Charley. 'But not tonight. It'll need careful handling. He's already half-convinced she's not coming back.'

'Don't!' Jon winced a little.

At that moment, Zizi came through the archway from the beach, towing a brown mongrel dog on a string. He was out of breath, dishevelled, and oddly frightened about something.

Instinctively, Charley folded her arms round him and hugged him close. 'Zizi? What is it?'

He did not answer at first, but burrowed his head against her arm in silent relief. Then he said, looking up trustfully from Charley to Jon: 'I brought a dog—for guarding.'

They looked from the small dusty boy to the cringing dog. It was not a prepossessing animal. What hair it had seemed to stand on end like a punk-rocker's, in spikes of brown and black and mingled grime. Its eyes were yellow and wild, and its legs seemed to have a permanent trembling twitch below the emaciated rib-cage.

'Guarding?' murmured Jon, thinking it looked more likely to die of fright than to protect them. He took a step towards Zizi and held out his hand, meaning to offer a tentative welcome. But it must have looked like a threatening gesture directed at Zizi, for instantly the dog bared its teeth, growled in its throat with warning menace, and tried to spring at Jon from the end of its string.

'You see?' Zizi was triumphant. 'He guards.'

'I see,' agreed Jon gravely. Then he came past the snarling dog, ignoring the snapping fangs, and carefully laid an arm round Zizi's shoulders. 'Do you think he will like me now?'

Zizi smiled seraphically. 'Of course. You are my friend.'

Apparently, the dog thought so too. It sniffed cautiously at Jon, and then at Charley, and finally sat down on its thin rump and looked at them out of its strange yellow-topaz eyes.

Selina had been watching all this with amazement, and she still stood frozen in the archway, not daring to move. 'Am I your friend, too?' she asked, trying a nervous smile.

Zizi considered her. 'Are you Charley's friend?'

She glanced at Charley, the smile becoming a little rueful. 'I hope so.'

'And Jon's?' He pronounced it 'Jean's' but his meaning was plain.

Selina's gaze went to Jon speculatively. There seemed to be some sort of challenge in the air. 'Jon?'

He had been staring at the dog, deep in some abstraction of his own, but now he started and looked up. For a moment fierce anger seemed to spark in the air like winter lightning—but then it was gone and he answered neutrally: 'Of course.'

Zizi had not missed the undercurrents. He was sensitive to atmosphere. He said cautiously: 'He will get to know you soon.'

Selina sincerely hoped so. The animal looked dangerous

171

to her. 'I suppose it hasn't got rabies?' she asked, her eyes on those far-too-visible teeth.

'Rabies?' It was a new word to Zizi, but he understood that it must be something derogatory about his dog, and he laid a hand protectively on its spiky head. 'He is only hungry,' he said. 'And no one has ever been kind to him. That is all.'

It was a simple statement. But it was spoken with such wisdom, out of such knowledge and experience, that Charley felt an absurd lump rise in her throat. That had been Zizi's own life he was speaking of—before Ankaret found him.

'Come,' she said, breaking the tension deliberately, 'let's find him something to eat. What is his name, Zizi?'

Zizi looked perplexed. There were stray dogs all over the village—particularly in the market. No one paid any attention to them, except to kick them out of the way. Did they have names? This one had simply taken to him because he threw it a scrap of food, and prevented another boy from beating it with a carpet brush. But a name? Where would a dog get a name?

'You must give him one,' said Jon. 'Let's see . . . what does he look like?'

He looked like nothing on earth, but they none of them said so.

'Tell you what,' said Charley, 'take him in the sea, Zizi, while I find him some food. He may look quite different when he's clean.'

That made good sense to Zizi, and he trotted off cheerfully with the dog loping along behind him on his grubby piece of string.

The other three turned to each other and sighed.

'It's a good idea, though,' admitted Charley thoughtfully, 'with that man, Aziz, about.' She looked at Jon in mute appeal. 'And—maybe having something else to lavish his affection on will be a good thing for Zizi just now.'

Jon nodded. 'Did he seem frightened to you when he came in?'

She agreed. 'I thought so—yes.'

172

'I wonder why?'

They strolled into the house again, and Charley rooted about in the fridge for something suitable for a starving dog. By the time she had got a plate of scraps together, Zizi was back with a transformed, no-longer-cringing dog. The spikes had gone, and he now seemed to glow with a soft fuzz of hair almost as yellow as his eyes—except for a ring of longer tawny fur like a mane which framed his face, and a small, dark tuft at the end of his tail.

'But of course—Leo,' said Charley at once. 'He is just like a lion-cub.' She put the plate of food down on the floor in front of him. 'There you are, Leo. Try that for size.'

The dog looked enquiringly at Zizi, as if unable to believe his luck, and then bent down his new clean head and wolfed the lot.

Zizi watched him and then said to Charley seriously: 'He will get slower—when he is used to it.'

Charley nodded, wondering painfully if Zizi had also wolfed his food when he first came into Ankaret's care.

'Come on,' she said. 'Our supper's waiting, too. Humans next.'

*　　*　　*

Late that night, the storm broke. Charley was lying awake anyway, worrying about Ankaret and what to tell Zizi, and about Selina's arrival and the dark tensions it seemed to arouse in Jon. She heard the first distant growl of thunder over the Atlas mountains, and then the sky began to be lit with sheet lightning and sudden sharper flashes of jagged blue-white brilliance. There was no rain as yet, but the air was thick and heavy with menace, and she knew the clouds would open soon and fill the rivers with their winter torrents. She wondered how soon the water would reach the lake, and how much the levels would rise—and found herself smiling at the thought of how much the birds would rejoice at their growing water margins.

The sky was now a spectacular sight, riven with light behind the piled clouds, glowing with strange incandescence one minute and drowned in massive onslaughts of darkness the next . . . Fascinated, Charley got up and decided to go out and watch the storm from the beach.

Zizi now slept in a corner of her room on his familiar sleeping mat, scorning the offer of a camp bed, and Charley paused to look at him as she passed. He was fast asleep, with one bare brown arm flung over his head. As Charley stooped over him, an extra vivid flash of lightning lit the room, throwing the sleeping child into sharp focus, and she saw on his lifted arm the marks of a large, dark bruise. She leant a little nearer to look at it and drew a sharp breath of shock when she realised that she was looking at the imprint of a man's fingers pressed cruelly deep into the soft flesh of the child's arm.

Fingers? A man's hand, grasping him tightly, probably twisting his arm as well? Who? A fight with a bigger boy? Or a market trader? Had he been caught stealing? Or was it because of the dog? Or could it have been Aziz? No wonder he had looked frightened when he came home. But he had not complained—not about anything. He had been far too busy championing his dog . . . Sighing, Charley pulled Zizi's thin blanket up a little higher and went quietly out of the room.

On the verandah, the dog, Leo, stirred on the end of his string and opened a baleful yellow eye. But when he saw it was Charley, he sighed and closed the watchful eye again, and even managed a slight wave of his tufted tail. Smiling a little, Charley patted his head and stepped over him.

It was cool on the beach, and the lightning seemed brighter than ever. It lit the sea in liquid-silver flashes, and gave the clouds sudden extraordinary profiles. Charley stood gazing, heedless of the approaching thunder, awed by the majesty of the storm and its brief and glorious revelations. One moment there were mountains—then they were gone. One moment there was a wide expanse of shining sea—and then it was plunged in inky darkness, with only a faintly winking riding light or two appearing in the gloom. And then it was bright again, as clear as daylight, and even the footprints in the sand stood out black and strong, and the ripples at the water's edge were etched in silver.

She wandered on, closer to the sea, and stood looking out, her face lifted to the sky as the first heavy drops of rain began to fall.

'Charley—' said a quiet voice behind her, 'still obsessed with light?'

'I couldn't paint *that*!' she muttered, not turning.

'I wouldn't put it past you.' An arm came round her shoulder, and they stood for a moment watching the storm together.

'Couldn't you sleep either?' Her voice voice was soft with welcome.

'Haven't tried. I was in the studio, working.'

She turned then, reproachfully. 'Oh Jon! You can't exist without sleep.'

'No,' he admitted, gazing in fascination at the sheet lightning flickering across the sky. 'I wish I could.'

She heard the faint note of pain in his voice and understood it all too well. Dreams and nightmares still haunted him.

'I don't think you should let Selina upset you,' she said gently. 'All that is over now.'

He rubbed a weary hand through his hair and sighed. 'That's what I keep telling myself.'

'She doesn't mean any harm.'

He laughed shortly. 'Selina never means any harm. But she always succeeds in setting everyone by the ears.'

'Then you mustn't let her.' She reached up her hands and laid them on his shoulders, turning him to face her. 'This is a tranquil place—remember?'

'Even in a thunder storm?' He was smiling now, crinkling his eyes at her in a kind of tender amusement.

'Well—' Charley grinned, 'this sort of mighty tantrum seems less—er—personal than our own!'

His laughter was genuine this time. 'Oh, Charley—there's no one like you for cutting things down to size.'

She still stood before him with her hands on his shoulders, her face lit spasmodically by the brilliant lightning. But now she looked faintly surprised. 'You have always been the strong one of this partnership, Jon Armorel, and you know it,' she said crisply, 'How would I have survived otherwise?'

Something in his face seemed to change then, and he let out a curious sound between a groan and a sigh. 'Charley . . .' he murmured. 'Oh, my dear, idiotic girl!' and he stopped suddenly and kissed her long and hard on her rain-wet upturned face.

She did not move at first, but in a little while, involuntarily, her own arms reached out and clasped themselves round his neck, pulling him closer.

They stood in the falling rain, still lit by bright flashes of blue light, oblivious of the storm around them.

But at last Jon seemed to become aware of the increasing hiss of rain pouring down on to the sea, and he drew her into the protection of his arm and said, none too steadily: 'Come on. You'll get soaked . . . These lightning idylls can be dangerous!'

She couldn't tell if he was dismissing that moment of sudden revelation as a mere figment of the storm, but she thought, by his shaken voice, that he was not. In any case, she told herself, no words of his could change it. She knew now what she felt about Jon—and it seemed to her irrevocable and entirely right, but terrifying, too. She didn't want to be assailed by such a heart-shaking wave of feeling—she wasn't ready for it and the enormous possibilities it engendered. The changing pattern of her life was much, much more profound than she had bargained for . . . But that didn't in the least mean that Jon felt the same. Almost certainly not—and she must never let him know what he meant to her, or try to ensnare him, like Selina. Jon was a loner—he had told her so. He was just finding freedom from a tragic past, and emotional commitments were the last things he needed right now.

All these painful thoughts surged through her mind as she made her way, side by side with Jon, through the stinging rain back to the shelter of the verandah.

But there, Jon paused and drew her close against a comforting arm. 'Don't let me throw you, little Charley,' he said. 'Maybe the storm possessed me—but you are much more precious than you know.'

176

Charley said nothing to that. She could not. But when he kissed her again, gently and slowly this time, her eyes were full of tears.

*   *   *

The next day, Jon elected to work on alone in the studio, leaving Charley to entertain Selina.

But Charley had her own ideas about that. She had not failed to note the shadows of fatigue under Jon's eyes, and she knew that he was finding it a struggle to edit and cut his film without help.

So she bundled Selina into a taxi and sent her off to visit Tunis and Carthage, and gave Zizi some money to go and buy Leo a new collar and chain. Then she marched into the darkened studio and demanded to be useful.

'I kept notes of everything you were filming,' she said. 'And I've got my sketches to refer to—and the bird books. We've got plenty of ways to check all the shots—and make our own rough commentary. They'll need one to work from, won't they?'

Jon was looking at her in astonishment. 'How d'you know so much about it?'

'I've been finding out,' said Charley, setting her mouth in a firm and obstinate line. 'And I *can* be some help, so you might as well use me.'

Jon shrugged, none too graciously, and said in a tired voice: 'All right. Let's see what you can do.'

But in a little while he had to admit that in this, as in other things, Charley was invaluable. She recognised the birds he did not know, reminded him which shots were duplicating earlier ones, refused to let him cut his good shots for the sake of brevity, saying only: 'No. It's too beautiful to waste. Leave it in. Let them decide later.'

Jon found himself getting through twice as much work as he had expected, with Charley's clear decisive eye to stop him going through agonies of choice. And Charley, for her part, was amazed at the sheer beauty and imaginative brilliance of Jon's film.

It was early evening before they stopped work—and

177

even then it was Zizi who made them take a break. He knocked very politely on the door, and then came in carefully carrying two mugs of tea.

'You are tired,' he stated. 'You stop now.' He looked from one to the other of them in the shuttered room. 'Besides, Leo is hungry.'

They both laughed and gratefully drank their tea.

'Is Selina back yet?' asked Charley.

'*Oui*. And she is hungry, too.'

Charley looked at Zizi playfully. 'And you?'

'*Moi aussi*,' agreed Zizi. Then he added, in the voice of weary, streetwise experience that sometimes assailed him: 'But I can wait.'

Charley put down her empty mug. 'No, Zizi. You shall not have to wait. I'm coming *now*.'

Somehow, the thought of Zizi patiently waiting until someone thought to feed him was rather upsetting. She glanced apologetically at Jon and went through into the kitchen with Zizi by the hand.

To her surprise, Selina was busy cooking something on the stove. At Charley's startled look, the other girl flicked back her blonde hair with a slim hand and said mildly: 'I'm not entirely useless, you know.'

Charley grinned. 'Did I look so incredulous?'

'You did rather.' She began to stir something vigorously, and Charley's nose gave an appreciative twitch.

'Smells good.'

'Spaghetti bolognese. It's the only thing I'm good at.'

Charley sighed with pleasure. 'One of my favourites. Jon likes it, too.'

'Yes, I know.' Selina gave the sauce another fierce stir. 'Is he coming?'

'I hope so.' Charley went over to the fridge and found some scraps for Leo who was looking hopeful but shy in the corner. 'Here,' she said, smiling. 'Stop looking so anxious. It's all yours.'

Zizi said, by way of explanation: 'He is not used to eating every day.' Once again there was infinite knowledge in his voice.

Charley sighed. 'I suppose not.' Her hand lingered for a

moment on Zizi's dark curly head. 'It will take time.'

Zizi agreed. But he added, by way of defence: 'I bought a chain, like you said. But he stays by the door without it now. Don't you, Leo?'

The dog, already beginning to recognise his name, looked up out of his strange amber eyes and waved the tuft on his tail. Then he went back to the serious business of eating.

'This stuff is ready,' announced Selina. 'Give Jon a shout.'

But at that moment the phone rang. Charley had been waiting for it all day, and she knew very well why Jon was driving himself to work so fiercely. They were both desperately anxious about Ankaret, both afraid of what news the evening might bring.

Now, Charley went across to pick up the phone with a shaking hand. 'Yes? Charley Gilmour here.'

'Oh Charley—' It was Jean-Paul's voice, sounding close and warm. He did not waste time on preliminaries. 'Ankaret has come through all right so far.'

'Thank God,' breathed Charley, hearing the reservation in Jean-Paul's voice with misgiving. 'How is she now?'

'Asleep.' His tone was still guarded. 'It will be some days before we can really tell how she is.'

'But—the operation was successful?'

He seemed to hesitate a little before he answered. 'Oh yes. In itself. But her condition was quite serious. She will need to have chemotherapy here before she goes home.'

Charley sighed. 'When is that likely to be?'

'I don't know, Charley. It's early days yet. We shall have to see . . . Perhaps I shall know a little more in a day or two.' He also seemed to sigh down the line. 'I wish I could be more positive.'

'It's all right, Jean-Paul. At least you have told us the truth.' She paused and then added: 'Please give her our love when she wakes. And tell her Zizi is fine and he has got himself a dog called Leo.'

Jean-Paul chuckled a little. 'I will tell her. And I will ring again the day after tomorrow. At about this time?'

'That will be fine.'

179

'You can always ring the hospital if you are worried. But they will not know any more than I do—in fact, not as much!'

'That's what I thought. We trust you, Jean-Paul. We'll wait for your report.'

'*Mon dieu*,' he said soberly. 'To be trusted is a great responsibility, *ma petite*. I will do my best.'

He rang off then, and Charley fancied he was more upset than he cared to admit. Sighing, she turned away to relay the news to Jon, and found him close beside her, with Zizi, wide-eyed and scared, behind him . . . I meant to tell him this morning, she thought, with a start of guilt. And then I got so involved with Jon's film, I forgot. How could I? And now he hears it like this! What am I to say to him? . . . But there was no chance to say anything—no escaping those large, accusing eyes.

'Is something wrong with Mia-Ankar?' he said, in a small, frightened voice.

Charley took his hand in hers. 'She has been ill, Zizi. But the hospital is making her better. She will be coming home soon, and you and I will look after her. You'll like that, won't you?'

'Better?' he asked, grasping essentials at once. '*Vraiment?*'

'Really better,' repeated Charley firmly. 'Dr Jean-Paul is taking care of her. He is a very good doctor, isn't he?'

'The best,' answered Jon, with equal firmness. 'He will make her well.'

'Soon?' The dark eyes were anxious, fixed on his face in mute entreaty.

'As soon as he can.' Jon's voice was gentle. 'We must all be patient, Zizi.'

Charley thought it was hard for a small boy to be patient. But then she remembered Zizi saying earlier: 'I can wait'— and she knew that he had learnt patience in a hard and bitter school.

She leant forward and folded her arms round him comfortingly. 'She'll be all right, Zizi. And we will look after the house for her till she comes back, won't we?'

The small dark head nodded silently, and then Zizi said

180

in a tight, controlled little voice: 'Leo will look after it, too.'

'Of course. He will be very useful.'

'Come on,' called Selina despairingly. 'Aren't any of you going to eat this food?'

'Yes.' Jon suddenly took command. 'All of us are. The news is good so far—we can all relax.'

'Well, thank God for that,' Selina retorted, and ladled large mounds of spaghetti on to everyone's plate.

Charley thought privately: Selina's no fool. She knows quite well what's been biting Jon. I don't believe she's as heartless as he makes out.

Beside her, a small determined voice said: 'Before Mia-Ankar comes, I will learn to cook.'

* * *

Charley and Jon intended to go out to the lake alone the next morning. They knew Selina would not want to get up at five, although she had demanded to come and see the birds of Ichkeul for herself, so Charley volunteered to come back for her in the jeep at lunchtime. Jon was surprised by this and wanted to know about her driving licence, but she told him tranquilly that she had kept up her old one for emergencies, and on the strength of that had acquired an international licence before she left England 'in case it came in useful'.

'Well, it has,' said Jon. 'What a girl you are, Charley. Prepared for anything.'

'Quite the little girl scout,' Selina had added flippantly when they were discussing the morning's arrangements late that night. Zizi had been asleep by then, and Charley made Selina promise to keep an eye on him and take him with her for a swim during the morning. She knew he wouldn't like being left behind, but she fancied Jon needed an uncluttered morning—and anyway, Zizi could come with Selina in the afternoon.

But in the morning, Zizi was up before Charley and had already been to the baker to fetch some fresh rolls for breakfast; when she told him their plans he refused to be left behind.

181

'What about Selina?' said Charley. 'She will be left alone.'

'She will sleep a long time, that one,' said Zizi wisely. 'And Myrrha will come. And there is Leo.'

'Yes, Leo. What will he do?'

'He will guard,' said Zizi in a flat, calm voice. Then he slipped a hand into Charley's and added, still calmly: 'And I will stay with you.'

She understood it, and could not bring herself to refuse. Ankaret was ill and far away. His safe, secure world was suddenly very precarious. And Charley, she supposed, was the next best thing to Ankaret's all-embracing affection.

'All right.' She smiled into his taut, determined little face. 'But you must keep very quiet. Jon will be busy today.'

Zizi did not say: 'Don't I always?' but it was clear in his expression. Why bother to tell him? He understood the necessities of the day's work.

They set off in a cool, clear dawn, leaving Leo chained on the verandah. Myrrha, Zizi explained, would let him off when she came. Then he would not try to follow them. But even so, the golden dog lifted his head and howled when they left, and Zizi's own small head was turned to watch him as he followed them out through the villa to climb into the jeep.

The lake was full and busy that morning. Great clouds of geese flew up and settled in a babble of excited voices and a snowstorm of wings. The rivers and small tributaries seemed to be pouring new water down the slopes to the flat levels, chuckling over stones and boulders, and swirling out into new eddies and currents over the smooth surface of the lake. There also seemed to be more animal wildlife about than usual—perhaps disturbed by the storm—and Zizi exclaimed in delight when a whole family of wild boar went trotting by, making for the slopes of the mountain on the far side of the lake. Charley did her best not to scream a warning when a young jackal appeared, busily stalking an oblivious, wading avocet. She was sure those spindly legs would falter and the predatory jaws would strike; but the bird darted away into deeper water, and the disappointed jackal gave up and slunk away.

Jon had already gone to film the new water cascading down the slopes into the lake, but he turned his camera on the jackal, and on the retreating family of wild boar now scrambling up the rocky slopes of Jebel Ichkeul. But what pleased Jon most was a sudden arrowhead of ripples in the water, and the sleek wet head of an otter swimming purposefully into the reed beds close to the shore. Jon loved otters. They seemed to have a special quality of grace and friendliness, and they were curiously unafraid of man— even a man with a camera. Jon hoped they were right.

The fishermen were out this morning too, trailing a long string of boats across the far end of the lake, and one of them hailed Jon quietly and stopped his flat-bottomed craft to talk to him. Charley saw their two heads stooping close together while a long, serious conversation took place. Jon seemed totally absorbed, and for once did not look impatient at the interruption.

Zizi had elected to stay close to Charley this morning and was crouched down beside her, watching her sketch the birds. As her pencil moved across the white page of her sketch book, a thought occurred to her and she said without turning: 'Do you go to school, Zizi?'

'Sometimes,' he answered carelessly, more concerned with the image of wings growing on the page.

'Why not now?'

He seemed to hesitate, trying to find English words. 'Mia-Ankar said . . .'

'Yes?'

'I must learn to write a little first.' He looked away at the lake of teeming birds, and there was sadness in his glance. 'She . . . teach me.'

'I see.' Charley drew another stroke with her pencil, and then tore off the page and found a clean one underneath. She tore this off too, and handed it to Zizi with a pencil. 'While she is away, I will teach you. Show me what you can do.'

Zizi turned and looked at her, his dark eyes alight with hope. 'You will teach me?'

'Why not?' Charley smiled. 'I can write. And read. So can you if I show you how.' She drew him close to her and leant over to write on his new clean page: '*I am Zizi*', and underneath she wrote in equally clear, bold letters: '*Je suis Zizi*'. She didn't know the Arabic even for this simple statement—but maybe that was just as well, for the Arabic script was much more complicated.

'What does it say?' demanded Zizi, poring over the letters, and when she told him, he leapt to his feet, delighted, and started capering about, chanting: '*I am Zizi. Je suis Zizi.*' Charley let him dance about unhindered, but after a few minutes of wild exuberance, he settled down and dutifully copied all her letters in a determined if inexpert hand.

'Ankaret will be pleased,' murmured Charley, offering another carrot. But, she reflected, this small donkey doesn't need any new incentive. He *wants* to learn.

After a while she saw Jon break off his conversation with the fisherman, who gave one thrust to his oar and returned to his friends fishing in the deeper reaches of the lake. Jon stood for a moment gazing out after him, and then turned to pick up his camera. Charley thought, by the sudden squaring of his shoulders, that he was already tired, and she sent Zizi after him to suggest a break for coffee and rolls.

'Tell him I want to ask him something,' she said. 'Then he will come.'

Zizi grinned at her like a true conspirator and ran off down to the reed-fringed shore.

When Jon came, she invented some query about a purple gallinule, and Jon looked at her quizzically and said: 'Delilah.'

Charley blushed. 'Well, you looked tired.'

He flopped down beside her and gratefully accepted a cup of thermos coffee.

'What did the fisherman want?'

Jon screwed up his face in a small frown. 'He wanted me to protest to the government about the damming of the rivers. He says the fishermen's livelihood will be threatened—as well as the birds.'

'Will it?'

'Probably. Especially if they filter the outflow to the sea.

At present the fish come in to spawn in summer.' He sighed. 'People don't realise—the whole eco-system will be changed.'

Zizi, who had been listening seriously, said: 'Will the birds go away, too?'

Jon sighed again. 'Some of them, Zizi—if the lake changes.'

'And not come back?'

'Perhaps. We don't really know what they might do . . . Or they might come back and find there wasn't enough room. This is the last great oasis before the Sahara—the only stopping place they have . . .' He watched a long skein of geese come in across the sky, swoop down in a circle, and come skidding in to land on the shining surface of the lake. 'They have nowhere else to go,' he murmured, finding a curious lump in his throat as he watched those snow-white wings settle in such supreme and trustful confidence on the calm refuge that they knew.

'There have been birds here always?' asked Zizi, wondering.

'Always—since the lake was formed, I suppose.'

'And fish?'

'Oh yes.' He paused. 'Though I don't know how soon the sea crept in . . .'

'And fishermen?' Zizi was pursuing a thought.

Jon laughed, and waved a half-eaten roll at the line of fishing boats in the distance. 'So they tell me. Since Allah decreed that there was a lake and there were fish for the taking, there have been fishermen to take them. From time immemorial. It is their right, and they do not see why it should be taken from them.'

'Nor do I,' said Charley.

'Nor do the birds,' added Zizi, his small face set.

Jon grinned and reached out a playful hand to ruffle his hair. 'You've got the right idea, Zizi. A proper champion.' As he spoke, his eye fell on Zizi's bare arm and the large, tell-tale bruise upon it. 'What's this?' he asked. 'Did this young champion have a fight?'

Zizi snatched his arm away. *'C'est rien,'* he said, his English deserting him. Then, looking to Charley in appeal, he added:' 'It was about the dog.'

'The dog? Leo? Why?'

He seemed to hesitate, and Charley fancied his small brain was working overtime to invent a plausible explanation . . . Why?

'He—thought Leo would bite him. He was angry.'

Jon was about to ask another question, but he caught Charley's eye. 'Oh well,' he said easily, reaching for another roll, 'a warrior wears his wounds with pride. It is a handsome bruise!'

Zizi did not quite follow this, but he understood the faint note of approval in Jon's voice and grinned his relief.

'I have written my name,' he said shyly, and held out his piece of paper. 'Look!'

Jon looked and admired. 'Well done. You are a scholar as well as a warrior. Soon you will be too clever for me.'

Zizi was enchanted.

The morning seemed to pass with magical swiftness. All too soon, Charley realised she would have to go back for Selina. Doubtfully, she left Jon knee-deep in water, crouching in the small hide he had built himself on a reedy islet, trying to get closer to a flotilla of diving pochards.

Zizi insisted on coming with Charley, so they set off in the jeep together—Charley fumbling a bit with the unfamiliar gears.

They found Selina talking agitatedly to Myrrha in the kitchen, and Leo looking rather sorry for himself, with a small deep gash over one eye.

'What happened?' asked Charley, and Zizi flew to put his arms protectively round his scared yellow dog.

'A man came,' said Selina. 'I heard the dog barking and barking, and then he gave a sort of yelp and I came out to have a look.'

'What time was this?' Charley's voice was sharp.

'About—I don't know—not long after you left. It was still very early.'

'After we left . . . and before Myrrha was due to come,' murmured Charley to herself. 'That figures.'

'What does?' Selina looked from Charley to Myrrha. 'What's going on?'

186

'What did he look like?' pursued Charley. 'What was he doing?'

'He was standing on the terrace, just out of reach of the dog, staring at the windows. He was—oh, darkish and smallish and—er—very surprised when he saw me.'

'I'll bet.' Charley's voice was grim.

Myrrha's smooth golden face was clouded with anxiety. 'Madame Ankaret would not like.'

'No. She would not. But the dog seems to have done his stuff.' She turned to look at Zizi and Leo, entangled in a loving embrace. 'How is he, Zizi?'

'Frightened,' said Zizi flatly. 'And his head hurts.'

He must have thrown a stone,' muttered Selina, eyeing Leo with some distrust.

'Like this one?' Charley had gone across the verandah to look at Leo's gash, and now she stooped and picked up a jagged piece of rock lying on the bare stone floor. 'So what did this darkish, smallish man say?'

'He looked at bit startled—as I said. Then he asked if Madame was at home. And when I said no, she wasn't, he bowed quite politely and said he would call another time.'

'Did he give his name?'

'No.' Selina looked confused. 'I didn't think to ask. Should I have?'

'It doesn't matter.' Charley looked at Myrrha. 'I think we know who he is.'

'The gate was locked,' said Myrrha defensively. ''E must 'ave climb the wall.'

Charley nodded, and stooped to pat Leo with a gentle hand. 'Good dog, Leo. You saw him off, didn't you?'

'Will he die?' asked Zizi anxiously.

Charley laughed. 'Good gracious, no. It's only a small cut. I'll bathe it with some disinfectant. It'll soon heal.'

Zizi looked doubtful. But he led Leo, unprotesting, into the kitchen, where Charley dealt with the gash on his head and then looked round for an extra scrap or two to cheer him up.

'I brought meat,' said Myrrha, opening a parcel on the table. 'For kebabs. And the—*boucher*?'

'Butcher,' agreed Charley.

'The bootcher gave a bone,' she explained anxiously, 'for the boy's dog, 'e say.'

Zizi's grin grew wide. 'Can I give it him now?'

'Why not? He's certainly earned it.' Charley's voice was warm with approval, and Leo heard it and wagged the absurd tuft on his tail.

'There you are, Leo.' Zizi watched delightedly as Leo looked from him to the enormous bone with a mixture of incredulity and ecstasy in his yellow eyes. 'For me?' they seemed to say. 'Really? For me?' . . . and then he took the bone delicately in his mouth and ran away with it on to the verandah.

'We'd better get back to Jon.' Charley was looking wildly at the clock. 'He's probably fallen in and drowned by now.'

'I bought *casse-croûtes*,' announced Myrrha, producing yet another parcel.

'Myrrha, you're a marvel,' said Charley, and scooped them into her shoulder bag. 'Zizi, are you coming back with us?'

He looked from Charley to Leo with agonised indecision. 'No,' he said at last. 'I stay with Leo.'

Charley looked anxious. But Myrrha said at once, with sturdy good sense: 'I stay also. Till you return.' And then, by way of excuse: 'There is much to clean.'

Charley nodded, and grasped the Arab girl's arm for a moment in friendly acknowledgement. 'Thanks. He won't come back, I'm sure. Now that Leo's scared him off.'

'*Je pense*,' agreed Myrrha, smiling at Zizi. 'We will be guardians, all three—*n'est pas?*'

'We will,' agreed Zizi soberly. 'But first he must be free. Come on, Leo, we will run.' And he took the yellow dog with him down the path, through the now open gate and out on to the wide, smooth sands.

'We'll be back for supper,' called Charley, and Zizi waved a cheerful hand, and went on running towards the sea with his dog who was as yellow as the sand.

*   *   *

Selina was quiet on the journey back to the lake, except to ask abruptly: 'Who is this man, Charley?' .

Charley changed gear to negotiate a particularly bumpy piece of track and spoke carefully, her eyes on the unreliable ground ahead. 'His name is Aziz. He *says* he knew Ankaret's husband.'

'And—?'

Charley would have shrugged, but the jeep gave a spectacular leap over a boulder just then, so she merely said: 'We think he's up to something—but we don't know what.'

Selina agreed. 'I must say, I didn't like the look of him.'

'Nor did we.' Charley swung the jeep round on the last bit of safe dry ground and brought it to a halt. 'And nor, it seems, did Leo.'

'I suppose,' admitted Selina doubtfully, 'dogs usually know.'

Charley looked at her sideways and laughed.

Selina was enchanted by the lake and its myriad population of talkative birds. Charley left her gazing in fascination, and went to find Jon. As she expected, he was still crouched on his reedy islet filming, but his camera was tilted skywards to catch the dark, menacing silhouette of a marsh harrier cruising above the unsuspecting small birds below.

Charley had learnt never to interrupt a shot, and she settled down to wait, automatically bringing out her sketching pad and trying to capture the shape of the harrier's long-fingered wings . . . Presently the powerful bird swooped on some unknown prey, swerved upwards, balancing its wings on a rising air-current, and drifted away.

Jon lowered his camera, flexed his aching shoulders and noticed Charley sitting there sketching on the shore.

'You need a break,' she said, noting the tired set of those eloquent shoulders. 'And Myrrha sent some fresh *casse-croûtes*.'

'Now you're talking,' smiled Jon, and waded somewhat stiffly towards her. 'Is Selina here?'

'Admiring the view.'

Jon grunted and rubbed a weary hand over his face. 'As long as she keeps her predatory eye on the birds.'

Charley grinned, and led him back along the shore. 'I

189

think you're a bit hard on her,' she said mildly. Then she remembered Aziz, and related the morning's curious incident as they made their way back to Selina and the welcome bag of food.

'You know,' said Jon thoughtfully, 'Jean-Paul told me how to open the safe and get some money out for Myrrha. I think we'd better take a look inside.'

Charley nodded. But just then something startled the geese on the lake, and they flew up in a sudden swirl of the white wings and a great shouting of voices before they decided that it was a false alarm.

Selina seemed almost stunned by their numbers—the air seemed to throb with the wind of their flight and the sound of their incessant calling. 'I didn't know there *could* be so many birds!' she murmured.

'Only here,' said Jon, and there was sadness in his glance and in his voice as he stood looking out at the shining lake. 'Only here there is enough water—enough space to breathe—enough to eat.' He turned and waved an expressive hand southwards. 'Out there—less than two days' flight away—there is only desert. Only the Sahara and a few oases. This is their last refuge.'

Above him the blizzard of dazzling wings swirled and sank and settled again, covering the surface of the lake with a floating glaze of bobbing heads. Jon watched them settle back to their peaceful feeding and sighed.

'Come on,' said Charley, feeling his sadness on her like a weight of grief she could not dispel. 'Even cameramen must eat.'

Jon's sombre gaze lightened as he turned to her. 'Charley,' he murmured, and sudden tenderness crept into his voice. 'What would I do without you?'

Beside him, Selina looked thoughtfully from one to the other of them and said nothing at all.

*　　*　　*

That evening after supper, Jon called Charley into the living-room and opened Ankaret's wall safe. Selina, of course, elected to come too, and Jon did not try to stop her.

190

Zizi, naturally, was there already beside Charley, but he did not seem particularly interested. He had seen the safe opened before.

It was placed in the wall behind the tall carved chest which Jon had mentioned before as being of some value. Charley didn't care much for that style of furniture—it was too ornate for her—but she supposed its Moroccan splendour must appeal to some, and it was probably quite old. Now, she and Jon took hold of its curly gilt handles and moved it aside. The safe stood revealed, square and ordinary, with a routine combination lock.

Jon turned to Zizi, smiling. 'Do you know the combination?'

He looked puzzled. 'Com-bination?'

'The numbers—to open it.'

'Oh.' He nodded vigorously. '*Oui.* Mia-Ankar taught me. In case.'

In case of what? thought Charley, and wondered, not for the first time, if Ankaret had known she was ill for longer than she admitted.

But Jon clearly knew the combination too—for Jean-Paul had told him—and now he and Zizi stood side by side and recounted to each other every turn of the dial as they made it. 'Six—zero—zero—five—three—double-one—zero—seven—seven.'

The lock clicked easily into position, and the safe swung open at Jon's touch.

Inside were several bundles of notes which, when they counted them, made up about £500 sterling and an equal amount in French francs, together with a fairly thick wad of Tunisian dinars which they didn't bother to count. Behind these was some family silver wrapped in a green baize cloth, and a smaller parcel tied up with pink tape wound tightly round a box in a linen case.

They looked at the silver first. There were a pair of heavy candlesticks, a couple of smaller ones and some vases, a silver rose bowl and some ornate tableware with crests on the handles.

'Not specially wonderful,' commented Jon. 'And it would have to be melted down, with those crests.'

191

He took out the linen-covered box and began to unwind the pink tape. 'What about this?'

Inside the linen covering was an oblong box made of dark red morocco leather, old and stained, but still intact. Carefully, Jon lifted the lid, and there—lying on a bed of yellowing silk—was the Berber necklace. In fact, there was not one necklace, but three, with all their gold and silver links and filigree patterns heavy with jewels, and with them sets of equally heavy ear-rings, bracelets, rings and head-pieces to match.

'A bride's dowry,' murmured Jon. 'How romantic Jacques was.'

'Fabulous!' breathed Selina. 'What do you think it's worth?'

Charley said nothing, but fell to examining the beautiful workmanship, waiting for Jon to answer.

'Hard to say.' Jon shook his head. 'It depends on its age. But—knowing Jacques—I should think it's pretty old, and almost priceless.'

'But—could he sell it?' Charley was not deflected from their reason for opening the safe.

'Aziz? . . . Probably—in the right quarter. Or if he actually had a buyer.' Jon frowned in thought. 'But antiquities are very carefully controlled nowadays—if the authorities find out.' He paused. 'I believe the reputable dealers keep a list. If anything like this came into their hands, they'd be bound to report it.'

Selina laughed. 'Unless they got a big rake-off.'

'Exactly.' He looked at the glittering display almost with dislike. 'And our friend Aziz is no fool.'

Charley said suddenly: 'Zizi, I am glad you brought Leo.'

'*Moi aussi*,' agreed Zizi, nodding a solemn head.

'Put it all back, Jon.' Charley shivered a little. 'I'd rather it was safely out of sight.'

Jon looked as if he was about to echo Zizi's usual catch-phrase, but Selina leant forward and protested: 'Oh, do let me have a look at it first.'

They waited, none too patiently, while Selina handled the heavy jewellery with loving fingers. But at last she sighed and pushed it all away from her, saying: 'Yes. Put it away, Jon. Before I get too envious.'

Zizi said suddenly: 'It is unlucky.'

'What, Zizi?' Charley looked at him inquiringly.

'Mia-Ankar would not wear it—not after her man died.'

They stared at one another in silence—remembering that Ankaret now lay in hospital in Paris, possibly fighting for her life.

Still silently, Jon put the jewellery back, wrapped in its careful packing, pushed all the silver and bundles of notes in after it, and shut the safe with a decisive click.

'Well, now we know,' he said. 'We'd better watch out for Master Aziz. I wonder if I should take it all to the bank?'

Charley nodded. 'You could ask Jean-Paul when he rings. But he'll probably say he doesn't want Ankaret worried.'

'Probably.' Jon rubbed his hair up the wrong way in exasperation. 'I wish people didn't hoard possessions. It makes life so complicated.' He sighed again. 'It's not like Ankaret, either.'

'This was special,' said Zizi.

Charley understood this better than the others. Jacques had loved Ankaret. It had been a gift of love, and this was all she had left of him—this and the little villa by the sea . . .

At this point the phone rang again. It was Jean-Paul, and this time Jon received the latest bulletin. Ankaret was holding her own, but she was still very weak, and still in intensive care. She wouldn't be out of danger for a day or two yet. But Jean-Paul was still confident that she would be on the mend soon.

About the Berber necklace, Jean-Paul was non-committal. 'You do as you think best,' he said to Jon. 'She is too ill to ask.'

Jon looked at Charley, troubled and uncertain. 'Very well,' he said, and sighed as Jean-Paul rang off. Then he added, still looking at Charley: 'I shall be taking another batch of film into Tunis soon. Maybe I could put it in the bank then.'

He began to cough then—something he always did

193

when he was extra tired or confused—and Charley took charge.

'Tea,' she said. 'Tea for everyone. And then bed—especially for Zizi and Leo. It's been a long day.'

No one contradicted her.

*   *   *

The next few days passed peacefully enough. Charley and Jon went off to the lake early as usual, leaving Selina behind. Sometimes Zizi came with them, and sometimes he decided to stay and play with Leo. But if Selina elected to join them out at the lake, Charley insisted that Zizi came too. She didn't like the idea of leaving him alone in the house—even with Leo to guard him—and Myrrha could not always stay on late.

Zizi protested at this, explaining with great seriousness that Leo needed someone to look after him, especially since he had been hit on the head with a rock.

But Charley said firmly: 'Zizi—he is there to guard the house. You brought him there yourself. It is absurd for you to stay at home to guard your own guard dog!'

'What is "absurd?"' asked Zizi, wide-eyed and innocent.

Charley sighed. But she made Zizi come with her. And Jon, seeing the boy's anxiety, went down to talk to the local police about the wandering Aziz, and Ankaret's absence in hospital and their responsibility for her villa. The friendly policeman, Habib, was sympathetic and said he would keep an eye on the place and stroll by from time to time, but he clearly didn't take Jon very seriously.

*   *   *

The winter population of birds on the lake seemed to become ever more numerous and more varied. Flight after flight of geese came in, and besides these regular visitors, all kinds of weary migrants, driven south by the icy winds of northern Europe. Jon was totally absorbed in trying to capture them all on film, especially the long-distance travellers who were flying on to even warmer places beyond the Sahara, and Charley found herself equally fascinated and equally driven on by the urgency of Jon's ceaseless recording. Selina did not seem to share their enthusiasm, although she came quite often for the afternoon. But this, Charley supposed, was more to be near Jon than anything. So far, she had given no indication about how long she was staying, or when her holiday leave would be over— although she had protested rather tartly that Jon never seemed to have time to take her out.

'God forbid!' muttered Jon, when this was raised again. But he agreed, grudgingly, to take them all out for a meal in the town, eyeing Charley fiercely and repeating, 'All of you,' in a determined voice.

Selina gave in gracefully to this, and they all spent a cheerful evening sampling the local cooking and drinking rather too much local wine. But of course the next day Jon had a conscience about stopping work early, and decided to stay on beside the lake to film the sunset against the dark contours of Jebel Ichkeul, and the long lines of geese coming in to settle for the night.

This time, Selina had decided not to come out—in fact, Jon had said bluntly that he couldn't spare Charley to go back to fetch her at mid-day—and Zizi had also felt guilty about Leo and decided to stay at home.

Charley watched Jon grow tired, but she said nothing until the light was almost completely gone, and the glowing western sky was deepening into African night. There were no soft English twilights out here, she reflected, with some sadness . . . But at last she followed Jon into the whispering reedbeds and touched him gently on one aching shoulder. She did not speak until he stopped filming and the sound-tape stopped turning. Then she said in a gentle voice: 'Come on home, Jon. You've done enough— and it's too dark to see.'

He sighed. 'You're right. I can't do any more.'

He followed her out of the forest of reeds and stopped to touch one feathery seed-head with an appreciative finger. 'I was trying to get these silhouetted against the after-glow.'

Charley smiled, and also touched one gently. 'They're so delicate.'

'Mm.' But Jon's voice was absent, and he seemed to be looking at Charley's profile against the fading primrose of the west, not at the reed-heads at all.

'Charley—?' he said, and stopped.

She turned and waited for him to go on. 'Yes?'

But he said nothing more, only laid one hand against the line of her cheek in a curiously tender gesture, and then moved on towards the dark bulk of the jeep waiting for them on the stony shore.

'I suppose we'd better get back,' he said. But there was reluctance in his voice.

'There's still some coffee left.' Charley was still worried about the exhausted line of his shoulders. 'And one roll . . .'

He accepted them without protest, and leant against the side of the jeep, staring out at the gleams and shadows of the tranquil lake.

'What I would like,' he began, without looking round, 'is to stop for a meal on the way back—on our own.'

Charley looked at him in surprise. 'Selina will be expecting us.'

'I told her we'd be late.'

'And there's Zizi.'

'He won't mind. He's used to a flexible regime with Ankaret.'

And before, thought Charley. She remembered the small, resigned voice, full of streetwise experience, saying: 'I can wait'.

'He'll be hungry—' she murmured.

'I told Selina to give him his supper. He was up very late last night.'

'True,' sighed Charley. But somehow she was not happy about it. There was a sense of unease at the back of her mind.

'Of course if you'd rather not—' Jon's voice was suddenly cold.

Charley was horrified, and unthinkingly put her arms round his tired shoulders. 'Don't be so silly. You know I'd love to. But—'

'But you're too conscientious about Zizi . . .' He was

196

smiling again now, and did not move away from her light embrace.

'It's not that—' she tried to explain. 'I—just have a feeling . . . we should go back.'

He stared at her for a moment in the darkness, trying to assess the seriousness of her mood. Then he seemed to accept it and to relax under her touch. 'All right. Your instincts are seldom wrong!' And then his arms came up round her, and he kissed her soundly before letting her go. 'And nor are mine!' he growled, and began to laugh.

Charley laughed too, in relief and sudden gladness. She did not stop to ask herself why this welling surge of joy assailed her. She knew, really—and it was better not to examine it too closely. Jon was laughing, and they were friends again. The moment of sudden tension was over. It was enough.

Together, they climbed into the jeep and made for home.

*   *   *

When they got to the villa, a scene of chaos awaited them. All the lights were blazing, the doors were open, and Selina was standing in the little kitchen with Myrrha and the friendly policeman, Habib.

'What's happened?' asked Jon and Charley in one breath.

Selina, the cool blonde, was almost wringing her hands. 'The safe—' she said. 'Broken into—'

'Where's Zizi?' Charley's voice was sharp.

Selina looked at her, pale with fright. 'Gone.'

'What d'you mean—gone?' Jon's voice was even sharper.

'Disappeared. He must have—could he have . . . ?'

'No!' said Charley. 'He couldn't have. He loved Ankaret. He was *guarding* her house—remember?'

'Where were you at the time?' Jon's tone had got crisper and crisper.

Selina went even paler. 'I—only went down to the shop to buy some suntan oil . . . He said he would be all right. I was only ten minutes . . .' She looked at Jon defensively.

197

'Weren't there any signs of a struggle?'

She hesitated, and gestured vaguely towards the living-room. 'Yes. No—I don't know . . . Chairs overturned—and one of the big blue vases smashed . . . And the safe wide open—' She looked at Jon piteously. 'Only—only Zizi knew the combination.'

'He would never tell.' Charley's voice was flat. 'I know Zizi.'

'Out of the question.' Jon's reply was just as uncompromising.

Selina stared at him in growing horror. 'Could—could this man, Aziz, have *forced* it out of him?'

'I doubt it.' Jon was watching Charley's increasing pallor. He badly needed to reassure her. 'An experienced thief can usually crack a safe—particularly an ordinary run-of-the-mill one like this. And he may have known the combination somehow, anyway—especially if, as he says, he was a colleague of Jacques.'

He heard Charley let out a slow breath. But she spoke with the same sharp urgency: 'What about the dog? Leo. Why didn't he stop him?'

Selina gulped and looked at Myrrha. 'He—come and see . . .' she said, and let them helplessly on to the verandah.

The yellow dog lay on his side, his teeth bared in a snarl, a little froth clinging to the edge of his muzzle. On the stone floor beside him were two uneaten hunks of meat. He was clearly dead.

'Oh!' cried Charley. 'The poor thing!' and bent swiftly over him.

'Don't touch him!' snapped Jon. 'We don't know what the poison is.'

Charley looked down at him sorrowfully. Poor, wretched creature, she thought. He had such a short time of happiness with Zizi . . . And Zizi? Where was he? What had happened in that disordered living-room? Why had he disappeared? If he had surprised Aziz and tried to prevent him, had he been hurt? Or killed, like Leo? Or kidnapped? . . . She shuddered.

'We'd better have a look at the safe,' said Jon, taking

command. 'Leave the dog—and the meat. It'll have to be analysed.' He turned to Habib. 'Won't it?'

Habib agreed, though he didn't see why they were so perturbed about a poisoned dog. Still, the rest of the crime looked interesting. Burglary was fairly routine, but the boy? An inside job? . . . He didn't think so. He knew Zizi. All the village did. He was a good boy—in spite of his background—and he had much reason to be loyal to Madame Lejeune. She set great store by the boy. Adoption papers were already in hand, he understood. She would be very distressed if anything happened to the boy.

'Come,' he said importantly. 'We will examine the safe.'

There was nothing in it, of course. Neither silver nor notes, nor the Berber necklace.

Habib took careful notes, and asked, pencil poised: 'What was the necklace like? Could you describe it?' He turned from Selina to Charley inquiringly.

'It's not important,' said Charley impatiently. 'It's Zizi we're worried about.'

Habib nodded. 'But if, as you suspect, it is this man Aziz—he will try to sell the jewellery. And that way, we may be able to trace him. You understand?'

Charley sighed. 'I could draw it for you,' she said suddenly, and brought out her sketch book. She had examined the necklace with an artist's critical eye, admiring the workmanship. She had a clear picture of its intricate design in her mind, if only she could set it down on paper.

'Selina,' she prompted, 'you looked at it, too. Help me.'

Together, they worked out the details—the gold and silver filigree, the inset jewels, the dangling medallions and chains, and the set of ear-rings and bracelets and head-dresses in their matching designs.

'That's the best I can do,' she said at last, looking up at Habib with entreaty. 'Will that help?'

'It will indeed, *mademoiselle*.' He bowed to her politely. And then another thought struck him. 'Could you also draw the man Aziz? It might help us—especially if he tries to sell the goods.'

'Or if he has a record,' added Jon drily.

Charley looked doubtful. 'I'm not very good at portraits. But I'll try . . .'

For a while her pencil moved swiftly on the white paper, and gradually an image appeared. It was Aziz all right—the slightly hooked nose, the small, penetrating eyes, the black hair flat on his head, and the thin, cruel mouth with its bright, false smile. (That mouth frightened Charley.)

'He's small,' she said, still sketching in bits of detail, 'and he smiles a lot. And he has very long hands which he waves about.' She handed the sketch to Habib, shuddering a little. Jon almost shuddered too—the drawing was all too like the original.

'That's him,' he corroborated. 'That's Aziz.' He glanced at Charley approvingly. 'You're very clever.'

Charley did not smile. Her face was almost as pale as Selina's. 'So long as it helps to catch him,' she said, and her voice was grim.

Habib said delicately: 'Of course, we do not know that it is this man, Aziz. But we will take finger-prints, of course. And we will make enquiries.'

Charley was gazing at him. 'Mr Habib—if it is Aziz, what would he do with Zizi?'

The policeman's face seemed to close. 'There are—several possibilities,' he replied carefully.

'Such as?'

'He might—er—keep the boy as a hostage. He might ask for ransom—since he probably knows how much Madame Lejeune values the boy.' He paused there, and Charley prompted him, driven by a dreadful urgency.

'Or?'

'He might—get rid of him.'

'How?'

The question hung in the air between them. Poor Habib understood Charley all too well—and, like Jon, he wanted to reassure her.

'He might sell him—or give him away . . .'

At Charley's horrified look, he shrugged and said mildly: 'This is a strange country, *mademoiselle*. And some barbaric customs still persist.'

Charley nodded, almost too distressed to speak.

'Presumably, the boy caught him in the act and could identify him,' went on Habib thoughtfully. 'So he would have to make sure he was taken a long way away—where he could not be a nuisance . . . And it is likely that once the man had sold the goods, he would disappear himself.'

Still he had not answered Charley's question—the one she dared not ask.

But Jon asked it for her. 'Would he—kill the boy?'

Habib shook his head. 'I doubt it. He might ill-treat him. But murder is another matter. He sounds to me like a petty thief—not a murderer.'

Charley sighed, only half-believing him. 'I hope you're right.' She was still deathly pale, and beginning to shiver.

Jon laid a hand on her arm protectively. 'We'll find him, Charley. We'll find him somehow.'

'What are we to tell Ankaret?' asked Selina, also still very pale.

'Nothing,' said Charley flatly. 'It would kill her. We must find him without telling her he is lost.' She turned back to the troubled policeman. 'Mr Habib, you must help us. *Zizi has got to be found.*'

*   *   *

None of them could sleep that night—and next day wasn't much better.

The policeman, Habib, sent someone up to dust the safe for fingerprints, and someone else to take away the dog. He told them he would be 'making enquiries', and the best thing they could do was wait for news. Either Aziz would telephone about the boy—or he would try to sell the necklace and someone would report it. Either way, there was nothing they could do but wait.

Only, Charley could not wait. Images kept going through her mind of a small boy, lost and frightened, tied up in some filthy hovel, hungry and neglected and perhaps beaten-up as well. She blamed herself for not getting back sooner from the lake—though she had refused Jon's offer to stop on the way home, and their moment of bitter-sweet dalliance had not been long. But even so, while she was

201

kissing Jon and wondering how to hide her turbulent feelings, Zizi was fighting Aziz and trying to protect Ankaret's belongings . . . And now he was missing— hidden somewhere in the dark mazes of the *medina*, in Bizerta or Tunis . . . Where could they begin to look?

Jon had suspended all work on the lake until there was news. In the meantime, he had intended to do some editing in the darkened studio while they waited for news—but he could not concentrate and soon gave that up as well.

Selina had more reason to blame herself, although Jon told her bluntly that it was not her fault. No one could be expected to live a life where they couldn't go out for ten minutes to the shop—and anyway, Aziz would almost certainly have found another time to strike. Even so, Selina was pale and quiet and kept looking from Jon to Charley appealingly, as if she was sure they blamed her. There was a certain puzzlement in her glance too—at their enormous distress at the loss of Zizi. To her he was just another small street urchin, one of Ankaret's strays, and no doubt she could find plenty more needing her attention—just like a homeless kitten, or a mongrel dog like poor Leo . . . But to them, inexplicably, Zizi was a person, a real member of the family whom they loved . . . Selina had always maintained that she did not like family ties, didn't understand them and was better off without them. Now she was not so sure.

In the end, Charley rebelled and said to Jon: 'We can't just sit here doing nothing. For God's sake think of something we can do.'

Jon nodded, seeing how it was, and stopped his restless pacing. It was time he organised some kind of action, however useless, or Charley would go crazy.

'Selina,' he ordered, 'stay by the telephone. If Aziz rings, inform Habib. He's left his number.'

Selina looked at him, nervously flicking the gold hair away from her face. 'What are you going to do?'

'I don't know.' Jon was thinking hard. 'First, I'm going to see Habib. Come on, Charley. We'll see how far he's got.'

Selina looked so forlorn and troubled standing that he turned back for a moment and patted her kindly. 'Bear up. You've lived through worse.'

She flashed him a startled glance, and there was suddenly a crackling tension in the air. But then Jon turned away and caught hold of Charley, steering her out through the door.

In the street, Myrrha was just hurrying up to the villa, her face half-hidden in her white sifsari. 'Is there news?' she cried, as soon as she saw them, and when Jon shook his head, the brightness seemed to go from her face. She loved Zizi, too—all the village did. He was so cheerful and friendly, so willing to run errands for them all, and so devoted to Madame Lejeune.

'I have ask my 'usband,' she said slowly, ''E 'as many friends in the souks. Maybe 'e will find.'

Jon smiled at her encouragingly. 'Good. Every bit of information may help. Will you stay with Selina? We are going to see Habib.'

She nodded, and glided in through the front door archway with the special liquid grace of the true Arab woman.

Jon and Charley climbed into the jeep and went up the hill to the local police station to look for Habib. They found him elbow-deep in copies of Charley's drawings.

'We are sending these to all the big dealers in jewellery in Bizerta and Tunis,' he said.

'Why not the little ones?' asked Jon.

'Because the big ones are reputable and will report back,' he replied simply.

'And the little ones might take it and say nothing?'

'They might. But of course the price would be lower.'

Jon nodded. 'But suppose someone—not a policeman—called at their shop to make inquiries, with money in his hand?'

Habib looked at Jon, and a suspicion of a drooped eyelid accompanied his non-committal response. 'It is said that money talks.'

It was enough for Jon. He seized two copies of Charley's drawings and smiled at Habib over his shoulder as he left. 'Thanks. We'll be in touch. Selina, the other English girl, is at home by the phone.'

Habib did not have time to reply before Jon and Charley were outside in the street again, climbing back into the jeep. Once there, Jon sat for a moment, thinking hard. 'Bizerta—? Or Tunis?' He wondered.

Charley did not know. In either place there were walled *medinas* and sprawling *souks*—big shops and little shops, streets of jewellers and backyard stalls with shady dealers and small back rooms with even shadier characters lurking inside . . . In either place there were dark archways and shadowy alleyways, shuttered windows and crumbling hovels where a small boy might be hidden.

Where to begin?

'Let's try Bizerta first,' she said. 'It's nearer. He could go to ground sooner.'

So they tried Bizerta.

All day, they went up and down the teeming streets of the *medina*, showing Charley's drawings, asking questions, and sometimes not even bringing out the drawings at all but inquiring innocently about Berber jewellery—real or fake. They were shown a few pieces, but nothing as fine or resplendent as Ankaret's, and one dealer pored over Charley's drawings and said strangely: 'This is the design of the gold links? You are sure?'

'Yes,' agreed Charley. 'I am sure. Why?'

He seemed to hesitate, and then said slowly: 'In Berber work, each design is—how you say?—unique. Each one belongs to a certain family. It is passed on from mother to daughter for her wedding, down many generations. This one I recognise. It is very old, and from a very ancient family . . . How did it come into your possession?'

Charley looked at Jon helplessly. 'It was not mine,' she said. 'It belonged to a lady called Lejeune. It was brought for her by her husband.'

'Jacques Lejeune?' The clever eyes lit up.

'Yes.' Jon was watching his reaction. 'Did you know him?'

'I knew him well. He was a good man. And a good lawyer. It was very sad that he was killed.'

'It was.' Jon's voice was clipped. 'So you will understand why Madame Lejeune would be very sorry to lose it.'

'I understand well,' agreed the shopkeeper gravely. 'And it was stolen, you say? When?'

204

'Last night. And with it, a small Arab boy who was Madame Lejeune's ward.'

The shopkeeper clicked his tongue in protest. Then he said sadly: 'For goods like this, a man might risk much.'

Charley felt her heart grow cold. Much? How much? Would he consider a small boy's evidence dangerous? Dangerous enough to be suppressed? For ever?

She came to with a start, to hear the shopkeeper saying to Jon: 'If you would return tomorrow . . . I have many contacts in the city . . . I will make inquiries.'

'It is the boy,' said Charley suddenly, tears in her voice. 'The necklace is only goods—but the boy . . .' She looked at the dark Arab eyes out of her own startlingly blue ones and willed the man to understand how important Zizi was. In this country, life was cheap. The fate of one small boy didn't matter much. It was as Allah willed . . . But to Ankaret it mattered terribly. And—she suddenly realised—to Charley herself, too. *'Please,'* she said. 'Help us to find him. Madame Lejeune is very ill in Paris. I think it will kill her if he is not found.'

The shopkeeper nodded slowly. 'I understand, *mademoiselle.* I will do my best. Come again tomorrow.'

It was all they could do, and by now they were both exhausted. They tried two more shops without success, and then wearily made for home.

There was no news waiting for them. No one had telephoned. Selina had cooked them a meal which nobody wanted to eat, and Myrrha had gone home to question her husband about news from the *souks.* There was no news from Habib.

They all went to bed very late, worn out with worry but not expecting to sleep. But Charley and Jon had walked for long hours in the crowded streets of Bizerta, and they were bone-weary. Before long, in spite of her deep anxiety, Charley fell into a deep, exhausted sleep.

So did Jon. But late in the night, his old shouting nightmares returned. Whether it was the presence of Selina stirring old memories, or the tensions and anxieties of the day and his secret fear that Zizi was dead—something triggered it off, and he found himself fighting unknown

205

opponents, stumbling over unseen obstacles, and trying to run on legs that would not move, struggling to reach Richard and push him down on the stony ground before the sniper's bullets reached him, and at the same time trying to reach Aziz who stood poised and smiling with a knife in his hand, while Zizi lay bound and kicking at his feet. 'No!' Jon shouted. 'No!' and lunged at Aziz—at Richard—at a smiling, malevolent fate that always decreed he would be too late . . .

Charley climbed back out of heavy sleep to hear Jon's voice shouting. She knew at once what had happened—even guessed why—and leapt out of bed to go to his room.

Outside in the passage-way she met Selina, dishevelled and sleepy but looking as ravishing as ever, even in the midst of her alarm.

'What on earth—' she began, clutching at Charley's arm.

'It's all right.' Charley pulled herself together. 'It's only Jon.'

'*Only*? I thought he was being murdered.'

'Not him,' said Charley clearly. 'Richard.'

Selina's eyes went wide. '*Richard*?'

'He still has nightmares. Didn't you know?'

Selina shook his head, still wide-eyed with shock. 'No. I didn't. *Still*? How awful.'

'It is rather.' Charley looked at her straight. 'Shall I go in—or will you?'

Selina backed away. 'I'd only make things worse, wouldn't I? It's probably because I'm here that he's remembered . . .'

'Probably.' Charley's voice was terse. 'And the worry about Zizi.' She was still looking at Selina, and bright challenge hung in the air. 'All right, if you won't go in—go and put the kettle on.'

To her surprise, Selina turned obediently and went into the kitchen without another word.

As Charley went towards Jon's door, he called out again 'No!' at the top of his voice, and there was a heavy, muffled crash from inside the room. Charley rushed in and found him lying in a tangle of limbs and crumpled duvet on the floor. Instinctively, she knelt down beside him and put her arms round him, pillows and duvet and all.

'Jon, it's me. Charley . . . Wake up. It's all right.'

She felt the tension go out of his limbs, and for a moment he went slack in her arms. Then his body straightened and his own arms came up and held on to her in a convulsive, desperate embrace.

'Oh, Charley,' he said, in a voice still broken with nightmare, 'oh, *Charley*! . . . Thank God you're here.'

They did not speak after that for a while. She just held him close, rocking him in her arms like a child, and he clung on, seeming unable to let go.

But at last he slackened his grip and said huskily: 'I'm sorry—you don't deserve this . . . What you put up with at my hands!' and got shakily to his feet.

Charley knelt where she was and looked up at him. 'Was it Richard? Or Zizi?'

'Both,' he sighed, and turned away, ashamed of his weakness. He began to cough again, painfully.

Charley could not bear the dispirited droop of his shoulders, and got swiftly to her feet. 'But don't you see—' she said, putting her hands on those weary shoulders and turning him to face her. 'If it was Zizi, too—you have walked out of the past. It is just present anxiety—not guilt any more.'

'Isn't it?' He seemed to be still talking in a dream.

Charley shook him gently. 'You've brought it up to date. To the *present*. It's Zizi who matters now—the rest is over and done with.'

The veil of dark dream seemed to clear from his eyes as he looked at her. 'Yes,' he repeated, 'it's Zizi who matters now.'

They stood gazing at one another, while a different kind of tension seemed to rise between them. There was longing in Jon's face, and longing in Charley's too. She knew what she ought to do now for Jon's comfort and reassurance . . . It was patently obvious—but she couldn't bring herself to make the first move. She just stood there, helplessly caught in the intensity of his glance.

'Charley?' he whispered, as he had done at the lakeside

207

before, and there was the same thrill of tenderness and awareness in his voice.

'Yes,' she answered. 'Yes, Jon.'

But Jon, seeing her there, so vulnerable and unguarded, so full of loving generosity, could not exploit that moment of truth. So he bent his head and kissed her with the utmost gentleness, and laid an arm round her shoulders and murmured softly: 'Bell, book and candle, little Charley . . . You are better than any priest—and more potent, too.'

Potent? thought Charley, with a desperate flick of laughter. It is you, Jon, who are potent. You, with your poet's eye, and your desperate need of comfort. What am I to do?

But aloud she only said in a shaken voice: 'Tea is quite potent, too, as a ghost-breaker,' and led him towards the kitchen.

Selina was sitting at the table, her hands clasped round a mug of tea, and her golden hair swinging forward, hiding her face. Two other mugs of tea were steaming on the table.

'All this anxiety is getting me down,' she said, carefully not looking at Jon or Charley. 'Have some tea.' Then she looked up and smiled a little wanly. 'Perhaps there'll be news in the morning.'

But in the morning there was no news, and Habib, when they spoke to him on the phone, said he was still waiting for reports to come in.

This time, Selina refused to be left behind, saying she would go mad with nothing to do but wait, and pointing out that at least they could cover more ground with three of them to visit the traders in the souk. So they arranged with Myrrha to stay and man the phone, and decided to return to the shopkeeper in Bizerta late in the evening, giving him more time. Instead, they spent a fruitless day in Tunis. No one seemed to have heard of Aziz, or to be interested in Berber jewellery (though Jon knew this couldn't be true). And in those teeming narrow streets, with their hordes of street traders, beggars and darting street urchins, who would know or care about the fate of one small boy?

Despondently, they came to the conclusion that they were doing no good, and that the trail to Aziz was cold. During the long mid-day siesta most of the shops were closed, and they walked aimlessly through the maze of alleyways and arches, past narrow slivers of houses standing blind and shuttered against the open street, past gleaming white domes and mysterious courtyards, and glimpses of filthy yards full of rubbish and scavenging dogs.

When Selina complained that her feet hurt, they stopped at a nearby café for the inevitable mint tea—but all of them felt that the search was in vain. Charley in particular was somehow convinced that they were looking in the wrong place. Bizerta seemed more likely. Tunis was too big and too open, with its wide streets and boulevards—too westernised and commercial. Even the closed *medina* and the *souks* with their crowds and wandering tourists seemed more casual and impersonal than the dark, secretive atmosphere of the winding alleys of Bizerta.

She said as much to Jon, but he shook his head uncertainly. 'That might be the very reason Aziz would choose Tunis. It is more anonymous—easier to disappear.'

Charley knew it made sense, but she still obstinately clung to her feeling about Bizerta. There was something about it that tugged at her mind. Some of the people had known Jacques Lejeune. They might even have known Zizi—though probably they would have forgotten. One small boy was very like another. But still, they had not been unfriendly, or indifferent. They might be willing to help.

'Let's go back to Bizerta,' she said. 'We're doing no good here.'

When they went back to the small jeweller's shop in the *souk*, the shopkeeper made them all sit down and brought them coffee.

'I have not found out much,' he said, spreading his hands apologetically. 'But two of my friends say the man, Aziz, approached them.'

'When?' Jon's voice was sharp.

'I think, before the robbery. He told them he would have a valuable piece to sell. He described it to them, and asked how much it would be worth to them.' He looked from Jon to Charley, and then to Selina—and his eyes lingered in undisguised fascination on the golden glints in Selina's hair. 'I think—my friends think—that he already had a buyer, but he was—how do you say?—testing the water.'

'Yes.' Jon nodded. 'Was this in Bizerta?'

'Oh yes. Certainly in Bizerta.' He paused, and then added, putting the tips of his fingers together delicately: 'Though I daresay he has asked in Tunis also.'

'I daresay,' agreed Jon drily.

'But—' Charley was pursuing it urgently, 'has he been back to them since?'

'Not yet.' The shopkeeper saw her disappointment and added kindly: 'But my friends think he will.' He reached out a surprisingly gentle hand and patted Charley's arm. 'Be patient, *mademoiselle*. They say the man Aziz is a meddling fool. He will make a mistake before long.'

'I hope so,' breathed Charley. Oh God, I hope so.

They thanked the shopkeeper, who asked them to call him Ahmed, and the three of them went back to their aimless wandering in the street. But Jon could see that the girls were tired and disheartened, so he decided to cut their inquiries short and go home.

Charley had been walking alone ahead of them along the narrow cobbled street, looking up in despairing hope at the huddled houses, wondering if any of them held a frightened small boy behind a locked door.

Probably lots of them, she thought bitterly. There are lots of Zizis dying to be rescued. *Dying*? She shivered, and turned in relief when Jon laid a hand on her arm.

'Come home, Charley. We'll try again tomorrow.'

Tomorrow? she thought. It was two days and two long nights since Zizi had gone. What would tomorrow bring?

On the way home, Jon stopped at the police station to ask Habib if there was any news, leaving the two girls outside in the jeep.

'News of the boy, I have not,' said Habib, looking at Jon cautiously. 'News of Aziz, I have.' He paused, and added kindly: 'I am glad you are alone. I would not wish to alarm the ladies.'

'Tell me,' said Jon, his own alarm bells already ringing in his head.

'It seems you were right. Aziz has a record. For several robberies. He was also employed by Jacques Lejeune as a clerk in his office, but he was caught stealing from office funds and dismissed.'

'I see.' Jon's voice was bleak.

'He then worked in another office as a clerk—one that installed safes in private houses. He was dismissed from that position as well . . . And they have recently reported a break-in. Their filing system was tampered with.'

Jon whistled. 'No wonder he knew the combination.'

'*Exactement.*'

'How do you suppose he knew of the Berber necklace?'

'Jacques Lejeune purchased it through a friend. It was a private transaction. But his office remembers the occasion—and that he kept a receipt of the sale in his desk.'

They looked at one another somewhat grimly.

'It all seems far too clear.'

Habib nodded, far from happily.

'Do you think—?' Jon began, and then did not know how to voice his fears aloud.

'I do not think he is capable of much violence—no. He is a small man, in every sense. But—' he sighed, and looked down at his desk for a moment before facing Jon's challenging gaze, 'he is also a frightened man. And for that reason, I do not want to move too fast.'

'Yes,' Jon agreed. 'That makes sense.'

'We must wait for more news,' Habib told him. 'In the meantime, you may tell the ladies what you think fit. But do not alarm them too much. We will do everything in our power to get the boy back.'

Jon thanked him, and went back to the others heavy of heart. He told them most of it—but omitted Habib's remark about Aziz being frightened. It was all too obvious to Charley anyway. It did not need saying.

'At least we know it wasn't Zizi who gave him the combination,' said Selina, trying to offer comfort.

'We knew that anyway,' snapped Charley, her eyes sparking blue fire.

*   *   *

That evening, Jon went for a walk along the beach on his own—trying to dispel the various doubts and terrors that assailed him. He was worried about Zizi, and desperately afraid that something had happened to him, though he did not say so. He was worried about Selina, who clearly felt responsible and needed reassuring. He wished she would go home and leave him alone. She reminded him of too much he wanted to forget . . . And he was worried about Charley, and their growing closeness which he could neither ignore nor deny. Indeed, it was perilously sweet, but he knew he must not allow it to grow any stronger. Charley was young and inexperienced (at least, he thought of her as young—years and years younger than he with his wide and sorrowful experience of disillusioning life), and she was generous-hearted and loyal to a fault. Her very innocence was a danger in itself, and he had no right to take advantage of it. Besides, she had only just broken free from a life of drudgery and grey restriction. She had all the world before her, and he must do nothing to prevent her flying off like all the free wild birds of Lake Ichkeul. If he was getting much too fond, that was his own look-out. He had known from the start how appealing she was, and how her happy companionship had warmed his heart . . . And then there was his health—and try as he might he could not disguise from himself that his lungs still hurt and got far too exhausted by far too little work . . . Charley had already nursed one invalid. And she was already committed to looking after Ankaret when she came home. He must not add to her cares by allowing himself to rely on her gentle loving-kindness. It was not fair . . .

Pursued by these thoughts, he walked long and far, and at last turned back towards the villa, feeling drained and tired and with nothing resolved.

*   *   *

Left behind, Charley and Selina looked after his retreating figure, and gave a mutual sigh.

'He's quite wrong, you know,' said Selina.

'About what?'

'About Richard. He was the reckless one, not Jon.'

'Was he?' Charley was looking at her in surprise.

'Mm. Jon was always trying to prevent him doing something rash.' She was not looking at Charley, but staring down into her tea as if the past was mirrored in its surface. 'Guilt,' she said, in a voice suddenly heavy with knowledge, 'is a bad thing to live with.'

Charley did not know how to answer that. She had been climbing out of that nightmare herself, ever since her mother's death . . . And her heart had often ached for Jon, who clearly blamed himself for something he could not prevent. But Selina seemed almost to be talking of herself, not Jon at all.

Impulsively, Charley laid a hand on her arm. 'You're not to blame about Zizi.'

Selina looked almost surprised. 'Zizi? . . . Oh yes, I am. But I was actually thinking of Richard.'

'What do you mean?'

'It was much more my fault than Jon's.'

'Why?'

'Oh, I—egged him on. Made him take risks and follow up dangerous leads.' She shook her head, and the blonde hair swung and gleamed in the light. 'I wanted him to shine—our intrepid reporter, braver and handsomer than all the rest—you know the scene.' She sounded faintly contemptuous of herself. 'And Richard was a bit of a show-off, you know. He loved success.' She sighed again. 'A lethal combination. All that burning brand stuff— passionate commitment, gazing white-hot into the camera (with Jon there to make the most of it!), fearless and heroic and all that jazz—while Jon tried desperately to steer him out of the line of fire . . .'

Charley could see it. 'Were you in Beirut, too?'

'Oh yes. With the office back-up team, sending through his reports. We all lived in the same hotel—until things got too hot.'

'And then?'

'I got sent home. After Richard was killed.'

'And Jon?'

'Got sent home, too—on a stretcher.' She paused, and then added, almost defensively: 'I didn't go to see him in hospital. I thought he might be blaming me for Richard's death. It never occurred to me that he would blame himself.'

'Didn't it?' Charley thought, knowing Jon, that it would have occurred to her at once. But she realised she had sounded inexplicably abrupt, and added in a gentler tone: 'Why are you telling me all this?'

Selina looked up and smiled. 'Partly to take your mind off Zizi. And partly, I suppose, because I hope you'll tell Jon.'

Charley shook her head. 'Only you can do that, Selina.'

Selina's smile became distinctly rueful. 'When do I ever get the chance? He never lets me get within a mile of him.'

Charley laughed. 'That's only because he thinks you're after him.'

Selina laughed, too. 'I'm not, you know.' Then she turned to Charley quite seriously. 'I really only came out to set his mind at rest. Someone at the office told me he was all hung up over Richard. In fact,' she explained, in a surprisingly shy and uncertain voice, 'they sent me here—to finish the cure, they said.'

Charley was staring at her in astonishment. 'I see . . . Then I think you'd better tell him that.'

Selina tossed the hair out of her eyes. 'I'll try—if he'll give me half a chance.' Then she looked at Charley and added, half-smiling: 'If you don't object.'

'I? Object?' Charley was mystified.

'Seeing how things are between you and Jon.'

Charley's eyes went wide. 'Things aren't any way between me and Jon.'

It was Selina's turn to look astonished. 'You could've fooled me.' Then she added, with genuine curiosity: 'Anyway, why aren't they? Lovely place—plenty of opportunity—the perfect set-up . . . And he relies on you a lot.'

'Yes,' sighed Charley. 'I know. And I rely on him.'

'Well, then—?' Selina looked frankly disbelieving. 'Why aren't you having a ball?'

Charley wondered how to answer her. At last she said slowly: 'I don't know . . . I suppose—we are neither of us casual enough.'

'You don't have to be casual. In fact, looking at you two

214

together, I don't think you could.'

'No,' agreed Charley sadly. 'That's the trouble.'

'No commitments either?'

Charley shook her head. 'Not for Jon,' she said, but her voice was low.

'What's not for Jon?' said a voice from the doorway, and they looked up to find Jon standing there, smiling in on them.

It was at that moment that the phone rang.

They all thought it would be Jean-Paul with news of Ankaret. But it was not. It was Aziz.

'Do you want the boy back?' said the voice, silky and full of menace.

'What do *you* want?' countered Jon, and signalled to Charley and Selina to come close and listen.

'Ten thousand dinars,' said Aziz promptly. 'And no questions asked. And no police. Understand?'

'I understand,' agreed Jon, his voice deadly cold. 'Where are you speaking from?'

'Ah,' Aziz laughed quite pleasantly. 'It would be foolish of me to tell you, would it not?'

'Even more foolish not to,' snapped Jon. 'Or how will you get the money?'

'As to that,' Aziz purred, 'I will let you know. When you have got the money.'

'It may take a little time.'

'There isn't much time.' The menace was back in his voice. 'I am leaving the country soon.'

'When?'

There was a pause on the line. Then the disembodied voice said, 'I will be in touch,' and the line went dead.

They stood looking at one another in grim dismay.

'At least we know he's alive,' said Jon, and seeing Charley's pallor, went to pour her a drink.

While he was gone, the phone rang again, and after a moment's hesitation, Charley picked it up. It was Jean-Paul.

Keep your head, she told herself. Don't let him suspect anything is wrong. He can do nothing to help up there, and it would only add to his anxieties.

215

'Yes, Jean-Paul,' she said, sounding a little breathless. 'How is Ankaret?'

'She is a little better today.' Jean-Paul's voice was warm with reassurance. 'We are hoping she will be out of intensive care by the weekend.'

'That is good news,' breathed Charley. 'Is there anything she wants? Can we send her anything?'

'That is all taken care of.' He almost sounded as if he was smiling down the line. 'But in a day or two you could write to her. Perhaps Zizi could write something, too? She would like that.'

'Yes,' agreed Charley, her heart shaking within her. *In a day or two*? 'Of course.'

'Charley, *chérie*? You sound a little strung up.'

'Do I?'

'It is going to be all right, you know.' The kindness was back in his voice, even stronger now. It made her want to weep.

'Yes, Jean-Paul,' she whispered. 'Of course it is.'

'Don't cry, *ma petite*.' He was far too acute for comfort. 'She will return to you soon.'

She took a shuddering breath of control. 'I'm sorry, Jean-Paul. We have all been—so anxious.'

And that is true, she thought. All day. And all night. Anxious about Ankaret. Anxious about Zizi . . .

'Give her our love,' she said at last, 'when you can. And tell her—tell her not to worry about a thing. Just get well.'

She hoped her voice sounded steady. But Jean-Paul accepted her distress anyway,—and that made her feel worse than ever.

'Do not fret, little one,' came the comforting voice down the line. 'All will be well.' And he rang off before she could reply.

Jon had been standing close by during this exchange, but when he came forward and handed her a drink, he saw that the tears were running down her face.

'Here,' he said gently. 'Drink this. You did very well.'

'I've never—never lied like that before—'

'You didn't lie.' Jon was smiling a little. 'You simply didn't tell all the truth. You were very clever.'

216

Charley gulped. 'I feel awful.'

Jon brushed the tears off her face with a gentle hand. 'You were fine. Have your drink, you'll feel better in a minute.' He watched the colour begin to return to her face, and then went over to the telephone to ring Habib.

Charley did not protest. But he saw her increased anxiety and said, with his hand on the phone: 'I've got to, Charley. We can't handle this alone.'

She nodded silently, and took another gulp of her drink. Beside her, Selina had brought over a chair and now pushed Charley into it, saying with unexpected sympathy: 'Sit down, Charley. You look like death.'

They waited while Jon talked to Habib. His instructions were to do nothing, and wait for Aziz to call again.

'I can't raise that kind of money,' said Jon.

'Don't try. Just agree to everything. Arrange to meet him. And tell us. We will do the rest.'

'You must not—'

Habib interrupted him. 'I know. We must not bungle it, or take risks with the boy. Don't worry, my friend. We will be very careful.'

They agreed to meet again in the morning to discuss the next moves. But they both knew there was nothing they could do but wait.

*　　*　　*

Aziz did not ring for two days. By this time, Charley was getting desperate. Reports had come in from two jewellers who had been approached—one in Tunis and one in Bizerta. The curious thing was, Aziz had not produced the Berber necklace itself, only described it in some detail. Both dealers had stalled and asked him to call again when they had consulted experts about the price, and when he could actually show them the goods in question. He had not called again.

At last, Charley could stand it no longer. She begged Jon to take her back to Bizerta and to the small shopkeeper, Ahmed, who might have a bit more news.

Selina agreed, rather nervously, to stay and answer the

217

phone in case Aziz called again. But she begged Myrrha to stay with her because the thought of talking to Aziz made her distinctly scared. Jon reassured her, saying Aziz could not harm her on the end of a phone, and arranged to ring back during the day in case of news.

So he and Charley went to Bizerta again. Ahmed told them—over the ritual mint tea—that one of his friends had been approached again by Aziz. He had not brought the necklace with him, but had asked for a higher price. When his friend asked for time to consider, Aziz had gone away.

'Where was this?' asked Jon urgently. *'Where?'*

'Here, in Bizerta.' Ahmed looked at him out of shrewd but reassuringly honest dark eyes.

'How long ago?'

'Yesterday.' He paused and added in a trader's knowing voice: 'We think he is having difficulty selling the goods.'

Jon and Charley looked at each other. 'That might explain the ransom demand.'

'Ransom?' Ahmed looked startled. Buying and selling he was used to—even a shady deal or two now and then—but ransom? That was outside his experience. And it was dangerous.

'Where is your friend's shop? Could I talk to him?' Jon was insistent.

Ahmed looked inscrutable. 'There is no shop. He is a dealer. He met Aziz by arrangement.' But then, seeing Jon's frustration, he added carefully: 'I could arrange a meeting.'

'Soon?' pressed Jon. 'It must be *soon*. The boy is in danger.'

Ahmed nodded. He had already worked that out for himself. 'Wait here,' he instructed, and waved a polite hand towards the back of the shop. 'My house is yours.'

Jon and Charley found a low divan piled with cushions behind the beaded curtain, but neither of them could bring themselves to sit down and relax. They stood together uncertainly, filled with a dreadful sense of urgency.

'I hope—' began Charley, voicing their fears, 'he won't panic.'

'So do I,' Jon's voice was grim.

218

They both had nightmarish visions of a small, defence-less boy whom they had mysteriously grown to love, caught in the toils of a greedy and ruthless man.

Presently, Ahmed returned with a slightly taller verson of himself, also dresser in a white *jellaba* and red *chechia*. He bowed to Charley politely, and held out his hand to Jon.

'I am Ishak. I will tell you what I know. But it is not much.'

Coffee was produced this time, and not until they were all seated on cushions and sipping the black, sweet liquid, would Ishak proceed.

Charley and Jon chafed at the delay, but they knew they could not hurry him. The customary ritual had to be observed.

At length, prompted by Ahmed, Ishak began to speak. 'We met in a café. Word had been passed to me.' He glanced at Ahmed. 'My friend here had already warned me—so I was careful to ask for a delay.'

Jon nodded.

'He seemed in a hurry. He was very impatient.' Ishak raised his eyes heavenward. 'In business, you understand, such transactions take time.' A glimmer of a smile touched his mouth. 'In the end, I agreed to meet him again today— at the same place. But he did not come.'

A sudden coldness seized Charley as she listened. *He did not come.* Why not? Had he already taken fright and fled— with the necklace still unsold? . . . Or had he sold it to another dealer? And if so—where was Zizi? *What had he done with Zizi?*

Jon laid a cool hand on hers for a moment, and murmured: 'Hold on.' Then he turned to Ishak and asked urgently: 'Did you see where he went?'

Ishak's eyes—as brown and shrewd as Ahmed's, and almost as honest—narrowed a little. 'I had a boy watching him—but he lost him in one of the *souks*.' He looked apologetic. 'They are so crowded—especially with the tourists—and there are many stalls.' He paused for a moment and then added with a sudden edge to his voice: 'But we will watch. There are many eyes in the *souks*.' His gaze met Jon's—as hard now as his voice. 'Transactions we

219

are used to—whether honest or not. But *ransom*—that is another matter.' He did not add his own puzzlement that anyone in their right mind should want to ransom a small boy who had once been no better than any of the other street arabs in the *souks*. But it was clear to him that these two anxious people really cared about the boy. Who was he to question it? The ways of the West were a mystery to him.

Jon rose to his feet. It seemed that they would find out no more from Ishak today. 'Thank you,' he said gravely, holding out his hand. Courtesy mattered very much in these matters, he knew. 'You have been most helpful.'

'Do not worry, *mademoiselle*,' said Ishak, rightly interpreting Charley's silence and pallor. 'We will find him.'

Charley also held out her hand. 'Soon, Mr Ishak,' she pleaded. 'Please make it soon!'

* * *

Ishak's boy was called Ali (most of the *souk* boys were either Ali or Abu, and answered to either) and he was cross. He had failed to keep track of the man Ishak wanted followed, and he had lost the few millimes he had been promised as well. Ishak was a good master, and not ungenerous when a job was well done, but he didn't like failures, and—as he often told Ali—he didn't pay the boy to be a fool. It seemed to Ali, therefore, that he had better do something about this man Aziz they were supposed to be looking for, so he called his friends together and told them to keep their eyes skinned and report to him.

The streetwise urchins of the *souks* ran about like dogs among the stalls and alleyways, and their bright, observant eyes missed very little. But they did not find Aziz. They reported back to Ali, and he shrugged philosophically and said: 'He has gone to ground. But he will come out. He must eat. So keep looking.'

They kept looking—and one small boy in particular kept haunting the kebab stalls, partly because he was hungry himself and people sometimes dropped things, and partly because he thought it would be the quickest and most anonymous way for Aziz to grab some food in a hurry. He was dodging back down an alleyway, having snatched a fallen kebab for himself when the stallholder wasn't looking, when he thought he saw the man he was looking for crossing the street ahead. The police had put his picture on several posters round the *souks*, and Abu thought he recognised that dark, shut-in sort of face. He ran very fast up the alley to the corner of the next street and stood looking up and down it. Half-way along, there was a dark archway and another alley leading out of it. He thought he caught a glimpse of the man slipping inside the archway, but when he got there and looked down it, there was nothing to be seen except an old yellow dog lying in the sun. Puzzled, he began to saunter along the alley, looking from right to left at the closed doors and shuttered windows. Had the man gone in there? Or had he simply gone on to the next street and yet another dark alleyway? He did not know.

He was pondering what to do next, when something small and hard hit him on the head from above. He looked up in surprise at the slit of hot blue sky between the narrow leaning houses with their blank, secretive faces. There was nothing up there, though, he decided. All the shutters seemed closed, and the shadowy alleyway seemed to brood in heavy silence. He glanced down at the dusty cobbles and piles of refuse at his feet, and saw a small round stone with a piece of paper wrapped round it. Curious, the boy picked it up and unwrapped the paper. One side of it was an advertisement for western furniture, with pictures of tables and chairs and fat-looking sofas. He could not read the writing on it, though—in fact he could not read at all, whether in Arabic or French—but he understood the pictures all right. He turned the paper over and saw that on the other side someone had tried to write something with a very smudgy pencil—or it might have been charcoal or a burnt match-stick. He looked at it both ways up and then sideways, but he still could not read it. In any case, it didn't look very important, more like a child's scribbling than anything, and he almost threw it away. But then he thought of Ali, and how cross he would be if the piece of paper was important after all, so he held it carefully in his hand and ran off to look for his friend.

Ali couldn't read either, but it seemed to him that people didn't throw stones wrapped up in paper with writing on it without a purpose, so he took it along to Ishak.

And when Ishak saw it, he whistled.

'What does it say?' asked Ali, intrigued.

'It is in English,' answered Ishak, and hurried across the Street of the Coppersmiths to talk to Ahmed in the Street of the Goldsmiths.

'Where did you get this?' barked Ahmed, and listened intently while Ali questioned his friend Abu, the small boy who was hungry, and found out which alley he had been running through at the time.

'Go back there,' commanded Ahmed. 'Both of you. And watch the doorways near where the stone fell. Do you know where that is?'

'It fell from the sky,' said Abu, who was rather bewildered by all these questions. 'No doubt it was sent by Allah.'

'No doubt,' agreed Ahmed grimly. 'But go now and watch. And if the man Aziz appears, one of you must run here to tell me.'

The boys departed, and Ahmed went into the back of his shop with Ishak to have some mint tea. Then he got hold of his ancient telephone and rang the number Charley and Jon had given him.

When they arrived, breathless and anxious, having driven crazily at breakneck speed from the villa, parked the jeep where they could, and run all the way through the *souks*, Ahmed carefully laid the crumpled piece of paper before them.

Charley looked down at it in disbelief. But there was no doubt about it. There, in faintly scrawled letters, painstakingly scratched with something black and smudgy, were the words '*I AM ZIZI*'. It was the phrase she had taught him to write. Almost the only thing he *could* write. Her eyes misted with tears as she thought of that small, imprisoned boy remembering what she had taught him, and having the sense to use it. For the paper had been wrapped round a stone and pushed out of one of those dark, shuttered windows in one of those crowded, shabby

222

houses . . . And that meant Zizi was there—and safe enough, alive enough, to write those three important words . . .

'We must tell Habib,' said Jon.

'I have already taken that liberty,' replied Ahmed, with dignity. 'He is coming.' He smiled at Charley's blazing white face, and added gently: 'Will you take some tea while we wait?'

'But—we ought to go there,' began Charley, her voice sounding strange and broken. She could not quite believe that Zizi was really found—or trust the enormous wave of relief that was threatening to overwhelm her.

'Not yet,' said Jon, laying a restraining hand on her arm. 'Better wait for Habib.' He looked at Charley urgently, willing her to understand. He did not want to put into words his own dread of sudden action—of what a frightened man at bay might do to one small, vulnerable boy.

Charley did not miss that look. Sighing, she turned away and followed Ahmed and Ishak into the back of the shop.

'The boys are keeping watch,' said Ishak in his soft, soothing voice. 'They will tell us. We only have to wait.'

It seemed a long wait to Charley, agonisingly slow, but at last Habib came. He inspected Zizi's note gravely and nodded his head as if it confirmed his own thoughts. 'You are right, *mademoiselle*. No one but the boy would write this.'

Charley wanted to scream at the slowness of things, but she merely agreed, and then added with rising impatience: 'What next?'

'I will collect my men and place them discreetly.'

'Do you know which house?' asked Jon, with almost as much impatience as Charley.

'No. But we know the street. Sooner or later the man Aziz will come out—or go in. We have only to wait.'

'Yes, but—' began Charley in desperation. Another wait seemed impossible.

'We must move very carefully,' said Habib, observing Charley's mutinous face with sympathy. '*Very carefully*, *mademoiselle*, if we are not to alarm this Aziz. You understand?'

223

'I understand,' Charley answered, but something inside her ached with terror at what might be happening to Zizi.

At this point, the boy Ali appeared, out of breath and excited. 'He has come out,' he panted. 'But only to get food. He is at the kebab stall. Abu is following him. I came to tell you.'

'Now at least we know the house,' said Habib, and went off at a run to collect his men.

The street child, Ali, looked hopefully at Ishak. 'I did well?'

'You did well,' approved Ishak. 'There will be much reward when the boy is safe.'

Ali's brown face split into a cheerful grin. 'That will be soon!' he said, and prepared to go back to his vigil outside the marked house in the street.

'Wait,' exploded Charley suddenly. 'We're coming with you.'

Jon looked up, startled, and the two Arabs glanced swiftly at one another, clucking their disapproval.

'We must not alert Aziz—' Jon began, in reluctant protest.

But Charley interrupted. 'I have to *be* there.' Her voice was rough with anxiety. 'He might be frightened when the police go in—all those men charging about. He might bolt or something.'

Jon did not comment on this. Knowing the man, Aziz, he thought it unlikely that poor Zizi would be able to bolt anywhere—until they freed him. But he did not say so.

'*Please*, Jon,' she begged. 'I can't stay here doing nothing.'

Jon sighed and capitulated. 'All right,' he agreed, for it was clear to him that Charley could stand inaction no longer.

But before they could move, the gentle Ahmed spoke. 'Forgive me, *mademoiselle*,' he said, regarding her flushed, determined face with concern. 'If you will permit me—' and he reached up to his wall and carefully removed a long white silk scarf from its hanging beside a garnet-coloured rug suspended above his head. 'Please,' he murmured softly, offering it to her with exquisite courtesy, 'to cover

224

your beautiful hair.' Once more his eyes met Ishak's with hidden messages. 'It is better so.'

Jon agreed, smiling. 'It is certainly conspicuous,' and he helped to drape the clinging silk over her telltale auburn hair. 'Will that do?' he asked Ahmed, standing back to admire the effect.

Ahmed gave an eloquent shrug, but there was a hint of a smile behind his dark, observant gaze. 'She is still beautiful,' he remarked gravely. 'But not so—noticeable.'

'A couple, sight-seeing,' said Ishak softly. 'Stay well behind Ali—and do not appear to hurry.'

Jon nodded, thanked the two of them for all their help, and followed Charley and a round-eyed Ali out into the street. 'Not too close,' he told Charley. 'Just strolling—remember?'

The street urchin, Ali, slid effortlessly through the crowded *souks* and led them unerringly down the narrow streets of the *medina* to a dark, almost empty alleyway behind a tangle of warehouses.

On one side there was an arcade of small shops beneath a leaning jumble of narrow, shuttered houses. Across the cobbled path was another row of thin, blind-faced houses huddled together in shabby profusion, their roofs a medley of flat parapets, ancient tiles, flaky blue paint, and unexpected glimpses of white domes and minarets in the old city beyond. From one of these slender towers the call to prayer came thinly on the air, and a few of the faithful hurrying by promptly knelt down in the street and bowed their faces to the ground before moving on about their lawful business. Or unlawful? Was Aziz among them? Charley wondered. She shivered a little, and Jon, sensing her distress, drew her into a darkened archway and said softly: 'It's all right. Habib's coming.'

She nodded, for a moment unable to speak, so great was her anxiety about little Zizi.

'We'd better wait here,' Jon went on quietly. 'We can see Ali—just across the street.' His eyes ranged from the small boy idly playing jackstones in the gutter to the dark opening beneath a tall grey sliver of a house just behind him. He looked innocent enough, Jon thought, and not particularly watchful. But, clearly, Jon and Charley must not be seen to approach him.

'Be patient,' Jon breathed to Charley's white-swathed head beside him, and he took her hand comfortingly in his.

Charley did not answer, but she squeezed his hand tight for reassurance. The wait seemed endless. Nothing moved in the house opposite, and there was no flicker of life behind those tightly fastened shutters. Was that where the stone had come from? She tried not to picture what might be happening in that upstairs room. And she tried not to forget to be cautious and go rushing up those stairs like a cavalry charge to rescue Zizi, without waiting for Habib or anyone else . . . She knew really that she must not. It might put Zizi's life in danger if she went in too soon. But it was hard to wait, to do nothing, when he was within reach at last. So she went on waiting, half-hidden in the cool obscurity of the archway, with Jon beside her.

A couple of cats skittered by like lean and hungry shadows, and the same yellow dog came close to them, sniffing, and then cringed away when Charley moved. It reminded her of Leo, and she felt a lurch of fear when she remembered what Aziz had done to Zizi's dog. He was pretty ruthless. Would he hesitate to hurt Zizi?

Suddenly Jon stiffened beside her. A man was coming along the narrow cobbled street—a small man with dark hair and a swift, jaunty walk. And behind him, slipping from shadow to shadow at a discreet distance, was Ali's quicksilver friend, Abu.

'Aziz . . .' breathed Charley, and Jon turned to her deliberately, with his back to the street, and put an arm round her, apparently engaging her in earnest and loving conversation. To the casual observer, it was just any lover's tryst, and Jon carefully clinched the matter by drawing Charley close and kissing her soundly on her trembling mouth.

Aziz did not give them a single glance. All the same, he did look up and down the street somewhat nervously before disappearing inside the door of that tall, thin house.

'Street door not locked,' muttered Jon. 'Probably a rooming house.'

'Separate locks on all the doors?' Charley was not slow to

226

understand. She shifted anxiously under Jon's casual arm and added in a fretful voice: 'I wish Habib would come.'

'I have come, *mademoiselle*,' murmured a voice at her ear. 'We can move now, since our friend has arrived. But carefully, you understand?' *Very carefully.*'

Jon turned to him in relief. 'Is there another way out?'

'My men have surrounded the house,' replied Habib quietly.

Charley looked at him, surprised. 'We didn't see you.'

Habib surveyed Charley's enveloping white silk shawl with approval. '*Mademoiselle*, we also have learnt to be inconspicuous.'

'What do we do now?' she asked, including herself in the action with intent.

Habib looked thoughtful. 'We need to surprise him. No breaking down of doors, if possible. Nothing that gives him time to react. A frightened animal can be very vicious.'

Jon said gruffly: 'Charley, I think you'd better keep out of it.'

'No.' Her response was instant. 'How can I?'

Habib still looked serious. 'It might be dangerous.'

'It is dangerous now—for Zizi.' Charley's voice was flat. There was no denial to that.

Habib spoke slowly. 'The boy who works for Ishak—is he here?'

Jon nodded. 'Across the street.'

Habib looked across at the dark archway where Ali was now carelessly playing jackstones with his friend, Abu, and not apparently paying any attention to anyone. But when Habib lifted his hand in a small, imperious gesture, the boy came strolling across the alley and stood beside him. A short, very quiet conversation in Arabic took place, and young Ali nodded his head vigorously. 'I can do,' he said in careful English, with a hopeful eye on Charley and Jon.

'Can do what?' asked Charley.

'Go up to the room and say he has a note from Ishak,' murmured Habib. 'It may bring him to the door. Once it is open, even a crack, we can go in very swiftly. That way—if we are very quick—we should be able to prevent him harming the boy.'

Charley nodded. But Jon said obstinately: 'I don't like bringing Charley. It's too risky.'

'Zizi is at risk,' retorted Charley—as if that eclipsed every other consideration. 'He may need me.'

The two men looked at each other. It was clear that they couldn't deflect Charley from her purpose. Habib was used to Arab women who did as they were told, and this was a new experience for him. He shrugged fluid shoulders and cast a rueful glance at Jon. 'Very well,' he said.

Quietly, not seeming to hurry, they strolled across the street and into the darkened doorway of the house, pushing open the unlocked outer door.

Behind them, two more unobtrusive shadows slipped into the silent hallway. Carefully, making as little sound as possible, they mounted the stone steps, with Habib's men close behind. On the landing there were three doors, all with shiny new Yale locks. Habib looked around him, trying to place where he was in relation to those shuttered windows on the street. Ali and his friend Abu had followed them silently up the stairs, and now the two boys consulted together earnestly. Then Ali looked at Habib and pointed to the door almost opposite. Habib nodded again, and handed the boy a folded piece of paper. Then he stood to one side of the door, with his men behind him, and Jon and Charley ranged themselves on the other side.

Ali went across to the closed door. Once more he looked round inquiringly, waiting for Habib's nod. Charley, watching him, suddenly shut her eyes in a silent prayer. Oh God, don't let Zizi get hurt, she thought. Then, as she opened her eyes again, Ali lifted one small brown hand and knocked softly on the door.

For a few seconds nothing happened. But presently footsteps came close to the other side of the closed door, and the voice of Aziz spoke in soft and cautious Arabic. Equally softly, the boy answered, and Charley recognised the name Ben Ishak as he spoke.

There was another pause. Then the door was unlocked and opened a small crack. A hand came out to accept the note. Fearlessly, young Ali held out Habib's folded slip of paper and thrust it into the waiting hand of Aziz.

At that precise moment, Habib acted. He flung the door back with his foot, and Jon and he erupted into the room, with Charley close behind them. They were very quick, but Aziz was quicker. He whipped out a knife and whirled round, leaping across the room to where a terrified Zizi crouched in the corner. The boy was dirty and dishevelled, covered in bruises, and his hands were tied together in a cruel knot—but he was alive, and a huge gladness seemed to come into his eyes as he saw Charley and Jon in the doorway.

'Don't move,' Aziz snarled, 'or I will kill the boy.' And he held the wickedly-gleaming blade of the knife against Zizi's throat.

There was a pause. Habib had been afraid of this. But he had his two men just outside the door at the head of the stairs, and more surrounding the house. He did not think Aziz would get far. The only trouble was, the boy might get hurt in the ensuing fracas.

'Aziz,' he said mildly, 'it is useless. My men are outside.'

Aziz took no notice. His eyes glittered with rage and fear. Charley thought: Habib is right. A frightened animal is very dangerous. She had time now to take in her surroundings. The room was bare, save for one rickety chair and a sleeping mat on the floor behind the door. Zizi was crouched close to the window, and she saw that the rope binding his hands was attached to one of the thick iron bars across the glass of the window behind its tightly fastened shutters. Tied up like a dog, she thought, shuddering—like poor, poisoned Leo.

A this thought, a sudden wave of fury came over Charley. She had not known she could be so angry—or so reckless. For she suddenly shouted at Aziz, with all the pent-up rage and anxiety of these last awful days in her shaking voice.

'How dare you!' she yelled, sounding absurdly English and outraged. 'You horrible little rat!' Her voice came out in a rush of anger. 'Take your filthy hands off that child!' And before the startled Aziz could do anything but stare at this virago, she had launched herself forward, unwinding the white scarf as she ran and hurling it straight at the face of

229

the astonished man before her. Its clinging folds descended over his head, blinding him and entangling itself in his knife-holding hand.

Zizi, seeing his chance and being as brave and resourceful as ever, promptly butted the blinded Aziz in the stomach, throwing him off balance—and at this point Jon leapt forward and seized the knife-hand in his own powerful grip, wrenching Aziz over so that he collapsed in a heap on the floor. Jon fell on top of him, and the two men rolled and fought and grunted in a struggling heap, with Jon trying to wrench the knife away and Aziz trying desperately to strike upwards at Jon with its lethal point. At last Jon managed to land a sharp jab at Aziz' jaw with his left fist, but not before the wildly slashing knife-blade had made contact with his arm. Both men grunted, but here Habib and his two men got close enough to grab Aziz and hold him down. The fight was over.

Charley knelt down on the dusty floor and gathered Zizi in her arms. 'Oh, Zizi,' she wept. 'Oh, darling Zizi, you're safe.'

Zizi did not weep, but he buried his head against Charley's shoulder and tried to grasp at her with his tied hands.

'Give me that knife,' said Charley.

But Jon was before her. He had already cut the rope attached to the iron bar, and now he also knelt down and cut Zizi's bonds. The boy's wrists were chafed raw, but he did not seem to notice. At once his arms went round Charley and clung on as if they would never be able to let her go.

But Charley had noticed Jon's gashed arm, and now she reached out for the white scarf lying in a crumpled heap on the floor. She seized one end to tie up Jon's arm and stop the bleeding, and somehow contrived to turn the other end into a passable sling.

Jon looked at her, and then at the white silk scarf, with a smile twitching at the corners of his mouth. 'Well, it certainly came in useful,' he said.

'Worth its weight in gold, I would say,' agreed Habib, smiling in undisguised admiration at Charley.

'That arm will need a stitch,' stated Charley severely, and stood up, lifting Zizi with her. 'And we might as well get Zizi looked at, too.'

'I can walk,' said Zizi, wriggling in her arms. 'Put me down. Did you find my letter?'

'I did indeed. Or rather, Abu and Ali did.' She glanced round, expecting to see the sharp, eager face of Ali in the doorway, but he was nowhere to be seen. At the first sign of real action, the two boys had fled. Charley did not blame them. They knew all too well where such violence could lead. Sighing, she set Zizi down gently, and brought out the crumpled piece of paper with his message, which she had retrieved from Ahmed's shop. 'I think we ought to frame this,' she told him, smiling. 'What did you write it with?'

'A match.' Zizi pointed to a small heap of cigarette ends and spent matches beneath the shutterd windows. It spoke volumes about the nervous vigils of Aziz looking out at the street, and the patience and ingenuity of one small boy waiting for Aziz to go out and give him his one opportunity for communication.

'The stone?' queried Jon, also intrigued by Zizi's initiative.

'A bit of the wall,' said Zizi, pointing to the cracked and flaking plaster. 'I—picked it out with my fingers.' He tried earnestly to explain. 'But I was slow because of being tied.' He looked from Charley to Jon a little anxiously. 'I couldn't write very well . . . Could you read it?'

'Of course,' grinned Charley. 'We all read it. You are very clever.'

Habib had gone down to watch his men bundle the handcuffed Aziz into a police car. Now he returned and looked searchingly at Jon who was a little grey under his tan. 'I have another car here. Where is your jeep?'

'The other side of town.'

'*Exactement*. And you should not drive it, and Mademoiselle Charley is also tired. So I will take you home.'

'A doctor first.' Charley's voice was firm.

'*Certainement*. The hospital is not far.' He looked round

231

the room and added: 'My men will search here.'

'It is not there,' said Zizi suddenly. 'I know where it is, but I did not tell him.' And then his voice seemed to fade on a sigh and he slid down into a small heap on the floor.

                              *   *   *

When they got home—Jon with his arm in a (professional) sling, and Zizi still pale and grubby but smiling all over his face—Myrrha burst into tears, and Selina went white with relief and rushed over to pour Jon and Charley a drink.

'Thanks,' said Jon. 'But I think Zizi needs it more.'

So Zizi was given a drink too, and everyone toasted him and waved their glasses and laughed.

Then the baker from down the road, who had seen them all go by in Habib's car, came running with some of Zizi's favourite sweet *maqroudh* and a basketful of hot *briks* straight from frying. After him came Myrrha's two brothers who had been working on a building site and had seen Zizi's arrival from up on the scaffolding, and with them a small boy who had been hodding bricks and was Zizi's friend. And behind them came several of Myrrha's neighbours, usually quiet women but now chattering excitedly and coming forward to offer small gifts—an orange, a bunch of flowers, a packet of western biscuits, a cluster of purple grapes, a piece of syrupy *baqlawa* and some equally sticky stuffed dates—even a pomegranate. Last of all came Myrrha's husband who had run all the way from the market stall he was tending when he heard the news, and with him was a shy, thin man who stood on the verandah clutching something in his arms.

'My friend here,' said Myrrha's husband, 'has a small dog—in case the boy is sad about Leo.' He looked at them doubtfully. 'He is young,' he apologised, 'but you could train him to guard.' Then he beamed suddenly and added: 'Though it is hoped you will not need a guard now.'

Zizi looked at Charley with large, hopeful eyes, and she looked at Jon who nodded faintly.

'That is a very good idea,' Charley said, smiling at the shy man outside. 'Zizi—go and see.'

Zizi went quickly over to the verandah and looked at the bundle of fur in the man's arms. It was small, certainly, but it had long gangling legs and he could see that it would grow, and its golden fuzz of fur was very like Leo's. As he reached out a tentative hand, the small dog lifted its head and the brown, tufted ears cocked themselves in alert inquiry. Two eyes as brown and liquid as Zizi's own looked up at him in an assessing stare, and then the soft yellow muzzle thrust itself into his hand confidingly.

'He is beautiful,' whispered Zizi. 'Beautiful—aren't you?' And the small dog licked his hand as if it thoroughly agreed. 'Can I really have him?' he asked the man, looking up into his face with serious entreaty. 'I will take care of him.'

'He is yours,' the man replied, blinking a little at Zizi's sudden dazzling smile, and he placed the furry bundle gently in Zizi's arms. 'May he learn to guard you well,' he added in liquid Arabic.

Zizi understood him, and so did Jon and the rest of the company. Only Selina and Charley did not—but they made a good guess.

Jon, meanwhile, had seen the shadows under Charley's eyes and the tiredness that was creeping up on a small, gallant boy who would never give in, so he turned to the roomful of people and said in friendly dismissal: 'Tomorrow we will have a party. All of you are invited, and as many more of Zizi's friends as you can find. But now I think he should rest. It has been quite a day.'

You can say that again, thought Charley, suddenly realising how exhausted she felt—and if she felt like this, what about Jon who had been fighting Aziz as well and suffered a gashed arm in the process? And what about young Zizi? God knows what he has suffered during those long days and nights of imprisonment, she thought. And probably he will never tell me.

But the villagers understood Jon very well. They each came up and shook Zizi by the hand, and then Jon and Charley and Selina, and went away smiling and talking about the great blessing of Zizi's return and the prospect of a real party tomorrow.

Behind them, Zizi stood with the new little dog in his arms, looking small and brave and very tired.

'It is good to be home,' he said.

* * *

When Habib questioned him—which he did next day, very kindly and gently—Zizi told him that the persecution from Aziz had gone on much longer than they knew. The man had come up to him in the market several times, demanding to be let into the house. He had threatened Zizi with violence if he did not agree—violence either to him or to the other people in Ankaret's villa, particularly Charley. Aziz had clearly deduced that the boy was fond of Charley. But his worst threat—one that he used both before and after he kidnapped him—was that he would sell Zizi back to his former thieves-kitchen master. He knew who he was, and where he was. He was not in Tunis or Bizerta, Aziz told him, but down south at Zarzis. It was near the borders of Libya, which was where Aziz was going when he had completed his transactions. Once Zizi was taken down there, he would never escape, never get back to Bizerta or Raf-Raf, and never see Ankaret Lejeune again.

It was a cruel threat—much worse than actual violence to Zizi—and it was clear to Habib, and to Jon and Charley listening, that the boy was still frightened by it. If Habib was surprised by this devotion to his absent benefactor, he did not say so, nor did he make any comment about the obvious concern and affection felt for this small waif by Jon and Charley . . . In fact he was beginning to be quite taken by the child himself, with his big, anxious eyes and painfully honest answers.

Zizi also told Habib that Aziz repeatedly asked him for the safe combination, and got very angry when Zizi said he didn't know it. Once he tried to twist Zizi's arm, but Leo sprang at Aziz and almost bit him. Aziz was very angry about the dog, too, Zizi said. Charley could imagine that. She remembered the bruise on Zizi's arm.

'I didn't tell him,' said Zizi suddenly, turning to Charley and Jon in piteous appeal.

'Of course not,' said Charley. 'We know that.'

'All that money . . . and the candlesticks . . . I couldn't hide them, they were too big,' he said apologetically. 'But Mia-Ankar's necklace, that I hid before.'

'Before what?' asked Jon.

'Before Aziz came,' said Zizi simply. 'I knew he would come. So I hid it.'

'Where?' demanded Habib.

'I will show you.' Zizi took Charley by the hand, as if for protection, and led all three of them out of Ankaret's sitting-room and along the corridor to Jon's studio. There he went in without hesitation and walked over to the jumble of camera equipment stacked in the corner.

'You said that one was broken,' he told Jon, 'so I knew it would be safe,' and he pointed to the small video camera that Jon had dropped in the lake some days before. It had been left in the sun to dry and then put away among the empty film cans to be cleaned up later. Confidently, Zizi went over to it, and pulled the back off to expose the empty loading space. Only, it was not empty. Neatly tucked down inside the black plastic camera case was Ankaret's Berber necklace.

'There!' said Zizi proudly. 'It is safe. Will Mia-Ankar be pleased?'

Jon and Charley looked at each other, and could not speak. All that dreadful anxiety, and the life of one small boy in danger—for the sake of this pretty, useless bauble. And Zizi, suffering untold miseries for its sake, and for Ankaret whom he loved.

But Habib spoke for them. 'Yes. She will be pleased.' A smile lit up his dark face as he looked from the glinting gold of the necklace to Zizi's anxious eyes. 'You have been very clever—and very brave. Now I will tell you two good things.'

They all looked at him in surprise.

'First of all, Aziz will go to prison, so he won't be able to bother you for a long time. And secondly, I have heard that your adoption papers have come through. You are going to be Madame Lejeune's own boy, and no one can take you away from her. Is not that good?'

235

For answer, Zizi did what he had not done in all his long and frightening ordeal. He burst into tears.

*　　*　　*

That evening they had the promised party. Almost the whole village came, it seemed, and they spilled out on to the terrace, into the small garden and beyond on to the sandy beach. Everyone brought gifts of food, and someone lit a fire on the beach and cooked lamb in the traditional way on a spit over a smoky flame.

There was singing and dancing—though Jon didn't know where that sprang from either, except that someone had brought a guitar and another produced something that looked like a Greek bouzouki. Even the two jewel-dealers, Ahmed and Ishak, came to pay their respects and told Jon seriously that Aziz was not Tunisian, he must understand; their people were mostly honest, especially in the small villages where everyone was known, and the man Aziz was just a rogue outsider. Jon saw that it was a matter of pride among the traders, and assured them gravely that he understood, and thanked them for their help. He then thanked the two boys, Ali and Abu, who had also come (rather shyly) to the party, and made sure that they received their due and just reward.

Charley had made a cake for Zizi. No one knew exactly when his birthday was, but this seemed as good a day as any to celebrate. She had written on it, in large pink letters: 'I AM ZIZI'—and everyone cheered when she told them why, and cheered again, even louder, when he cut the cake.

'You must make a wish,' she said, smiling at his serious face.

He looked at her, puzzled. 'What could I wish for?' he wondered, as if he already had the whole world at his feet. But then his expressive face changed and he added gravely: 'Except for Mia-Ankar to come home.'

Charley nodded. 'Wish for that, Zizi. It will happen soon.'

Selina and Myrrha had been busy dispensing tea and

236

coffee from the kitchen—since most of the company was strict Muslim and did not drink alcohol. Charley was rather amazed at Selina's willingness. She seemed to be so relieved about Zizi's return (especially as she felt she was to blame for his snatching by Aziz) that she would do anything to help make the party a success. But now she came out on to the terrace looking for Jon, and said, under cover of the singing and clapping: 'Jean-Paul is on the line.'

Jon sighed and turned to go inside. He knew the time had come to tell Jean-Paul what had been going on—and he was more than a little ashamed that his guardianship of Zizi and Ankaret's property had not been better.

He was gone a long time. But when he returned he was smiling. He went straight to Charley and Zizi, who were standing hand-in-hand watching the bonfire.

'Ankaret is getting better,' he said. 'And I've told Jean-Paul everything.'

'When is she coming home?' asked Zizi, putting first things first.

'In about two weeks, Jean-Paul thinks. If all goes well.'

Zizi gave a little skip of joy. 'Can we have another party?'

'Why not?' Charley was smiling at his exuberance. It was good to see him capering about with the little yellow dog at his heels.

Zizi danced back to them and slipped a hand into each of theirs. 'This is a special day,' he said.

*   *   *

In the morning, since Jon could not work with his arm in a sling, they decided to take the day off. Jon had demurred, saying he could perfectly well edit film with one hand (which was blatantly untrue), but Charley was adamant.

'No,' she said. 'We all need time to recover. Relax, Jon— and enjoy yourself. You've earned a rest, God knows.'

So they all lazed about on the beach, while Zizi scampered about with his little new dog.

They had decided to call it Dingo—because it was even yellower than poor Leo. Zizi didn't know the story of Yellow Dog Dingo, but when Charley told it to him he was

237

delighted, and somehow the name seemed to suit the long-legged ball of yellow fluff. So Zizi and Dingo danced together on the edge of the sea in the mild Tunisian winter sun, and the others could hear Zizi's voice calling from time to time: 'Dingo! . . . Come on, Dingo . . . It's only the sea . . .' And they raced together along the wet golden sands, without a care in the world . . .

Selina was rather quiet during the day, and she kept looking at Jon in a tentative, questioning way. At last she said when they were eating their picnic lunch: 'Jon, I think I should go home tomorrow.'

He looked up, surprised. 'Tomorrow?'

She nodded, and the gold hair swung and gleamed in the sun. 'I've been here too long already—but I couldn't go while Zizi was missing. So—now that he's back, and you've got good news of Ankaret . . .' She shrugged and did not finish.

'Well, if you're sure—?' Jon sounded as neutral as possible.

'Oh yes, I'm sure,' answered Selina, staring out at the sea. But her voice was bleak.

'Have you done what you set out to do?' asked Charley deliberately.

Selina turned and looked at her, and sighed. 'No. But maybe it's not necessary now.'

'I think it is,' said Charley, and got to her feet. 'Come on, Zizi. We'll take Dingo for a walk.'

'Charley—' protested Jon, his voice full of reproach—and he scrambled to his feet and followed them as they set off along the sand.

But Charley stopped him. 'Jon.' She laid a hand on his good arm. 'Do you remember when I was ill?'

He screwed up his eyes at her against the sun. 'I remember.'

'I couldn't make myself go back to my mother's house. I couldn't even face Uncle Hal.'

There was a pause. Jon wasn't stupid. 'You think I'm running away?'

'I know you are.'

There was another pause, even tauter than the last.

'What has Selina been saying to you?'

'Only what she ought to be saying to you.'

He sighed. 'It won't help, Charley.'

'Oh yes.' She sounded quite definite. 'I think it will.'

'You promised to protect me.' His voice was rueful.

'I am protecting you. From a quite mistaken sense of guilt which is destroying you. Go and talk to her. *Please*.'

He looked into her face for a moment as if he would say something else. But in the end he only reached up and touched her face gently and murmured: 'Little Charley— brave as a lion for other people!'

And a hopeless coward about yourself, thought Charley, as her unguarded heart lurched at his touch. But she did not say it. Then Jon turned on his heel and went back to Selina, who was still sitting on the sand, gazing after him with an expression of mingled exasperation and affection.

Charley took Zizi's hand and began to run rather fast along the beach. Dingo ran after them, his gangling legs seeming to skid all over the place. But even so, he covered the ground faster than they did. They went a long way, and only turned back when the shadow of the palm trees on the shore-line grew longer as the sun sank low in the sky.

But presently they saw Jon coming towards them with long strides along the wet sand at the edge of the sea. And he was alone.

'Selina's gone in to pack,' he said, smiling at Charley's anxious face. 'And then we're all going out to dinner.'

'*Moi aussi*?' asked Zizi, dancing up and down from one foot to another.

'But of course, you also!' smiled Jon. 'How can we celebrate without our hero?'

'Are we celebrating?' Charley's voice was not as innocent as it sounded.

'We are.' He linked his good arm through hers and hugged her close, turning her to look at the sun setting far across the western sea. 'The light is wonderful tonight,' he said.

Charley was looking mischievous. 'Did Selina let some in?'

'Daylight. Into a very thick and obstinate head. Yes.' He

turned his head to look at her, and his eyes were suddenly vivid and strange. 'But as a purveyor of light, she isn't a patch on you.'

Charley had nothing to say to that. There didn't seem to be anything she could say. So they walked along together by the shore, following the path of light across the sea.

*　　*　　*

They saw Selina off the next day at Tunis airport. To Charley's surprise, Selina hugged her hard and whispered: 'Fight for him, Charley. He's too good to waste!' Then she waved a cheerful hand at Jon and Zizi, and disappeared through the boarding gate without looking back.

Charley was a bit shaken by that farewell, but she did not speak of it, and Jon never told her what he and Selina had said the night before.

PART V
LIGHT INESCAPABLE

They returned to the lake with a sense of enormous relief. The storms were over for the moment—the water lay still and calm, and the birds were still there in their myriads, resting and feeding, flying up in silvery clouds and settling again, unconcerned with any affairs except their own.

Charley had persuaded Jon to do half a day of filming at a time until his arm had healed, so they came out soon after dawn and stayed till mid-day, and then went home to lunch. Jon chafed at the waste of filming time, but Charley pointed out that if he slowed up the healing of his arm, he would be in worse trouble. Sometimes, though, he got too impatient to wait, so they came back in the cool twilight and filmed the birds returning to roost and settle on the smooth, unbroken surface of the darkening lake. Zizi came with them now, always, but Jon would not let Dingo come in case he disturbed the birds. Instead, the little yellow dog stayed with Myrrha and learnt to guard the house by day, and greeted them ecstatically when they returned.

Although Charley had hoped that the dark tensions within Jon would have been resolved by Selina, sometimes he seemed as remote and filled with brooding sadness as ever. She did not know how to dispel these moments of darkness, but she and Zizi did their best to distract him, and Zizi often made him laugh with his attempts at identifying the birds in their English bird book.

'That is a golden plum,' announced Zizi, pointing a brown finger at the illustration of a bird.

'Are you sure?' Jon's voice was laced with laughter. 'Don't you mean golden plover?'

Zizi frowned at the book, and retraced the words with his fingers. 'It says golden plum—'

'And on the next line, -age,' explained Charley, also

laughing. 'Plumage means feathers, Zizi.'

'Plum-age?' He said it again, carefully. 'Then why do they not say fevvers?'

And at their helpless laughter, he laughed too. Nothing could quench Zizi's thirst for knowledge in that halcyon time—and nothing could quench his bubbling happiness, either. He danced through the days, with little dog Dingo at his heels when they were at home, and Charley as his sheet-anchor by the shores of the lake.

Jon, observing Charley's indulgent smile as she watched Zizi lean down over the water to look at a pair of bright-hued pochards floating by, said suddenly: 'Charley—are you getting too fond . . . ?'

Her heart lurched in terror. Had he uncovered her secret thoughts? Was she so transparent? But before she could answer, he went on, half to himself: 'He's such an engaging child.'

The terror within her subsided—but the ache it left behind seemed even worse. 'Zizi?' she said. 'Of course I'm too fond.' She sighed. 'Fond and foolish, I daresay. But I wouldn't have it otherwise.'

'Wouldn't you?'

Something flashed in Charley's eyes—Jon wasn't sure if it was scorn or anger, or even a brief, inexplicable joy. 'You can't stay cautious for ever,' she said. 'You've got to let love in somewhere. What else is living for?'

There was a long, pulsing silence, and then Jon said in a shaken voice: 'Oh, Charley—how you put me to shame!'

* * *

The days slid by, and the gentle Tunisian winter was almost over. The rains had fallen, the streams had cascaded down from the Atlas mountains and filled the rivers, the lake was brimming with fresh, clear water, and the first of the spring migrants were returning from across the Sahara. And with their coming, Ankaret also returned to the safe haven she knew.

They had got the house ready as far as they could. Myrrha had polished everything till it shone. Zizi had gone out and come back with masses of flowers from the market, and Charley had arranged them in all the vases she could find. Jon had mended the long garden chair that was folded up on the verandah, and set it out so that it looked at the sea.

Jean-Paul was travelling back with Ankaret, to see her safely through the journey, and he had told them not to try to meet them. They would take a taxi out to the villa, and not expect too much of a welcoming party at home.

But of course there was a welcoming party—how could it be otherwise? Zizi was on tenterhooks all day, jumping up and down like a demented frog, and rushing to the door every time he heard a car in the street.

At last, towards evening, they came. Ankaret looked pale and tired, and she had lost a lot of weight, but she was as smiling and serene as ever. She walked slowly, leaning on Jean-Paul's arm, but as soon as she saw Zizi she stopped and stood up straight, holding out her own two arms to him. Zizi ran straight into them and buried his face against her side. '*Tu es revenue!*' he whispered. 'You have come back!'

'Zizi,' she murmured, holding him very tight. 'Zizi . . . I'm sorry I was so long . . .'

For answer, Zizi just clutched her harder and did not say anything more at all. But he had been primed by Charley not to be too exuberant or to tire her, so he straightened up almost at once and took her hand, saying: 'Mia-Ankar, we have a special chair for you—and Charlee is making tea.'

Jon and Charley were inside with Myrrha, but they all came forward then to help, taking the suitcases inside, installing Ankaret in her chair, and telling her how glad they were to see her back again.

It was a happy homecoming, and nothing was done to mar it. But later on, when Ankaret was resting in her room, Jon and Charley walked on the beach with Jean-Paul and asked him how things really were.

He sighed, and his doctor's professional gravity descended on him, quenching the cheerful, lighthearted Jean-Paul they knew. 'It is not very good,' he said. 'As far as surgery goes, we have removed what we can—as much as we dare. She has had a course of radiotherapy—also as much as we dare. Now she must rest and regain her strength. We hope she is in remission. But if it returns—' He shook his head sadly. 'There is not much more we can do.'

Charley said hopefully: 'But she is so brave. I am sure she will fight it. She has such a zest for life.'

'Yes,' agreed Jean-Paul. 'I am sure she will beat it if she can.' He paused and then added, looking at Charley: 'We must just help her through, that's all.'

'You know I—' began Charley, and Jon spoke at the same time: 'Just tell us what to do.'

Jean-Paul smiled, and grasped both of them in a strong and friendly grip. '*Mes amis*, I do not need to. Just be there. She doesn't need much nursing now. But she needs comfort—and encouragement. I am sure you will give her both.'

'We will try,' they said, and walked on with him down the sand.

Presently Charley asked: 'How much of the Aziz affair have you told her?'

The young doctor laughed. 'Most of it. Especially the bit about Zizi writing that note. She was very impressed by that!' He glanced at Charley, still half-laughing. 'And by your courage, *ma petite*, and Jon's too, of course . . .' But then he grew more serious. 'I have purposely kept it light— for her sake. Though I know Zizi must have been very frightened—and you were no doubt extremely worried. But I think it may be better—for Zizi, too—if we treat it all as a rather splendid adventure in which he acquitted himself extremely well. Don't you agree?'

'Yes,' Jon nodded. 'I think that's very sensible.' He turned to Charley in mute inquiry.

Charley grinned. 'You're brilliant, Jean-Paul. We were wondering how to mention it without getting Zizi all worked up again.'

Jean-Paul was grinning, too. 'What did you do with the famous Berber necklace?'

'It's in the bank,' said Jon. 'Along with the silver and most of the money which the police recovered from Aziz's room. It seemed the best thing.'

'Much the best,' Jean-Paul agreed. 'She should have put it there in the first place.' His smile became a little wary. 'But don't tell her I said so!'

They all laughed, and turned to stroll back to the house.

'How long can you stay, Jean-Paul?' asked Charley anxiously, feeling she needed his support.

'Not long, I am afraid, *chérie*. I have to be back at my *clinique* by the end of the week . . . But I will stay a couple of days to see Ankaret settled in.'

'Good.' She looked at him with the same anxious appeal, but said nothing more. She wanted to ask a hundred questions about how to look after Ankaret—what to guard against, what signs to look for—and when to be worried enough to send for Jean-Paul again. But tonight, when they were all so pleased to see Ankaret home at last, seemed hardly the time. She just hoped Jean-Paul would understand her anxiety and explain things to her before he left.

'Don't worry, Charley,' said Jon's voice softly beside her. 'You are very good at keeping the darkness at bay.'

And when she looked at him in astonishment, he reached out a hand, unconcerned by Jean-Paul's presence, and gently pushed the springing red-gold tongues of hair out of her eyes. 'Just concentrate on the light,' he murmured, and turned away, leaving her speechless on the shore.

*   *   *

For the rest of Jean-Paul's visit, Jon went off to the lake on his own all day, saying that Ankaret had enough people fussing round her. Charley felt bereft, and found that she missed those marvellous dawns beside the water-margins profoundly, but she did not say anything. The only concession she made to her own sense of loss was to get up as early as Jon and see that he ate some breakfast before he left. He protested at this, but she was adamant.

'You work too hard as it is,' she said severely. 'And if you don't eat, you'll be tired.'

It was logical, and Jon submitted, mutinously but

happily, to the pleasant hardship of demolishing an English breakfast before he left.

Ankaret was an easy patient, undemanding and appreciative. Charley could not help comparing her in her mind with the imperious, demanding tyrant of the bedchamber that had been her mother—though she felt guilty even thinking it. But Ankaret was different—full of calm acceptance. She did not get up till mid-day, and then had a kind of brunch on the verandah, lying on her chair, with Zizi and little Dingo frolicking round her. She did not each much, and instructed Myrrha and Charley with a smile to make her helpings very small and then they wouldn't be disappointed. She did not attempt to do anything about the running of the house or to interfere in Charley's and Myrrha's arrangements. She read quietly in her chair, or lay gazing out at the sea, and sometimes roused herself to give Zizi a reading lesson, and in between talked to Jean-Paul about the problems of his clinic, and the dreadful effects of drought and malnutrition on his patients, particularly the children.

But talking seemed to tire her, and Jean-Paul rationed it strictly, going off to deal with his own arrangements, and spending much time on the telephone planning shipments of food and medicines through the Red Cross and the relief agencies to the stricken area of Somalia to which he was returning.

Zizi was Ankaret's devoted slave, and indefatigable in fetching and carrying for his beloved Mia-Ankar. But he had also learnt how to be quiet and not disturb her. Often, Charley came to have a look and found Ankaret dozing in her chair, and Zizi sitting cross-legged on the floor beside her, watchful and silent. He did not seem unduly worried by Ankaret's tiredness, but accepted it philosophically and adapted his own pattern of behaviour to suit her needs.

Charley was amazed at his grasp of the situation. It did not seem natural for a small boy to be so wise and so considerate. But when she tentatively suggested he might like to run off and play with his friends for a change, he shook his head decisively and said: *'Je reste ici.'*

Charley did not pursue it. Clearly, Zizi knew very well

what he was doing. But he surprised her by saying suddenly: 'She will not go away again? If we are careful?'

'No.' She began to understand his reasoning. 'Of course she will stay here. She is getting better all the time.'

Zizi was staring beyond Charley at the long shadows of the palm trees on the sand beyond the villa garden.

'My mother got sick,' he said.

Charley was startled. She did not dare to question him about this sudden memory. He had never talked of his past before. But now he went on, in a voice of dark dream: 'They took her away in a white sheet. And she didn't come back.'

There was a long silence. Charley was too appalled to speak. What nightmares, what unspeakable tragedies and privations, had this small boy suffered before he came to the safe refuge of Ankaret's house—Ankaret's love and protection . . . ? And what would he do now, if Ankaret—?

She did not let her thoughts go farther. Instead, she acted instinctively and gathered Zizi into her arms. 'She will be all right, Zizi. We will make her well, between us . . . Everything will be all right.'

Zizi's taut small body suddenly relaxed in her arms for a moment, and he allowed himself to be rocked and comforted like a baby. His arms crept round Charley's neck and he clung there, at last admitting his desperate need for reassurance. '*Oh, Charlee, je t'aime,*' he said.

'*Moi aussi,*' responded Charley, smiling, and held him close till the terrible shadow of death had receded from his mind.

But Zizi would not admit to such weakness for long. He was made of sterner stuff than that. After all, he was not a baby—however good it felt to be treated like one sometimes. No, he was a boy—Ankaret's own boy, Habib the policeman had said, and it was up to him to look after his Mia-Ankar properly.

He climbed down from Charley's lap and squared his shoulders in a determined manner. 'I will make tea,' he announced. 'Mia-Ankar will be awake now,' and he trotted away to the kitchen.

Charley did not stop him.

Jon came home late now in the evenings. At first Ankaret

decreed that they should wait for him and all have supper together—the only real family get-together of the day. But the long-awaited mealtime clearly exhausted her when it came, and after the first day, Charley refused to let her stay up for it.

'No need to wear yourself out,' she said gently. 'Have something on a tray. You'll be much happier in your own quiet room.' She looked at Ankaret and smiled a little shyly. 'Am I bullying you too much?'

Ankaret laughed comfortably. 'To tell you the truth, I love it!' She leant back against her cushions and added, still smiling: 'You are a blessing, Charley—do you know that?' and closed her eyes in peaceful surrender before Charley could answer.

Jean-Paul stayed four days, and on the last evening he walked on the shore wtih Charley and gave her what instructions he could—together with a phone number where he could be reached in an emergency. He had been watching Charley's treatment of Ankaret with growing relief—and not a little admiration. Now he said cheerfully: 'I have no qualms about leaving her in your care, Charley-*chérie*. But I am afraid it will somewhat restrict your freedom.'

'I don't mind that,' Charley assured him, untruthfully, but with a smile. 'So long as we can keep her happy—and as well as possible.'

Jean-Paul nodded. His mobile, expressive face was suddenly serious. 'Charley—I have something I want to ask you. But first of all, how are things between you and Jon?'

Charley's unruly heart missed a beat. But she spoke evenly enough. 'I am very fond of Jon, of course . . . And he is much better now—as I am, too. But—'

'But?' His voice was questioning and a little wistful.

She hesitated. 'He likes his freedom too, you know.'

There was a small silence while Jean-Paul paused for thought. At last he asked mildly. 'And that is all?'

'That is all.' She sounded calm and firm—but something within her twisted and protested, knowing it to be a denial of the truth.

'Then I can say what is in my mind,' Jean-Paul continued,

in a relieved tone. 'Charley-*chérie*, I think I fell for you when I first met you—but now I feel even more sure. I suppose you wouldn't consider marrying me?'

'Jean-Paul!' exclaimed Charley, astonished. 'But you scarcely know me.'

'Oh yes, I do, *chérie*. I know you are brave and loyal, and an enchanting companion. I know you are compassionate and kind, both to Ankaret and to Zizi, and a most competent and sympathetic nurse. And you speak beautiful French! What more could a struggling doctor want?'

'Love, perhaps?' said Charley, eyes innocent and wide.

'Ah, love, *chérie*. The out-of-reach dream . . . ? But I have already said I fell for you at the very beginning . . . And you are a delight to the eye, and especially beautiful when you laugh.'

Charley was laughing now. 'Oh, Jean-Paul, you are incorrigible. But it won't do, you know.'

'Not?' He sounded absurdly disappointed. *'Mais je suis desolé . . .'* He looked at her searchingly. 'Tell me why not?'

'Because—well, for one thing, you are going to the other end of Africa, and I cannot leave Ankaret.' Or Jon, she thought, in desperation. I cannot leave Jon. But one day soon, Jon will leave me.

'I am talking of the future, *chérie*.' Jean-Paul's voice was serious again, and Charley could not mistake the note of sorrow behind it.

'Is that why you mentioned Zizi?'

He nodded silently, and then explained: 'I have suggested that Ankaret might make me his guardian—just in case. And . . . he is very fond of you.'

'And it would be very convenient if you and I could agree to marry and take him on?'

'I think it would relieve Ankaret's mind very much—and mine as well.' He looked at her sadly. 'You do not like the idea?'

'I do, Jean-Paul. And I am very honoured.' She drew a long, shaken breath. 'But I cannot do it.'

'Pourquoi pas?'

Because I love Jon, she thought. I love Jon, and no one else will do. 'I am sorry, Jean-Paul,' she said, genuinely

251

distressed at having to refuse him. 'It sounds like the ideal solution—and you are so good . . .' And I am not getting any younger, and I ought to be grateful for any offer—let alone one from anyone so prepossessing and successful as Jean-Paul . . . Her thoughts churned on, making her tongue sound halting and strange. 'And—and I am very fond of Zizi, and very fond of you, too—but I—I am old-fashioned about love.'

'And you are afraid of a commitment without it?'

And even more afraid of one with it, she thought, with a despairing flick of self-reproach. But aloud she only said: 'It would not be fair on you.'

'I would take the risk,' Jean-Paul told her, looking ardent and boyishly appealing.

'No.' She laid an affectionate hand on his arm. 'No, Jean-Paul. You deserve more than that. I would love to be able to say yes—but I have to say no.'

'Think about it, *chérie*. You need not decide anything yet. I will ask you again when I return.'

She shook her head. 'Please, Jean-Paul—don't make it harder for me. You know I will always help with Ankaret—and with Zizi . . . But, for the rest, I could not let you settle for second-best. One day you will find the perfect wife.'

Jean-Paul looked at her for a moment without speaking, and then he drew her close and kissed her with great tenderness. 'Dear Charley,' he murmured, 'I think I have already found her. But I see now that she is not for me.'

He did not say any more, and remained charming and good-humoured right up to the end of his stay. But Charley felt guilty and not a little saddened by her own refusal. He was so nice, and he so much deserved to be happy with someone. It was such a pity that it could not be her. And it was true that it would settle Zizi's future and relieve Ankaret's mind . . . When her thoughts reached this point, she felt guiltier than ever. But she could not bring herself to change her mind.

Jean-Paul said goodbye to her with a kind of rueful sweetness, and murmured in her ear under cover of the flurry of farewells: 'I shall try again, you know. *Au revoir, ma petite.*'

She watched him go with a mixture of sadness and relief, and turned to find Jon regarding her with a strange, almost angry expression in his eyes.

'So you turned him down,' he said. 'I wonder why.'

Charley stared at him, confused by the edge of bitterness in his voice. 'A marriage of convenience is not really my style.'

'Oh?' He sounded inexplicably cold and distant. 'What is your style, Charley? I'd like to know.'

She did not answer him at first—still too confused by his sudden hostility to know what to say to him. But then she laid a gentle hand on his arm, ignoring his disapproval, and spoke simply and directly to him as if there were no unexpected barriers and defences thrown up between them. 'I'm sorry if it's upset you, Jon. He's been a good friend to us all, I know—and simply marvellous with Ankaret. I ought to be grateful—we all ought—but that doesn't mean I ought to marry him—not even for Zizi's sake.'

'For Zizi?' Jon looked mystified for a moment. 'Did he bring that into it as well?'

'He did.' She sighed. 'And that was the only argument that might've won me over.' Once again she looked at Jon, almost apologetically. 'But I'm afraid it didn't.'

Jon was still gazing at her, but the taut anger seemed to be draining out of him at her touch. 'Zizi?' he said again, as if the thought was new to him. 'But you love him very much.'

'Certainly. I've already told you.' She smiled, and then went on fiercely: 'But in any case, that argument doesn't apply. We're going to get Ankaret well—and nothing's going to stop us!'

Jon nodded, shaken by her insistence. 'Of course, Charley. Of course we are.' But he was still regarding her with that strange, smouldering glance. 'And freedom is more important than security—is that it?'

'That's not it at all,' retorted Charley, her eyes flashing blue fire. 'But love can't be given to order, Jon Armorel. It's

253

as ungovernable as the light.' Her voice sank, as if scared of its own ring of truth. 'And just as inescapable,' she whispered, almost to herself. And before Jon could answer, she had turned away and gone into the house—alone.

* * *

After Jean-Paul had left, Jon insisted on coming home to lunch—in case, he said, Ankaret needed anything, or Charley was worried.

Charley had to admit she was glad of his support. Glad of his company. She missed him more and more each day— and the strange, unspoken communion that had grown between them as they watched the ceaseless comings and goings of the birds on their tranquil lake.

Now, their closeness seemed to be held in abeyance, over-ridden by their mutual concern for Ankaret and her painfully slow recovery. All the same, from the moment Jon had started going to the lake alone, Charley had insisted that they spend some time each evening when he came back logging the work of the day, recording each species he had been filming or watching, and looking up any strange unknown visitors in their various books of reference. That way, she told him, there would not be any gaps in his story of the year's migratory cycle, and the making of the commentary to the film would be that much easier.

Jon agreed to this plan of campaign thankfully, although he knew that Charley must be tired after the day's chores. But he also knew that it was important to Charley—to both of them—that she should still be part of the project. Besides, her clear and observant eye was very valuable to the progress of the film.

By the end of the second week, Ankaret was walking about the house, albeit slowly, and even venturing out on to the sandy stretch below the villa garden, although she could not yet walk down as far as the sea. She was beginning to look a little less frail, though her weight did not increase and she was still inclined to get exhausted over trifles.

However, she was well enough to receive the policeman, Habib, who recounted all the happenings with Aziz, and informed her that Jon and Charley might be asked to give evidence, but Zizi would not—he was too young, and anyway he had given them a statement already. It would not be right to frighten the boy further. Ankaret thankfully agreed. Then she asked if Habib had any idea who had wanted to buy the Berber necklace.

Habib told her he had. Word had spread through the *souks* that a certain wealthy Berber chief, who owned many camels and whose family possessed a fortune in jewels for the dowries of their daughters, had claimed Ankaret's jewellery as his own. It was a family heirloom, he said, that had been stolen long ago, and he was willing to pay handsomely for its return. Aziz had somehow discovered all this from showing a photograph of the necklace which he had removed from the file in Jacques Lejeune's office soon after the goods had first been purchased. When Aziz did not immediately close the deal—presumably because he hadn't actually got the necklace—the traders in the *souk* supposed it was just the thief's natural desire to play off one dealer against another. But somehow the original Berber chief got wind of the crookedness of the deal, and went cold on the transaction. That was when Aziz got desperate enough to try the ransom bid instead. He had almost certainly tried to get the whereabouts of the necklace out of Zizi by force—and failed—and it had obviously occurred to him that Zizi himself might be more valuable to Ankaret than a piece of jewellery. Just as well, added Habib drily, for it had certainly kept Zizi safe from serious harm.

Ankaret was thoughtful for a while after all this information, but that evening she sent for Jon and Charley after supper.

They found her resting peacefully on the piled-up cushions of her wide divan, her dark blue kaftan spread round her, and a silk scarf tied like a turban over her newly-growing hair which was recovering from the ravages of chemotherapy.

'Sit down, my dears,' she said, waving a graceful hand. 'I want to talk to you.'

255

Dutifully, they sat—Jon on a chair and Charley perched on the end of the divan.

'What is it, Ankaret?' Charley sounded faintly anxious. 'I hope Habib didn't tire you.' She knew the policeman had been there rather a long time—too long in her opinion, although she had not liked to interfere.

'No.' Ankaret was smiling. 'But he set me thinking. Could we get word to this Berber tribesman that the necklace is still for sale? Legitimately, this time.'

Jon considered. 'I dare say Ahmed and Ishak could find him.' He looked at Ankaret seriously. 'Are you sure that is what you want to do?'

'Yes.' She was quite definite. 'I don't want it back in the house. It's caused enough trouble already. 'I think Zizi is right—it does bring bad luck. It should go back where it belongs.'

The two of them were silent at this. They could not deny that it had caused a lot of terror and distress.

'In any case,' Ankaret went on smoothly, 'the money may come in very handy for Zizi—later on.'

Charley looked at her with hidden anxiety. There were blue shadows under her eyes, and her skin seemed far too transparent, almost luminous in the darkening room. She did not seem to be in pain, and never complained of discomfort, but how well was she, really? How much did this slow recovery really mean?

'I suppose it's a good idea to build up a fund,' Charley agreed easily. 'He may want to go to school or something . . .' She reached out and took Ankaret's hand in hers. 'Though you seem to be teaching him plenty at the moment.'

'You taught him the most important thing.' Ankaret was smiling.

'What was that?' Charley sounded mystified.

'That writing has a practical use!'

They all laughed at this, and their eyes strayed to the small new frame on the wall which contained Zizi's historic note. Thank God, thought Charley, thank God Zizi had so much sense! But Ankaret and Jon both thought: Thank God for Charley.

Then Ankaret made her next suggestion. 'Charley, I think you should go back to work with Jon.'

Charley was shocked. 'Oh, but, Ankaret—I can't leave you.'

'Yes, you can.' Her voice was firm. 'After lunch. Each day.' She shook her head at Charley's protesting face. 'I am much better now. And Myrrha and Zizi will be there. I shall be perfectly all right.'

Charley looked doubtfully at Jon. 'What do you think?'

Jon said, half-smiling: 'I think Ankaret is a very difficult person to cross!' Then he turned back to Ankaret seriously. 'But you must promise to tell me when I come back for lunch if you want anything or need anything done—and most of all, if you should be feeling less well, or extra tired . . . Otherwise, I know Charley won't agree to go.'

'Quite right,' agreed Charley. 'I won't.'

Ankaret looked lovingly at them. 'You are both the most awful bullies,' she said. 'All right.'

* * *

It ought to have been all right, but somehow it wasn't. The old, easy companionship seemed to have gone, and all sorts of new dark tensions seemed to have crept into their Eden. Sometimes, Jon seemed cold and aloof, wrapped in an icy professionalism that kept him filming for too long at a stretch and made him snap at Charley if she protested. Sometimes, he seemed moody and disconsolate, lapsing into long silences, brooding and unresponsive. But at others, he suddenly relaxed and looked at Charley with an expression of curious tenderness and delight, saying huskily: 'Oh, Charley—how I've missed you!'

She was mystified by his behaviour. The only excuse she could make for it was that he did not seem all that well at present. His cough had returned, and his voice was husky even when he wasn't being suddenly affectionate.

The birds still delighted them both, of course. Especially now that spring was coming. The gorse bushes were in flower again, and all kinds of wild flowers—marigolds and blue borage and purple gladioli, yellow verbascum and pink oleander, were springing up in the open land round the edge of the lake. And, with the return of the flowers, came the migrating birds. First came the cranes, flying in long lines across the sky, calling to each other as they came in to land. They stayed for a while to feed and gather strength for the last lap of their long journey back to Europe, stepping delicately in and out of the reeds on their thin legs and nodding to each other gracefully in the beginnings of their courtship dance which they would be displaying as soon as they got to their final spring breeding grounds. And after them came the swallows, exhausted and ravenous after their long flight across the Sahara, swooping on the myriad insects flying above the waters of Lake Ichkeul.

Charley particularly loved the swallows—and so did Jon; they seemed so brave and tireless, though Jon said many of them perished on the way across the desert, too weak and hungry to fly any farther. But the ones that did make it swirled overhead in blue-black circles, and made Charley's heart lift with delight at every tilt and turn of their scything wings. Their flight was so ecstatic and so joyous.

Perhaps it was the return of the swallows that prompted her, but she suddenly couldn't bear the strange rift between her and Jon any longer.

She had managed to persuade him to take a short break from filming a purple gallinule's nest in the reeds, and he was drinking a cup of coffee and gazing up at the swallows as they darted and swung over his head, their thin cries higher and sharper than any of the other multitudinous voices on the lake. But his expression was sombre and remote—not reflecting any delight in the lovely sweep of wings above him. Almost, he seemed not to see them, and Charley was suddenly filled with sorrow that their wild ecstasy of spring flight failed to move him.

She went across to him and knelt down on the dry reeds beside him so that she could look into his face. Tentatively, almost shyly, she touched his arm. He seemed so remote.

'Jon? What is it? . . . Does the spring make you sad?'

He turned his head and screwed up his eyes, as if seeing her so close dazzled him. 'The spring?' He spoke slowly.

'No.' But he looked so lost and confused that she could not leave it there.

'There must be something upsetting you—is it Ankaret?'

He was staring at her now, almost blankly, seeming unable to understand the words she was saying. 'Ankaret? No.' Then he roused himself a little to add: 'Why? She's getting better, isn't she?'

'Yes. Slowly.' Charley was still groping for an explanation for his strange, disorientated mood. 'Then is it me? Is it something I've done?'

His expression changed then, and light seemed to flow back into the strange darkness of his eyes. 'Charley—don't be so humble. Of course it isn't anything you've done.'

She looked at him despairingly. 'It must be something . . . Would you rather I didn't come with you? Is it a nuisance coming back to fetch me?'

'No!' He sounded quite explosive. Then he seemed to realise that he was being unreasonable, and shook his head at her apologetically. 'I'm sorry,Charley. I told you I was a moody devil . . .' His voice trailed away. He didn't seem able to offer any excuse.

'Jon—' she sounded near to tears, 'please tell me what it is. I can't bear to see you like this.'

He sighed—a long, shuddering sigh—and closed his eyes for a moment as if in pain before he answered. 'I can't tell you, Charley—I don't know. But sometimes . . . the fragility of the world seems too much to bear.'

She nodded. This she could understand. It was part of her own trouble. 'The cracks show?'

He smiled a little at her instant comprehension. 'They do, little Charley, they do . . . As well you know.'

She was silent for a moment, marshalling her forces. 'Yes, but—surely not here.' Her eyes rested lovingly on the tranquil, unbroken surface of the lake and its myriad population, and then returned, with the same loving awareness in them, to Jon's face.

'Even here . . .' he murmured, and waved a vague hand at the crowded shores close by. 'Life is precarious for them, too. Some of them make it, some of them don't . . . There's always a shadow hanging over them—' His eyes lifted to

259

the silhouette of the marsh harrier sailing overhead on the spring wind. 'And even this paradise of theirs is threatened.' His voice was suddenly heavy with grief. 'As paradise always is threatened—and always destroyed in the end . . .'

'Not always,' protested Charley, somehow pleading for more than she understood. 'After all, the light's still there.'

Something—like light itself—flashed in Jon's face then, and he turned back to Charley, suddenly ablaze with unexpected power. 'Oh, Charley!' he said, 'Oh, my dear, clear-sighted Charley—how right you are!' He seemed to be looking at her now as if he had never seen her so clearly before, and all at once he seized her in his arms and kissed her with a kind of fierce despair, and said in a strange, broken voice: 'I might have known—of course the light's still there . . .' before he kissed her again, more wildly than before.

But when Charley responded, unable to hide her longing to comfort and console him, he drew back a little and held her away from him to look at her again with searching tenderness. There were tears on her face, and he brushed them away with a hand that shook.

'Don't be too kind to me, little Charley,' he said. 'I don't deserve it.' He leant forward and kissed her again, more gently this time. 'Just remind me of the light from time to time—that's all I need!'

Charley did not understand him, and could not answer. There seemed to be nothing she could say.

But in a little while she asked in a small, uncertain voice, rather like Zizi's when he wasn't sure if he'd done right or wrong: 'Is it all right now?'

He laughed and hugged her close. 'Of course. Don't you always put things right? . . . I'm sorry I was such a boor.'

As he spoke, the family of wild boar went by at the edge of the lake, the father leading, the sow behind, and the small stripy young ones grunting and squealing behind. It was so comically on cue that both Jon and Charley collapsed in saving laughter, and the moment of extraordinary tension between them passed in a haze of affectionate good humour.

After that, the barriers seemed to be down, and Jon was almost his old self—but Charley was still a little troubled by the undercurrent of sorrow which she had not quite managed to dispel.

*　　*　　*

When they got home that evening, Ankaret had already gone to her room to rest. Charley was a little perturbed by this, but when she looked in, Zizi was perched on the divan, poring over a book, and Ankaret was leaning up on her cushions, pointing to something on his page. She looked up as Charley came in, and seemed to be as serene and calm as ever.

'Are you all right?' Charley's voice tried not to sound anxious.

'Yes, of course.' Ankaret's smile was entirely spontaneous—loving and without guile. 'I was a little tired, so Zizi and I decided to do some reading.'

She was looking at Charley shrewdly, and inquired with seeming unconcern: 'Did you have a good day?'

Charley laughed. It was hard to describe her day to anyone—not least to herself. 'You could say so.' She paused, and added slowly: 'I think Jon's a bit tired, too.'

Ankaret made no comment, except to suggest that they came and drank coffee with her after their meal. Jon agreed to this readily, and was so charming and tender with her, and with Charley, too, that both of them were a little dazzled.

Finally, he went off to check his cameras for the morning, and Zizi decided to take young Dingo for a walk, leaving Charley and Ankaret alone.

Charley looked rather severely at Ankaret and said again: 'Are you sure you're feeling all right?'

Ankaret nodded and smiled. 'I told you. Just a little tired.'

Charley shook her head at her, half-playfully. 'So long as it's only that.'

Ankaret did not bother to answer. Instead, she attacked on her own. 'Are you and Jon friends again?'

261

Charley stared. 'Ankaret—you're positively uncanny.'

It was Ankaret's turn to laugh. 'Oh, Charley—your face is too expressive. It was not hard to see.' She paused, and then went on calmly: 'That's why I insisted on your going back to work at the lake. I thought he was missing you.'

Charley grinned. 'He had a funny way of showing it.'

Ankaret was watching her quietly. 'Jon is a complex person.'

'You can say that again!' She sighed. 'Sometimes I think I don't understand him at all.'

'Give him time,' said Ankaret serenely. 'I dare say things will become clear to you both quite soon.'

Charley looked at her in amazement. But Ankaret did not say any more. She merely reached out a hand and patted Charley in affectionate understanding.

Feeling suddenly near to tears at her kindness, Charley leant forward and hugged her close. 'Ankaret—you're a witch.'

'A white one, I hope,' murmured Ankaret sedately, and lay back again her cushions, smiling, and closed her eyes.

Charley looked at her face for a moment, wondering again about that startling pallor—and then went quietly from the room.

*   *   *

It was a day or two after this that Jon failed to come home for lunch.

Charley did not fret at first. She thought he had probably forgotten the time. But as the afternoon wore on and there was still no sign of him, she began to worry in earnest. Nightmare pictures of disaster kept creeping into her mind. The jeep overturned in a ditch—or Jon floundering in deep water—or climbing the cliffs on the edge of Jebel Ichkeul to film the marsh harrier's nest, and falling off . . . All kinds of absurd possibilities assailed her.

At last, she could stand it no longer, and went down the village street to find some transport. Myrrha said the baker's brother had an old van and might take her out to the

262

lake if he wasn't busy. A taxi from Bizerta would take longer.

Charley explained the situation to her friend Youssef the baker, and soon found herself rattling along in an ancient Ford van beside his brother, Mavrouk, who was bearded and wild and drove like a maniac.

They arrived at the lakeside in a flurry of dust and groaning springs. Charley leapt out and stood looking round the lake in growing anxiety. The jeep was still in its usual place, parked on the last bit of firm dry ground by a group of gorse bushes. There was no sign of Jon.

She turned to Mavrouk, who was possibly less piratical than he looked, and asked him to go one way along the shore, while she searched the other way.

At first neither of them found anything, but then she remembered the purple gallinule's nest in the reeds, which Jon had been filming before. Perhaps he had been making another attempt at some closer shots. He might have built himself a better hide. She paused for a moment to get her bearings, and then set off again in a different direction. It was somewhere over there, in that thick island of reeds, and she would have to wade across to it, as Jon had done.

All kinds of birds flew up at her approach, but they didn't seem to be unduly frightened and soon settled again to their own preoccupations of eating and squabbling and preening . . . Some of the reeds were trampled down as if Jon had been through them before her. She pushed past them into a denser tangle of green arms and spiky reed-heads almost tall enough to shut out the sun—and there she found him.

He was lying on his back, half in and half out of the muddy water, with his camera beside him on the squelchy ground. When Charley lifted his hand, he groaned and muttered something unintelligible, but he did not open his eyes. She put out a hand and felt his forehead, which was burning hot to the touch. He was clearly in the grip of some kind of fever, and in a way this reassured Charley. At least he was not injured—even if he did look half-drowned—and fevers could be dealt with.

263

She stood up and called across the water to Mavrouk for help.

* * *

Together, they carried him to Mavrouk's van and laid him flat on the floor, deciding that it was less bumpy than the jeep. Then Mavrouk drove him home, attempting to be less wild as a driver, at Charley's urgent request, while she followed more sedately in the jeep. Once back at the villa, the two of them put Jon to bed with a minimum of fuss, after which Mavrouk smiled charmingly behind his beard and said he would go at once to fetch the doctor who lived in a villa quite nearby, and after that he would return to ask if there was anything else she wanted him to do. Charley was too worried to do more than breathe a thankful sigh that the local people were so kind, but she managed an answering smile and that was enough for Mavrouk.

The doctor when he came turned out to be a courteous Frenchman who told Charley reassuringly that Jon had a chest infection and was in a high fever, but antibiotics would be sure to cure it. He would give him an injection now, and send some tablets up later. The fever would lessen soon, and he would be much better in a day or two. He was, of course, a bit susceptible with his history.

He went away, promising to call the next day—but not before he had gone to see Ankaret, too. He told her that Jean-Paul Latour had asked him to call from time to time to keep an eye on her, and he hoped she did not object.

Ankaret replied smilingly: 'How could I refuse?' and asked him all over again about Jon's condition.

When he had gone, Charley took a deep breath, told herself not to panic, and went to make everyone a cup of tea. She didn't know if Jon would be able to drink his, but at least she could try to rouse him.

Zizi came in then and said gravely: 'Mia-Ankar says you need a helper.'

Charley smiled at him, touched by his concern and his instant offer of help. 'You can take this tea to Mia-Ankar. Would you like some, too?'

264

Zizi put his head on one side and considered. 'Are you going to have some?'

'In a minute—I must see to Jon first.'

'Then I will wait,' he said simply, and carried Ankaret's mug of tea carefully into the other room.

Charley was dimly aware that she had a staunch ally there who was trying to prevent her being overworked and harassed. But she had no time to consider the matter now. She went back into Jon's room and found him tossing and muttering to himself, still only half aware of his surroundings. When she tried to lift him up enough to drink his tea, he nearly knocked the cup out of her hand, so she decided to wait until he was calmer.

But as she turned away, he opened his eyes and for a moment they focused on her face. 'Charley—' he whispered. 'Damn nuisance . . . Sorry . . .'

'Hush,' said Charley, and stooped unselfconsciously to brush the hair out of his eyes. 'Go to sleep. You'll be better soon.'

Obediently, he closed his eyes again, and drifted off into restless sleep.

*   *   *

It took three days to get the fever down, and then he was left very weak and exhausted.

Charley nursed him cheerfully and without fuss, merely grinning at him and telling him to shut up when he tried to apologise. He was a docile enough patient on the whole, until he noticed that Charley was looking tired, and then he protested.

'It's absurd to wait on me hand and foot—I can manage now perfectly well.'

'Oh yes?' Charley looked at the shadows under his eyes, and the weary tilt to his head.

'Besides, you've got Ankaret to look after—she's much more important.'

Charley smiled. 'If you say so—' She watched him begin to cough, and noted uneasily that tears of pain still came into his eyes. When the paroxysm was over, she picked up a glass of fruit juice and handed it to him.

'Listen to me, Jon. You've been quite ill. And you're nowhere near ready to cope on your own yet. I doubt if your knees would hold you up, for a start.'

He glared at her mutinously. 'I can try.'

'You can *not*.' She glared back. 'You can wait until that nice French doctor declares you fit enough to move. You'll only make yourself ill again if you try to get up too soon. And that would be more trouble to everyone.'

He sighed. Charley was talking sense, and he knew it. 'It's not fair on you.'

'It'll be less fair on me if you have a relapse,' she retorted. And then relented, smiling. 'Besides, I rather like being indispensable.'

He looked as if he was about to contradict her, but then the words seemed to die on his lips and a strange look of vivid grief came into his eyes. At last he shook his head at her in despair and said in his new hoarse voice: 'Oh, Charley—you are.'

She did not quite understand his distress, but she thought she had probably quelled that first rebellion, so she hurried away to see if Ankaret needed anything. In fact, she was more worried about Ankaret than Jon at present. For Jon had a curable illness, and he was getting over it. But Ankaret seemed to be frailer and more tired each day—and her illness was much more serious. For a time she had seemed to be getting better, but now she was not—and however serene and uncomplaining she continued to be, it was clear to Charley that she was getting weaker.

Charley tackled the pleasant French doctor about it one morning, after he had seen both his patients, but he was evasive and kind. 'There are bound to be set-backs,' he said. 'Ups and downs, I think you call them.'

'I understand that,' agreed Charley. 'But this seems . . . rather more than a temporary "down".'

He regarded her gravely. 'We can't be sure of that.'

'No, but—isn't there anything else we can do?'

He seemed to hesitate for a moment. Then he said carefully: 'Dr Latour left her case notes with me. From what I have seen, the hospital in Paris did all they could. Further

266

surgical intervention would be too dangerous. She has had one course of chemotherapy. Possibly another might be necessary, if there were indications that it was spreading farther.'

'How would we know?'

'She would have to go in for further tests.' He was still looking at her, concerned and cautious. 'But she has told me she does not wish to do that at present.'

'I see.' Charley did see—and what she saw dismayed her. But she thanked the doctor calmly and did not try to detain him.

She did not try to tell Jon about it either—since he was still too shaken by his own illness to deal with any more shocks. So she worried about it alone and in secret, until she decided that she had better tackle Ankaret herself before sending for Jean-Paul.

Ankaret was lying on her chair on the verandah, gazing out at the sea and the golden sunset in the west. Her expression was remote rather than sad, and Charley felt almost afraid to disturb that tranquil stillness. She looked round for Zizi, and saw that he was romping with Dingo not far away on the smooth warm sand.

'Ankaret,' she said, sinking down beside her on to the verandah floor, 'do you think I should send for Jean-Paul?'

Ankaret stayed quite still for a moment, and then she turned her head and looked at Charley. 'No.'

'But—'

'No, Charley.' Her voice was firm.

Charley sighed. 'You know you are not as well as you should be.'

Ankaret nodded quietly. 'It's all right, Charley. I know exactly where I stand.'

Only you're not standing, Charley thought desperately. You can scarcely get from one room to another. But aloud she only said: 'I don't like to leave things to chance—not if there is something else we could do.'

'There is nothing else,' said Ankaret. She smiled, seeming quite calm, and then her gaze returned to the far horizon. It was almost as if the present failed to grasp her attention.

267

But there is Zizi, thought Charley. We have to think of Zizi. How can I say this to her?

Ankaret turned back to Charley, still faintly smiling, and reached out a hand to pat her arm. 'Let be. It will all work out. I am a great believer in fate.'

Her tone was so loving and so tranquil that Charley wanted to shout: Don't you see? There's a small boy who loves you. You've simply got to fight—for his sake, if not for your own! . . . But she didn't know how to say it. She didn't know how to put her fears for the future into words—especially in the face of Ankaret's quiet courage.

As she was wrestling with her own recalcitrant thoughts, there was a shuffling sound on the verandah, and she looked up to see Jon standing there, pale and shaky, and clearly weaving on his feet.

'You idiot,' she said, springing up. 'Wait while I get a chair.'

Obediently, Jon clung to the archway stones until Charley produced a chair and steered him into it.

'What brought this on?' she asked, pretending to sound extremely crisp and disapproving.

'I wanted to see Ankaret.' His voice was still a bit husky. 'I wanted to be sure—I mean, I was anxious.'

'*You* were anxious!' snorted Charley. 'Jon Armorel, I could shake you.'

'You can if you like,' offered Jon demurely. 'Much good may it do you.'

Ankaret looked at them both and laughed. 'It's a bit like a convalescent ward out here. Stop bickering, you two, and admire the sunset.'

Jon made an apologetic face. 'I only came to see how you were.'

'I'm fine,' said Ankaret, with supreme and unhurried confidence. 'Nothing to worry about here.'

She looked at Charley, who seemed about to explode, and added cheerfully: 'What about some tea, Charley? I'm sure we all deserve it.'

Charley accepted her warning look, though with misgiving, and went inside to boil yet another kettle. When she came back, Jon and Ankaret were teaching Zizi backgammon with a set Zizi had found in Ankaret's room, and the little dog, Dingo, was busy chewing the leg of Jon's chair.

'*Viens*, Charlee,' said Zizi. 'We are having a game.'

Ankaret looked up and smiled. 'You'd better help Jon. He's losing.'

Jon was staring at Charley with an extraordinary expression on his face. He seemed to be riven with some kind of sharp awareness of grief—his eyes far too bright and vivid with something beyond pain . . . For a moment she fancied she saw the anguish of farewell in his glance, and she was pierced with sudden terror.

But he only said: 'Yes, Charley. I'm losing.'

*   *   *

The next morning, when Charley took in Jon's breakfast tray, she found the bed empty, the room stripped of his possessions and his travelling bags gone.

She couldn't believe her eyes. Jon gone? Where? He wasn't fit to walk yet, let alone travel anywhere. She rushed outside to look for the jeep, but it was still there, standing by the kerb where she had left it. But if Jon hadn't taken the jeep, how had he gone? By taxi? And where to?

She went back into the house, and on an impulse went into the studio. Jon's cans of film had gone, and so had his cameras. But her latest light-study was still there, propped up on its easel—and lying beside it, a note.

With trembling fingers, she opened it.

Dear Charley,

I have gone to London to deliver the first batch of film. I couldn't bring myself to argue with you—forgive me. I hope you and Ankaret will be all right—and Zizi and Dingo, of course. I have made arrangements at the bank in Bizerta for some funds which are owing to you, so do use them.

I hope to be back to finish the film sometime, but

269

there are things I have to do first. You can always reach me through the office. Ankaret knows the address.

Love,
Jon

She still couldn't believe it, and read the note through again with eyes that were blurred with tears. It was so unlike Jon—to go off without a word, without saying goodbye. But then she remembered suddenly that look of anguished farewell she had fancied she saw last night. It was no illusion. Jon had already decided then. He *was* saying goodbye—in silence and despair.

But why? What had she done to drive him away? She had thought after that day at the lake when he had kissed her so wildly that things had been better between them. And when he was ill, he had seemed content to let her look after him. She had been careful not to fuss over him too much— she knew he hated it. And he had not seemed unhappy to have her near him then—rather the reverse . . . So how could he go like that—and leave all his work half-finished? She couldn't understand it.

Then she remembered, with sudden burning shame, how her own arms had crept round his neck as he kissed her, and how she had responded in love and terror, unable to disguise her feelings any longer . . .

And now he had gone—swiftly and silently—before he could be entangled any further in a relationship he did not want.

Oh Jon, her heart wept. I didn't mean to scare you. I never meant you to know. There was no need to run. I would never have asked anything of you—never expected any recognition. It was enough for me to work beside you and help you to keep the dark dreams at bay. I wanted nothing more . . . Why did you have to go?

She found that she was still standing in the studio with Jon's note clutched in her hand. Blindly, she turned and walked out of the room, stumbling a little as she went. I shall have to tell Ankaret, she thought. Will it upset her, I wonder? But I can't keep it from her. She will have to know.

Ankaret looked up as Charley came in with the tray, and said at once: 'Charley? What has happened? You look like death.'

'Jon's gone.' She put the tray down and stood looking helplessly at Ankaret, as if she didn't know what to do next.

'Gone? Gone where?'

'To London. To take the film back, he says.' She held out the note to Ankaret, and went on standing there, rigid and pale with shock.

Ankaret read the note gravely. 'I see,' she said. Then she held out her hand to Charley and drew her close. 'Come and sit down. You're not going to faint, are you?'

'No.' Charley's voice was blank. 'I never faint.' (But she had once—long ago when she was ill—and Jon had been there to comfort her.) She was silent for a moment and then said jerkily: 'He wasn't fit to travel. What possessed him to go off like that?'

But she knew what possessed him, really. Terror. The fear of being trapped. Only, that was not like Jon either. He was never afraid—except in dreams.

Ankaret was saying quietly: 'It was partly my fault, I'm afraid.'

'Why?'

'He asked how I was, remember? And I told him I was fine.'

The two women looked at one another. The implication was clear. Charley's expression changed. She felt even more ashamed. What Ankaret had to face was infinitely worse than Jon's sudden desertion.

She took a deep breath of resolve, and kept tight hold of Ankaret's hand. 'Ankaret—I think we ought to talk about Zizi.'

Ankaret smiled, saluting Charley's courage. 'Yes. About Zizi?'

'Jean-Paul said . . . he was going to be Zizi's guardian.'

'He *offered* to be his guardian.'

Charley stared. 'You didn't accept?'

'Only provisionally.'

'But he said that he . . . that I . . .' She floundered helplessly.

Ankaret was still half-smiling. 'Was that the bait he used? Zizi's future?'

'And—and your peace of mind.'

'He's an unscrupulous devil, Jean-Paul, when he wants something badly.' Her voice was still flecked with faint laughter.

'Ankaret—I'm sorry I couldn't . . .' she blurted out, unsure where the conversation was leading.

'I never thought you would.' She shook her head at Charley. 'It would never have done—for Zizi, either.'

'Why not?'

Ankaret sighed. 'Jean-Paul is a dedicated doctor. He loves his work out there in the disaster areas. He would never leave it . . . For Zizi, it would either mean boarding school in France, or moving from camp to camp with Jean-Paul. And that is the life he has just escaped from. He shouldn't go back to it. He needs stability.'

Charley nodded. 'I can see that.'

'And you would have had to choose between Zizi and Jean-Paul every time he left for a new trip into the interior. Not an easy decision.'

Charley said slowly and deliberately: 'I would always choose Zizi.'

Ankaret looked at her—a strange, piercing look of tenderness and triumph. 'Would you, Charley?' She was silent for a moment, and then asked carefully: 'Are you saying—?'

'That I would take Zizi on, and bring him up to the best of my ability. Yes.' Her eyes were fixed on Ankaret's face. 'You know I love him dearly already.'

Ankaret sighed and nodded thankfully. 'I know. And he loves you . . . But I could not ask it of you.'

'You don't have to *ask*.' Charley sounded almost indignant.

'It's a big responsibility.' Ankaret gave a gentle warning. 'It takes away your freedom at one stroke.'

'Freedom without love is a barren future,' said Charley bleakly.

Ankaret made no comment on that for the moment. Instead, she said quietly: 'His adoption papers are through now. He has a name and a passport . . . And of course he will have what money there is, and this house . . .'

'I have some money of my own,' protested Charley. 'We—we would be all right.' She still had hold of Ankaret's hand, and now she grasped it even tighter. 'But in any case . . . this may never come up. We mustn't assume—'

Ankaret's smile was tranquil. 'I'm not assuming anything. But I can face the future now.'

Charley met her smile with a brave one of her own. 'We will face it together,' she said steadily. 'You and Zizi and I.'

But her heart denied it. How could she face a future without Jon?

*   *   *

The next few weeks passed in a haze of unhappiness for Charley. Daily, Ankaret grew more exhausted and needed more care. Though she never spoke of it, pain was a constant companion now, and the kindly French doctor produced stronger and stronger painkillers which she now took without demur. She spent quite a lot of time in heavy, drugged sleep, and for this Charley was thankful, because it meant that at least there was some respite from the continuous onslaught of gruelling pain.

Respite too for Charley and Zizi, who often went out for walks together along the shore by the sea, leaving Myrrha to watch over the sleeping Ankaret. They never went far; they were always within call. And little yellow dog Dingo also learnt to come when he was called . . . *But Jon did not come back.*

Strangely enough, the thing that troubled Charley most about Jon's disappearance was the interruption to his work. It was April now, and the spring migration was in full swing—in fact, almost over, for many of the passing visitors had already flown on to Europe. The lake was teeming with new arrivals, and Jon was not there to see them. In a desperate attempt to keep some of his work together, Charley paid several short visits to the lake, bumping along in the jeep at breakneck speed so that she wouldn't be away from Ankaret for too long. She gave herself just enough time to make a hasty record of all the new arrivals she could see and recognise—and then drove home in a wild hurry and a mounting sense of guilt to make sure Ankaret wasn't needing her. In the evenings, when Ankaret was asleep, Charley settled down to make a record of all the Lake Ichkeul new arrivals, working up as many sketches as she could into recognisable portraits of the birds. Her own light-study picture she could not touch. It stood on its easel still unfinished—just as she had left it. The meaning behind it and the memories it evoked were too heart-shaking to bear. Jon understood about light—as no one else did in this dark world. But Jon was gone.

Sometimes she took Zizi with her to the lake, knowing he needed relief from his patient vigil beside Ankaret. But he would not leave her very often, and Charley did not insist. She worried though, increasingly, about what she should say to him about Ankaret—how much warning she ought to give him about the future—or whether it was better to say nothing.

However, Zizi as usual surprised her by doing it for her. He came up to her one evening as she was leaning on the verandah rail looking out at the sea, and put his hand in hers.

'Charlee—are you going away like Jon?'

She turned to stare at him. 'Going away? No.' Then she saw the doubt and fear deep down in Zizi's eyes, and knew what this was all about. She knelt down beside him and put both arms round him and hugged him hard. 'Never, Zizi. I'm never going away from you. I will always be here as long as you need me.'

'Until I'm big?'

'Yes. If that's what you want.'

'*Oui. Je desire*,' he said, and clung on to her very tight. For a few moments he did not speak, and then he said in a curiously flat, toneless voice: 'Mia-Ankar is going away.'

Charley's far too vulnerable heart gave a lurch of dismay. How could you explain death to a small boy who had already spent most of his life alone—and had only just got used to being loved and protected by Ankaret?

'Zizi . . .' she began, 'Mia-Ankar is very tired . . .'

'I know.' He sounded quite calm, though his voice still had that flattened quality. 'She told me. People have to rest when they are tired, she said.'

Charley was silent. Ankaret had clearly paved the way for Zizi's acceptance of the situation. What more could she say?

'*Comme un aimant*,' he said, still sounding strange and brittle.

'Like a magnet, Zizi? Why?'

'She said—Mia-Ankar said—it is like a mag-net . . .'

'What is?'

'The earth.' He was staring out at the sea, to where the far horizon and the pale evening sky show the faint curve of the turning globe. '*La terre* . . .'

'Go on, Zizi.' Charley was beginning to follow Ankaret's thoughts.

'*Il tire* . . .' he said dreamily. 'The magnet pulls . . . and you feel heavy. But when it lets go, you feel light.' He searched in his pocket and brought out a small red-painted magnet with a metal bar across its end. 'See?' He held it up. 'Mia-Ankar gave it to me.' He pulled the metal bar off the magnet and tossed it up and down in his hand. 'Light,' he said, working out a thought. '*Legère* . . . And then she can fly . . . She says she has always wanted to fly, *comme les oiseaux*.'

Gravity, thought Charley sadly. The heavy pull of ancient mother earth, holding you down . . . *And when it lets go, you feel light* . . . Oh Ankaret, how wise and brave you are.

'Like Jon's birds,' added Zizi suddenly. 'She says to remember Jon's birds.'

This time, Charley could not answer him at all.

*   *   *

There came a day when Charley knew she must send for Jean-Paul, whether Ankaret liked it or not. She also decided that Jon must be told—whatever the consequences. Jean-Paul, she knew, might not be reachable, for he was apt to go off into the interior to visit other outlying clinics, and could

275

only give his headquarters as an address. She sent him a cablegram, and hoped it would reach him somehow.

As for Jon—she had got his office number out of Ankaret, but she guessed he would not be there. Still, she could always tackle Selina—and it was too late now to worry about how it would look. Besides, in the last few days she had almost convinced herself that it was only right and natural for her to want to know how he was . . . Almost, though she was still too shy to make the first move on her own. But now, with Ankaret so ill, she felt she had the right to ask.

So she rang Selina and told her bluntly that Ankaret was dying, and Jon had got to know, so would she please tell her where he could be reached.

There seemed to be a long silence on the other end of the line, and then Selina said a little breathlessly: 'I'm not supposed to say—but since it's you, Charley, and Jon's all kinds of a fool—I will. He's in Romania.'

Charley felt herself go cold with shock. '*Where*?'

'Romania. He came home, dumped the film, and demanded to be sent on another assignment.'

'Was he fit enough?'

'No. Shouldn't have travelled in that state. We all told him. Like I said, the man's a fool.'

'How long will he be away?'

'Can't tell. While there's news to report, I suppose.' Selina sounded clipped and faintly contemptuous. 'Said it was time he got his act together.'

Charley sighed. 'You'd better not tell him, then. About Ankaret, I mean.'

'Why not?' Selina sounded even more contemptuous. 'He's got to make up his own mind where his priorities lie.'

'I thought he had,' said Charley bleakly.

There was a pause at the other end. Then Selina spoke crisply: 'Go and see him.'

'What?' Charley sounded totally blank.

'My God,' said Selina, 'the girl's a fool as well. *Go and see him*, you dope. Don't be so damn prickly. The poor sod probably needs you.' Then she added slyly: 'Bucharest's not that far away.'

276

Charley was silent for a moment, swallowing tears. 'I can't,' she said. 'I can't leave Ankaret now—or Zizi either. It's impossible.'

'Charley—' Selina's voice was exasperated, but there was somehow kindness in it as well. 'I told you to fight for him.'

'I know,' agreed Charley sadly. 'But I can't run after him. He walked out on me, remember?'

'Balls!' said Selina rudely. 'He went off to rebuild his working career, that's all.'

'Exactly.' Charley's voice was flat. 'Without encumbrances.'

Selina swore a bit more. 'Has it occurred to you, Charley, that he might think *he* was the encumbrance?'

There was a startled silence. Then Charley said shakily: 'N-no. It hasn't.'

'More fool you.' Selina sounded even more exasperated. 'You don't understand a thing, do you?'

'No,' Charley whispered, too close now to tears. 'Not a thing.'

'That last bout of illness was the last straw,' said Selina, spelling it out for her. 'He thought he was over it, and he wasn't. So he had to go off and prove to himself and everyone else that he was fit enough to cope with his own life. He felt he was a failure and a tired old crock. See?'

'Yes, I—I think so.'

'So what are you going to do about it?' Selina sounded downright belligerent now.

'Nothing,' sighed Charley. 'I can't . . . Selina, you don't understand.'

'I understand very well,' she retorted. 'Monumental idiots, the pair of you. Shall I tell him you called? He rings in most days.'

'No,' said Charley. 'Yes. I mean—if he's interested, give him my love.'

'I'll do that.' She paused and then added more gently: 'I'm sorry about Ankaret.'

'Yes. I—I'll let you know what happens.'

'Keep in touch.' It sounded casual enough, but suddenly her voice seemed to get nearer and warmer on the phone.

'Charley—do you hear? *Keep in touch*. It may be important.'

'I will,' promised Charley, and rang off before the tears engulfed her completely.

As she laid down the phone, feeling somewhat shaken by Selina's forthright words, she heard Myrrha's voice remonstrating with someone at the front door. For a moment she felt a sharp flick of alarm. Could it be Aziz, making more trouble? But then she remembered that Aziz was in prison, awaiting trial for theft and abduction. He posed no threat to them at present.

She went through the living-room and along the passage to see what it was all about. Myrrha sounded very fierce and forbidding.

'What is the matter?' she asked, as she came up behind her.

Myrrha turned an outraged face in her direction. 'This man—' she said, gesturing towards a tall, shadowy figure standing outside, with one foot firmly placed in the door, 'he says he knows you.'

Charley went forward and stood beside Myrrha, looking out at the stranger in the street. But it wasn't a stranger. It was Gerald Farmer. Dressed in smart and faintly ridiculous new holiday clothes, with an outrageously garish shirt besprinkled with red and blue palm trees, he stood confidently on the villa steps, smiling his particularly irritating self-satisfied smile.

'Hello, Caroline. Surprise, surprise.'

Charley stiffened. 'Gerald? What are you doing here?'

'On holiday,' he smirked. 'Down the coast. Thought I'd look you up.' He looked into her closed, uncompromising face in genuine bewilderment. 'Aren't you pleased to see me?'

'Not very.' Charley's voice was clipped.

He did not appear very taken aback. 'Oh come. Old friend. Foreign country, and all that. Must find out how you're getting on.' He smiled, even more engagingly. 'Don't you think I'm clever to find you?'

She gazed at him coolly. 'How *did* you find me?'

The only person who knew her address was her Uncle Hal, to whom she had written reassuringly from time to time. But he disliked Gerald Farmer almost as much as she did. Surely he wouldn't have told him where she was?

'Your friend the colonel,' said Gerald, sounding even more pleased with himself. 'Remember him?'

She remembered all too well. And how when his letter came, via Uncle Hal's office, she had been relieved to find that the old man was at last reconciled to living again, and even grateful for her intervention. He was going to live with his son, he told her—not actually with him, but in a flat in the same house. He would see the grandchildren— even do some baby-sitting—and life once more had a purpose. He would always remember Charley, and always bless her for giving him back the things he might have missed . . . And Charley, touched by his gratitude, had sent him a cheerful, sunny postcard with 'Raf-Raf' written on it as her address.

'Met him in the street,' explained Gerald proudly, 'and I made inquiries. They knew all about you in the village— and about the film of the lake.'

He came a bit nearer, placing his other foot in the doorway too. 'Aren't you going to ask me in?'

Charley hesitated. All her instincts told her not to—he would only cause trouble. But he was a visitor from home, and he had obviously made a great effort to find her. She supposed it would be churlish to refuse to see him after he had come all this way . . . and she was lonely.

'Very well,' she said, somewhat primly. 'But you must understand, Gerald, that we have an invalid in the house. It is not very convenient to receive visitors.'

She sounded like the old-fashioned spinster she used to be, she thought, and was not surprised when Gerald took little notice of her protests and pushed his way past Myrrha through the door.

'So this is your hidy-hole,' he said, looking round him at the elegant arches and cool white walls of Ankaret's villa. 'Rather stark, isn't it?'

Charley, remembering the overstuffed sitting-room of her mother's house where Gerald had done his early courting, shuddered inwardly.

'Would you like some tea?' she offered, leading him

279

through to the kitchen, with Myrrha glowering behind.

'Tea?' He laughed gustily. 'I might have expected it from you! Isn't there anything stronger?'

'This is a Muslim country,' said Charley severely, and exchanged a secret grin with Myrrha as she put the kettle on. 'Tea or nothing.'

'Oh, very well,' grumbled Gerald, and lowered himself into the nearest chair.

At that moment, hearing a man's voice in the kitchen, Zizi came running in, a spark of wild hope in his eye. But when he saw it was a strange man, and one whom Charley did not seem to like very much, the spark died very swiftly, and he went up to her and slid a quiet hand in hers.

'Mia-Ankar is awake,' he said.

'Would she like some tea?' asked Charley, smiling at his instant grasp of the situation, and his instant loyalty. 'Go and ask her, Zizi, will you? . . . And tell her we have a visitor from England—Gerald Farmer. 'I'll bring him in to see her if she feels strong enough.'

Obediently, Zizi went back to Ankaret. Charley thought he would give her his own warning—and she would have a chance to say she did not feel up to seeing Gerald, if that was how she felt.

'*Who's that?*' asked Gerald, staring after Zizi with astonished disapproval.

'Zizi?' Charley smiled at him sweetly. 'He is Ankaret's adopted son. And my responsibility, too, at the moment.'

'*Your* responsibility?' He sounded even more outraged. 'Why?'

'Because Ankaret is ill, and she can't look after him at present. Not that he needs much looking after.' She looked at Gerald's annoyed, uncomprehending face, and added, almost in defiance: 'And I am very fond of him.'

Gerald seemed about to explode, but instead he fired another question at her—one she had been dreading.

'And where is the intrepid film-maker—the great Mr Jon Armorel?'

'In Bucharest,' said Charley flatly.

'Bucharest?' Gerald was thunderstruck.

'On another assignment.'

280

'You mean you're here alone?'

'Not alone, Gerald, no. As you can see, there's Myrrha, and Zizi and Ankaret. We are quite a family party. Here is your tea,' and she plonked down a mug of steaming tea in front of him.

Zizi returned then, and said: 'She would like some tea. And she wants to see your friend.'

He's no friend of mine, thought Charley, in fierce protest. She could feel Gerald's growing hostility like a cloud settling over the villa, and she didn't want anything to disturb Ankaret's hard-won serenity at present.

She gave Zizi Ankaret's mug of tea, and with a murmured apology to Gerald, followed the small, carefully-stepping figure into the other room.

She looked at Ankaret anxiously. 'You don't have to see him,' she said to that fragile, transparent face. 'He's not a very—um—sympathetic person.'

Ankaret returned her look with equal concern. 'An ex-suitor? . . . Jon told me about him.' She held out a hand to Charley. 'Don't let him rile you.'

'Do I look riled?'

'No-o. Just a little at bay.' She smiled at Charley's expression. 'Bring him in.'

Charley hesitated. 'He might tire you.'

Ankaret replied with a touch of spirit: 'So what? I'm a bit bored with my own company—and with being cautious!'

Charley sighed, the protest dying on her lips. In the face of Ankaret's unwavering courage, how could she refuse her anything—however unwise it might be? 'All right,' she agreed. 'But mind you throw him out when you've had enough!'

They grinned at each other, and Charley went to fetch Gerald.

'You must understand,' she told him severely, 'that Ankaret is not very strong. Everything tires her. So don't ask too many questions—and don't stay too long.'

Gerald smiled his bland smile. 'I'll be the soul of discretion.'

If only you would, she thought. But you don't know

281

how . . . She took him into the airy room and sat him in a chair facing the bed and the long view of the sea from the window.

If Gerald was shocked at the fragility of the woman lying on the divan, he did not show it. He put on his best party manners and took her outstretched hand, saying easily: 'How nice of you to see me. I'm sorry to hear you're not too well. I thought I must make myself known to Caroline's new friends.'

'Of course,' agreed Ankaret, smiling up at him with a hint of mischief. 'And how do you find us?'

'What?' He was flummoxed by this.

'Do we come up to expectations?' Her voice was entirely innocent.

Challenge was bright in the air. Ankaret knew very well why Gerald had come, and how surprised he must be at the curious set-up he found. But for once Gerald Farmer seemed at a loss for words.

'I—er—I'd no idea . . . you were so near the sea . . .' he finished lamely. 'It must be—very convenient.'

'Yes.' Ankaret's smile was positively roguish. 'Charley and Zizi swim most days . . .' She paused, and reached out an arm to draw Zizi close to her with deliberate emphasis. 'You've met my son?'

Charley thought Zizi seemed to stiffen and hold himself straighter as she spoke. He was clearly very proud and very reassured by that small word.

'Yes.' Gerald gave him a brief, dismissive nod. 'Hello, Zizi.'

He was not, Charley thought, very good with children. He didn't seem to know what to say to them. Not like Jon, who loved Zizi almost as much as she did . . . Not like Jon . . .

'I'm sorry you missed Jon,' Ankaret was saying serenely.

'Yes. I'm sorry, too.' He sounded a bit grim now—as if there was some kind of conspiracy going on. 'Will he be back soon?'

'I hope so.' Ankaret still sounded entirely tranquil. But her eyes were on Charley as she spoke.

The conversation seemed to be getting nowhere, and the

tension was rising in the quiet room. Charley knew she must end it quickly.

'I think Ankaret is tired,' she announced firmly, refusing to meet that faintly rebellious glance from the divan. 'I'll walk along the beach with you, Gerald, if you like. It's worth seeing. And then I'm afraid you'll have to go. We keep rather strict hours here while Ankaret is convalescing. I'm sure you'll understand.'

There was nothing he could do but agree. She waited while he made polite farewells, and then led him out through the kitchen on to the verandah and down to the shore . . . As far away from the house as possible, she thought desperately. And I wish he'd go away altogether without this final scene that I know is coming. But of course he won't.

They walked for a while in silence, and then Gerald stopped, laid an angry and possessive hand on Charley's arm, and swung her round to face him.

'How long has this been going on?'

'What?'

'This incredible set-up?'

'What's incredible about it?'

'Looking after a sick woman—playing nursemaid to a street-Arab.'

'Gerald!'

'Well, that's what he looks like.'

And that's what he was, thought Charley sadly. But not now. Not ever again, if I have anything to do with it. And I *have*.

'I thought you were supposed to be escaping from all that.' Gerald's voice was sharp. 'Helping to make a film, you told me—a life of comparative luxury on the shores of this wonderful lake—assistant to a brilliant camera-man . . .' The sneer was unmistakable now. 'And what do I find? The famous Jon Armorel has gone off somewhere else, leaving you literally holding the baby! You're nothing more than a drudge here, Caroline. Worse off than before. You'd better pack up and come home with me right away.'

Charley looked at him in astonishment. 'Pack up? Are you serious?'

'Of course I'm serious. It's obvious you can't stay here.'
'Why not?'

'Well—' In the face of her cold disbelief, he began to bluster. 'What's going to happen to you in the future? I thought this Jon Armorel was supposed to be looking after you. Some looking after, I must say!'

'He couldn't help it.' Charley flew to Jon's defence. 'It's his job to go where he's told.'

It was Gerald's turn to look at her in disbelief. 'Oh, really? Very convenient.' He sounded even more exasperated. 'Caroline, have some sense. That poor woman in there isn't going to last much longer by the look of her—and then what?'

Charley winced at his blunt, insensitive words. But she answered him steadily enough, and with a certain dignity. 'I could not possibly leave Ankaret now. Or Zizi either. I am much too fond of them.' Her eyes sparked ice-cold blue fire. 'In my book, friends don't walk out on each other when they are needed most.'

Some of the old bitterness at Gerald's earlier desertion seemed to creep back into her voice—and she saw that her words had struck home . . . I sound like a prig, she thought, but I can't help it.

An uneasy flush was creeping up behind Gerald's pink and white English skin. 'Armorel seems to have done so,' he said nastily. And seeing the flash of refusal in her eyes, he went on remorselessly: 'What will you do when she dies?'

'Stay here and look after Zizi,' said Charley calmly.

'Are you mad? What future is there in that?'

'Zizi's future,' she stated, still in the same calm voice.

'And what about yours?' shouted Gerald, exasperated now beyond all reason.

'That is my own affair.' Her tone was as cold as her glance.

He tried another tack. 'Look here, Caroline—you can't tie yourself to someone else's child for the rest of your life. You're not getting any younger, you know, but you could still marry and have children of your own. Have you thought of that?'

She regarded him levelly. 'Yes, Gerald. I have thought of that.' And then some imp of mischief made her add brightly: 'As a matter of fact, someone asked me to do just that not very long ago.'

Gerald's gape was not very flattering. 'Who?'

'A French doctor called Jean-Paul Lafitte. Not that it's any business of yours.'

'And you turned him down?' It was almost a squeak of disbelief.

'I did.'

'Why?'

It was her turn to look exasperated. 'Because I didn't want to marry him, Gerald. That's why. It may not have occurred to you, but for a woman today there are other things in life besides getting married.'

He looked unconvinced. 'A single woman—bringing up a child alone? It won't be easy.'

'I shall manage very well.'

'What will you live on?'

'I can earn my own living.'

He snorted. 'You'd do much better to come home and marry me.'

Charley drew a long, steadying breath. 'Thank you, Gerald. I'm afraid that's the last thing I would want to do.'

There was a tingling silence. Gerald at last began to see that he was wasting his time. She really didn't want him. Extraordinary female.

'Well—' his voice was full of the tight venom of a snubbed man. 'If you prefer to remain a frustrated spinster for the rest of your days . . .'

She looked at his red, discomfited face and wondered whether to hit it or not. But instead, she laughed. His reactions were altogether too predictable.

'The only frustration I feel at the moment,' she told him clearly, 'is that I am too well brought up to smack your face.' She watched him blink at her words, and her laughter became suddenly goodhumoured. He was only a clumsy, rather stupid man, after all. 'Go on, Gerald. Enjoy your holiday. I'm sure you'll find lots of other girls to de-frustrate.'

She held out her hand in frank and friendly dismissal. He ignored it.

'Is that your last word?'

'Goodbye, Gerald.'

'Huh!' he said. 'You're out of your tiny mind.' And he turned on his heel and stormed off down the golden beach.

Charley looked after him and sighed. That's the end of a beautiful friendship, she thought, suppressing a hysterical desire to giggle. But there was too much on her mind now for her to spare the retreating figure of Gerald Farmer more than a passing thought. His visit had been a nuisance, as aggravating as an angrily buzzing fly. She brushed it off, and returned to the real problems of the day.

Jon was alone in a foreign city, trying to rebuild his life without her, when, according to Selina, he still needed her. But was that really true? How could she possibly go and ask him if he still wanted her in his life? Supposing he didn't? What would he say? Her face seemed to burn with humiliation at the mere thought of it. And in any case, Ankaret was far too frail to leave—she might slip away at the merest breath—and she relied on Charley now more than ever for comfort and reassurance . . . And so did Zizi. There was no way she could leave them now, however much her heart denied the rightness of her choice. Ankaret, with her fragile hold on life, and Zizi with his anxious, grief-filled eyes, must come first. Of course they must.

Sighing, Charley went to see if Gerald's visit had really tired Ankaret. She found her wide awake and restless, sitting up on the divan with her favourite blue kaftan spread round her.

'Charley,' she said, 'could you take me out to the lake? I would so love to see Jon's birds.' She did not add that she also wanted to see some of the stress lifted from Charley's face, for there was clearly something more than the visit of that tiresome young man, Gerald Farmer, troubling her.

Charley looked at her with alarm. It was hard to refuse Ankaret anything these days, but a journey in the jeep across those murderous potholes and tufts of reeds . . . Could she stand it?

'I needn't get out,' pleaded Ankaret. 'I only want to look.'

286

Charley sighed. 'All right. But I don't know what the doctor would say.'

Ankaret's reply was soft. 'It's too late for caution now, Charley. Let be.'

There was no answer to that. Charley capitulated. She piled the jeep with cushions and blankets, and told Zizi to hold on to Ankaret tight to protect her from the bumps.

They drove to the lake just before sunset, when the birds were just returning for the night. The sky was alive with wings—long skeins of honking geese, a rosy cloud of flamingoes, a string of cranes calling to one another as they came—and below them a cacophony of voices arguing and shouting as they settled down to rest on the quiet water . . . And above them all, the swallows darted and planed and rose in wide circles in the clear blue air, spending their last day of rest in ecstatic flight before they flew on across the sea to bring the summer to Europe.

They will be going to Bucharest as well as London, thought Charley. I wonder if Jon will see them and remember . . . But the memory of Jon's sudden passionate explosion sparked off by the swallows made her shiver and turn away.

'Oh!' breathed Ankaret, in a hushed voice of dream. 'Aren't they beautiful.'

She sat for a long time, rapt and silent, watching all that teeming life with wonder, and with no sense of sorrow or regret. Life goes on, she thought. Even if I shall not be here to see it—life goes on, and the world still turns . . .

The sunset laid fiery fingers on the surface of the water, turning it to rose and gold, so that the whole world of sky and lake seemed aglow with light. And not until it began to fade into blue dusk did Ankaret stir.

'You can take me home now,' she said finally. And she put an arm round Zizi and the other round Charley and hugged them both close for a moment. 'Thank you for bringing me,' she murmured. 'It was worth the risk!'

Charley had nothing to say to that, but she answered her smile with one that was almost as gallant.

They drove home through a still-golden afterglow, though the darkness was coming fast now, and when

287

Charley got Ankaret inside again, she put her back to bed, afraid of her startling pallor. But Ankaret seemed calm and happy, and kissed them both goodnight with unshaken serenity.

'I shall sleep now,' she said.

And in the morning, when Charley came in to look at her, she was dead.

*　　*　　*

There was quite a lot to do, and Charley did it alone. It seemed to her that the world had shrunk to this little villa by the sea, and Zizi's small, bewildered face, and the many comings and goings of lawyers and doctors and embassy officials, and a host of other kind people offering help.

Jean-Paul had not come back, and a return cable from his headquarters told her: *'Regret unable contact Dr Lafitte at present. Will do so as soon as possible.'* So that was that. And Jon, of course, was too far away and too busy to be told about Ankaret's death. There was nothing he could do, anyway.

So she was alone. With Zizi and a small dog to comfort and look after—and a mass of papers and local regulations which had to be dealt with somehow. Well, she would cope, she told herself. She would cope and not think. Not remember the golden days by the lake with Jon—nor Ankaret's serene and courageous presence, which she missed almost as much as Jon's. Zizi missed her badly, too, she knew. Better to concentrate on reassuring him, and fill her days with the mechanics of living—and not think at all.

People were astonishingly kind. Myrrha, tearful but determined, insisted on taking over all the domestic arrangements for the moment, cleaning and polishing in a frenzy of distress, and producing meals that no one could eat.

Habib, the kindly policeman, arranged all the immediate notifications, and tactfully sent up the village undertaker, who was also the local carpenter and a relation of Myrrha's. The baker, Youssef, came up to say that his brother, Mavrouk, could provide a smart-looking car for the funeral, and it would not cost her a single millime because they had loved Madame Lejeune too, and she had always been so good to everyone in the village. Someone—she thought it was the embassy official who had known Ankaret and Jacques Lejeune quite well—found an English priest and a small Anglican church in Tunis. Charley didn't know much about Ankaret's religious beliefs—except that she was tolerant of everyone else's, and once smilingly said she thought Allah and God were just labels for something too big to name.

Maybe, she thought, confusedly, I ought to invite a Muslim priest as well. The call to prayer at the top of the white minaret on the hill had been part of Ankaret's daily life, after all. But it seemed too complicated to arrange, and anyway she thought Ankaret would probably laugh at all the fuss.

At this point, a picture of Ankaret laughing came into her mind with such force that she had to go away by herself and take a lot of deep breaths to stop the tears.

So they buried Ankaret quietly in the little English cemetery, and Zizi's small wreath of white roses went with her. At the last moment, he did something very curious. He took the magnet out of his pocket and carefully pulled off the clinging metal bar. Then he tossed the magnet into the grave after his white flowers, and threw the small piece of metal high in the air so that it spun and shone in the sun and then fell somewhere into a pink oleander bush and lay there, unmarked.

Charley took hold of Zizi's hand and held it tight. She did not say anything, but he knew she understood.

And so it was all over, and she had to take stock of what she had in the way of assets, and what she was going to do next. What would be best for Zizi—that seemed to be paramount.

It was at this point in her thoughts, when she was standing irresolutely in the empty villa, that her Uncle Hal rang her from England.

'Caroline, my dear,' he said, sounding quite close and crisp, 'I had a visit from that tiresome young man.'

'Gerald Farmer? I thought you might.'

'Yes. Well, as you know, I don't give much credence to his extravagant assertions. But what he said about your circumstances out there did make me a trifle anxious. Is everything all right?'

'Yes, Uncle Hal.' She drew a slow, steadying breath. 'Everything is all right.' And that was true, she supposed. There was nothing more to be done. She could manage now on her own.

'How is your friend Ankaret?'

She hesitated, and then said quietly: 'She died a few days ago.'

'My dear, I'm so sorry. Would you like me to come out?'

She was startled. 'No, Uncle Hal. Don't do that. It's not necessary. I mean—everything's been taken care of.'

'How are you managing?'

'Quite well,' she lied. 'People have been very kind.'

'Are you all right for money?'

'Yes, Uncle Hal, thank you. That's no problem at present.'

'What are you going to do now?'

She paused, wondering how to answer him, and the silence went on so long that her uncle's voice prompted her, sounding sharp and insistent.

'Caroline? Are you there?'

'Yes, I'm here,' she answered. Yes, I'm here when anyone calls. When Ankaret calls. When Jon calls. I'm here. Only, they aren't here to call any more. Only Zizi is here to call now—and that I must be here to answer, always.

'Caroline?' he repeated, puzzled by her silence.

'I—I'm not sure what I'm going to do,' she said slowly. 'Not yet. I shall probably stay on here for the time being anyway. There is Zizi to think of, you see.'

'Yes, I have heard about Zizi.' It was his turn to pause fractionally before he added: 'Are you sure you know what you are doing?'

'Yes,' she said. 'Quite sure.' And then, by way of reassurance: 'There is nothing to worry about.'

She heard him sigh on the line. But he was too wise to argue further. He merely said in his kind, precise voice:

'Well, I respect your decision, Caroline. Just let me know if there is anything I can do.'

'I will,' she said, thankful that there was to be no more argument. 'I will, Uncle Hal. And thank you for being so concerned.'

'My dear girl,' he said surprisingly, 'you are all the family I've got.' And then, as if to spare her any further embarrassment, he rang off before she could reply.

She stood there for a moment, trembling with reaction. But before she could recover from the ordeal of having to explain things to Uncle Hal—even though it hadn't been as much of an ordeal as she had expected—the phone rang again. This time it was Jean-Paul, speaking on a very distant-sounding crackly line, and sounding quite heart-broken about Ankaret. She let him talk on for a bit, unable to think how to comfort him, and then explained to him what had been done so far.

'*Chérie*, I am so sorry to leave it all to you. I would have been there if I could.'

'I know that, Jean-Paul.'

'We have an epidemic here. And the other doctor is sick . . . I have asked for a replacement, but he cannot be here for at least another week . . . I may be able to get away then.'

'Don't worry, Jean-Paul. We can manage.'

She meant herself and Zizi, but it occurred to her then that Jean-Paul did not know that Jon had gone, and would assume that the 'we' meant that she had Jon's help and support. She did not disillusion him.

'How is young Zizi taking it?'

'He is very brave, Jean-Paul, as you know. He does not make a fuss.' She hesitated and then went on: 'But of course he is sad. He needs a lot of comfort just now.'

'Which I am sure you will give him, *chérie*.' Once again there was a pause on the line, and then Jean-Paul spoke even more earnestly: 'Charley-*chérie*, have you given any more thought to—my suggestion?'

She sighed. 'Yes, Jean-Paul. Of course I have. But I'm afraid the answer is just the same.'

'Even now? In spite of—all that has happened?'

'I'm afraid so—yes.'

'And Zizi? . . . Have you considered what it might mean to him?'

'I have, Jean-Paul.'

'It will be difficult for you, alone.' He sounded sad and faintly reproachful. 'For both of you.'

'I know.' She sounded sad, too, but unshaken in her resolve. 'I'm sorry, Jean-Paul. But there it is.'

He seemed to sigh, but when he spoke his voice was determinedly cheerful and friendly. Jean-Paul was incapable of bearing a grudge. 'Well, never mind, *chérie*. We will talk again when I come . . . You will be all right till then?'

'Yes. We will be all right.'

'Give my love to Zizi.'

'I will.'

'The rest is all yours,' he said, and his voice came in a sudden burst of warmth and closeness and then faded. '*Au revoir, chérie.*'

She found this time when she put the phone down that there were tears in her eyes. She wasn't sure if they were for Jean-Paul who was so devoted and kind and so persistent, or for herself, or for Ankaret whom she missed so much . . . She only knew she was tired—her mind was tired—tired of trying to cope with all these conflicting emotions and tugging loyalties, and she felt somehow besieged by all these people who wanted her to do things she didn't want to do . . . If only they would let her alone to pick up the pieces and put her life together again as best she could . . .

There was Zizi to consider. He was the one who mattered now. It was no good grieving for Ankaret, no good thinking of Jon. No good feeling bereft. She could make a go of it alone—she knew she could. It must be possible to make one small boy happy—even if her own heart wept inside and wouldn't be comforted . . .

But just now she was too tired to be rational or self-controlled, or any use to Zizi. Her mind ached with too much thinking. She shook the tears out of her eyes, and went outside to get some air.

She was standing on the verandah, staring out at the sea and trying to put some order into her churning thoughts, when she heard a step behind her.

She turned and saw the silhouette of a man standing in the doorway. It was a shape she knew—she would have known it anywhere. She would have followed it from heaven to hell and back again, and if it had held its arms out to her, as it seemed to be doing now, she would have run to it without question and left the whole wide world behind . . . But was it real? Maybe it was a figment of her dreams . . . God knows she had fought off its haunting image often enough . . .

'Jon?' she whispered at last. 'Is it you?'

For answer he came forward, and with a cry she ran straight into his arms. He held her close for a long time while she shuddered and wept in the safe darkness of his embrace.

'My poor girl,' he murmured. 'My poor, darling girl. Why didn't you send for me sooner?'

At last Charley dared to look up into his face. He was gaunt and haggard, there was a day's stubble on his chin, and his eyes still held that look of dark, unexplained sorrow that had so shaken her before.

'How—how are you? What are you doing here? Did Selina send you?' The questions came tumbling out.

Jon smiled and drew her close again in a swift, convulsive hug before saying unevenly: 'One thing at a time. Zizi sent for me.'

'Zizi did?' She was astounded. 'How?'

'He wrote me a letter. Remember, you taught him the value of the written word!' He was still half-smiling, but his voice shook a little.

'But—how did he know where to write to?'

'I suppose Ankaret must have told him. Or maybe he had seen it on the film cans. Anyway, it came to the office—he had copied the address faithfully. And Selina had the sense to send it on.'

'What—what did it say?'

For answer, he brought out a carefully folded sheet of paper and handed it to her. Charley smoothed it out with clumsy fingers. The painstaking script said baldly: '*Mia-Ankar is ded. We need you. Zizi.*'

'When I got it,' Jon was explaining. 'I was out in the field. I had to do some handing over. I came as soon as I could.' He rubbed a rueful hand over his face. 'I'm sorry about the beard.'

'Zizi?' said Charley, wonderingly. That little grief-stricken boy—in the midst of all this loss and confusion—having the sense to send for Jon.

'There's more to that one than meets the eye!' said Jon, a fleck of shaken laughter in his voice.

As he spoke, Zizi came out of the kitchen door. He did not seem surprised to see Jon, and he was carrying another letter.

'This is for you,' he said and offered it to Jon.

The envelope was addressed in Ankaret's clear, decisive hand.

'Where did you get this?' Jon asked.

'Mia-Ankar wrote it. She said I must give it you when you came back.' He looked at Jon anxiously, and added by way of explanation: 'I did not send it—in case you were not there. It was too—?' But here words failed him.

'Precious?' said Jon gently.

Zizi nodded. '*C'est ça.*' He glanced warily from Jon to Charley, gave them a fleeting grin and ran back into the house.

Jon watched him go, and then turned back to open Ankaret's letter in puzzled silence. '*Dear Jon,*' flowed Ankaret's untidy scrawl. '*I want you to ask Charley a question. Why did she turn down Jean-Paul? She has just said to me: "Freedom without love is a barren future." Think about it. Love always, Ankaret.*'

Jon stared and stared at the letter, as if he could not take in the words on the page. '*Freedom without love is a barren future*'? Oh, Charley, he thought helplessly, how well I know that to be true.

He raised his head at last to look at her, and something far down in his eyes seemed to leap and flare with hope. And Charley saw that uprising spark, and her own disbelieving mind sprang to meet it, so that when Jon asked his question, she knew how to answer him.

'Because I love *you*,' she said.

She thought Jon was going to faint, he went so pale.

'Are you—are you sure?' he stammered. 'I thought—'

'Of course I'm sure.' She sounded almost cross. It seemed so obvious to her. 'I think I've loved you since that first day when I stood on a bench and screamed.'

He began to smile—but shakily. 'You're not going to scream now, are you?'

'I might—if you don't believe me.'

'But I'm much too old for you,' he said. 'And my damned health is a liability . . . and as for my career—'

'Stop babbling,' said Charley. 'This is serious. Jon Armorel, do you love me or not? I like to get things clear.'

'Of course I love you,' groaned Jon. 'Why do you think I went away?'

Charley was silent, understanding a lot of things in a very short space of time. 'Selina said I was a fool,' she murmured.

'She said I was, too,' admitted Jon.

They looked at one another, and suddenly all their doubts and anxieties seemed to dissolve, and there was nothing between them any more but a great welling tide of love and thankfulness.

Her face transfigured now with a joy she could not hide, Charley held out her arms to him and said: 'Oh, Jon . . . welcome home.'

He did not answer. But there was no need. Their bodies seemed to flow together as one.

Zizi, standing in the doorway, looked out at them for a moment in silence. Then he said softly, to someone not far away: 'Mia-Ankar. It is all right now.'

As he spoke, a whole swoop of swallows flew down out of the sky, swirled round the cool arches of the little villa as if in valediction, and flew away across the light-filled sea.